THE ELEPHANT

THE ELEPHANT

THE ELEPHANT

RICHARD RAYNER

TURTLE BAY BOOKS

A Division of Random House

New York 1992

Copyright © 1991 by Richard Rayner

All rights reserved under International and Pan-American Copyright Conventions. Published in the United States by Turtle Bay Books, a division of Random House, Inc., New York.

A portion of this work was originally published in different form in Granta.

This work was originally published in Great Britain by Jonathan Cape, London, in 1991.

Grateful acknowledgment is made to the following for permission to reprint previously published material:

EMI MUSIC PUBLISHING: Excerpt from "Love Me Do" by John Lennon and Paul McCartney. Copyright © 1962, 1963, copyright renewed 1990, 1991 MPL Communications Ltd. All rights reserved for the U.S. and Canada controlled and administered by Beechwood Music Corporation. All rights reserved. International copyright secured. Used by permission. SHAPIRO, BERNSTEIN & COMPANY: Excerpt from "Yes! We Have No Bananas" by Frank Silver and Irving Cohn. Copyright 1923 by Skidmore Music Company, New York. Copyright renewed. Used by permission.

Library of Congress Cataloging-in-Publication Data

Rayner, Richard
    The elephant: a novel/by Richard Rayner.—1st ed.
        p.   cm.
    ISBN 0-679-40725-1
    I. Title.
    PS3568.A94E44   1992   813'.54—dc20   91-75239

Manufactured in the United States of America
98765432
First U.S. Edition
Text set in Bembo
Book design by Debbie Glasserman

For my father and stepfather,
with love

". . . this was anything but a regular bee: in fact, it was an elephant . . ."

Lewis Carroll, *Through the Looking-Glass*

". . . a man that has pleased himself at home with his own resolution, will, in the hour of darkness and fatigue, be content to leave behind everything but himself."

Samuel Johnson, *A Journey to the Western Islands of Scotland*

A DISCOURSE ON THE ELEPHANT

Part One

Yesterday I met a woman, very beautiful, it was in one of those modern art galleries, you know the kind of place, all grey paint and grey steel chairs with big holes where you're supposed to sit and a grey-jacketed assistant whose haircut is presumably part of the exhibit, and I looked her up and down, thought I'd give it a try, so after I had smiled and introduced myself, noting—casually—that her eyes were those of Leonardo's *Madonna,* her grace was that of a Degas, and her cool allure would have left Renoir gasping, while her intellect, her intellect shamed the Tate Gallery's entire twentieth-century collection, after I told her that my one remaining desire, the only thing of any consequence to me now, was to beach my life, wreck it for ever if she should only wish, so I could spend a few moments, an hour, perhaps a night, even a *lifetime* in her company (oh God, I exclaimed, I'm out of control, I don't believe I'm saying this, I adore you, it's everything, from your thick dark eyebrows which don't quite meet to your slim legs tucked into blue socks and Doc Martens, I have a pair also, no, not legs, though obviously I do, no Long John Silver me, but shoes like that, cue: cheesy chuckle), and after I had produced the yellow carnation bud kept behind my back until this moment, she smiled in return and asked me to repeat my name which was the cue for further word-play—it was like fencing, I swear: lunge and thrust, party, thrust again with one hand and with the other beat death aside, *rinverso tondo ELA!*—and then off to a hotel, it was easier than her flat, she lived in Baron's Court or somewhere beyond the back of beyond, where we drank cool wine from tall glasses, slowly, undressed, slowly, kissed slowly but with a growing and eager passion, and whispered and laughed and licked and bit, then fucked each other to oblivion.

Didn't happen.

Another of those rare occasions. In other words: me, telling a lie. And that's not what I want. This is not the story of my life, at least not the story of all of it, but it is the story of me, my father, and women we loved, and now that at last the time has come for me to dive in and tell it, what I want is an honest job, no tricks; well, not many tricks. Honestly. The truth is apple pie and mother. Nobody could be against it. True, there is a problem, but it has nothing to do with the truth, it's this: I don't know where to start. That's not true. I know precisely. The story, my confession, begins where it ends, and that point of arrival and departure is not an event, not a conversation or a remembered emotion or a portentous moment in history, but the name of my birthplace.

Composure. Is not, of course, the name of the place in question, or the name of any place as far as I know (a sleepy hollow in the American heartland, perhaps—Composure, Iowa, pop. 637, it could be home to an evangelical church of unusual fanaticism, or the township chosen by alien pod-people to begin their conquest of earth), but I want to say a few words on the subject, on composure, and on the fact that I used to have it and now I don't. Time was when I would sit alone in a restaurant or a railway carriage and my composure would be remarked upon. "Look at that fellow over there," it would be said, "doesn't it strike you how *composed* he is?" I had many friends. I didn't approach people, they approached me, attracted by my composure. Now it's different. On a bad day I'm like the bums you see in the street. People debate with themselves whether there should be a statue of me for the edification of future generations. I talk to myself and fidget and feel lost and there is a certain point in the dripping damp corridor of the hotel where I live which fills me with such terror and despair that when I pass it I no longer know who I am.

What am I saying?

My name is Headingley Hamer.

Absurd, I admit, but that statement is true, and it's not that I don't want to tell this story, nor that I feel impelled to do so and am trying to stop myself, just that I'm having trouble getting going. Bloody British stories—never start first time. I'll try again, and this time it'll be the whole truth. That's the good news. Now for the bad. My story is utterly immoral, by which I do not mean that it consists merely of sex and comedy and thrills (though: of course, of course) but that it has no message, nothing to prove.

Morality: I'll tell you something. Morality is not a regular fellow. Morality makes promises which he doesn't keep. Morality makes demands and gives nothing back. Morality does not buy his round. Now I'm returning the favour. But for morality I would never have met Maclaren, and would therefore never have followed him into the hellish toilet of a pub called The Hand of Glory, and therefore would never have received the gun from the blackest black man I ever met, only hours after the police had shocked an Indian cook into heart-attack and death while searching for looted silverware in the gurgling curry cauldrons of his Lumb Lane restaurant, thus precipitating the worst riot in the history of Bradford.

I've said it.

Bradford is the place I've been trying not to mention.

I was born in Bradford.

Bradford is in the north of England, and was once a city of mill chimneys and grotesque Victorian statuary. Now it is a city with no identity. But for me Bradford isn't a city at all, rather the dream of a department store at the top of a hill so vertiginously steep it seems the whole building must break loose and roll down at any moment. I am on the top floor, lost, wandering among lawn-mowers and garden furniture, and then I am in the lift where the lift operator works a wheel with a shiny brass handle as we descend, at first smoothly from floor to floor, but then dropping at alarming speed and freefalling at last with no hope of a stop.

For me Bradford is fear. I think of the place as a personal enemy and I know I am right. In Bradford it was always a damp, drizzly November of the soul, and Bradford is where it starts.

But let me tell you about where I am now. I live in Wonderland, a crumbling hotel at the north end, the end populated by muggers and screamers and mad poor people, the *wrong* end of the Holloway Road in London. I'm alone most of the time. Wake up alone, brush my teeth alone, wash my hair alone with a mild anti-dandruff shampoo (it says you can use it as often as you like, no split ends), spend much of the day alone in my room, take a solitary drink in a pub and talk to no one, go to sleep by myself and dream dreams which involve only me. It hasn't always been this way. I've been married, I've been in love, I've been so alive that I wanted to shout for joy in the street. Now I suffer what the poet Goethe called *Weltschmerz* (dissatisfaction with the world) and *Ichschmerz* (dissatisfaction with the self). Only someone possessed of a truly Teutonic thoroughness could have thought up the combination; that Goethe, I tell you, I have my doubts concerning him. He must have been a barrel of laughs.

Back to business.

I was born in Bradford, and at night Helen slept among the coffins downstairs. Helen was my sister by the way and that's not another of those flashy first sentences, though I admit I love the beginnings of stories, the way they hold the promise of all that is to follow and propel the hero—unaware of his chances of success or failure—into the world and his adventure.

Where was I?

It was the winter of 1959, when my father hadn't died even once and at night Helen went downstairs to sleep among the coffins. She would pick one at random and climb in. Sometimes a corpse was already in occupation, but she didn't mind; not for her the taboo of the unclean dead.

Let me tell you something about heroes. A hero should do his heroic stuff and make his exit, otherwise he finds himself tempted to become boss of the new order he has created, turns himself into a tyrant, and spends nervous years looking over his shoulder for the next hero in line. Look what happened to Perseus, Theseus, Oedipus, all those Greek fellows: betrayed by a wife, thrown from a cliff, eyeballs punctured. No good, that's what happened, because they didn't stride into the Greek sunset when they had the chance.

Think what Jesus would have been like thirty years on: alone and lonely in the palace of cool white marble built by followers in honour of His successful revolution, worrying that He can't quite manage the tricks with the water and loaves and fishes which used to engage the populace so, worrying that the Christian splinter groups are getting uppity in Northern Judaea and that each hand He touches could be an assassin's, worrying that He can no longer control His bladder and the last drops always leave a stain on His kingly robes, worrying most of all Mary Magdalene is at it again with Peter (never should have trusted that one after the cock and the Garden of Gethsemane). What a drag! Ignore the brotherly love. The Son of God's best move was to get Himself up on the Cross, where He was actually begging the Romans to do the business with the nails and thorns and spear. They had no idea, those witless helmet-heads, they were dupes of His scheme to die and become immortal. That's the trouble with heroes, you see: you can't trust their motives. Not like me, you can trust mine, but then I'm no hero.

It was the winter of 1959 when my father, and so on. At night Helen would go downstairs, etc. She would pick one at random and climb inside. Sometimes a corpse was already resident and she would spread herself across it, her face pressed against a dead face, her lips breathing on dead lips, her fingernails snagging on the fine wool of the best, and previously, unworn, clothing in which Bradford men and women were often buried because Bradford men and women pinched pennies when they were alive so they could die beyond their means. Then Helen would listen to the songs of the dead. These rose from the pores of the skin and told her of many mysteries. She was only four years older than me, yet she had already the experience of a hundred lifetimes. At least, that was Helen's story.

She was eleven and I was, well, work it out for yourself. No, please don't bother. I dare say you're too lazy to go back and I certainly don't want to risk losing your attention. So, you win, I was seven and my sister reminded me of Joan of Arc. Alright, I'm imposing on childhood the judgments and language of—oh dear— maturity, but that's what she was like. She had a pale face and short black hair. Her voice was solemn and deep, and filled with passion. She told me that our grandfather invented the submarine, that the

River Aire flowed through Bradford on a bed of diamonds, that the Nazi dagger with the swastika sawn off which our father had was in fact a sword with magic powers, and I believed her. But not about singing dead people in coffins downstairs. I dared not believe that.

She had other scary ideas. For instance, she read the stories of Edgar Allan Poe as if they were newspaper reports, dispatches from a battlefield or a pit disaster. Her world was made up, therefore, of derelict mansions, the fear of burial alive, razor-edged pendulums which descended towards helpless victims, and a plague which was not a matter of fiction but raged in fact in Busby's department store at the top of Manningham Lane, transmitted among the glass counters—from hosiery to perfume to ladies' lingerie—by hissing pneumatic tubes normally used to convey cash and change.

During daylight, she said, our house seemed normal: a tall Victorian building of soot-blackened stone, on a hill overlooking the city, with gables and a big white door and steps leading down to the outside entrance of a cellar. During daylight you could look through the windows and see curtains, light-fittings, glass bird ornaments on the mantelpiece, and our brother Keith's bike propped against the living-room wall, where its chain had spread an oily smear on the paint. But at night, she said, at night it was transformed and filled not only with singing corpses, but with candles lit to protect dead souls from demons, non-corporeal women demanding satisfaction from equally non-corporeal lovers, and an aborted foetus pickled in a jar in the kitchen.

Gosh!

Then, on the day with which I begin my story, Helen came up with an extra twist.

She said, "Remember the pendulum that was in the story I told you about?"

I did.

"It's in the cellar. Our dad's had it fitted, down there with all the coffins."

"He has?"

"It's a torture chamber. Just in case one of the bodies doesn't want to sing." She imitated the pendulum's long and terrifying arc. "*Swish* down, and *swish* up and, *swish* down and *swish,* cut out your heart, I'll eat it from a dish."

My sister could talk in rhyme.

"You're a laugh," I said.

"Is that right, little brother? Imagine choking on a fly. Its wings are in your throat, rattling and buzzing. You feel its life. It's *there*. And then it's gone, you've swallowed it, you don't feel it any more. But it's not gone really, its life has just become part of your life. The fly is *you*."

"Get lost."

She tapped a finger on her temple, saying, "The show is in our heads, you see. It's not ghosts in white and skeletons that walk around going *clank-clank-clank*. The big show is in our heads."

"Like on the telly?"

"Our kid, you've not got a clue. Not one single clue."

I knew she was right, that was how I felt, clueless. In those days I had no character. So adults said. For them character was the conceptual opposite of bad reports, skipping school, leaning forward to kiss the backs of girls' necks in class, spending too much time scared by Helen's stories, and being clueless. "You're like your father," I was told. "No character." Later I would develop lots, too many perhaps, different characters for different situations, a sweep of characters such as Mr. Charming, Mr. Melancholy, Mr. Passionate, Mr. McLiberal-Feminist (a Scot—yes, I can do voices), and Mr. Disgusting After Eight Pints and Three Greasy Hamburgers. Even *I* don't like *him* very much. And that's enough of those Comic Capitals. Just to say: I was able to twist my soul at will. My soul was, is, made of rubber. This was, is, especially so with women. I expect you want to know how this has affected my love-life. Well, later. You'll have to wait.

For now it's back to Helen. "You'll see," she was saying. "There's a man down there now, in the cellar. He's waiting, he's not ready yet, not opening up his valves. And you ought to see them, they're huge things like on the organ in the church at the bottom of the lane. He'll be ready one day soon, we'll go down there, you'll see the pendulum swing, hear a dead man sing."

I didn't argue. You couldn't disagree with Helen. She thought things, therefore they were so; always the totalitarian metaphysician, my sister. None of which would have been of the least concern, it wouldn't have mattered at all, had it not been for a curious fact: there *were* coffins in the cellar, towering stacks of them, black and smelling sweetly of varnish.

I went to see my father, but to get to his office I had to go first through the garage, where Billy Crow had a bucket between his boots on the stone flags and was washing the black Rolls-Royce. He saw me and held a sponge over his head as if it were a trophy. A vast fist squeezed and soapy water came in a torrent, gushing over his head, down his cheeks and neck, rolling from his bare shoulders and puddling on the floor. I said, "You're an idiot, Billy," which was true, though I didn't know it then. At the time Billy Crow was just something else I was scared of. My father called him The Human Horse because Billy had once carried a piano on his back all the way from Bradford to Blackpool, over forty miles. I was scared of his shaggy size and strength, scared of his lurching walk and his lumpy arms, scared most of all of his cavernous, crack-toothed grin. "You're daft, Billy," I called as I ran up the wood steps to the office, not looking over my shoulder to see if Billy was grinning the grin. I knew he would be.

My father lay on the floor, surrounded by books and bills and magazines. His hands were clasped behind his head and he glanced mournfully at an empty glass which rocked on his chest.

"Hello, Headingley old man," he said.

I said, "Dad, tell me about the cellar."

"Fellow I knew spent two thousand pounds on whisky in 1947. In *1947,* can you believe it? Forty pounds a week, thirty-six shillings a bottle, two bottles a day. That's what I call drinking."

I said, "Dad, I wanted to ask you something."

"Birds or fish, Headingley, what do you think?"

"Dad?"

The phone started ringing. My father took a hand from behind his head and waved it vaguely. "Would you mind?"

I was about to pick up the phone when he protested, "Not the phone, Headingley, *the bottle*."

I poured whisky into his glass.

"There's a fellow in Manchester sells birds' eggs. But not just any birds, oh no, these are extraordinary birds. Eagles and peacocks. Vultures and kestrels. Condors. And not just any eggs. We could have an aviary up in the loft, because these eggs are *fertilised*. Birds will hatch from them. Huge exotic things. We'll have to train them so they'll always come back. Think of the feathers, yellow and black. Or red, burning like poppies. And think of the beat of their wings. What a picture!"

The phone stopped. I said, "Helen's been saying something. About the cellar."

"Or fish. We could get a big tank. They make one in the shape of a Sputnik. They do, there's a picture in one of the magazines. Think of that, Headingley. Local fish, tropical fish, fighting fish. *In orbit*."

I realised it was no good trying to talk to him. He had an expression for when he was like this: he would say that he had gone to see the elephant. At the time I didn't know what he meant, but when he said the words, *see the elephant*, his voice was resigned, and somehow thrilled, as if he were discussing a natural catastrophe, an earthquake or tidal wave, that could be explained and even fore-told, but never prevented.

"It would be amazing," said my father, and went into a reverie, sipping at the whisky, ignoring the phone which had started to ring yet again. He was silent for some moments. Then: "Indeed it would."

I said, "Dad, it's about the coffins. And the phone's ringing."

"Fish, yes I think so, definitely fish. It's the more practical option. In the Sputnik tank. Or birds? I wonder."

"Dad," I repeated.

"Not to worry, a decision has to be made so I suppose a decision will be made," he said, examining his watch. "Now it's time for an adventure."

Thus: my father. It's right that he should make his entrance this way, with a big lunatic close-up, since he is at the centre of this in a way that my mother, for instance, is not. In the end she proved the stronger—she was gutsy, volatile, determined—but it was he who became the myth by which I believed myself doomed to live.

My father had a thin moustache and a flair for melodrama. Loved cricket, hated work. Cultivated an air of suave disinterest, bor-rowed from Fred Astaire and the musical comedies of the 1930s.

Was interested in any woman who wasn't my mother. He had been a pilot in the war, flying bombers, Wellingtons and Lancasters, first from a desert airfield in North Africa and then from the chalk escarpments of Lincolnshire. His memories of that time were not what you would expect. No comic-book heroics. He remembered that in the air he had stuffed Penguin paperbacks in his flying boots to keep his feet warm, that between missions in England he had driven a battered Alvis along roads built faultlessly straight by homesick Romans nearly two thousand years ago—"Think how old this country is, Headingley, no wonder it's tired out," he said—that he had spent his twenty-first birthday in Alexandria where he had his own three feet of polished zinc at the bar where the lager was pulled from brass pumps into frosted glasses and where he ate and drank all night for ten shillings.

My first memory of him? We are in a car, he is driving fast and a little recklessly, driving (in fact) like a madman. He grins, nods in the direction of the speedometer—it reads 105 miles per hour—and lifts his hands from the wheel. Then he laughs the laugh which people say I have inherited from him, a joyful and raucous and out of control sound, the laugh of someone who senses his trolley could spin off the rails at any moment. And he sings the song he says he'd sooner have written than the Magna Carta: "Yes, we have no bananas, we have no bananas tod-a-a-ay." He calls it The Banana Masterpiece.

That's not true. It's true that it happened and true, certainly, about the laugh and the song, but my first memory of him is something else and concerns not him but rather his absence. I am four years old and he tells my mother he is stepping out of the house. We need some milk, he'll only be five minutes, he won't even take his coat, but soon it's six hours, twelve, a day later and still he hasn't come back. A policeman comes to the house and stares at my mother's legs as she gives her report, and smiles uneasily when he sees I'm staring at *him*. He squashes my hair with a fat hand and asks if I would like to wear his helmet. It drops over my head on to my shoulders and suddenly I am in a bell tower, dark and echoey, listening to his booming voice as it announces that there is nothing he can do, that it's a family affair, and that in any case all Bradford knows Jack Hamer is a bad 'un but he always turns up in the end, more's the pity. After a week we're short of money.

While Helen and Keith are at school, my mother and I act as guides for an Irish piano tuner, blind, going with him from house to house to earn extra cash. One afternoon, as reward, my mother takes me to Lister Park where there is a zoo and a snake, a python I think, its once opulent skin now resembling a mouldy rug. Perhaps it doesn't like the cage. Perhaps it doesn't like Bradford. I remember thinking that either way I'd rather be the python than the hamster, white and gold and with brown eyes, and each hair standing on end, backed into a corner waiting for its co-tenant to wake up and wonder about tea. After twenty-two days my father comes back, with no explanation but with a bottle of milk in either hand.

He says, "I got two, just to be on the safe side."

He was in the death business. It doesn't seem accurate to describe him as an undertaker, a word which suggests stove-pipe hats, pale faces like watery mashed potato, and long black coats ballooning in the wind. That was scarcely my father's style, though he *was* an undertaker. In 1946, aged twenty-four, he had put himself in charge of the business. One war was over and for him another began. The problem was that Bradford had a surfeit of undertakers, men who'd been doing the job for a long time with great skill, career undertakers with undertakerly names: Twiggy Fawcett, Amos Bass, Hirsh McMahon, Ebenezer Cryer, and (I'm not making this up) Herbert W. Tristram Coffin. For more than ten years stubborn Bradfordians refused to die in sufficient number and the result was a race for each corpse, the sabotage of funerals. My father seemed unconcerned. He did not dream the diligent undertakerly dreams of Amos Bass, whose heavy boots were always the first to creak up any mourner's path, or the devious undertakerly ones of Twiggy Fawcett, who carried not one ounce of flesh on his bones and whose skeletal frame stalked moonlit cemeteries with a spade filling in graves which had been dug in advance. Instead he dreamed of a coup. Like Napoleon, he believed the opposition could be dealt with at a stroke, once and for all, *spectacularly*. But in 1959 business was at a low and he was still waiting for Austerlitz. Hence the coffins, bulk-bought from a carpenter in Boole and piled high in the cellar. My father said he was laying in an arsenal for the campaign.

.   .   .

They were filming at Taylor's Mill and we went there, not part of my father's campaign for supremacy in the undertaking war, but the adventure he mentioned on the day I was talking about, which begins the part of the story ending with my mother's death. She was tall, black-haired, and dressed in red, a wicked queen from a fairy tale. No, not my mother, I'm not talking about her now, though I realise this is a moment when you might expect me to do so, but about the film actress Diana Farrell, an important character in my life, and my father's; of the women in his life she was, in some way, the *one,* if only because she remained a little beyond his reach. She stood among a crowd of technicians and other actors, laughing and talking with them, yet somehow apart, stamping her feet on the slick and shining cobbles, crossing her arms over her chest and hugging her shoulders as if she were cold. My father offered his coat.

Not an innocent gesture.

"Come with me," he said.

Nor an innocent command.

The brown eyes of one of Diana Farrell's companions looked my father up and down. The man was tanned and handsome, and wore a natty tweed suit. He said, "And w-w-w-w-h-at have we here? B-b-bradford's Sir Walter R-r-r-r-alegh, I presume."

This stammered pronouncement brought laughter from the rest, including Diana Farrell. It wasn't that my father ignored this amusement, he didn't even notice. He was back in the war, landing a plane in dodgy weather. She was the beacon from which he dared not look away; all else was fog. He had gone to see the elephant. He said, "You must come. There's something you have to look at. I wish I could tell how important it is. Come on. Please."

The man said, "Oh, Diana, for God's sake, this one looks like R-r-ronald Colman after two g-gins t-t-t-oo many."

The others hooted their appreciation, but this time Diana Farrell did not join in. Instead she gave a casual twirl to the bag which hung from her wrist. She looked at me, saying, "And you? Who are you, soldier?"

My father did not take his eyes from hers. He said, "He's my better half, my trouble shooter. I'd be lost without him. I tell you, he's quite a fellow my kid brother, and an invaluable adviser on my business affairs."

"I bet he is," she said. "And what is that business?"

"I'm an architect. I'll rebuild your life, you'll see."

I heard the languid and honeyed voice once more. "That's r-r-ight, Diana. You go slumming. See where it lands you. N-n-n-eck deep in it I shouldn't wonder. Bloody yokels. They resent everything we stand for. Beauty, wealth, and t-t-talent."

But by then my father had already taken Diana Farrell's arm and we had already turned our backs; so much for the brown-eyed handsome man.

We went to the cooling tower. Not every mill had one but because there were so many mills it seemed that the city was dominated by these hourglass structures of blackened brick, 150 feet high, looming over the terraces and streets, and over the men and women who trooped to work each day in flat caps and formless coats.

My father said, "These things are miracles of design. The safest shape for a building of this size, the most economical shape for a building of this size, the most *practical* shape for a building of this size. It was proven by a team of engineers. Fellows from Finland I think they were."

He paused.

"Which is funny when you think about it," he said, and his hands made a mime of the female form. "Because *that's* what they remind me of. A regiment of monstrous women, standing guard over Bradford. Everywhere you look."

"Are you an architect or a comedian," she said. "Or just a woman-hater."

He told her he was a criminal millionaire, and I groaned inwardly. Even now I can think of few greater embarrassments than hearing someone else lying while in pursuit of sex. Or telling the truth while so engaged. When you come to witness my own efforts in this department your reaction will, I predict, be gratifyingly wince-free. Then she asked the question I was asking myself.

"And what would a criminal millionaire want from me?"

My father, of course, did not answer.

In the cooling tower we found piles of cinders and smoking ash, charred bales of spoiled wool, and pieces of old machinery, almost unrecognisable now, their shapes distorted and made wild by the heat that blasted them when the mill was working. High above us was the sky, an oval of luminous grey, and the light was strange, a faint clouding, almost like steam, as if it had struggled hard to get down this far and had then given up, but not before exhaling a last, dying breath.

She said, "What is this place?"

"I love you."

"Is it dangerous?"

"I have always loved you."

"Is it dangerous?"

"I will always love you. Dangerous? Only when the sheds are working. Not today. The mill is closed in your honour."

"Where do those go?" she said, pointing to steps which ran round the inside of the tower, up and up in a dizzying spiral towards the sky.

"Do you still do theatre? Or is it just films now that you've hit the big time."

"I hate theatre. It's just some man in black swanning around doing this," she said, and issued a theatrical sigh, *aaaaaghhh*. "Let's go to the top."

My father made a face. "You want to go to the top?"

"I want to go to the top."

So we did. I assure you it wasn't as easy as it sounds. Minute after minute went by and still we trudged, on and on, up and round, round and up, until my shins began to ache and my father's breath was a wheezing pant. Diana Farrell was unconcerned, however. She moved ahead, her step light as a dancer's.

I said, "Dad, what are we doing?"

He paused on the heat-cracked brick. He told me he'd been asking that himself. He was developing a theory. It concerned his own character. There were situations, he realised, when he found himself behaving in a way that seemed to have been predetermined. These situations concerned women and not questions of mere lust or momentary infatuation. True, he did sleep with some of the situations and some did last only a single night. But others went on for years. My mother, for instance, was one of those situations. He had known it the first time he saw her, realized he was just a bear led on a chain, unable to help himself. The other mystery was that he never knew when they would finish. It could happen slowly, or sudden as a gunshot: *bang,* mortally wounded situation. While they lasted, though, they were exhilarating. He invited me to stand outside myself and consider what we were doing: climbing steep and perilous steps in pursuit of an actress whose fascination was not her beauty so much as the fact that she reminded him of what it was to be younger and fresher to the world. And perhaps the fascination was not even that, perhaps it was just that she was a face he would not routinely see in Bradford. Perhaps he had no idea of the true nature of her fascination, but he was impelled. She was a situation, a chance to see the elephant. The erotic can turn to farce very easily, he told me, but he was prepared for that. His passport stated his occupation: sexual fatalist.

We made it at last. We were dirty and out of breath. Diana Farrell had somehow kept her red dress spotless, and had almost finished smoking a cigarette. The pack and lighter were on a ledge and as my father approached she made a slight adjustment of their position, not a nervous gesture, but quite conscious, even theatrical, as if she were building a protective wall.

My father was the gesture's equal. He crushed the wall and took her hand.

I sensed its closeness, couldn't see it, but heard—yes, there it was—its approach. *Thump-thump-thump:* the elephant.

"So," he said, still gasping. "Will you marry me?"

"You're barmy. Besides, you're married already and I'm filming in South America next month. Me and Carmen Miranda."

He sang, *"Braaaaaa-zzzil."*

"You are barmy," she said. "You were barmy all those years ago, and you're still barmy now."

So: they had met before, in 1951, when she had been starting her career and he, five years out of the RAF, had been a glamorous figure, with the war long over and the promise of his peace not yet entirely denied. He had been wearing a big bath towel as if it were a toga. He had been drunk, of course.

"I heard you were married. Some manager chappie."

"My agent. Had a sleepy eye and chewed everything in multiples of twelve. Turned out he was fucking one of the cocktail girls from The Moonlight. Before I left him I hit him hard enough to make his clients' book dizzy."

"Another man?"

"What did you say your job was now?"

"I work for the Devil. I walk the streets of Bradford with a case full of contracts and a wallet full of cash. Souls at a fiver a time."

"You don't say."

"I'm an undertaker."

"Now I really don't believe you."

Enthusiastic confirmation from me: "It's true, miss. There are coffins in our cellar. My sister says there's a pendulum as well, with a sharp edge like a sword, for torturing dead people."

"Your sister says *what*?" My father looked down at me, surprised for a moment.

"So you two are a double act," said Diana Farrell.

"Haven't you noticed? I'm the straight man, a terribly gloomy fellow. Just like an undertaker."

"Any money in it?"

"In Bradford, a bundle."

"Which you're making?"

"Not precisely, not yet."

"Competition?"

"Old men and gallant opponents, but not in my class, not at all in my class." He moved his face close to hers, as if to kiss her, and then withdrew. "Soon to be eliminated. And then we'll be top of the heap. Isn't that right, Headingley?"

Diana Farrell was laughing now. "You had a son," she said, "and you called him 'Headingley.' Why didn't you just tie a rock around the poor little devil's neck?"

Did I explain about my name? It was—need I say?—my father's idea. With my mother it would have been something respectable and unremarkable, like Mark or Matthew or Christopher, that was what she wanted, something saintly, and it was while she lay in bed recovering from my birth that my father slipped along to the registration office at Bradford Town Hall, a building whose design resembled nothing so much as a Venetian dream palace. Once there he played out an ornate fantasy of his own. You see, it was his theory that there was a magic in Christian names. Who, he said, would dream of calling their child Judas or Adolf? To do so would be the guarantee of such contempt and mockery that the child would certainly turn out, if not such a rascal as Iscariot or Hitler, at least a rotten fellow. Conversely, he argued, the right sort of Christian name could act as inspiration, and since he was obsessed with cricket, it was his only ambition for me that I should play for Yorkshire and aged nineteen score a maiden century against one of the despised southern counties, he called me not Herbert or Leonard (after Sutcliffe and Hutton, great batsmen) as those names had meanings beyond the game, but Headingley, which has one association only. Headingley is the home of Yorkshire County Cricket Club; I am named after a cricket field.

Now Diana Farrell was jack-knifed over the edge of the tower, waving with enthusiasm. The brown-eyed handsome man was below, not bothering to gesture in reply. "The director," she explained. "We've been having a fight."

"I suppose that means," said my father, "that you're fucking him."

"Is there something wrong with your lips? They seem stuck to your gums."

"My smile. I was thinking how splendid it was to see you again."

And then he leaned forward to kiss her, but she moved away, saying, "It's nice to see *you*. But I won't sleep with you. That was then, and now is this policy I have, not to sleep with men while their children are in the stalls."

"Who says I want to sleep with you? Who says he's my child?"

The cock crowed for the second time.

"Still the Don Juan, aren't you?"

"Don't talk to me about him. He was just an overpublicised Spaniard. Bloody fellow would have resented everything I stand for."

"And what's that?"

My father smiled: "Beauty, wealth, and t-t-alent."

That's just how it happened. I had no idea my father knew Diana Farrell already until we were on top of the cooling tower. They had been lovers some eight years before, not that I understood as much then. What I did understand was that I became his alibi on frequent elephant-viewing expeditions. "No need to let on to your ma," he said. "Tally-ho!"

It went on for weeks. Went on while he seemed to pay no attention either to the funeral business or his campaign. Went on in haphazard fashion because he refused to make arrangements, saying that people who did that needed to draw lines on writing paper and squeezed toothpaste from the bottom of the tube. So each afternoon he'd collect me from school and we'd go down the hill to Taylor's where the first question was always: would we find her? Sometimes the answer was quick, there she was, a slender arm raised high in greeting if she wanted to see him, or in dismissal if she didn't. Sometimes the answer took longer: she wasn't on set, or they were shooting, and we would hang around. It didn't seem to bother my father either way: he was content to wait, and then try to seduce her all over Bradford.

He took her to the reservoir at Wrose, where he got out of the car and lay in the mud in front of the wheels, saying he wouldn't move unless she told him she loved him in return. She said he knew it was impossible, because he was married with children and she was worried about James, her director, the brown-eyed etc.

My father: "I dreamed he killed us both. With his camera. Just crushed us with it. There we were, strawberry jam."

Her: "I *am* sleeping with him."

Him: "Loot. Or boodle. I'm going to get my hands on consider-able quantities of the stuff. Can James better that?"

He took her to the Wool Exchange. This temple to commerce resembled a cathedral more than Bradford's cathedral did. We stood among the pillars, gazing up at the vaulted ceiling and the murals which were on the walls beneath. He told her with a smile he was suffering somewhere, he'd always suffered, yet he was very jolly, he adored the colour red, his bird was the hawk and his aeroplane was a Merlin-roaring Lancaster but the moral engines were going and he was about to drop from the sky.

She said, "You talk too much," which he did, and so do I, it's another habit I picked up from him. But how was she to suspect, and how was I, that in this case what seemed lies was truth?

He took her to Saltaire and told her about the dance that was held each year, the *conversazione,* told her how the village itself came to be, built by the mill owner Sir Titus Salt, in the middle of last century, and modelled after a town in Italy. "Somewhere I probably helped bomb to blazes during the war," said my father.

We looked at the church, which was black, as everything in Bradford was black. (But so many blacks: blacks which seemed red, or yellow, or sickly green, blacks which glowed warm and cosy.)

The church, with its columns and rounded facade and octagonal tower like a pepper pot, was yet another sort: its black was deep like dulled black marble.

He said, "Salt didn't rate what the lads were getting up to all over the city. Brothels, robberies, twenty sleeping in a room, murders. Small wonder they wanted a revolution. Dodge City was nothing to it. I'd have paid the price of admission to see Gary Cooper sort that lot out. It was devil darkness and he'd have met his high noon alright."

My father paused, relishing the telling of the story, not bothered by her seeming indifference. "But that old Sir Titus, he was a foxy old bugger, he gave something. He gave this village, this church. It's the way they always do it, keep us down with a nice little village like this with a dance once a year and train outings to Morecambe. Or some other bit of excitement, like a war. To get us interested, keep us down. So here we all are, living in a world fit for like-minded Yorkshire pudding eaters."

"I hate to interrupt this wonderful monologue, the deepest thoughts of Jack Hamer," said Diana Farrell, "but I'm cold and bored and I'd like a drink."

He caught her by the waist and spun her round. "You're quite right, of course. Karl bloody Marx. Bet he couldn't do the rumba."

He took her for a drink, and another, and yet another, and sometimes he remembered to bring a bottle of pop and a bag of Smiths crisps while I sat in the car.

He took her to Crossley's Garage, down on Canal Road, where it was always dark, even on the most brilliant days, since it was sandwiched between cooling towers, and he looked contentedly across the forecourt. There were at least twenty cars, each the same, each black, and each made by Rolls-Royce: hearses.

"What's this," she said, "the bargain basement?"

"No," he said, laughing, "it's John Bertram Hamer doing the rumba around Bradford." He explained that at last his campaign had been brought to a triumphant conclusion. He and a few friends had toured Bradford with bags of Tate & Lyle, dumping sugar into the petrol tank of every non-Hamer hearse in the city, a quaint plan, which had worked.

Diana Farrell was delighted. She asked if this meant he was rich. She couldn't believe it. Had he really won?

But my father's delight was gone now. He shrugged. The fact of his victory seemed of no consequence; the intrigue and drama of its staging had been what mattered. It was another game, another attempt to charm the elephant. He said, "Only for a time, and then who knows?"

Then he smiled again. "A coup, a palpable coup. What do you say, Headingley?"

I said, "What's a coup?"

He said, "Tell me about the cellar. What's the problem? I know it's been worrying you old man."

He was right. The previous night, late, I had gone downstairs, asking myself about everything Helen had said, and had stood in front of the cellar door, knowing I wouldn't go down, just teasing myself, that was all. None the less, my heart drummed as my hand reached for the handle. Then a sound made me turn. Helen was at the bottom of the stairs, giving me that passionate stare of hers. "Pride, hunger, greed," she said, "are what make people tick. He told me, the one who's down there now. He worked at a steel mill, a cast broke, should have been replaced years ago, and boiling steel rolled towards him across the floor like toffee melting, all orange and bubbly. He tried to run. Too late, his brains were steam! Go down there, ask him any teaser you like." I pushed past, taking the stairs three at a time. Her voice had followed: "Think about it, little brother. This one's alright. If you don't listen to him, it could be much worse, someone with bad songs, evil songs."

I said, "It's the dead people."

But I no longer had his attention. A pallid, pudding-faced young man was waving from inside the office. He towelled oil from his hands, and came towards us with a bow-legged, rolling walk. My father wound down the car window and held out two ten-pound notes, to ensure—I suppose—that a delay would occur before the hearses were restored to working order. The young man smelled of chips and vinegar. He said nothing, took the notes, stared for a moment at Diana Farrell, and ambled away, his mind unreeling a film in which he was James Dean.

My father turned his head towards Twiggy Fawcett and Amos Bass who, dressed in black, were approaching along the Canal Road, behind a black Rolls-Royce which they pushed at funereal pace, as if the vehicle were a corpse.

"Morning Twiggy," shouted my father.

Twiggy Fawcett's bony face arranged itself into a scowl. "We'll get yer, yer young bastard," he said.

"On horror's head horrors will accumulate," said Amos Bass. "That's Shakespeare. Don't say you've not been warned, Jack."

"And a very good day to you too Amos," he said, throwing back his head and letting rip one last time with the Hamer laugh.

He took her finally to the cricket ground at Windhill where my grandfather once played with Learie Constantine, the West Indian who wore silk shirts buttoned always at the wrist, even on blazing summer days when the five poplars on the northern boundary stood motionless in the heat.

But now it was Bradford weather, brutish and black. We sat in the car. Rain thumped on the roof. My father had a half-bottle of whisky. The bottle was in the shape of a bell. He said, "I'm going to do something very strange. I'm going to be completely honest."

Oh, very smart that, very casual indeed.

"I'm in a spot of bother. There's a fellow called Redbecker. He's after my neck."

Diana Farrell was apparently unmoved. She wore a thin-lipped smile, as if she'd heard it before. My father pressed on. Perhaps he heard the elephant.

"Redbecker made a pile, selling cars with nylons stuffed in the gearbox. Muffled the noise, you see, so you couldn't tell how shot to pieces the whole crate was. He's a garage on the Leeds Road, a lock-up in Guiseley, a farm up Bingley way. Something else somewhere else. Stuff all over the place. Drives a Cadillac with a shotgun in the boot. Says he's shot three men, and I bet drool was coming out of his mouth while he did it. Not an amusing fellow."

She said, "Sounds like the booze talking."

"I don't drink so much, you know," he said, taking another life-size swig. "Just enough to keep a couple of shots ahead of reality. And Redbecker."

"Sounds like self-pity."

But my father shook his head and had another drink.

"I was wrong. You have changed. What happened to you, Jack?"

"I became an undertaker."

"You were always an undertaker."

"I remember when I met you. You wore a green satin hat and a dress like an explosion in a firework factory. Not a week has gone by when I haven't thought of you. Not a single week."

Had he heard that line in a film? In the car there was a smell of whisky and warm leather. The elephant was close.

He said, "Don't worry about me. I'll not be beaten by any of them." He laid a hand on her cheek. He stroked her arm. They kissed. I remember how I thought of it: like pulling a toy arrow from glass, the rubber sucker resisting at first then coming away with a wet plop. I was uneasy, fascinated.

"Headingley, old fellow, wouldn't you fancy a bottle of pop?" said my father, looking at me over Diana Farrell's shoulder.

"No thanks, Dad."

He winked and gave me a two-shilling piece.

"What's this for?"

"Go get yourself a couple of bags of crisps."

"Diana," I said. "Do you ever hear footsteps behind you in the dark? People coming for you from the past?"

She gave me a stiff little smile and reached in her bag for a cigarette. "No, I don't," she said.

"Do you think about what it will be like to be dead? Do you think you'll sing?"

"I don't know," she said, puffing smoke towards me. "I don't think about it at all."

I turned the two-shilling piece between my fingers. I had an awareness that I wasn't doing what they wanted; I quite enjoyed the feeling.

"Here you are," said my father, giving me another coin. I saw he was angry. "Now go on Headingley, be a good fellow."

"What are you going to do?"

"Headingley," he whispered, leaning over the back of his seat, putting his face close to mine. *"Piss off."*

"Go on, Headingley," said Diana Farrell, smiling. "Do this favour, just for me."

This question of men and women. Big, isn't it? And difficult. Here, for instance, is Diana Farrell: doing what my father wanted simply because he was persistent, or because he wanted it so much, or because he wanted it so much and she had at last decided she wanted it as well? Possibilities occur to me:

1. Men do not like women, fear that they are a widely distributed species of beast of prey, know that feminism is merely the equivalent of the medieval witch's *grand grimoire* and are therefore more intent than ever on trying to teach them not to talk or think.

2. Men like women, find that the reality is somewhat different from the expectation, discover that beyond a certain point women assume an unknown self, as water changes when it boils, and therefore try to teach them not to talk or think.

3. Men understand women. This sounds reasonable. Men are cool customers.

4. Men do not understand women. To confront one is to be faced with another person saying, "I am me, I am me, I am me." Men are themselves self-infatuated and self-deceiving, and thus certain to be shocked and outraged by this proof of the existence of un-me.

5. Men are interested in getting women to do impossible things. To do this it is necessary to find that bit of themselves which matches a bit of whichever woman they are talking to. Then, bingo! Which raises another question. Why do women suck men's penises? What could conceivably be in it for them? Search me. I mean: would you like to be force-fed tepid oysters?

6. Men are regular fellows. Women are not. Women, like morality, are reluctant to buy their round. Men know this and understand that women are capable of all sorts of beastly behaviour. A man could not have betrayed Christ, for instance. Iscariot, that miserable fuck, was a cross-dresser.

7. Men are quite right to want to spoil the fun. Women are planning a series of outrages against society. Men have played the fool for quite long . . .

Enough of this. I was on the cricket square in the rain, realising that my father had a life beyond the one I knew, beyond my own. It involved secrecy and deceit. I was thrilled, without quite knowing why, and resentful. I remembered a man I had seen one Saturday morning at the film club in the Victoria Cinema in Shipley market square, beneath the ugly clock tower which my father always called

Clegg's Clanger, after the architect who had built it. The man in the cinema sat in the back row, surrounded by children, pushing salty pop-corn into his mouth, turning from side to side, grinning, and then loudly laughing as Bugs Bunny, dressed in tall hunting hat and carrying a rifle, mimicked his pursuer, Elmer Fudd: "Be wery wery quiet. I'm huntin' a wabbit. I'll gwind his bones to make me bwead." The man, he was young, with a fleshy face and curly black hair, was actually leading the way in the laughter, as if he were the Pied Piper, and understood the world of children. He was joining in. The man was Redbecker, and I wished my father was more like that.

Did I sense even then that my father was sprinting after something he would never catch? I doubt if I did. Of course I didn't. It's only now that I ask myself whether he thought about what he was doing, that I wonder what he cared for really. The pursuit of sex, drink, money: these were probably on his mind, though he might not always have been aware of it; his was not an analytic disposition.

Did he care for the decencies of the human heart?

Do I?

I found a rotting apple, offbreaked it, and as it exploded on the wicket I imagined that I had fooled Constantine. The West Indian was on his way back to the pavilion, head down, silk sleeves fluttering. Looking back, I saw rain bouncing from the windscreen of the now gently rocking car.

It was the night of the *conversazione*. I was with Helen, Keith, and my mother. I realise I haven't told you much about my mother. She looked like she should have been in films herself: eyes of Garbo, legs of Dietrich, mouth of Hayworth. So I exaggerate. Her name was Lillian and she was small and pretty, with green eyes, though the most remarkable feature of her appearance was her red hair. Bradford people remarked on it. "Joost tek a look at that carrot top. Like a roman candle on bleedin' bonfire night." My father told stories about her. Once, for instance, he had arranged to meet two members of the Yorkshire cricket team only to be kept waiting all night because they were with my mother, drunk in The Oddfellows. Another time she thought he was with another woman in a Scarborough hotel room and arrived bent double in the dumb-waiter, leaping out with poker in hand. And then there was the occasion when mourners drove forty miles from Skipton to pay their respects to a dead relative in the Hamer Funeral Service Chapel of Rest (our living room) and she found that the body was not there, had been buried in error the day before. So she improvised, came on strong and serious, told them there was a crisis, she'd just had a warning from the Bradford Infirmary, a fever was being transmitted by a South African bug found in the orange boxes from which coffins were sometimes made. Dangerous dead men! Sick stiffs! She told them that the house was in quarantine. After that you couldn't see them for dust.

"Headingley," said my mother, "I want to ask you something."

I knew what was coming.

She said, "Have you seen your father in the last few days?"

What did I do? I'll tell you, but first let me ask: what was the most important moment in the history of our species? I imagine I am a professor about to deliver the first in a noted series: The Headingley Hamer Memorial Lectures. I am in a lecture hall, faced by students whose suggestions I have graciously invited. The blonde at the back, whose shoes rub and whose heels are covered with wrinkled plasters, raises a plump and enthusiastic hand. From her it's . . . the invention of the wheel. Oh yeah? I let her know what I think, namely that the wheel was just the first of those gimmicks whose purpose is to allow people in white coats to give bragging press conferences and make a lot of money easily. The wheel is only science, I say, and science is only Frankenstein and his monster. The blonde blushes. Then it's the birth of Christ, *you must be joking,* I shout, *that fraudulent Jew boy,* the gift of fire . . . *blind man at the helm* . . . and the formation of the first social group, which doesn't even merit comment but is dismissed with an imperious punching motion. There's a silence after that, and I'm careful to give the message, it's a beam I send them from my eyes, that I'm not in a temper. True, their proposals have been banal so far, but I'm sure . . . what? I smile at the flame-haired temptress who dresses always in short tartan skirts and who says it was the distillation of the first single malt whisky, *yes that's more like it.* We laugh and another silence before I at last divulge my own opinion. The most important moment in the history of the species? Was the telling of the first lie. It's true, I say, the human genius is for fabrication, for the creation of that which is not. As an Irish poet once said: false representation is the critical difference between man and horse.

So, on that night when my mother asked me if I'd seen my father, what did I do? I examined the lemonade which Keith had spilled moments before on the rubber mat beneath our feet in the car; the liquid was spreading through the grooves, taking the shape of a V. I demonstrated that I am no quadruped.

I said, "No, Mum, I haven't seen him at all."

She glanced at me then, saying, "Are you sure?"

"Yes, Mum, I haven't seen him for ages."

"He hasn't been picking you up from school?"

"No, Mum."

My mother sighed. "I'm sorry, Headingley. I didn't mean to accuse you of lying."

Shake, rattle, and roll! I like those Irish poets.

The party was on the first floor. I heard it faintly when we were half-way up the stairs and as we walked closer across the marble tiles on the landing, the music and conversation grew loud. I grasped Helen's hand.

"Isn't this great?" she said. "Like going into a haunted house on a dare."

We went into the ballroom. A band thundered. A fat man in a tuxedo was trying to sing like Frank Sinatra. He had a red carnation in his buttonhole and the face of a murderer. My mother looked around and saw him at the other end of the room; my father, I mean, not the villainous crooner.

"Jack," she said, "I might have known I'd find you here. Never miss a party."

But my father was smiling and already surrounded, busily ignoring the shouts of various others. She was just one more.

Billy Crow and his sister were there. "Us need that money, Mr. Hamer," the sister said. "Us need it now. It's not reet you not givin' Billy 'is wages."

Diana Farrell was there. "Weren't you keen to show me how well you can rumba?"

And the brown-eyed handsome man: "Can you imagine what

Bradford m-m-ust have looked like to the V-v-v-v-ikings when they came through. Not exactly like stumbling on M-m-mayfair, is it?"

"Yer've bin reet good tah Billy, Mr. Hamer, and ahm grateful. But bills'll not wait. Rent'll not wait."

"If you won't dance then I'll find someone who will."

"C-c-oming all the way from D-d-enmark in their helmets with h-h-h-h-orns on. Three m-m-onths in a bloody cold longship to f-find this. Or was it N-n-n-orway?"

"If you think I'm going to put up with much more of this, Jack, you're wrong. You're dead wrong."

He spoke at last, but not to my mother. Instead, he addressed Helen, Keith, and I. "What would you say if we moved away from Bradford? We'll have a big house and a cellar for disposing of unwanted guests. A house so huge that we will never run into each other and can meet only by appointment. A house so huge we'll need a map. I'll buy you each a compass. What do you think?"

"Will there be dead men in the cellar?"

That was Helen, of course, but then it was my mother once more, saying: "Jack, you haven't introduced me to your lady friend. That's rather rude, wouldn't you say?"

"Ah can't insist, yer knows that Mr. Hamer, and Billy'll allus do yer work 'cos Billy's like that an' don't know no better an' you're 'is friend."

My father took out his wallet and, without counting, handed over its contents. He said, "I hope it's enough. I have been remiss. You have my apologies. Billy, I'm very sorry."

I looked down . . . Billy's grin.

"D-d-d-iana. Shall we trip the light f-f-fantastic?"

"There's too much 'ere, Mr. Hamer."

"Please. Take it on account. I'm not sure when I'll be able to pay Billy next."

"Oh, very generous, Jack. Always the grand gesture. Meanwhile you haven't seen your family for a week."

"Are we going to rumba, or aren't we?"

My father pressed the palms of his hands to his temple. "By all means we'll rumba," he said. "But first I must be social secretary. Lillian, may I present Diana Farrell? Diana has a degree in philosophy. From Heidelberg University. We speak only of metaphysics and lager beer. And Diana, I'd like you to meet Lillian, another of my business associates. Isn't this what Saturday night should be? A regular do."

He looked at them both, and attempted what I imagine he thought a winning smile, which makes me wonder what my father understood about women. The answer, of course, is everything. And I understand even more. That's one of the issues at hand here, how well we have understood women, my father and I.

My mother hit him across the face.

My father took pride in her strength of character, which may seem curious, but he did. And when she hit him he didn't look surprised, though the blow sounded like a gunshot. Not that I know what a gunshot sounds like; that's not true, I do. Anyway, this violent unexpected sound amazed everyone except my father. There was a hush. Even the singer paused from his butchery of "Come Fly With Me."

"Oh yes," she said, "it's a regular do alright. Fasten your safety belts, we're in for a bumpy night."

"B-b-bravo, Bette Davis. I just adore amateur th-th-theatricals."

There was laughter and the band started up again.

"Now then, what's this? Happy sodding families?" said another voice, one we haven't heard before, with a mild Yorkshire accent. And thus, unannounced—typical, an important character makes his entrance: Redbecker, he'll be Captain Ahab, harpoon at the ready, in sullen and insane pursuit of something he nearly caught so long ago. The whale, the whale! Where is the whale? Here he comes: my father.

He said, "Bloody hell it's Redbecker," and slid an arm round my reluctant mother's shoulders. "Nasty nosy noisy in everything but the way he comes up behind you and that's because he's worried about wasting leather on his shoes. And that's because he's worried about money. Redbecker likes money, don't you old chap? If you drop it, presto! it doesn't break."

"You're a card alright, Jack," said Redbecker with a chuckle. "I like that about you. You're a bloody card alright."

"But my dear fellow. That's not so. You're the one. With that fabulous American car of yours. And the check suits. Bradford's Jimmy Cagney. You know you are. Drive around with your molls in the back, waving to your wife at the bus stop. And I'll tell you something else. Not only am I not a card, at the moment I'm sorry I'm the only man in Bradford who is not not Jack Hamer. Do you follow? Tell my associates here . . . ," pause for nod in our direction, ". . . that I want to change. I do. I want to live quietly, away from all this. Give me the Highlands. Do you know the Highlands old man?"

Redbecker did not know the Highlands.

"Or perhaps the Islands. There's always those. Do you know the Islands?"

Redbecker did not know the Islands.

My father let go my mother and took him by the arm. He said, "Tropical fish."

Smiling, Redbecker took a cigar from his pocket and rolled it slowly along a tongue black as Bradford. He told my father to go on for as long as he liked. He loved to listen, he said, he didn't mind at all. Spit gleamed and bubbled on the cigar.

"Guppies, swordtails. Zebras and Siamese fighting fish. Isn't there one called a Black Molly? I need to know all you know."

Redbecker just grinned.

And I grinned too, until I looked at Helen. She had turned white and was pointing. "I've met you before. I've heard a song about you. You're an evil man," she said. Her voice shook: Joan of Arc, recently introduced to the executioner. That was how it would turn out. I loved you Helen, I never told you, not really, but I did.

Redbecker was still grinning. I had a dizzy sensation. I too felt sick and afraid, though then I could not know how dangerous he was. He would do anything to achieve his goal. He believed without question he could make the world march to his own speed. Yet nothing of this was visible—he seemed almost babyish, with his hair slicked back, his pink shiny cheeks, and his loud, absurd suit—except perhaps his cigar. Alight now, it was like Redbecker: sleek and slightly plump and glowing with purpose. I am very much like Redbecker, it seemed to say, I am Redbecker, a born boss among cigars.

I hate people like that: tyrants with torture in their smiles. Don't you wish you could smash their complacency? I hate also those who are weak and so confused by their weakness that they can do nothing but wish everyone were as weak and confused as they. Spineless shits! And the people in between, I can't stand them either, the ones who carefully tread the line, neither too cocky nor too unsure, like a fellow I knew who wore a shiny grey suit and on Friday nights in subterranean wine bars grinned enthusiastically at his employer's bad jokes, you know how to get a nun pregnant, you *fuck* her, and whose like was tied up in the question of whether he could dump his girlfriend and thus afford to trade in his fast red car for a faster one of even greater redness. Mediocrity, worthless scum!

I am Hamlet!

Where was I? With Redbecker, saying, "You get nowt for nowt, Jack," and not taking his eyes from my father. "We had an arrangement, Jack. I did you a favour."

Redbecker had helped my father with the sugar and the hearses.

"And got well paid for it."

"We've yet to settle the other."

"A partner for Jack Hamer? There's no such person."

"Remember, Jack. Nowt for nowt."

"Lend me a fiver will you old man?"

Still Redbecker smiled as he handed over the note. My father held it up to the light, and with the deft and deliberate gestures of a professional magician, turned its crispness between his fingers. He said, "I have enchanting visions of what this could buy. Two bottles of Scotch. Delectable foods. A ticket for Lord's and a Dexter double-hundred. Wonderful, isn't it?"

He pulled out a cigarette lighter, and turned this between his fingers with equal wonder. "You know Redbecker, someone asked me a question: "What once lost, is never found?" The answer she wanted was 'the truth.' But the correct answer was of course the one I gave: *'A Dunhill lighter.'* "

There was a flame and the banknote was a butterfly of fire, hovering for a moment, then turning black and fluttering up towards the ceiling. My father said, to no one in particular, "Shall we dance?"

Then it was more magic. Having invited Diana Farrell and the brown-eyed handsome man to our house for tea the next day, my father didn't show up. And nor did Diana Farrell, so you don't have

to be Sherlock Holmes to deduce that being a heavy stick the dog
had held it tightly by the middle and the marks of his teeth were
plainly visible. In other words: they were together. While I played
a game, rolling a coin along the floor, and diving to catch it in front
of the floor-length glass windows in our living room, the brown-
eyed handsome man talked to my mother.

He said, "Why do you put up with it?"

"What?"

"Your husband."

"This morning I took Jack's clothes, every last stitch, and threw
them off the Pottle Street bridge in Shipley."

"Women. Fiendish in search of revenge."

"Sod that. I'm not interested in revenge."

"What would interest you? Some sordid business in your bedroom. With me, mmm?"

She said, "Your stammer, it's gone."

The brown-eyed handsome man arched an imperious eyebrow.
He didn't, but he did say, "I'm a preposterous character alright, but
please don't assume I'm the fool I sometimes pretend to be. And
your husband thinks I am."

"Well, I'll be buggered."

"If such is your preferred *modus operandi*." There was a pause.
"Do you love him?"

"Love?" she said. She thought for a while. She said he'd laugh
if she told him how she remembered it. She thought of those times
with such nostalgia and longing that they had achieved the quality
of a film, a big costume number, like *Gone With the Wind* or
Wuthering Heights, with my father and her, centre-screen, locked
in a passionate embrace. Absurd, of course, because she knew it had
never been like that. She knew also that she'd lost touch with her
feelings, they'd been swamped by an ooze of lies and absence, and
the affairs which Jack didn't even bother to hide these days.

She said, "And I spend too much time wondering, *what-the-
bloody-hell-next?* and chewing my nails, terrified of the answer. No,
I don't think I do love him any more."

That was when I dived for the coin one more time, missed, and
it was goodbye window, hello deep cut in my upper arm. The
drive to the hospital featured me leaking blood on Jaguar uphol-

stery and him begging to see her again. They could take a drive, he said, or go to the c-c-c-cinema.

She said, "I'll take the sordid bedroom business."

I don't know if my mother did sleep with the brown-eyed handsome man. In the days that followed, she was often absent from the house, and Helen, Keith, and I were even less than usually concerned with the routines of family and domesticity. Perhaps she was with him. I really don't know. I do know that I saw a lot of my father in those days and that I was learning more about the critical difference between man and horse. "Miss Antrobus gave me the afternoon off school," I said to him, and then, in exchange for my father's disbelieving glance: "It's true. She said I was pale and should play football. But I'd rather come with you."

He said I might, but he had a funeral at Undercliffe and I had to drive there with Billy Crow.

"Dad," I pleaded.

"Headingley," he said, and so it was decided.

Billy and I arrived early. Imagine a graveyard on a hill. Bradford is below, and through the pouring rain you see chimneys and cooling towers, too many to count, and the flattened hump of a reservoir on the other side of the valley. The graveyard is sootblackened and huge, with streets, like the city for the living down there, about which this other city, this city for the dead, can tell you a lot, namely, for instance, that Bradford people had a taste for monuments that was not particularly Christian (bordered, in fact, on the pagan: look, a pyramid, an obelisk, even a sphinx or two) and that Bradford people believed in a grim Bradford solidity they could carry beyond death. Billy has a map. Not really, but he does know his way around, and takes you past the unmarked graves of the damned, the modest graves of the poor and the ornate deathtemples of the rich. He wants you to see something.

Billy wanted me to see his favourite grave. It was covered with white flowers and marked off with a low rail of black iron. A slab of white marble stood upright with the curt inscription: MARGARET LEHMAN, 1923–1944.

"Beautiful, isn't it? Put new flowers on every Sunday I do. Only white ones."

"It's lovely, Billy."

"I never met 'er but she's the dead body I like best. I know 'er. She talks to me and I'm 'er friend. It meks me mad when I see as 'ow folks'll not look after graves of their own. Maggie's grave were terrible. I thought, mebbee, she 'ad no family. Man doesn't look after his family, he's no good I reckon."

He kneeled, plucked a petal or two from last week's flowers, stood up and lost his balance. I missed whatever it was that caused Billy's size 14 boot to skid across the grass and into a puddle. Didn't miss, however, the mud it left on my bare leg, a sandy splash with a tail behind it like a comet. "Billy," I said in protest, and it was then that it happened, then that I had a vision of myself, down there in the coffin, the wet earth warming the wood and cloth in which I had been interred, staring up at mourners staring down. Then the vision was gone.

I shivered. I said, "You're bloody daft, Billy, do you know that?"

Sighing, he heaved his frame upwards. Had there been a sun he would have blotted it out, but there was none, this was Bradford in November and the sky's most cheerful tint was a dull grey which matched the overcoat stretched thin across Billy's immense chest. Billy wasn't hurt, as I had at first intended, nor angry, as I had then feared, but opened his mouth in the familiar, terrible grin.

"Oh aye," he said cheerfully, "dafter than a lorry load of thin-gummies, that's me."

The funeral was of a teacher who, my father said, had a glass eye. Perhaps the one-eyed teacher had been lonely and without many friends. Perhaps the weather was too brutish for the Bradford living to buy a ticket to the city of the Bradford dead. Perhaps he had been homosexual, and Bradford was too prudish to come. Anyway, there was just the one mourner, a former colleague, an old and thin and rather nervous man who was crying and who, my father said, had taught him Dickens, badly, many years before. Dickens was the only writer my father cared about. The man's grief was muted.

It was dust-to-dust, the burial service routine, then Billy and the other gravedigger took hold of the webbings, which creaked and strained as they lowered the coffin. Again I saw myself inside, looking up. My father was there, and my mother; Helen, Keith, Billy himself, Redbecker, and others, many more, who I did not recognise, all open-mouthed, as if they were laughing at me. Why laughter? Didn't they realise I was trapped, like a fly in a down-turned glass, not dead, but something worse?

Snap! One of the webbings had torn, and the coffin crashed down, breaking loose the lid. The corpse wore a grey suit and as I moved forward to look it sat up straight, called to order by a school bell from the other world. There was a silence. I looked at the solitary mourner. His mouth was wide open in shock, or disbelief. I looked at Billy. Rain ran in streams down his face, and a meaty finger was pointing.

"Bloody 'ell," he said. "I know 'im. He were at the grammar school. I saw on the trolley once, puttin' in 'is eye."

And now the glass eye popped from the dead man's face and rolled along a pinstriped leg towards his shoe, like a ball heading for the skittles in a bowling alley.

"Marbles!" shouted Billy Crow, which made my father smile. The boy Headingley was not smiling, however. He was scared. He wondered if the man in the coffin was really dead. If so, was he about to sing? He wanted to ask his father, but decided not to provoke him, which was sensible, because his father wore a terrible frown now, as if trying to work out what had happened, and why, and what the consequences might be.

Redbecker was in the street outside, elbow on the roof of his car. He smiled when he saw my father. I looked at him, remembering Helen's fear, and he made a sign as if to slit his throat. "Weather fit for a dog," he said. I remember also his nonchalance; that, and the sense I had of something important happening, because he was with another man, with a dark suit and a shiny face, big and round like the moon: Charlie Laughton.

"Jack, I'm going to come straight to the point," Laughton said. "Big fish eat small fry, and you really must decide where you are, swimming with the sharks or frying in fat and about to be served from the pan. Put it this way: if you don't agree, I won't answer for the consequences."

"You know me, Charlie," my father said, "I don't bother myself with consequences, it's my creed."

"You're on top at the minute. But it won't last. I know that. That's the trouble, Jack. I *do* know you."

I'd heard stories about Laughton all my life. He'd been at the grammar school with my father, he'd been top of the class, he'd asked my mother to dance before my father, he'd been a groom at the wedding, he'd given my mother a gold brooch in the shape of a bird, a swallow, with emeralds for eyes and diamonds on the tail. He had been christened Henry John but was now known as Charles; he liked people to be reminded of the famous actor, who had been born in Scarborough. This Charlie Laughton was rich and famous in his own way. During the war he had convinced an army medical board of his insanity, by sneaking from the barracks at night and planting stones, shouting, "You will grow up a little Laughton, and so will you," and by combing urine through his hair. He had been discharged, which had suited him fine. Then he had become a black marketeer, very successful, and had cruised through Bradford in an ostentatious American car, a Duesenberg, sitting always in the back with muscle on either side, wearing silk suits and a cashmere coat with an astrakhan collar. My father smiled when Laughton's name was mentioned; his friend Charlie, the one-time gangster.

Laughton said, "There are those who think life rolls out wide and gentle as the sea on a calm day. You just bob up and down on the waves, leaning back, watching the sky and the clouds, and everything takes care of itself. You need no one. But life isn't that way for you, Jack. Your life's a leaky boat that's moving away from a harbour and the harbour is getting smaller and smaller as harbours do. I know, because I'm out here in a bloody great battleship with my eyes open, watching. And you do need someone. You need me."

"And him?" said my father.

Redbecker's smile was unperturbed. He said, "Standing here like a mug I am. Too wet to smoke. I hear you had some trouble."

"What would you know about that?"

"Your business is in a spot of bother, that's what I heard."

"You bloody little sod," said my father.

"Shame about this rain. 'Cos when I've got a cigar, it's all different. I'm Stanley Mathews on the right at Wembley, John

Wayne with a six-shooter, and that's not Bradford down there, it's New York, Jack, New York, and here comes Marilyn Monroe about to stand over a ventilator shaft."

"So it was you who fixed the funeral."

"Whatshisname, the vegetable?" Redbecker was looking at Billy Crow. "Tell him to piss off."

"*You* piss off," said my father.

Still the smile: "Not over-fond of me, are you Mr. Hamer? Grieves me. Mr. Laughton and me and our pals, we've got some clout in this town. We speak, it jumps."

"Join me, Jack."

"Join us. We're the future."

"Just listen to this. A thug and a philosopher."

"Oh aye. But I'm practical as well. I make things happen. Do you see the cartoon shows? I do, take the kiddies each Saturday morning to the Essoldo, and it's always disasters. You know. Weights falling, holes in the ground. Guns going off. But funny. I hear that's what your funeral was like today. A farce. Walt ruddy Disney. It's going to get worse, I reckon. I do more than that. I *predict*. Be like Wile E. Coyote and the ruddy Road Runner."

My father smiled at Redbecker. Then, slowly, deliberately, he turned to Laughton.

"I like you, Charlie."

"And I like you, Jack. Always have."

"It's the things you marry into." He nodded at Redbecker. "Jesus wept, and why not when he saw this. It's true then, what they're saying, about you and Elvis Presley?"

The story was that Redbecker had burned down a dance-hall on Manningham Lane. The hall belonged to one of Laughton's rivals and Laughton, recognising talent, not to mention possible competition, when he saw it, took Redbecker in hand, telling him that arson was not always necessary or even desirable in business, that subtler methods could be more effective, that—for example—the rivalry between the Bradford undertakers was an opportunity it would be criminal to ignore.

"Redbecker and I have interests in common, that's all. Like you and me," said Laughton. "What's it to be then, Jack?"

My father said, "It's no."

"No?"

"No, that's not it, it's not just no, it's do your worst and sod the both of you."

"So be it," said Laughton. "Say hello to Lillian for me."

"I will," said my father.

Redbecker was grinning. "I'll be seeing you, Jack," he said. "I'll be seeing you very soon."

I dreamed I was in a coffin in a row of coffins. The corpse next to me sat up and asked how I died. I said I didn't know, I couldn't remember. And him? Drowned, he said. He had pitched into the canal after five pints too many. A little girl said she'd gone that way too, having bet her sister she could hold her breath for two minutes in Shipley beck. She lost her bet. Far away there was a huge butcher, heaving himself upright, saying he liked a flutter himself. He wanted to know who'd won the last race at York. Then, from all around, came the clattering of wood on stone as the dead pushed away the lids from their coffins and sat up, eager for polite conversation.

I woke up. I lay in bed, breathing quickly, scared, waiting for my eyes to accustom themselves to the dark, and as I began to see the comforting shapes—the wardrobe, the dark rectangle which I knew was a picture of Johnny Mathis put there by my mother when this had been her work room, the sloping shoulders of a cricket bat propped against the wall below it—it occurred to me that there was a reason for all this, it all added up. The dream, the man sitting up straight, and the visions I'd had of myself in the coffins were a warning. There was a chance that I would die, soon, in a coffin, and therefore (most likely) in the cellar. Redbecker was involved. Helen was right after all. He was a bad man. He was the Pied Piper who called the dead from their coffins and marched them to a cinema which showed, not cartoons, but only films of war atrocities. I felt calm, now that I knew. To cheat death wouldn't be so hard. Simple: just don't go to the cellar.

So what did I do?

I went to the cellar.

But first I went to the window. I moved the curtain aside a little, and peeped out. I expected to see Redbecker, waiting in his big American car which had fins leaping from the back and a ton of polished chrome. The street was empty. So, thinking I was safe, I went for a glass of milk. As I walked down the stairs the house seemed hollow and silent, empty. But the light was on in the kitchen and Helen was there, knitting a grey jumper. I liked that jumper.

She didn't seem surprised; it was as if she had been waiting for me, as if she had summoned me. She said, "Tell me your dreams."

"No."

"I know what you were dreaming."

I must have looked blank.

"Tonight's the night. I knew you'd come."

I tried to continue looking blank.

"There's one down there now. I can feel him. He's tall and thin with black hair. He looked like death even when he was alive and he died horrible. His wife strangled him with a silk stocking."

I can't remember what I felt. Yes, I can: the neon tube buzzed in the silence and everything in the kitchen was terribly bright. Helen's knitting needles moved in clicking metallic patterns, zig-zags of fear. I felt terror, because I knew who she was talking about: it was the dead man from Undercliffe, the one who had sat up straight, come to the house to scare me again.

"Just a filmy thing. But it did the job. Life's so fragile. Now he wants to sing to you."

I tried to laugh. Couldn't make a sound.

"You'll remember tonight for the rest of your life."

That was no lie.

"Are you scared?"

"Don't be daft," I said.

"Come on, then. It's show time."

In the hall moonbeams came through the skylight. There were squares of brightness on the floor; it seemed to me that they were dreams, intense and peaceful dreams which did not involve going into the cellar where coffins rested on stone slabs alongside cob-webbed gas meters and jars of pickles and raspberry jam.

Helen walked on tiptoe like a cartoon burglar, pausing after each step on the black and white tiled floor, admiring the silence of her motion. My own walk was loud. I slapped my naked feet hard into the squares of brightness. The strategy was to wake up everyone in the house. I imagined myself sitting by the stove in the kitchen sipping cocoa from a white porcelain mug while my father lectured Helen on the importance of respect for the dead. Not to worry that he wasn't even in the house, nor that I had never witnessed him in any such display of reverence, since he didn't seem to bother about the dead one way or the other. It was a fine strategy.

It didn't work.

We were at the cellar door, shiny black with a knocker in the shape of a leering gargoyle. No it wasn't. It was an old oak door, an ordinary door, but it led to the cellar and I hoped my father had locked it up tight and tossed away the key.

He hadn't.

Helen turned on her torch. A yellow beam shot into the gloom, and we followed it, past flaking whitewashed walls, down worn and creaking wooden steps. There was a smell of mildew and something rotting. Fruit, I hoped. The cold damp of the cellar was all about me like iced water.

Down and down and down, each step taken slowly, carefully, until we were at the bottom. Helen turned and made another of her cartoon burglar gestures, this time raising her finger and tapping it against her lips to signal silence. I imagined mice burrowing and spiders tensing their legs as they heard our approach. It was possible there were rats beneath the flagstones. Or on top of them. It was very possible. The cellar was filled with a gnawing life.

Helen swung the torch and its beam picked out a coffin. It was long and black and shining, with carved panels and handles of polished brass. Expensive: someone wanted to surprise the neighbours with a final, unanswerable act of one-upmanship.

She whispered, "That's fifty quid's worth of box with a dead man inside."

"There isn't really a body is there?"

"Don't be so namby-pamby," she said, shrugging. Helen was always so sure of herself. Not me.

"I think we'd better get back upstairs before someone wakes up."

"I think we'd better get on with it."

I walked towards the coffin. My heart thumped so that I lost my breath. I thought my lungs would explode. I reached for one of the coffin handles and the feel, in my palm, of the cool brass, calmed me, slightly.

"Push off the lid."

There was silence. My chest shook. Time was rubber stretched so I could see through as it became thinner and thinner, like being at the dentist when it seems the tooth-plumbing will never stop and your mind can somehow review your life in its entirety, moment by moment, and then it snapped at last. I screwed shut my eyes and pushed.

"Go on our kid," said Helen, and now her voice was urgent yet gentle, a team coach encouraging a nervous rookie, as if she understood what I felt. "Look into the box."

So I opened my eyes. And saw Adam in despair and the serpent in the garden but Eve to blame as well, and a woman in Bluebeard's back room, the one painted after his name, face to face with the circumstances of her own death. I saw forbidden knowledge.

I saw a body, a man dressed in black in the coffin. It's true. This wasn't from one of the stories in Helen's book. This was real. I couldn't see all of his face because the forehead was wrapped with a white cloth and two shiny copper pennies were where the eyes should have been. I assumed it was indeed the man from Undercliffe. It seemed logical: the dead were able to move about at will.

From behind, Helen said, "His hair will go on growing for weeks yet. There are parts of the body that are stubborn. They won't give up the ghost. Like the parts that sing."

She moved the torch, and I remember another of those Edgar Allan Poe details, a figure, grotesque and hunchbacked, appeared on the wall; my shadow, leaning over the coffin. Then the torch was directly beneath her chin, shining up, giving her face a white and ghostly look. "And you thought I was lying," she said. "From now on you'll know I don't tell lies."

I thought of the man. Imagine your breath being cut off: a rattle in the throat while you still smell the apple that is still cut in two on your plate. I thought about his last supper.

There was a noise from the coffin. It was as if the man had read my thoughts and wanted to send a message. I told myself I must have imagined it. I said, "Did you hear that?" Helen did not say whether she had or not. Then, incredible as it seems, and it did seem incredible, the man in the coffin began to speak.

He said, "Are you sitting comfortably?"

Helen and I stared at each other. She looked as scared as I was.

She hadn't been expecting this. "The voice," she said. "It sounds different. It's not usually like this. It's usually wonderful, like a voice from heaven."

There was another sound, of metal bouncing on stone and rolling, as if two pennies . . . I knew without looking. The man was getting out of the coffin.

"Man has come into the forest," he said. "Bambi, your mother cannot be with you any more."

I knew that voice, and I saw from Helen's face that she did too. She shone the torch. The man was looking at the corner where one of the pennies still rattled and then he raised his eyes. He belched and the air was filled with the reek of whisky. It was our father. And the business about Bambi? Like Redbecker, he loved cartoons, and I remember the time he took Helen, Keith, and I to see the film. I hid under the seat when Bambi was lost in the forest and he joined me, saying, "I say Headingley, don't blame you at all, bit strong this."

"Dad," Helen said, "you're dead, aren't you?"

What if it were true?

"You're dead and you've come back."

"No sweetheart, I'm not. Dead people don't talk."

"But they do. They sing."

He was crying. His face was squeezed by grief. It was a time before he could speak again and then he told us that dead people did not sing. It was a beautiful idea but, like many beautiful ideas, untrue. He said, "It's about your mother."

I said, "She's gone. That's it, isn't it?"

My father stared at Helen, and then at me. His eyes were glassy. He told us: our mother had died, it had happened that morning, they'd taken her to the infirmary, a blood vessel broken in the brain, Laughton and Redbecker were to blame, scared the daylights out of her, now we were all going to have to help each other and be very brave. He stopped suddenly as if hearing a noise. The cellar hummed.

There was nothing, just Helen whispering, "She's dead?" and my own voice, not quite an echo:

"Mum's dead?"

Part Two

"Take me, for instance. White gloves are a tradition."

"White gloves?"

"In-bloody-violable tradition, that's what it is, Jack. The tragedy is that there's not a decent pair to be found in the whole of Yorkshire. Except Harrogate, maybe."

"Hate Harrogate. Place where bored rich people go to die. Funny thing, that. They get money, they have money in their pockets and elsewhere, lots of money, plenty of money, too much money, they are moneyed folk, and what do they do with those money-laden purses? Do they seek sex and sun and stimulation? They do not. They use their money to make even more money. Their millions breed like rabbits. I tell you old man, if I were rich . . ."

"We will be rich Jackie, just watch."

"I'd buy a plane."

"It's not as if we're doing bad even now."

"Put something pretty in the passenger seat and, *whoosh,* around the world."

"Un-bloody-controllably-rich. And soon."

"Paris, then south to Naples. And on through the night to Rio and Buenos Aires. What spectacle, what charm, what mighty magic. Perhaps I'd marry a lady in a veil and live among the palm trees like a sultan for ever."

"I'll have a lorry load of white gloves and I'll shit on the whole bloody lot of 'em."

"I'd climb the great wall of China."

"What's that?"

"A wall in China."

"I know it's a wall in China, and that's the point about it, that's why it's there, to stop cocky sods like you who think they can do anything. It's like I've been telling you."

"What's that?"

"Now before I go any further, I'll ask a question. Who's the boss, Jack?"

"I am, no doubt about it, not a question in my mind."

"You're the boss. But we're partners?"

"Absolutely."

"And we're friends."

"I trust so."

"Like a brother I feel to you, Jack, which is why I can tell you this. It can't go on. This pavilion caper. It'll ruin us."

"Ruin me, old man, not you. I'll be the one looking down both barrels. And frankly I don't give a monkey's."

"You're off your rocker, Jack, you know that?"

Hang on a minute. This story is in danger of telling itself, and that won't do. So, in case you'd forgotten, here I am, having moved on a few years, five to be precise, which makes me twelve, and the above conversation took place not in Bradford but in Scarborough, a seaside town with a hotel on the front. The hotel is big and creamy, I can picture it now, like a wedding cake. Not that the above conversation—between Redbecker and, of course, my father—takes place there. Strictly, it doesn't happen in Scarborough at all, not precisely, and since I'm committed to a new policy of truth, I'm shooting straight ink now, I'll tell you that it happens a little way outside the town on the Whitby Road, in a car on a cricket field on a cliff, the same cliff which, legend has it, sank the ship bringing Dracula to England. But the rocks against which the vampire wilfully wrecked himself are down there, beneath an ominous sky, and while under the same threat of imminent downpour, we're up here at the cliff's edge, snug in a red Jaguar 340S, the car preferred by spivs, wide boys, bank robbers, and gangsters of all description, a sleek and powerful Redbecker of a car, a getaway Jag.

Memory sees gulls tossed by the wind, sees also a bright yellow rescue helicopter heading up the coast and two, no three fishing boats bobbing on the sluggish grey swell. I'd like to brighten things, include strong shadows, dappled walls, a warm sun which we felt on our back, but it can't be done, because the second part of my story, like the first, happens in winter.

November.

And "we"? Are my father, Keith, Redbecker, and myself.

I was along only for the ride, but the others had their reasons. Keith had heard he could pick up a drum kit and a pair of cheap Marshall amplifiers for his rock group. He was impatient, looking at his watch, wondering how long it would be before we made it to Scarborough. Redbecker, on the other hand, was trying to find out something, about my father, who was here as part of another of his campaigns. Redbecker didn't understand what was going on and neither did I, though this time it seemed my father might be on the road to Moscow, and disaster. He wanted to buy a cricket pavilion.

"This," said Redbecker, "is going to cost heavy sausage."

Look to the other side of the field, through the rain which has just started to fall, and there it is, white with a red roof, a clock, and a weather vane like the one at Lord's in London, in the shape of Father Time. The pavilion: my father proposed to take it to pieces and rebuild it, seventy miles away in Bradford.

My father was out of the car, raincoat flapping behind him as he leaned into the wind and walked around the edge of the field. Redbecker stared after him. "Either of you lads know why he's doing it?" he said.

"Beats me," I said.

"Where the hell is he getting cash?" said Redbecker.

"Couldn't care less," said Keith.

"I look out for your Dad," said Redbecker, "I do what I can for him. I only hope he's not going to land issen in the soup."

With an air of beery (did I mention both Redbecker and my father were drunk?) condescension, he put his hand on my shoulder. A cigar was wedged between the first two fingers. It squatted there, leaking ash on my windcheater.

Redbecker was a smoker, in the habit of lighting one cigar after another, but not always the same type. Some were fat, some thin. Some issued only wisps of smoke, while others billowed pungent fog. Some wore gold bands like wedding rings, others were quite naked. They had names like Hugo de Monterrey or Montecristo or Flor de Forach and Schimmelpenninck or Gatti-Gazzati or Ogden-Krystovski-Upmann. Redbecker smoked with abandon. I imagined them, all those cheroots, panatellas, and coronas, a shoal of cigars nosing through Bradford like barracuda, unaware that they were about to be caught and gutted by a more ruthless predator.

There are other things I should tell you about Redbecker.

First, my father's rejection of Charlie Laughton's offer had been a gesture and, like most such, an empty one. Laughton and Redbecker did become partners in the Hamer business late in 1959. The opposition in the funeral war had been quickly beaten, driven to the wall, or taken over. There were no longer races for dead bodies all over Bradford. Instead, everything was run from an office in Little Germany: the intelligence of death was collated, coffins and flowers and embalming were arranged, and hearses dispatched by radio. Soon other enterprises had been added: two garages, a taxi service, a demolition firm. The partnership seemed, by 1964, to be doing well. I've never known how much my father knew about what Redbecker did to make sure that it continued to do so. I've never known exactly what Redbecker *did* do, I presume some of it was violent, but my father didn't seem to mind, or if he did, I never heard him say anything about it. Cash was rolling in, that was the main thing. He gambled now, on the horses, at Thirsk and Doncaster and York, and spent more and more time away from home, perhaps with Redbecker, perhaps not.

Second, Redbecker's name was not Redbecker. I know, I know. But that was his lie, not mine. When I first met him he was indeed calling himself Redbecker, but since then he had gone back to his family name, Schenk, a grim name, and appropriate, since Redbecker, or Schenk as I shall call him from now on, is the villain of the story. Of course. And let me warn you about the way he carried on: it will be very nasty indeed. But his villainy cannot be separated from my telling of it; thus, when he appeared at the *conversazione* I had it in a balloon above his Brylcreem-slick head: MEET THE BAD GUY. I might as well have armed him with moustache, mortgage, or machine gun, a riding crop even, and said to hell with it. Even Schenk deserves better.

So: some facts concerning Schenk and his origins. He was born in Germany. His father left in 1938, soon after his birth. Over the years Schenk had made outrageous claims: that his father had been a financier, a movie director who had abandoned fame and fortune, an arms manufacturer, an author of popular songs, a symphony orchestra conductor who refused to play Wagner at Nazi party functions. All very unlikely. It's sure, however, that Schenk senior arrived in Bradford and within a year was running a butcher's stall in Rawson Market. He was said to be intelligent and, while sober, a fine judge of meat. I imagine him working with dry lips and hangover-reddened eyes. In 1939 he was successful, co-owner of five butchers' shops and a slaughterhouse.

Schenk did not take up his father's trade.

And by 1964 his style was no longer borrowed from America. The Jaguar had replaced the big American car of five years before. His suits were of dark mohair; cloth from Bradford, narrow-lapels courtesy of Savile Row. His shirts were sent from Jermyn Street. He dressed as though he expected at any moment the invitation to pose for a photographer, not just any photographer, but one of those successful fellows who earned a fortune in London, taking pictures of film stars, pop singers, and skinny girls. Schenk believed he was going places. In fact, he rather overdid the man of ambition, hero of our time angle: he was a little too persuaded by his own public face; he was a 1960s crook who, like so many others, including the Kray Twins themselves, thought he was one of the Kray Twins. I see a handsome man with curly, shining hair and a chipped front tooth.

Schenk said, "You know why white gloves are a tradition with me?"

My father said he couldn't begin to guess.

Schenk turned to Keith, who said it was a mystery to him as well.

And Headingley?

I too was nonplussed.

Schenk said, "I only wear them on special occasions, they've got magic powers, see, but only sometimes, only when I pop little boys' eyes out. I squeeze and," he made pincers of his thumbs and forefingers, "pop!" he twisted his face into a horrible leer, "oooh nasty."

Schenk laughed and Keith laughed, and then my father, so I did too, joining in the joke.

"I don't know Jack," said Schenk. "I just don't know."

"What don't you know?" My father's face had an innocent expression.

"What I was talking about before."

"What's that?" My father: as if struck by lightning.

"This pavilion caper."

"Oh, *that*."

"Where's the cash coming from?"

"Don't worry."

"Thousands, it'll cost. And I'm not worrying Jack, I just want to know."

"I expect you're right."

"So you'll not do it?"

"Vision," said my father. "You lack a vision, old man. Not me, I have my vision, I see it now, I see the pavilion, rebuilt but better, on the field at Windhill. Just think of the publicity! The press are going to go crazy for it."

"For Christ's sake Jack, this is getting out of hand. I'll have to talk to Charlie."

"Go ahead."

"So you'll not take my advice."

But that of course was one of the things about my father, he hated to take advice, and I have to assume that Schenk knew this, was relying on it, that it was part of the plot. My father smiled and said: "Don't go on about it old fellow, you'll put me off my feed."

My father never seemed to expect us to love, or even obey, him. He never sat in a chair and instructed us to bring the cocoa in or a cup of tea or *The Sporting Life* so he could examine form and running conditions. His parental whim was never our law, and when he did ask for something, it was as if seeking a favour from an equal. Nor was it usual for him to display affection. We were on one train, while he was on another, running on a parallel track, and on a different schedule. Occasionally, through a freak of timetabling, his train would come alongside. Often he was nowhere to be seen. Or else there was a party, with a big band playing music he liked—Ellington or Miller, something with swing—and we would glimpse him for a moment, tossing a woman's hat in the air, but he would soon be lost among the joggling, jiving bodies, who held each other, if at all, only by the finger tips, hurtling together for a brief doing and, when done, spinning away to find a new partner. And there were those times when he was at the window, looking for us, but gaily ignorant of our troubles, or glum, even doomy, unresponsive to the party *we* were having. That was how it was with our father: we had neither rights nor duties.

And then, sitting with him on a bench in the rubble of a demolished pub on Fatty Cake Row in Scarborough: badababoum! He said, "Keith doesn't like me, does he?"

I looked over my shoulder to check that Keith wasn't there. He had gone to see about the amplifiers and drum kit. Schenk had gone off also, I don't know where, so I was alone with my father. I was amazed. A wrecked piano was in front of us. I said Keith loved him, we all did, and I remember the expression on his face, a smile of such happiness that he at once thought he had given something away by showing me it. It was there, and gone in a moment.

He said, "You all do? Even Keith?"

I said, "Yes Dad."

The truth was that Keith detested him and didn't try to hide it. When my father walked into a room Keith would walk away, or push out his lips and clap his hands above his head, a gesture learned from Mick Jagger on the television. My father usually pretended not to notice, though once he dropped to his knees, saying Keith had the right idea, Jack Hamer wasn't to be liked and especially not to be trusted, we should call for God and the coppers, have him banged up now; or send him back to the desert and his caravans of musk and ivory.

"Even Keith, eh? That's splendid."

He asked what I'd do if I were in a duel. I told him—oh I was ruthless then—I'd let the other fellow have it in the back before he'd taken his ten paces. He said he'd smoke a cigar and shoot in the other direction at a scarecrow.

"But what if you were hit?" I asked.

"I wouldn't be," he said. "And if I were I'd just fall down, rise again on the third day, and haunt the chap for ever."

Again my father: the suave hero of a period melodrama, flicking dust from his sleeve, a Scarlet Pimpernel—*zounds!*—preparing to give the revolutionary upstarts what for. Or so it appeared. I believe now that he was frightened, that he knew events were at last spinning beyond his control. Perhaps that is to allow coming events to cast their shadows, though I know, and felt even then, this was one sign I was able to read, that when he laughed it was the Hamer laugh no longer. Neither so joyous, nor so reckless, as before, the old man was on edge about something.

I noticed Keith coming towards us. It was hard not to notice Keith, since he wore a bottle green suit made from Harris tweed. Wore also a black silk shirt and black elastic-sided boots with built-up heels, and carried over his arm an army-surplus anorak with fur which Helen had stitched around the collar. Keith was single-minded about his clothes, and much else.

My father looked at him. Then he looked down at his rubble-whitened Oxfords. Perhaps he thought that, like his paternal feelings, the shoes could do with a polish. So he dusted them off. "Hello son," he said to Keith, smiling extravagantly.

Keith said he'd made the deal. A group he knew about were playing in Scarborough that night and he was going to stay. The man he'd bought the gear from would give him a lift back to Bradford. Keith said all this as if he expected an objection.

Instead our father said, "I expect you'll be needing some readies. Here's a five-spot. No, better make it a tenner." He handed over the note.

Now Keith was puzzled. "Thanks," he said.

"What about you old man?" he said, turning to me.

I told him that, if he wanted, he could get me something.

"Sin-sin-sinbad," he said. "Your wish is my open bomb-door." He looked at his watch. "And Keith, one more thing. I met a popsie once, not far from here, a dancer, her face never showed what she was thinking but you only had to look down, everything in her head went straight to her feet. Very expressive feet."

Keith looked impatient.

"What I'm saying is: take care, eh?"

"I won't have sex unless there are shoe-trees available and a hanger for my suit," said Keith coldly.

"I see," said my father, not knowing if Keith was pulling his leg. He pushed his hands hard across his cheeks, and as the skin was drawn back from the eyes his face seemed rubbery, about to take on a new shape. He was tired. "If you lads will excuse me, I'm popping off. Back in a jiffy."

He went down the promenade, turned, and walked along the top of the harbour wall. His left shoulder was suddenly higher than the right as he leaned to pick up something from beside a lobster basket. Then he was moving again, down a ladder—it looked like an ice-cream: the top half whitewashed, the bottom green with weed—and on to a cabin cruiser whose name I couldn't make out at that distance.

"What's got into the old bugger?" said Keith.

"I said you loved him," I said.

"Do you reckon this is forged?" He held up the ten-pound note to the light, squinting at the water mark. "I bet it's bloody funny money. Knowing him. What did you say you said?"

"I said you loved him."

"Maybe you should say it every day," he said. "What did you ask him for?"

I didn't want to tell him. I was a little scared of Keith.

"It was to do with *them*. Wasn't it?"

I said it wasn't, but of course it was.

Keith was impatient. "It's like I keep telling you. It's the thing about *them*. *They're* no good live. No good at all."

The Beatles were coming to Bradford. That was the thing; that was what I'd asked my father: to get tickets for the concert, which was to be at the Theatre Royal, and which had been announced the week before. My Beatle-activities had immediately stepped up a gear, not that I'd ever been slack in this department. I sent for autographed Beatle-photos, bought new records to replace ones only weeks old but already worn out, and also bought Beatle-boots and a grey collarless Beatle-suit, raising the cash for this spree by taking a gold watch, a half-hunter with an inscription on the back which I found in a desk in my father's office, and selling it to a pawnbroker on Hustlergate. Each morning I asked Helen to call the grammar school and say that Headingley was ill again, and then I would walk to the cinema on Manningham Lane where the Beatle-film *A Hard Day's Night* was playing. At the end of each show I would hide under the seat and wait for the next; I had already seen the film eleven times. Or else I would stage Beatle-parties, *Beatle-ins* at the house. School ditched, suit on, I listened to records and danced Beatle-style, keeping the feet still and moving the hips just a little, making quick stabbing motions with the hands.

I was the only guest at these parties. I was a lonely child, I suppose, though the fact didn't worry me; I was used to looking after myself. The Cryer brothers, nephews, or great-nephews, of one of my father's former rivals in the funeral trade, had been regular visitors at one time, but that stopped when Ivan Cryer's tonsils were sliced while he and Keith were fooling around with a fishing rod. I was always a little unsure as to why Ivan had the fishing rod in his mouth. Perhaps Keith had forced him to do it. Keith didn't hate The Beatles, he just didn't like them very much. His friend Lesley had seen them in Manchester and had not had a good time, conclusive evidence, for Keith, that his group, The Five Shades of Blue, were better. Lesley was dark and pretty, with glasses. When she came to the house a cigarette, held by Keith for a moment down at his leg, would point my way to the door. I would go to my room defiantly and put The Beatles on the turn-table.

Helen was also indifferent to The Beatles. She was sixteen and no longer went to the cellar to hear the corpses sing. The cellar doors were padlocked now and Helen was cooler, prettier, with ambitions. She wanted to be a newspaper reporter. She liked the way they wore trenchcoats and their hats tilted back on the head, though she herself dressed in mini-skirts, did her hair high in the style of Diana Ross of The Supremes, and danced each night with her boyfriend Victor at the Locarno Ballroom. Keith called him Victor the Drip.

We cooked our own meals and took irregular turns to do the

dishes which made mountainous heaps in the kitchen sink. It was my job to feed the fish in the Sputnik tank and, provided Lesley wasn't there, I could stay up as late as I wanted to watch *The Twilight Zone, The Outer Limits,* and *The Avengers* on TV. I had discovered masturbation. My first ejaculation came after watching Emma Peel, in black leather cat-suit, beat up some fellow. Yeah baby! From which you may draw no accurate inference concerning my sexual tastes. As I said before, patience, patience. For months I collected old tin cans and soldered them together to make a rocket, a little more than three feet tall, which I filled with gunpowder from fireworks and tried to launch on the day "She Loves You" went to number one. I had celebration in mind. The gunpowder failed to ignite, which was just as well, otherwise this story would have ended then and there. It would have been Undercliffe for me.

What else?

It was around this time that Keith took me on a trolley ride. The trolleys were lumbering giants—I'd jumped off one once and cracked my head on the road—but this one was especially terrible, old and rusty, with seats through which the springs were escaping. Breathing flashes and sparks, it swayed and shrieked under the electric cables. After this ride? A walk down an alley to a firedoor which a friend of Keith's had held open with a brick, and a cinema. The film? Was not *A Hard Day's Night* but *Psycho.* I leaned to Keith when Norman Bates had done the business with the knife in the shower. I told him that blood would swirl the other way down the plug in Australia. A question of gravity. I told him I'd read about it in one of the encyclopaedia in our loft, big books which creaked and breathed dust when you opened them. Then I stopped talking, I stopped because I'd seen a man in front of us, the muscles in his neck like steel wires, taut with the strain of moving his head so he could look Janet Leigh in the eye while she slid, dying, down the tiles of the bathroom wall.

Schenk.

Could I really have seen that, or am I making it up? No, it was Schenk. He had his arm round a woman's shoulders.

I realise that I'm telling you this ominous stuff, as if creating the atmosphere for a plot concerning my father, Schenk, and the mystery of the pavilion. But it was a plot about which I was in the dark, and am only now fumbling to understand. Then it was three children, left pretty much to ourselves, growing up in a big old house. My concerns were masturbation, The Beatles, and waiting for the beginning of the cricket season. I found everything so strange nothing was a surprise; it felt like an innocent time.

Rain fell on the windscreen like stair-rods. Rain bounced off like fish-hooks. We were on our way back to Bradford, with my father driving. We had come through York and Pool and Otley. The tyres of the Jaguar swished through the wet on the Guiseley Road. Schenk was asleep, with his head slumped on his chest, and from the back I saw how his hair had greased the collar of his shirt. The heater was on full and I too felt drowsy. Not far to go now. Then, through the arcs which the windscreen wipers sliced in the rain, over and over, I saw the cluster of pinnacles and pointy towers come closer, sharp against the darkening sky: Menston, the name of a village, and, more significantly, the home of a village-sized mental hospital about six miles outside the city—High Royds.

"Like rockets on the runway," said my father. "That's what those towers remind me of. Your great-uncle Thomas did his time there. Now there was a character. He could give money wings to fly with. He was quite expert at disposing of it. Ran up debts of twenty-three grand before he was twenty-one. That was in 1911. Six months in High Royds. What a performance, eh? But it didn't change him, not old Thomas. He had big ideas. He was court-martialled in the first war. Refused to go over the top in 1916. Not that I blame him. Loyalty to life, better than to a lost cause."

I asked what had happened to Great-uncle Thomas.

"Oh," said my father, casually, "they put him up against a wall and shot him. And now that Im on the subject, I'll let you in on another piece of Hamer history. Did you ever hear of your great-great-great-uncle Sir Richard?"

"*Sir* Richard?"

"He was quite a fellow. Wore a wig and was in on the Gunpow-der Plot. They were going to put a bomb under the Houses of Parliament. The equivalent of blowing up the BBC today. So the authorities were very brassed off. They took Sir Richard, hanged him for a while, and cut out his intestines while he was still alive."

I wasn't sure that I believed him. I said, "Did that really happen?" but my father didn't reply. Instead he asked if tragedies started again, over and over, if families were doomed to walk towards their own destinies by approaching their origins.

"Well Jack, you'd better get your skates on, and do something pretty bad pretty quick," said Schenk. I hadn't noticed him wake up. I wondered how long he'd been listening. " 'Cos they'll be doing away with capital punishment altogether before long."

"I'm talking about uncertainty, the vagueness of man's aims. And the saintly belief that an oath is not binding if made to infidels."

Schenk laughed, though I didn't see the joke myself, and I remember knowing, in spite of their partnership and this apparent good humour, that Schenk was not what he seemed to my father and that, while he might be full of jokes, he had done terrible things. I remember knowing it then as I know it now, and feeling scared, and a little impressed. I remember also how my father seemed smaller when he was with Schenk and how that diminishment made me feel, not scared, or impressed, or sad, but angry. And not with Schenk, who was saying, "Jack, I'm a little bit worried, I'm telling the truth, I really do think you're losing your marbles."

When it was built High Royds was considered ahead of its time. A hundred years ago on public holidays mill-owners and their families would drive out from Bradford in carriages to watch the inmates perform a Miracle Play, or a Nativity, or perhaps even Shakespeare, *A Midsummer Night's Dream* or *As You Like It,* and while Sir Titus or Sir Joseph or Sir Samuel or Sir Shadrachmesach-andabednego smiled sternly at his more sweetly smiling wife he would take comfort, perhaps even give praise, not because he wasn't like this, it didn't occur to him such a thing could be, *this*—look at that poor beggar who's the donkey, he's banging his head against the floor and screaming—wasn't really human (couldn't be), but because he was so wise and virtuous and charitable that he would spend a day coming to watch the poor creature. He thanked himself for himself and afterwards pressed a tenner, nay lad, don't overdo it, a fiver, into the hands of the asylum superintendent, who was himself rarely off the premises—there was a community here, with its own post-office, library, bank, grocer, and a butcher with flies buzzing thickly around the meat—that was the marvel of High Royds, no one who was there need be encountered outside, ever, even the staff—and then he went back to the big black house on a hill where he said goodnight to his wife, rubbed a squarish and very rational forefinger against his chin, and felt that, true enough, he was a man of realities, a practical man, but also a man whose life was spent in the service of mankind and the Lord.

I mention this, a sliver of the history of High Royds, for one reason that will soon be made clear and for another that will only be explained much later.

I mention this because characters in my story ended up there.

Bradford was fog.

We went to Schenk's farm above Haworth. I'd been there once before, during the day, when I had looked across the black moorlands, divided up by dark walls of stone, and had seen scarecrows with something strange about them. It had been the way they moved. I had realised that they actually were crows, dead ones, nailed at the wing between two posts. They had swung to and fro, chest feathers pushed into tufts by the wind. And that night, while my father and I sat in Schenk's car, I imagined crow-corpses.

I asked where Schenk had gone.

"To get changed. We're going to a party at Charlie Laughton's. You remember Charlie?"

I nodded, thinking of the crows. Presumably there would be maggots. I said, "You won't forget about the tickets, will you Dad?"

"Absolutely not. The Fab Four at the Theatre Royal. Old Henry Irving popped his clogs there." He tapped the side of his head. "It's stored, filed away in my knowledge-box, clear as doodah."

"Thanks, Dad."

I thought once more of Schenk. He made me laugh, sometimes, and on other occasions made me very afraid. I didn't know what to make of him, but didn't mention this confusion to my father because as I've said, I saw Schenk grow big, like a looking-glass insect, whenever they were together. My hope was that by keeping quiet I wouldn't upset him.

Schenk got back into the car. When he turned I saw he was wearing a red nose, a ginger wig, and a bowler hat several sizes too small; Schenk was a clown.

We went back towards the city, the Jag nosing through the fog, purring, to our house. Helen was on her way out. My father said, "I thought you were going to watch the telly. With Headingley."

Helen had a date with Victor. She was in a hurry. She was in a skirt short even by her standards. Pneumonia-clobber, I called it.

With a shrug, Helen said, "Call it what you like. Dinner's in the oven, fish-pie."

"Thanks, Helen," I said, and reminded her I didn't like fish.

"Tough," she said.

"Take a dekko at this one," said Schenk.

"So what am I going to eat?"

"Talks like a gangster's moll, she does. A real gooseberry-grinder."

Helen eyed Schenk up and down, up and down, and turned to my father. "What's the matter with Bozo?" she said.

"Not to worry," said my father, who knew smoke signals from the Apache reservation when he saw them, and knew that Helen disliked Schenk fiercely. "Say hello to Victor for me. Need any cash?"

"No thanks, Dad."

And then she was out of the door. Schenk's eyes followed as, wobbling a little on spiky heels, Helen walked down the path to the gate and turned into the street.

My father told me I had better get inside and do some smart thinking. I had to eat whatever there was and be ready, in my costume, in ten minutes. I was going with them to the party. I wondered about the gooseberry-grinder; perhaps it could be used in some way concerning the crows; perhaps, if the crows were fed into it, they wouldn't grow maggoty; perhaps . . . things were not clear in *my* knowledge-box.

All over, people in fancy dress were driving through the fog, peering and cursing through it, *fumbling* through it, out of the city and up the hill towards Baildon. Schenk, as I've mentioned, was a clown, while my father was Sinbad the Sailor, with turban and curling moustache. I'd put on my cricket whites and my father asked who I wanted to be: Bradman, the greatest batsman ever, or Dennis Compton, if I fancied a more cavalier evening, or perhaps a bowler—the demon quickie Larwood, or the off-spinner Jim Laker, whose wiles surpassed those of Ulysses. Which?

I was Keith Miller, the Australian all-rounder. He delighted even as he destroyed; or so I'd read in an article in the *Cricketer*. My father was pleased. He said he had been drunk as a lord with Mr. Miller on many occasions, not unfond of the pop was Mr. Miller, and partial to the ladies also, remarks which caused Schenk to give me a secret smile, inviting me to be his partner in his disbelief: *just one of my father's stories, another boast about the elephant.* I wasn't having any of it. I was loyal to my father; after all, he was getting me tickets for The Beatles.

The house Charlie Laughton lived in was a grand affair called Old Gables. Four storeys high and very long, made from soot-blackened sandstone, it was as big and black as one of the big black warehouses in Little Germany. Laughton had this house, another on the French Riviera, and kept a flat in London, in Mayfair. He owned four cars, and two of them were Rolls-Royces. He was rich, and no longer a crook but a legitimate businessman, or so it seemed, a builder on a big scale. He looked at it this way. If London was swinging, why should Bradford be left behind? It was his mission to drag the city forward from the Victorian age. Therefore he had approached the city council with a plan to knock down half of Forster Square and rebuild it in the modern style. The plan had been approved. Had this been a question of neatly typed forms, followed by closely fought meetings in dusty rooms, after which backs were thumped when, of all the judiciously considered proposals, his was judged the best? Well, no. He had bribed everyone involved.

Laughton stood in the open doorway, with fog around his ankles, dressed in a Roman toga. "Headingley," he shouted, and leaned down. A round, fleshy face, not unpleasant and smelling of something—what was it? lemons!—came towards me. "Face like the backside of an elephant, that was God's gift to me," he said. "When I was your age, I thought surgery was the answer. I could be made again, like Frankenstein's monster. That was my ambition. And now?" Laughton's face moved away. He stood up and spread his arms wide. "Now I am Caesar."

Schenk laughed, loudly. He was smaller now, dwarfed in the imperial presence.

"What about you, Headingley, what's your ambition?" said Laughton.

I looked to my father but his attention was elsewhere, on someone he had glimpsed beyond the door, in the hallway of the house, a woman dressed in green like Robin Hood. His expression suggested she was the first woman he had ever seen.

Laughton's face was expectant.

He said, "You want to be a cricketer."

I said, "No sir. I want to be like you."

"I'll be damned," said Laughton, laughing and turning to my father. "The boy's a diplomat."

"None finer," said my father, without taking his eyes from the Robin Hood woman. "Headingley's going far, all the way, aren't you old chap?"

Laughton took us inside, into a wide oak-panelled hallway with a wide oak staircase at the far end. "And you, Jack, what do you want?" he said.

"I want to come home at night and know there's someone waiting who'll be glad to see me."

"You're considering another marriage?"

"No, marriage is only another greasy law you can always slip out of." My father was still looking at the woman. "I'm thinking of something much finer."

"Oh and what's that?" she said, as if she had been listening all along. "I want to know about the something finer."

"Beware of this fellow," said Laughton. "He's hot mustard."

"Tell me about the something finer," she said, starting to smile, but now my father's attention was somewhere else again, on the staircase, where Diana Farrell was making an entrance.

"Here she is," said Laughton, delighted. "My serpent of old Nile. What do you think of her, Headingley? Isn't she ravishing?"

"Oh yes," I said, an adequate response.

Diana Farrell, or Diana Laughton as she was then, since she and Laughton had been married for three years, was dressed as Cleopatra: black hair cut in a fringe low on her forehead, a ton of bangles and jewellery, and a dress like she'd been dunked in gold. She had a bottle of Gordon's in one hand, while with the other she gave languid strokes to a snake, a live one, yellow and brown, which was snakily unappreciative of her caress. Presumably it did not realise it was playing in Act V of *Antony and Cleopatra*, to a Queen who was beautiful, belligerent, and drunk.

"She *is* a bobby-dazzler," said Laughton. "A little lacking in seriousness, perhaps. For Diana the war was a tedious intermission between *Gone With the Wind* and *Passport to Pimlico*. But then seriousness can be taken too far, I've always thought. Hello, my dear."

"Sod you, Charlie. Why's the bastard here?" She stared angrily at my father; he was the bastard.

"Lovelier than Elizabeth Taylor," my father said.

"She's taken a skinful," said Schenk in a whisper, smaller still, almost tiny now.

"I thought I asked you: no invitation for the bastard."

"Oh come on Diana, you didn't mean that."

"I thought we discussed it."

"Jack's a valued associate."

"I thought we agreed."

"And an old friend."

"I thought I *made* you agree."

"What is she, a witch?" said Schenk, whispering again.

"Jack and I have a business matter to discuss, something which just came up, the moving of a cricket pavilion, quite a job I understand."

"Oh yes, it's going to be a major operation alright. The full Kildare," said my father, winking at Laughton.

But Diana Laughton ignored them both, bored now with the angry performance and interested, to my alarm, in something else, me, saying, "Headingley, it's been too long, and I'm sure you hate it when people tell you this, but it's true, you've changed, you're quite the young man," and, giving a hand still warm from the snake she said, "I want to teach you something."

. . .

I am back in the lecture hall with my students. I am encouraging. I praise their efforts. I seek their opinion: what would they most like to have been taught when they were twelve years old, what would have been the most useful, the most—pause, ironic smirk—*life-enhancing*. The charming redhead is first up. She wished she'd met the adult you never do meet, the one who would talk sensibly about sex, answer all the questions and, instead of blahing about bunny rabbits and banana flys, understand that what a child needs is to know what actually goes on. Maybe even provide a demonstration, gently. The other students laugh, yes, they would go along with that. I am firm. Not good enough, not good enough at all, I say, with another smirk. The redhead is chastened, *corrected*. Anyone else? Self-confidence, says the newty type in the suede jacket that belonged to her father, a forgotten novelist of the 1950s. She wishes she'd been taught that self-confidence is a bluff, no one has it really, you have to trick yourself into believing you do. I say nothing at first, but instead answer this twaddle with a stare that lets her know she hasn't tricked herself nearly well enough. Then: pitiful, I murmur, quite pitiful. She melts. She does, just dribbles away. Soon there is only a pool of hair, fat, and steaming suede. How to handle a bank account, says a chowderhead, so far away at the back I can't make out her face. Or should it be *his* face? No, no, it's a she, because that drony voice is talking about sanitary towels. Sanitary towels! Cue for eyebrow-music from me, not melodic stuff, but dissonant violin twanging, and for anger from the woman who stands and walks up and down the aisle, marching fast, but also with a pretentious air, letting us know what she wishes she'd known, namely, that ideology, even when unfurled to its full length, is only ideology, that the victory of reason over animal instinct was a cause for tragedy, that man's onerous task is to learn how to be himself, and to do this he must first learn to respect others, not just men, but animals, trees too, and the planet, he must learn compassion.

Da-da-da-DA!

Wrong, I tell them, you're deluded, as I know because, aged twelve, I was granted one of life's most important lessons.

. . .

Diana Laughton had a separate room for dressing, just like when she had been a film star, and that was where she took me. The room was brightly lit. The room was filled with clothes. Clothes on racks and on hangers, on chairs, on the floor, in boxes, and, still in tissue paper, in cupboards behind sliding mirrors on the wall. Smells? Of clothes (of course), of make-up and perfume, and of something I couldn't identify.

She said, "Normally I don't let anyone in here, Headingley. I hope you know that you're a very privileged boy."

"Thank you," I said.

Diana Laughton was still beautiful, as I said, if now a little frayed. I observed that she made me feel uneasy, in the way that Emma Peel did on the TV. I wondered what I was doing here. I felt my feet sinking into the thick carpet.

She opened a mahogany wardrobe in the corner and a light went on, revealing, not clothes, but glasses, bottles of various descriptions, olives in a bowl, and lemon slices neatly fan-tailed on a white porcelain dish. There was a mirror at the back with the silhouette of an ocean liner. The wardrobe was a cocktail cabinet. Then the lesson began.

"To make a martini," she said. "This is what you do."

She lined up a cocktail shaker, an ice bucket, the dish of olives, two glasses, and two green bottles, marked Noilly Prat and Gordon's. And the snake? Was no invention. There really was a snake, which she had returned to the glass tank where it lived, on a table next to the cocktail cabinet. I remembered the snake my mother and I had seen in Lister Park. Unlike that one, this snake seemed happy enough; presumably it liked Bradford, or Diana Laughton.

"Follow carefully," she said. "I was taught this by a very famous man. From Spain."

"Right," I said.

"First: ice in the shaker."

I put the ice in the shaker.

"Now, you wash the ice. What do you wash it in?"

I guessed. "Water?"

Gong!

"No, with this, silly," she said, and gave me the first green bottle, Noilly Prat. "Bottle A. Really, strictly, if you were driving the straight and narrow about this, you would let a ray of sunlight shine through Bottle A on to . . ."

She held up the second green bottle, Gordon's Gin.

". . . Bottle B. I have a theory. It's like the Holy Ghost and the Virgin Mary. He saw, he conquered, he came, and he left without even introducing himself. What a dream! That's how it is with a martini. The Holy Ghost, Bottle B, has been there and miraculously left the gin untouched."

She continued, "But since we have no sunlight we achieve the same effect by pouring from Bottle A on to the ice."

I poured.

"Shaking."

I shook.

"Pouring away what you just poured in from Bottle A."

I poured away.

"Taking Bottle B."

Yes, yes.

"Pouring from it into the shaker and shaking."

I poured, I shook.

"Pouring into the glasses which are still all cold and misty from the fridge."

More pouring.

"And, the last touch, an olive."

The olives slipped from my fingers and it was plop! plop! Circles raced to the edge of the glass and bounced back.

"There," said Diana Laughton, handing me one of the glasses, and taking the other herself, "I give you something that any woman will find irresistible. Two of these and even the most unimaginative consumer will begin to know that she's not half so mundane as she thought, that really she's made up in equal measure of Mata Hari, Marie Curie, and Brigitte Bardot. Headingley, I give you the perfect martini."

I took the glass.

"Here's to you," she said.

"And to you. And to us two too," I said, rather raffishly, I thought. I had at least learned something from my father. That, and how to tie a half-Windsor knot.

Diana Laughton giggled, I sipped, she asked how I liked it. I didn't, the taste reminded me of petrol, I'd had some once, on a bet with Billy Crow, in the garage where he now worked for my father, cleaning the funeral cars and keeping their tanks filled. I drank it down in one. The martini, that is. I'd spat the petrol out.

"Lovely," I said.

"Attaboy," she said. "Your dad's up to something, isn't he?"

"He's buying a cricket pavilion."

"Why?"

"He's going to move it to Bradford. Seems like a good idea."

She filled up my glass from the shaker. "We never got to know each other, did we, all those years ago?"

It was true, there had been a time, after my mother had left . . .

That's right, I suppose you may have guessed anyway, so I'd better tell you, my mother wasn't dead. The pretence wasn't my lie, not at first, it was my father's, though sometimes I wondered if I had provoked him by saying the words—*she's gone?*—when he had got up out of the coffin. Oh yes, the business in the cellar did happen. He was drunk, and frightened, I suppose, and it was his way of blurring an uncomfortable reality. He had suffered a blow whose severity he could not acknowledge. Later he told us the truth: that my mother had left him, that she had run away and was living, not with the brown-eyed handsome man, but with a journalist, in Dewsbury. "Dewsbury," he said, "that's what's so fantastic about it. I heard the voice of Moses say: "I'd be embarrassed to die there, in Dewsbury." Scout's honour, old man, I swear, that's exactly what Moses said. Dewsbury. She might as well have opened the plane door and gone for a shit with a blanket."

After that Diana Laughton had often come to the house. She had cooked beans on toast and had asked if I thought my father expected her to give up films to look after us all. She had asked if that was what I wanted. I had said nothing, hating her for making my mother go away; I didn't realise until later that it was my mother who had performed that trick, at my father's prompting.

I had been glad when she had stopped coming, and a little alarmed when, some time after, my father had shown me an edition of the *Telegraph & Argus* with her picture on the front page. I hadn't understood why he was showing it to me. Was he asking for my approval? But relief came like a warm glow when I read the headline: FILM ACTRESS TO WED IN BRADFORD. The story, written by my father's friend, the journalist Budge Carter, said that Diana Farrell, star of films such as *Madeleine, The Honest Thief, Cats in the Coffee,* and *Sweet Sleep I Owned Yesterday* was abandoning her screen career to be married to the Bradford-born multi-millionaire and property tycoon Charles Laughton.

She stared into the mirror inside the cocktail cabinet. I wondered if she was thinking of my father. Or seeing herself in her films, remembering some of the parts she'd played. I was with a cunning spy, a young wife of a Spitfire pilot, a nightclub dancer who got a fellow to give her all his money. Not looking away from her reflection, she said, "I have sleepless nights, Headingley. Bloody hell, I do."

I wondered if she stayed up late watching her films. I thought I probably would. I said, "I've seen your films. You were bloody marvellous." Using the word in her presence made me feel grown up, so I repeated: "*Bloody* marvellous."

She looked at me. She said, "Headingley, come here."

I was uneasy again, thinking of Emma Peel. For a moment I was even scared. There was a possibility, I thought, of karate: a blow to the back of my neck.

Instead it was, "Do you want to kiss me?"

I was light-headed. Did this mean I was drunk? I said yes I did want her to kiss me.

"Then wait a minute," she said, and turned again to the mirror, this time not seeing herself in one of her films, but putting on lipstick. Soon a bright red mouth was coming towards me. I imagined those lips touching my own, breathing gin, filling me up. I thought perhaps I would drown from her kiss. I closed my eyes.

And heard her voice: "First you have to promise me something," it said.

I asked her what it was, eyes popping now, her mouth still so close to mine.

"Find out for me, about your Dad and what he's up to."

I said if she liked.

"You're as likely to find out what's going on in his life as anybody."

I said I'd certainly do my best.

"And there's something else."

"There is?"

"If he asked you to give me something, a message, you'd do it, wouldn't you, for us?"

I said nothing.

"Then you'd get the kiss."

"Not now?"

"*After*. Is it a deal?"

I nodded.

"Then let's find my husband and that slick gigolo dad of yours. Not to mention the other great luminaries of the great worstedopolis." She gave me her hand again. "Shall we?"

The house had filled up. In the living room people were already dancing. In the hall I saw Twiggy Fawcett and Amos Bass, who'd come as the gravediggers Burke and Hare, so they'd hardly had to dress up. Twiggy Fawcett had smeared mud on his pale and skeletal face, while Amos Bass had put on a flat cap and a suit two sizes too small. Heads bowed as if in prayer, they listened to a man dressed as a highwayman.

I went and stood next to my father, who didn't seem to notice me. He was talking to the Robin Hood woman. They were getting along pretty well. But she'd decided she was in Sherwood Forest, putting up a fight. She had a husband, she'd have my father know, he was a good bloke, bought the wool down at Illingworth's, a responsible position. Seven and a half thousand a year. Steady as Gibraltar.

"Oh come off it," said my father.

Twiggy Fawcett and Amos Bass came up, with their customary smells: flowers and a faint whiff of formaldehyde. Even then I thought Twiggy and Amos were a little strange. They seemed to come from another world, like Miss Havisham in *Great Expectations*. Now I know this was actually the case. They were relics of Victorian Bradford, the Bradford that was once the Florence of the North, the Bradford that was being smashed by Charlie Laughton's demolition gangs, the dying Bradford. Eccentric (in Twiggy Fawcett's case, often more than that), dour, determined not to reveal themselves, they trusted no living soul; even the dead were regarded with suspicion, for they had a tendency not to pay their bills. They were slow to feel; but once roused, their feelings were not easily forgotten.

Twiggy Fawcett spoke first: "Evening."

"Good evening," said Amos Bass.

"Dust tha feel honoured?"

I asked myself what I was supposed to feel honoured about.

"Regular honoured to be at a bazzin do like this with the hoity-toity, that's what I am. Ist tha honoured Amos?"

"I do too feel honoured. I cannot imagine what I might have done to deserve the glory of such hospitality," said Amos Bass.

I should tell you, not about Amos Bass's appearance—only the big, squeaky boots, such as might have been worn by Frankenstein's monster, were unusual—but about the way he talked. Not everyone in Bradford spoke true Bradford fashion, dropping the "h," making "water" rhyme with "platter," turning "do you?" into "dust tha?" and making the "o" in "over" rhyme with "hover." Charlie Laughton, for instance, did not, nor Diana Laughton, nor my father. But their diction did not compare in refinement with that of Amos Bass. His was improbably urbane. It gave him style, tone, and these, he knew, were regretted absences at most Bradford funerals. Billy Crow believed Amos Bass had made a deal. He had gone to the place where the chemical outflow from Wilson's Mill turned the River Aire into a boiling cauldron over which he had held a silver fob and watched it tarnish. He had met the Devil there. He had sold his soul. My father had another story. He reasoned that the Devil offered better terms. If Amos really had made an arrangement with Old Nick, he hadn't done too well out of it. Look at those feet. Besides he had heard the crackling 78s which Amos kept hidden from his wife in the locked top drawer of a mahogany chest. Only when she was out would Amos play them over and over, mimicking the voices he heard, Laurence Olivier in *Henry V* or Noël Coward in *Private Lives*. This affectation amused my father very much. He teased Amos Bass. "Amos," he had said once, "could have bested Johnnie Gielgud. But he had these *feet,* so big and flat, so bloody noisy they were that he couldn't talk on stage and move at the same time. It's gospel, old man, I assure you. I had it from the bald doorman at the Alhambra. Said

Amos did things with Shakespeare that you'd never believe. He'd never heard the like." Amos Bass had smiled. He had told everyone my father was very funny.

"No," Amos Bass continued, "I fear it will remain a mystery. Do you believe our fealty and loyal service have at last been rewarded?"

"Like hell," said Twiggy Fawcett.

"Nor do I," said Amos Bass.

They were interrupted by loud cheering. Their heads turned. Mine followed, and saw two women in the doorway, standing with a man in tweed plus-fours and tweed cap who had a bag of golf clubs over his shoulder. But I wasn't really looking at him. The two women were dressed as belly dancers, in rippling, filmy things which sparkled as they flounced about, milking the applause. The Dolly Sisters: one was blonde and pretty, the other blonde and spectacularly not.

"I've eaten my dinner off the best of plates and I've never seen anything like it. She has thighs like monuments. A face like a boxer dog," said Amos Bass.

"They say she'll do owt for 'alf a crown. Or a packet of Capstan full strength."

"This event will be strictly downhill from here on in. I beg you to slap my face if I'm wrong." His voice suddenly become quieter, and yet more purposeful. "We had better seek out Mr. Charles Laughton, we had better make our presence known," he said. As I looked up, across the acres of black cloth that covered the legs, the waist, the chest of Amos Bass, I saw him shut his left eye in a slow, deliberate wink. He said, "We have to move along quickly now. Forgive us, if you please."

The dismissal failed to bother me. I didn't wait to see where Amos and Twiggy went. Glad to be free of them, head down, weaving between pairs of legs, I ran back upstairs and stopped, thinking. What else had my father said about Amos Bass? That he was a shifty old sod, was Amos, coming and going with those big, cunning feet of his, always trying to play a flanker.

I wondered what was meant by that: *playing a flanker*? I didn't know. I decided to go to the bathroom and masturbate. Excited by the prospect, I broke into a run. I wondered if I'd break the record: once, in the chilly and damp bathroom at home, it had been trousers down, Emma Peel, and thirty-three seconds later, the feeling. But now, when I opened the door at the end of the corridor I realised immediately I'd made a mistake: not the bathroom.

A TV was on, a gangster film, and the room flickered in a ghostly light. Laughton and Schenk were there, in armchairs, in front of the set, but talking to each other. A woman was in Schenk's lap, head turned away, attention fixed on the TV. I waved, but nobody noticed; at least, nobody moved.

Schenk was saying, "Had to. I said to him, 'Just look around, think you'll find yourself a better situation? Like hell you will, you've never had it so good,' but he wasn't seeing it. So I did him. No alternative."

"Oh, for Christ's sake," said Laughton. "Were you discreet?"

"You know me, when have I ever not been, it was white gloves, as always."

"You're a deplorable fellow," said Laughton, as though he meant it.

Somehow I knew what I was overhearing. Schenk had killed someone. I wasn't shocked, far from it, I was thrilled; he really *was* a gangster.

"Charlie," said Schenk, laughing. "I'm a pure blood descendant of George Raft." His hand moved up the stockinged leg of the woman, towards the crotch.

Laughton turned his head away with a look of distaste: the imperial thumbs down. *"Headingley!"* he shouted. "Join us, please."

"Hello, little boy," said the woman. She was dressed as Nell Gwyn.

"It's Jack Hamer's kid," Schenk said.

"Dead spit of his father," she said.

I sat down, cross-legged, on the carpet. Laughton asked if I was enjoying the party.

"Yes I am. I'm enjoying it very much."

The woman yawned.

"Have you had a drink?"

"Yes sir, a martini."

The woman laughed. Obviously she did not believe me.

"I'd like another."

On the TV a man slouched into a gun shop, picked up a gun.

He asked, "How much?" "Twenty dollars," was the reply. The gangster smiled and there was a pause in which it became clear to the gunsmith, and to me, so I laughed, that what was going on was a robbery, not a sale. "Fifty dollars," said the gunsmith. Another pause. "One hundred dollars." And, at last: "Two hundred!" Grinning insolently, the bad man took the money.

Grinning also, Schenk said to Laughton, "Headingley's a sensible young man, a well brought up kid. Who'd have guessed he belonged to black Jack Hamer?" Then he laughed, loudly and, as usual when he was with Laughton, a little nervously.

Laughton was once again the Emperor. He asked Schenk if he and the woman would mind leaving. Immediately, if Schenk didn't mind. He wanted to talk to me. I don't know if Laughton intended an insult, but if Schenk felt one, he didn't show it. Still grinning, he eased the woman from his knee and stood up. "Reckon it's time to punish the ladies," he said. "Come on, Nell. I'll be seeing you later, Charlie."

Laughton was silent for a while after they had gone. I watched the film, waiting for him to talk again, and when he did, it was during the scene where the gangster snarled and pushed a grapefruit into a woman's face, his voice was speculative and sad. "Do you know what I see every morning?"

I weighed the question. I tried to answer with a seriousness appropriate to the tone in which it had been asked. I couldn't think of anything. Then I remembered what my mother had once said, about how she hated waking up when my father was absent. That would do. So: "An empty bed?"

Laughton was silent. I reasoned that he hadn't heard my reply and tried another: "Sausages on a hot plate on a tray?"

He said, "My father. I see my father, back from the dead, come to see me, and I hear him, whispering: eat your porridge. He was a Scot, you see, didn't come to Bradford until he was seventeen, mean as Diana's snake and proud of it. Believed he had discovered the secret of living to a hundred. Porridge. He was a sulky old bastard. Conversation with him, it was pretty much what I think hell would be, a miserable groaning that went on and on, often about porridge, on and on, about lumps and Tate 'n' Lyle and how I always put in too much salt, on and on and on. He was wrong about the porridge. TB got him before he'd turned fifty. Lousy father. Better off dead. I know I'd be a better father."

"You don't have any children of your own then?"

Laughton seemed depressed by my cheerful smile. His plump mouth quivered a little. He said, "Do you think about life after death, Headingley?"

I said I ate plenty of porridge. Laughton's expression was gloomy, as if he didn't know whether I was taking the mickey. I didn't know myself. Then he laughed: he said I would probably turn out to be quite a card, like my father.

"Do you know why he's buying this pavilion?"

"Everyone's asking me that."

"I'll tell you why. Because his father, your grandfather, built it, forty odd years ago . . . who's asking you?"

"About what?"

"The pav—"

"Oh *that*. Keith, Mr. Schenk, Diana."

"Diana?"

"Everybody."

"Really?" said Charlie Laughton. "So, you see, because your dad's dad built this pavilion your dad wants to bring it back to Bradford, to bring it home and built it all over again. He thinks it's a family cycle. That's shit, it's another kind of cycle, it's he did this so I think I must too, it's a cycle of *dung,* and I'm afraid that's what you land face down in if you live in the past. Believe me I've had to learn that. I've tried to tell him. I think of him like a son, in a way, your dad, I think of them both that way."

On the TV the belligerent gangster had been shot by a blonde.

"Do you know how powerful I am?"

I shook my head. I didn't know how powerful he was.

"Of course not. I tell you Headingley, and this is the truth, I'm on the edge of something so big, I might as well be God I'll be so powerful in Bradford. I'm already cutting it up like a birthday cake, deciding who gets what and why. I'm sitting up here, on my cloud, and what do I see when I look down? I see your dad and Schenk, dog-fighting, half-way between me and the dung-heap. They're flying, but gravity will get them if they don't watch out. It's down to me. I'm the one who can sort it out. It's me or old man Newton, I'm afraid."

The hero lurched along a street, and up snow-covered steps, where he took a long time to die. Laughton asked if I liked gangster films. I said I preferred *A Hard Day's Night* and *The Avengers*.

"I'm bored with gangster films," said Charlie Laughton, sighing, and got up and turned off the TV. I watched the white dot as it disappeared into the middle of the screen and was reminded of when Helen told me she'd stolen the moon. It had been from the River Aire where it curved behind the garage in Shipley. (That was one of the garages owned by my father and Schenk. My father took me there sometimes and invited me to pick the car in which I wished to be driven to school. "Headingley," he'd say, "what are we smoking today?" My favourite was an Aston Martin, white as a Yorkshire rose.) Helen said she'd caught hold of the moon in her hands and given it to her boyfriend Victor. She said the theft had not made her guilty. The memory made me laugh out loud and when I stopped I saw Charlie Laughton staring at me, as if he thought I was very strange.

I remembered I'd left an almost full glass in Diana Laughton's dressing room, and went to get it. The glass was on a table beside the snake-tank, inside which the black and gold snake was coiled, eyes open, immobile. Exhausted after a recent meal? I hoped so. I kneeled down and observed the snake through my martini; the liquid in the glass was a lens, magnifying the folds of the snake's polished skin, making it even bigger than it was.

"Bored with Bradford, are you?" I said, and downed the martini in one. "I am. Perhaps I'll leave tomorrow, with Diana Laughton. Maybe not, I'd miss The Beatles." I spoke again to the snake. "I hope you're warm enough. Bad for your skin that cold glass."

My head staggered a little from the sudden effect of the gin and my hand trembled—a slight pleasure, thrilling—when it met silk, a beige stocking which was on the back of a chair and which swung to and fro in response to my touch. Now I had other thoughts. A mirrored door would open, I would step in, slide shut the door, and begin the postponed masturbation. Glorious! *A wank.*

In the cupboard, I left the door open an inch or two so I could see what I was doing. I unzipped my fly, finding that it was now

Diana Laughton who wore the leather catsuit. Hoping the usual actress wouldn't be upset, I set about beating my record.

There was an explosion of noise, of conversation and jangling music and a man shouting "Up yours Freddie," and in she came, Diana Laughton that is, followed by my father, who quickly cut off the noise by closing the door behind him. My reaction? Was not embarrassment, but outrage. I remembered the cricket field at Windhill and a car bouncing in the rain. I wondered what was happening. He should be with the Robin Hood woman. It was going to be Windhill all over again, but worse this time, since the kisses he would be getting had been promised to me. Quickly I zipped up my fly.

But then it seemed my father wasn't going to get my kisses after all. He and Diana Laughton were arguing.

"I'll marry you."

"You'd be just like the rest of them, Jack, you'd do it and try to glue my legs together."

"I love you," he said, mustering as much conviction as he could.

"Not this time, Jack."

"I have always loved you."

"It won't work this time."

"I will always love you."

"What if Charlie comes in?"

She went to the cocktail cabinet and pulled out bottles, glasses, and shaker, as she had done before, when she had made the martinis. My father stood behind her, leaning close, as if about to whisper, but a disdainful expression suggested she wasn't interested. He said, "I'm in a fucked-up condition, Diana. I need you," and put his hand on her shoulder.

"Same old song."

"It was true then . . ."

Who was he kidding?

". . . and it's true now."

He leaned closer still, his fingers squeezing the naked flesh of her shoulder.

Diana Laughton sighed.

Was she about to give in? I wasn't about to give her the chance. I said, "Hello, Dad," and stepped from the wardrobe.

"Bang my drum," he said. "It's Headingley." Then an angry certainty replaced the surprise on his face. "What the hell are you doing here?" He seemed to be staring at the bulge in my trousers.

I said, "I came for another drink."

His face rearranged itself again, this time into an unconvincing smile. "You're holding up production, old man," he said. I could see that he wanted me to leave.

"My fault," said Diana Laughton, "I've been teaching Headingley to make martinis."

"I'd love another one."

My next memory is of my father's face and a glance, almost of hatred.

"And that's what you'll have," said Diana Laughton. She asked if I remembered how. I went to work with the shaker, trying not to look at my father, whose mood had changed again, so that he was jolly Jack Hamer now, asking if I knew the one about the Englishman, the Irishman, and the Scotsman with the pineapple. I drank another martini and asked where the pineapple fitted in.

My father stepped nimbly over a dress and a shoe left on its side so I saw the dark print of Diana Laughton's heel. He put his fingers in my ribs and tickled until I was helpless. "That's the joke!" he said, and from behind pushed me towards the door, but instead of guiding me out of it, rushed to the side, towards Diana Laughton and the cocktail cabinet. We wheeled about the room. "Yes," we sang, "we have no bananas."

Noise was louder. Noise had colours and came from the radiogram in balloons that were red and blue and British racing green. My head was floating. I realised I was drunk. I thought: so this is what it's like, this is interesting. There was brilliant yellow cheering as my father appeared, chaired aloft by the Dolly Sisters.

"Jack Hamer, in his rightful position," said Charlie Laughton.

"Top of the world, ma!" boomed Schenk.

It started casually, with my father kissing a woman, not Diana Laughton, or a Dolly Sister, but the Robin Hood woman. He was with her again. This was confusing. Soon others followed the example and noises were different. Now they were purple and scarlet ahs ohs mms and yesyesyeses. And dark, sweet, Coca-Cola black moanings. Schenk and Nell Gwyn were on their knees, moving towards each other across the floor. They opened their mouths and kissed. A Dolly Sister straddled the head of the golfer and lowered herself towards his face, inch by inch.

"You're muttering, Twiggy," said Amos Bass.

"In situations like this, Amos, a man's best friend is his mutter," said Twiggy Fawcett.

"Look at her backside," said Amos Bass. "It's a public scandal."

Outside the wind was howling. Rain beat against the windows. The frames were rattling. I walked about. People were fucking in any old place. Schenk was in the bathroom, with his accent sliding.

"Come on yer little beauty . . . give it ter me." He was ramming again and again, straining now as if he had a pain. "Ugghhgh come on I'll drive out yer demons yer gorgeous little Paki."

Nell Gwyn stated, matter of factly, that she was not, as it happened, from Pakistan.

"Mmmumugh," said Schenk. He cried out that he couldn't help himself. It was too much. He couldn't hold back. "Yer beautiful yesyesmmmsobeautiful aaghm*aaagh* black bastards taking over Bradford BITCH!"

"Will yer look at that?" said Twiggy Fawcett.

"Oh yes indeed," said Amos.

"If yer can't beat 'em."

"Enjoy the party."

My father rushed about, supervising the mayhem. His costume was in disarray. The moustache was gone. Nell Gwyn wore it. She'd got away from Schenk. She was with the golfer, there he was, plus-fours round his ankles, holding out with a deft stroke of his mashie-niblick.

"FORE," shouted my father.

Somewhere, someone was howling. It was Charlie Laughton. He rolled over and showed Diana Laughton his arse. She hit him, first with her hand. Harder! he cried, harder! She did her best, but the demand still came: HARDER. She looked around and saw me. Of course! The cricket bat. I gave it to her. Thwack! Aaaagh, that's more like it. THWACK! THWACK! She dug her nails into his flesh and squeezed. He heaved like mad, bellowing, begging for mercy.

My father was with the Robin Hood woman now. His head was in the hair between her legs. There was a milky coffee-coloured sucking noise. She ground her teeth and wriggled. From the radiogram came a voice of sticky honey, "Your baby won't be near you any more." She drooled a little. "We're through," continued the honeyed voice and then, more emphatically: "IT'S OVER . . . IT'S OVER . . ."

"Yes . . . mmm . . . yes," said the woman. "Yes. YES!"

". . . IT'S OVER."

I said, "Dad."

He looked up. "Diving for pearls, old boy."

"Oh Jack," said the woman, laughing. "You rotten sod."

I was in the bathroom again. Twiggy Fawcett fucked the uglier of the Dolly Sisters. Amos Bass supervised the operation. "Mount her Twiggy, do it like a beast." Laughton came in and watched with a big smile on his moony face.

On the landing Beau Brummell was fucking Florence Nightingale up against a wall, and Mata Hari urged King Charles to get on all fours and bark like the spaniel he was. I met Schenk and the prettier of the Dolly Sisters. Schenk had a cigar on the go. She looked me up and down. She said, "A cricketer, is it? Well, I've just had the golfer. I like ball games. Come on, little man."

Charlie Laughton was at it again: "Woof! Woof!"

"I'll teach you how to cover drive," said the Dolly Sister.

"How's about it, Headingley?" said Schenk. "Shall I give you to her?"

"Go on," said the Dolly Sister.

"Shall I?"

"I want him."

"I don't have time to explain sex to you, you see I'm in a hurry myself, and besides you'd probably not believe me. I didn't believe it when my dad told me and you wouldn't if I told you. So I'll give you to her."

"Ooooh," said the Dolly Sister.

Suddenly Schenk decided he'd had enough of this game. He pulled on his cigar. "You're coming with me," he said to me.

"Are you bent or something?" said the Dolly Sister.

"Piss off, slag."

"Aren't you the witty one?"

I went with him down the stairs, through the kitchen, and out to a covered terrace from which steps led to the garden. In the distance I saw a pond with a little stone windmill at one end. The cold air made me feel faint.

Schenk tossed aside his cigar. He said he was worried. Concerned about my father. There was something wrong and it was to do with money and women. Beneath the surface, once you got beyond the good fellow-ing, the old man-ing, the now-listen-here-my-good-chapping, my father was a complicated customer. Usually he managed to come out tops. This time, however, he was in over his head.

"Some of us get older, some of us die, and he'll be cashing in his ticket if he don't watch out. I'm talking man-to-man," said Schenk. He wanted me to help him help. He needed to know where my father was getting the money from to move the pavilion. "He's not got it from the bank, I know that, and if he's borrowed from down London we could all be in the shite, tomorrow or the day after or the day after that. Soon."

Moreover, he believed Diana Laughton to be involved. She was bad luck to my father, he said, and if I saw them together, he knew I knew what he meant, this was talking *man-to-man,* I was to tell him for sure. There was a tenner in it for me, and I'd be doing my father a good turn. "You saw what he was like in there. Shooting about like a ball on a billiard table."

I could have asked myself what Schenk was after. I could have told him that I wanted the money, or that I didn't. I could at the very least have acknowledged that I'd heard what he said. I did none of these things, because my stomach was in the school playground, on the roundabout, heaving like mad. I ran out into the garden. The last sound I remember of that night is the yellow, green, and carroty-orange mmmumumouaaah roaring from my mouth as I vomited martini, and much else, on to the goldfish in Charlie Laughton's pond. That's not the last sight I remember, however. Throwing up finished, I rolled over and looked back towards the house. Schenk was still outside with another cigar going. Its glowing tip bobbed in the air as he strolled to the other end of the terrace. Someone else was there, drunk, flat out on her belly. I thought it was the Robin Hood woman. Schenk stood over her. Perhaps he was reflecting on the power of life and death. He elected to let her live. But he did grasp her hair and lift up her head. And then he let go, bashing her face against the slabs.

This is what makes the memory of that winter so troubling; I found none of it troubling. Such events didn't seem odd. Change was expected, the outlandish was my norm. Nor was it unusual for grown-ups to talk to me about my father as though I myself were grown up. His character was a puzzle, fascinating, and not only to Schenk and the Laughtons. Everyone had a different view. "A hero," said Miss Antrobus, my English teacher at the grammar school; "a dodgy and quite possibly criminal customer," said Budge Carter. "Nowt's good enough for him, and nobody," said Twiggy Fawcett, though Amos Bass shook his head and pronounced the judgment unfair, my father was no snob, he'd drink with whoever happened to be at the bar; "respects nothing and hates himself," said Keith, "cuts himself shaving because he can't stand to look in the mirror"; "worships himself," said Budge Carter, "can't smell his own shit for the incense." There were other voices: "simple," "complex," "sad and embittered," "euphoric and generous," and so on. It was confusing. The truth is that I did not, do not, know my father and the harder I try, the more I tell you, the easier he slips away. I am elephant hunting and the species is elusive, if not extinct.

Charlie Laughton was a better guide than most. He cared for my father, was faithful to him, but was too concerned whether my father was faithful in return. My father didn't believe in fidelity. He didn't believe in infidelity either; he denied the concept even when caught in the act. And a part of what was going on was that Schenk *was* hoping to catch him, red-handed with Diana Laughton, with his rasher in the frying pan, as my father would say.

Arrogant, seigneurial, perhaps a little lazy, Charlie Laughton didn't see how he could be harmed by war between Schenk and my father, his make-believe sons. He got that wrong. Giants tumble. The noise they make is a sign by which we know them.

My father did not admit the possibility of death, though he had spent a lot of time around it. It happened to others, to Geoff Taylor and his crew whose Lancaster had taken a hit in the starboard fuel tank above Mannheim. The plane didn't go down, but BOOM!, ceased to be, eight lives extinguished. Happened to Dudley Delacourette Snooke who nursed a sick Hampden back across the Channel, crash-landed, and impaled himself on the railings of St. Matthias Church in Lincoln. Happened in less bizarre fashion to the Bradford corpses it was his job to handle. But not to him. He saw himself as a Messiah; things might get tricky, but he would always come again. If and when he did die, and he wanted me to know it wouldn't be for a long time, if ever, he would accept neither burial nor automised cremation. Old Nick, the Devil that is, was to be made aware of the arrival of a damned unusual customer. Therefore my father wanted something spectacular, a big bonfire on a beach, at Filey perhaps, or Scarborough, with a squadron of Lancs booming overhead.

"Headingley," he had said, meaning me, not the cricket field, though we were there when he told me this, watching a young batsman named Boycott grind to a century. "I want you to see to it, if I have to go out, if it has to be the eternal toasting fork, let it be like a bloody Viking or one of those Romantic poet chappies. Have you ever seen someone burning? The head goes off like a bomb." Afterwards, he had said, his ashes were to be put in a Rolls-Royce, in the passenger seat (he refused to travel in the back of any car, even a Roller), and brought here, to Headingley, where they would be sprinkled over the wicket. "Splendid show!"

As I said, the funeral business had big new offices in the centre of the city, in Little Germany, in the last building on a narrow cobbled street which curved steeply into Forster Square. Custom came in the front, past a window display which featured mourning flowers, a brass crucifix, and (even in winter, somehow) a choir of frantic bluebottles, proceeded through the reception area and the radio room, where the immaculate voice of Mrs. Peachy could be heard instructing the drivers—"You're late for the cremation, Number Three, proceed immediately to Nab Wood, and please remember Mr. Olliphant has a wooden leg"—stayed a while on trestles covered with purple velvet in the Chapel of Rest, was carried through to the back to one of the waiting hearses, and only then, at last, driven to the cemetery or crematorium. Since the garage-area at the back was some forty feet higher than the window at the front, my father called the process "The Ascent to Hades," but all it reminded me of was *Billy Liar,* a film I'd seen, where the young hero worked for an undertaker and dreamed of escape to London. I was pleased by the idea. If Bradford was getting its inspiration from stories, so could I.

It was two or three days after Charlie Laughton's party that I went to Little Germany. I was to meet Helen there, and we would go for tea with our mother. Did I tell you that my mother wasn't dead, that it was only my father's drunken pretence? I did.

What I saw as soon as I arrived was, not Helen, but Amos Bass, his big black boots creaking as he went up the stairs at the end of the reception area, with Twiggy Fawcett following, lifting his thin legs high, almost prancing as if he were a horse. They were there for a few seconds only, and then gone; I wondered if I'd been seeing things.

I went upstairs myself and realised I hadn't. They were in my father's office, behind the desk with the green leather top. All the drawers were open. My guess now is that Schenk had sent them and they were looking through accounts and bank statements, searching for evidence that money had gone missing from the business.

"Why he-*llo,*" said Amos Bass. "Headingley, how are you?"

I said I couldn't grumble.

"Why not?" said Twiggy Fawcett, with no hint of a smile.

They really did make an excellent team.

It had been my father's idea to let them keep fifty per cent of their business. Schenk had been against it. "Bury 'em," Schenk had said. "Only way wi' buzzards like that. They nearly put you under once, now it's their turn." Laughton had also been doubtful, warning that some people would forgive you anything, except doing them a favour. But my father had insisted. Now it was Schenk who had offered a deal: if they would go to Laughton and confirm that my father was defrauding both him and Schenk, they would get back the other fifty per cent. Twiggy and Amos, being Twiggy and Amos, and therefore suspicious, wished to satisfy themselves that my father was doing what Schenk said. The farcical, dead-serious plot thickens.

They were pushing shut the desk-drawers. They did it calmly, in no hurry. They discussed the problems posed by various deaths.

They spoke as if they had been thinking of little else for months, years, the whole of their lives. It was probably true.

Car crashes? Were unfortunate, since bad damage to the face was often the result, and that was what the bereaved concerned themselves with most, the face of the loved one, who must be seen journeying to his Maker with a serene smile. A hanged man? Of surprisingly little concern, said Amos Bass, he had dealt with three in a single day, brothers who had chopped up their father, September 27, 1949, he remembered it well, the date not of the murder but of the executions at Armley Jail in Leeds. Lots of work for Mr. Roper! Back in the old days, before the art of hanging had been mastered, before civil servants had prepared white papers on the subject, it might have been different. The occasional decapitation. Messy. Speaking of which . . . a shotgun blast. Oh aye, said Twiggy Fawcett, that could be a guzma, a regular guzmaroo, 'specially if it were to the 'ead. Remember that chap up Bingley way in '58. Did he? Amos Bass did. Phew! He'd have eaten, forgive the language, a yard of his own *excrement* not to have seen that.

"Of course," said Amos Bass, "I have wished often to visit the United States where I understand the burn marks left by the electric chair would provide an opportunity to relish. Not that such an opportunity will present itself."

"Not now. Not bloody likely."

"Not with mortality as it is, and longevity run riot. Not with this epidemic of deathlessness."

"Oh aye, that's progress for yer, that's the nineteen-soddin-sixties," said Twiggy Fawcett, making it sound like the Black Death, not longevity, run riot.

"Not," said Amos Bass, looking around, "that it seems to have affected some as bad as the rest of us. In fact, some seem to be doing rather well at this particular time. Mister Schenk, for instance, and Mr. Hamer, who, I notice, have invested in new office equipment, new employees, new motor cars, not to mention . . ." pausing, as if he really had been thinking of not mentioning it, but had decided to after all, "new *birds*."

"Dolly birds," said Twiggy Fawcett, in gloomy confirmation. "Taint reet."

"You're right, Twiggy. It isn't right. Right is what it is not. Think of the boy. A different woman with his father every week."

"Oh aye, reet it ain't."

"Is this any sort of education for a boy?"

"Taint."

"What do you think, Headingley?"

This was a puzzler, but this—to my relief—was when Helen came in. "Oh God," she said, "it's Mutt and Jeff."

Twiggy and Amos looked at each other. They did not smile.

"What are they doing here?" said Helen, and turned to me, not really expecting an answer.

Amos Bass said he had thought my father would be in.

"Like hell," said Helen. "This is the last place on earth anyone in their right mind would expect to find him. After all, it's his place of work."

"A *logician*," said Amos Bass. He said he and Twiggy had thought they'd come over anyway, they had some papers to deliver.

"What papers?" said Helen.

Twiggy Fawcett nudged an envelope across the desk with the tip of a finger. "These."

The skeletal finger withdrew and Amos Bass, watching it, said, "Those. And now that we've delivered them and established your father isn't here and given our greetings both to you and to Headingley,"—lordly nod in my direction—"Prince of all the Hamers, we'll be on our way."

"Oh aye."

They came from behind the desk and moved towards the door. "Drowned bodies is 'orrible too," said Twiggy Fawcett, looking back over his shoulder, "all blue and puffy."

Helen picked up the envelope and fanned herself with it. "Those two are up to something," she said. "Do you think I should open this."

"No."

She went ahead anyway, but the envelope, torn by scarlet fingernails, revealed nothing. It was empty.

"There's something going on. Have you noticed?"

"Not really," I lied.

"You wank too much, that's your trouble." She said it was to do with Dad. She'd heard the police would be after him.

"Who told you?"

"Perhaps I'd better mention it to Mum. Do you think I should?" she said, again not expecting an answer. "Nah. I don't reckon so. She'd not thank me. Wants to forget him for ever, that's what I think."

My mother.

The daughter of a mill engineer.

Had won a scholarship to Bradford Grammar, the best school in the city, quite an honour even now. She had been twelve, and her parents had told her the important thing was, she had proved herself to be one of the best. But they couldn't afford to pay for the uniform, or the extra bus fare. So her place at the school was given to someone else, and she went to another, less prestigious, closer to home and where no uniform was required. When the war came along the girl who had taken her place got an important job, supervising one of the production lines at Avro in Yeadon where they built Lancaster bombers, while she worked as a secretary for a trumped up Ministry of Defence desk-jockey in Ilkley. Sometimes, to liven things up, she spiked his tea with laxative. Then the war was over. She was nineteen years old and looking for something. My father came along in his blue Royal Air Force uniform, they married two years later, and when Helen was born he walked the wards of St. Luke's, looking at charts and asking people how they were. They had assumed he was a surgeon and he, smiling, with his fondness for trickery and jokes, had encouraged them.

Helen and my mother were good friends. From time to time she would leave Bradford for a few days to stay in the flat in London where my mother now lived with Robert, or The Brown Man, as my father called him. Keith and I were invited, but we never went; nor did we reply to the regular letters she wrote. I might have wished that my relationship with my mother was closer; but it wasn't, and I didn't. She had left, and I hated her for it. I had no wish to see her, but every couple of months she would come up to Bradford on the train, and we would meet for tea. So: four in the afternoon, on the top floor at Busby's, my face bulgingly reflected in a polished silver tea-pot. Five old women at the next table, still in their overcoats, slurping tea loudly. They looked like teddy bears.

"What do you say, Headingley? Scones or toast? Or a chocolate éclair?"

I withdrew my face from the tea-pot and eased back into my chair of red velvet. I considered my mother's question. I said nothing.

"Éclairs," said Helen. "They're great here, all gooey."

"Three of those then," said my mother, pointing to the éclairs on the trolley. "Where's Keith?"

Helen explained: Keith was busy these days, with school and with his group. "They're going to be famous," she said. "Like The Beatles. Isn't that right, Headingley?"

I studied the carpet. The red and blue patterns on it were of extraordinary interest.

My mother asked me to tell her everything. "How are you? How's school? Are you still having trouble with history? I was the same. Could never get the kings in the right order. All those Edwards and Henrys in the fourteenth century. Very tricky."

One of the teddy bears was telling the others to "Listen, listen, listen." She tried to whisper, but her voice was like a cricket ball in a tin bath, booming. I imagined that I was one of the kings my mother mentioned, commanding silence, or punishment. The rack for teddy bears!

"You'll do well at school, won't you?"

I said, "Crossley, that's my friend Sam, his mum and dad pay him for every class he comes top in." I leaned back once more, a slip fielder, catching my mother's stare and tossing it back with an insolent smile.

"Ten bob," I said. "Dad has promised to put in five if you'll put in the other." A lie, of course. The idea might have appealed to my father, but I hadn't put it to him and therefore he had made no such promise. Was she going to check? Like hell.

My mother said I should try hard and do well, not to please others, but—this was the important thing—for myself.

"Take it or leave it," I said, a tycoon now, hard as a fifteen-minute egg, standing in front of a skyscraper that went up and up and up.

"Alright," said my mother.

"You shouldn't give in to him," said Helen.

My mother laughed. "No, we should applaud his business instinct. Though I can't think where the hell he gets it from in this family," she said. And to me: "I'll expect results, young man."

I smirked, saying that I was top already in English, history, and maths. "That's fifteen bob you owe me."

She opened her purse, took out two half-crowns and a ten-shilling note, and laid them on the white tablecloth. The purse shut with a snap.

I pocketed the money.

Helen said if I didn't start behaving myself she was going to knock me into the middle of next week.

I gave an innocent shrug. I said I had no idea what she was talking about.

"Look," said Helen. "Mum didn't want to go. He forced her into it. Don't you see? She couldn't do anything else. It was that, or pick up a carving knife, or stick her head in the oven. You know what he's like."

I told Helen, "I know what he's like."

My mother said, "It was very funny at first being married to your dad, I loved him very much and we danced the tango beautifully," she said. "And I'm not sure when we began to go downhill. But we did and soon we weren't dancing together any more, but he still wanted me always to be there when he came home from a hard day of being Jack Hamer, or an even harder day of Jack Hamer being someone else. And sometimes it wouldn't be a day. A week, a month, even two. I'd be at my wits' end. I don't know how I should live. I do know I couldn't live like that any more."

She said, "I miss you all very much."

I was a glass, flowing over with unacknowledged emotion. I was: sulky, angry, proud, afraid, and cunning. I said nothing, but looked instead at the patterns in the carpet. If I concentrated hard enough I thought I could make them dance and whirl.

We went to see my grandmother, my father's mother, who lived in a bungalow in a nondescript estate above the city. The bungalow was always hot and damp, with condensation steaming up the windows and steaming down the pale yellow paintwork. My grandmother was frail, her blood so thin that unless the temperature was tropical she felt the cold terribly. She was so considerate and good-natured, however, that she would always offer to open the windows, and would be told not to worry. Everyone adored her. She believed that people were good and that my father could do no wrong and therefore no wrong could be done him. A Catholic, she believed that her God would protect us all. She was wrong.

I inspected the small brass animals which were lined up on top of the TV set, next to a silver-framed photograph of my parents on their wedding day. I have it in front of me now. I've looked at it, I don't know, hundreds of times; it's part of my history. My father stands up straight in his blue RAF uniform; my mother is in white, with a bouquet and an uncertain smile. It used to seem to me that she was the one who didn't know what she was getting into.

I tried not to listen to my mother, grandmother, and Helen who were on the sofa chatting about this, about that, about I don't know what, and my father came in. That's not right. He didn't come in, he *made an entrance,* pausing at the door, looking at the sofa, then rocking on his heels and looking away, and looking back again, and looking away again, before at last walking towards me.

"Need your advice my dear fellow," he said. "This is the situation. The buggers didn't even listen to what I had to say. Buggers didn't bend their ears even a fraction. That's banks for you. So I went ahead and signed the papers. Was I right? I think I was. Sod 'em, let them stew in their own bile, did they think I saw my future grinning at me out of their arses, I did not, that's what I told them, and I'm sure you agree I did the right thing."

At last he turned. He changed his tone, saying, softly, "Mother, Helen . . . *Lillian.*"

"Jack," she said. "Didn't I always say you should have been an actor. Where's your tennis racket?"

He smiled, she smiled, so did my grandmother. Even I joined in. Not Helen. Now she was the sulky one, spreading her fingers and inspecting her nails in a very deliberate way.

"I require reformation," he said. "I require instruction and correction. I humbly await your orders."

"That aside, how are you?"

"Oh, I don't know, still trying I suppose. Dance, drink, dance, work a little, drink, dance some more."

"Same old Jack."

"Same old me. I've yet to find a partner as good as you of course."

"Someone with my peculiar talents?"

"Someone with grace and spunk."

"I didn't mean that, stupid."

I remembered the last time they had met. It had been here, in this room, not long before my mother and The Brown Man moved from Dewsbury to London. Different circumstances: the divorce had been under way. My father had behaved as though he couldn't care less. "There may be trouble ahead," he had sung. And then, savage all of a sudden: "If you think you can go doggo, run off with some chap and then double up to win first prize, if you imagine for a moment you can get custody after this little lot, you've got another think coming."

"Headingley," said my grandmother, "let's you and I and Helen go into the kitchen. Come on."

"Why?" said Helen.

"I think we'd all like a cup of tea."

"We would?" said Helen.

"The kitchen," my grandmother said, and the three of us went there, leaving my mother and father together.

My grandmother filled up the kettle. Put on the gas, and brilliant blue flame lit the afternoon dark. Said: "You miss your mum, don't you?"

I knew what she wanted to hear, and this may have been the moment I became conscious of something obvious, but important, about telling a lie: knowing what the other person wants, that's the greater part of the battle. The truth? Is irrelevant. The truth did not help Wellington at Waterloo. Superior acquaintance with the terrain and the arrival of Marshal Blücher, knowledge and power, helped Wellington at Waterloo. The truth was that I didn't miss my mother at all. I wanted to, I tried to, I had been made to feel I should. At my eighth birthday party, for instance, when my father had been called away. "Terribly sorry old man, um, business, look, here's a few quid, get yourself something, sorry about this, but *noblesse oblige*." In other words, a woman. So Aunt Louise had taken over, gazing at me all the time with such concern and pity that I had felt obliged to blubber. Blubbering was easy. I could screw up my face and do it to order. Missing my mother was what I couldn't get the hang of. I did miss her sponge cake. She had made excellent sponge cake.

"I miss her very much," I told my grandmother, who turned to Helen and asked her. For Helen it was a different question, because her feelings were divided; she didn't answer.

I took in the tea. My father was on the sofa, next to my mother, talking about the plan to move the cricket pavilion. Sounded expensive, she said, and mad. Oh yes, he agreed, quite mad. She asked why he was doing it, and he said why not. She smiled at him, he smiled at her. I handed over the cups. Conversation died.

"It's a bloody big operation," I said.

"Is it?" said my mother.

"Oh yes. The full Kildare. Isn't it Dad?"

"Come on, Headingley," said my grandmother.

"Do I have to?"

"Helen's in the back room. Let's go there."

I walked slowly to the door and glanced back over my shoulder, to see my mother and father standing now, by the sofa. There was the sound of wool rubbing against wool, the sound of hard breathing, and then another sound, wet and sloppy. I thought of tea-drinking teddy bears. My mother and father were kissing, with increasing passion.

What did I feel?

Shame? I don't think so. Nor embarrassment. Surprise? Not that either. After all, I was used to witnessing behaviour which adults try to keep private from children. I think of Charlie Laughton's party, or going to work with my mother when we were short of money. Or a time in Scarborough, at the cricket festival, when I had been in a dark hotel room, very late, awake, listening as my father haggled with a woman about how much he should pay for the night. Five pounds? Six? No, she wanted seven, she needed the seven to buy a winter coat for her little girl. I had heard paper rustling as he counted it out.

I'm not sure what I felt. I do know I was confused, not by the kissing, but by the ease of their intimacy, by their not bothering to hide it. And fascinated by a drop of spit on my mother's lip, swelling and shivering, not wanting to fall. She said, "Jack," so softly I almost didn't hear, and I wanted to move closer. I was about to take a step, but then I was pulled out of the door and the door was shut behind me. It was my grandmother, with one bony hand on the knob and the index finger of the other pressed against her lips.

I giggled. We were pantomime peeping toms. My grandmother went, *"Sssh,"* and began to giggle as well.

"What's going on?" said Helen, who had come from the back room. "What's so funny?"

My grandmother motioned us away from the door. "It's your dad," she said in a whisper.

Helen sighed. Exasperated, as if she were discussing a small and badly behaved child, she asked what the hell he was up to now.

"Wouldn't you like it to be how it was?" said my grandmother.

But there was a thumping of feet, the living-room door flew open, banged against the wall, and my mother rushed out, with my father following close behind.

"Lillian . . ." he said. "Listen."

She was in a rage. She gave it to him fierce and hissing. "I nearly did. I must have been out of my mind. A sensible woman might have learned by now, but not me, not Lillian."

"I wish you'd stay."

"One wish that won't come true."

"Things will be different. You have my word."

"You'll end up in Blackpool, Jack, selling rubber ducks on the Golden Mile, just like you've always been afraid you would. And I'm buggered if I see why I should help this time."

She turned to my grandmother. She was sorry, she said, she hadn't wanted there to be a scene. She immediately repudiated this sentiment. How very English of her, she said, to apologise. In fact she was bloody glad there had been a scene. That bastard, she said, staring at my father, had asked if she could lay her hands on five thousand pounds.

My father? Had a sheepish grin.

"Perhaps it will burn the message into my brain once and for all."

"When I saw the two of you just now . . ." said my grandmother.

"Oh Nan," said my mother, close to tears, "two minutes can't make up for twenty years."

I picture her as she turned quickly to my father. She told him to look after us.

"Lillian, calm down, get a grip for pity's sake," he said, but she ignored him. Helen said she would go with her to the station.

"Be good, Headingley," said my mother, and pressed my face into her fur coat. She kissed my grandmother, and was gone.

My father talked to himself. "That's right, get back to Dewsbury or wherever it is. Your behavior is comical, my dear, bloody comical. Look at me, I'm laughing."

He wasn't.

"Ha-ha-ha."

"Jackie," said my grandmother. "Jackie, sweetheart. Talk to me about it." She paused, waiting. I believe that her love for him was trusting, total, that she didn't really expect him to reply, that she had decided this was the only way it could be, because nothing would come of trying to question or influence or change him, and I also believe that as she stood there, a rosary swinging on her fingers, she knew he would break her heart.

"Nothing to tell, Nan. Everything is tickety-boo," he said, shrugging, as if to add: you know me. "Why don't you get some more tea on?"

My grandmother looked at him for a moment and went into the kitchen.

After she had gone he stood quite still and pressed the palms of his hands against his temples. Then he ran across the room, lifted his foot, and kicked hard at a large red and gold cushion which had been booty from North Africa in the war. "Life," he said. "What a bloody pot-luck arrangement."

His behaviour was getting wilder. In theory he was at an age, forty-four, when he should have been slowing down, paying the mortgage, perhaps thinking about marrying again, in any event *toeing the line*. The reality was different. He was never himself when at home with Helen, Keith, and I. He feared the order of it. His restlessness would betray him. He would stare at the fish in the Sputnik tank, pick up the paper, toss it aside, inspect his collection of Toby jugs in the cabinet in the corner of the room, move one of them an inch or two, scratch his crotch, try the paper again, or the TV, and announce (as if he himself was surprised by the deci-sion) that he was off to The Oddfellows, or The Cricketers, or The

Hand of Glory (which, at the time, I presumed was connected in some way with my masturbatory habit). I imagine his arrival at these favourite haunts. The door would open and it would be instant Jack Hamer, strolling to the bar, "My round, I believe!" laughing in just the right way at jokes, telling stories about another from the seemingly endless list of his great-uncles, Goliath Hamer the bottom-pincher or Harry Hamer, rejected in love, who had thrown himself off the Thornton Viaduct. Chatting up women. "Happy as a pig in shit old girl," he would say. "Couldn't be happier if I were wading cock-deep through a lorry load of cash. You look *lovely* tonight."

His tastes had always been for euphoria, for risk, for sex and money, for transferring his disappointments to others, and for sentimental and expansive declarations of love he didn't know whether he felt or not. Now he was desperate, going down fast, in bad trouble with Schenk and Laughton, not falling, or bouncing (as Schenk had suggested) but *diving*.

The pavilion was taken to pieces, plank by plank, and each plank was numbered and stored in sequence on a truck. When that part of the job was over, the trucks, there were four, were driven west across Yorkshire, arriving at Windhill cricket field when it was still dark. Fifty men were on hand, ready to start work at first light. My father had promised each of them a ten-pound bonus if the job was finished by two in the afternoon.

A concrete foundation had been put down already. Long beams of wood were bolted into it, and boards were laid across to make the floor. Door frames were put in place and the doors themselves were fitted. Whitewashed planks were taken from the trucks, slotted in, and nailed down. Progress was slow at first. By eleven the pavilion had reached only the height of my chest; half an hour later, my chin, another half-hour after that, the top of my head. Then everything began to speed up. Even the weather obliged: it was cold, but fine.

A crowd gathered, at first just a few, but soon twenty or so, then more and more. Laughton was there, with the boot of the Rolls open and a crate of champagne inside. Perhaps he disapproved of my father's profligacy, but he was gracious. "Jack," he said, handing out the bubbly. "You might be losing your shirt on this but I reckon today will be a legend in Bradford."

My father, who had not slept, was hungover, and had bashed his hand hammering a nail a few minutes before, was filled with demon energy. He said, "The balcony, old man, that's the key to the whole caboodle."

"Calm down, Jack," said Charlie Laughton.

"The balcony is what could cost me the whole show."

"Have a glass of champagne."

"No thanks, Charlie."

My father: refusing a drink? Habits are hard to break. He must have fancied a bash. But he resisted.

"You're bleeding, Jack."

"I've got a bet with a sportsman in Scarborough. Two-and-a-half grand that I wouldn't get this lot up by two-thirty. It's a sobering tale. I'm bleeding worried." He was still worrying about the balcony when, at one-thirty, another truck pulled up and there it was, on the back, complete, assembled by the carpenter in Goole, his old associate in grandiose schemes. Men immediately went to work with ropes and pulleys. The balcony was hoisted into position and held there while long screws were sunk into holes already drilled in the supporting struts. By two-ten he was beaming all over his face, handing out tenners to each of the workmen. He knew he had won. The pavilion was all but finished, and Billy Crow was on top of it, his enormous legs straddling the red-tile roof. He was ready to apply the finishing touch, waiting with the black steel weather-vane in his hands, shouting, "Shall us do it now, Mr. 'amer?"

But my father had disappeared. Puzzled disappointment moved across Billy Crow's face. At that moment the crowd was shaken by a shrill blast on a trumpet from inside the pavilion, and a few moments after that my father came out on to the balcony. He was dressed as a priest. He intoned, "Father Jack Hamer, recently de-frocked, banished from Rome."

I was down on the field, in the crowd.

"The man has lost his marbles," said Amos Bass.

"Ahv 'alf a mind to say her not wrong," said Twiggy Fawcett.

"I've been trying to talk to him. Can I get a word? I cannot, not with the high and mighty Jack Hamer."

"Yer not wrong."

"Action must be taken."

My father gave the blessing, "In the name of the Father, and the Son, and the Holy Famous Grouse."

"Ahm still not shoo-er, Amos."

"Twiggy, for pity's sake, he's a sinking rat, you're going to insist we go down with him?"

"Bless this pavilion, and all who play, and drink, and do whatever other fancy tricks, in her," said my father, looking up towards Billy Crow. "All right then Billy. You can do it now."

Grinning, Billy Crow pushed the weather-vane into the hole which I had myself prepared for it on the chimney at the edge of the roof.

"Crikey, worrisit?"

"Twiggy, it's a weather-vane."

"Ah knows *that*."

The weather-vane was modelled after Botticelli's Venus, birthed from the ocean. I had taken a look before Billy had carried it up.

"It's a woman."

"Of course it's a woman."

"Nekkid."

My father fingered his dog-collar and smiled benignly: a bishop who'd been at the sherry. "Isn't she beautiful?" he said and, as the weather-vane began to swing in the breeze, there was first applause, then cheering.

Not from Amos Bass. He made a face as if he smelled something bad, as if he smelled shit. "Hamlet, counterfeiting the madman," he said. "More ways of acting the fool than Heinz has varieties. I'm going ahead. Doing what Schenk asked."

"D'yer trust 'im?"

"Don't know, don't care. Jack Hamer's played us for cunts for long enough. I'm going to Charlie Laughton," said Amos Bass. He unbuttoned his coat and pushed through the crowd. Twiggy Fawcett waited, uncertain, with a hand on the back of his neck, bony fingers bending and straightening as they scratched, and then pranced after him.

"The time is . . ." said my father, who paused to look at his watch ". . . twenty-six minutes past two, and certainly time for refreshments, which will be found inside, because I am about to declare this pavilion gloriously open." He brought bat and bottle together, smashing the bottle and sending whisky-balloons, up and up, which then burst and fell, soaking our upturned faces.

The pavilion was not built just on a bet. Nothing concerning my father was so obvious. It was neither the fulfilment of a dream, nor the making good of an obligation to his own father (he had lied to Charlie Laughton about that), nor merely a plan to make money (though it was, it did), but something more. My father was building an image of himself. This is Jack Hamer, the pavilion said, I *am* Jack Hamer. It was also, in a way, his last will and testament. When he came down from the balcony, however, and opened the door, it was a moment of glory with people surrounding him everywhere. He walked through the main room, where bottles of champagne were lined up on a table. "Soldiers waiting to go over the top," he said, popping a cork, "certain to be slaughtered." Handing out glasses, he explained where trophy cabinets would be. He mused over whose picture should go where. Pride of place on the back wall to Sutcliffe, or Hutton, or Trueman? Or some other cricketing icon? Hedley Verity, maybe. He walked through the two dressing rooms, discussing plumbing. He was historian, tour-guide and interior designer. Style would be simple, he said: white Dulux all over. Billy Crow was going to see to it. Billy Crow nodded enthusiastically.

I was an eavesdropper through all this, as I was for most of that day. Helen talked to Schenk and Budge Carter, who was tall and ginger-haired. Pale skin. Helen told him he was too good looking to be a journalist. She had supposed journalists to be along the lines of Spencer Tracy. Honest, but with wrinkled faces like walnuts. He was more like Albert Finney. She liked Albert Finney.

"A dab flattering hand," said Schenk. "First time I ever saw Budge we blabbed about something he'd written about yours truly. Told him he'd made errors of fact. Was thinking of his journalistic integrity. Budge went goose-turd green. Must have thought I had something else in mind."

Budge Carter went red in the face.

"Now he's blotting paper," said Schenk, not laughing. "A colourful character, is Budge."

I walked about. It was Diana Laughton and the time she met Larry Olivier. It was Amos Bass and the notable dead he had known, Twiggy Fawcett and the geometry of digging a grave. Keith and when his group could start playing. But most often it was the grim Bradford relish with which my father's champagne was drunk and the possibility of his ruin contemplated. He'd been reckless and got away with it. But he'd gone too far. This little caper must have cost hundreds. *Thousands*. Even Don Quixote, Budge Carter said, didn't stop to build the windmill before he took a tilt at it.

It began to get dark. People were leaving, drifting into the November twilight, but that was the moment, when it seemed the party was over, that my father, the magician, turned his best tricks. At first it was just a pair of headlights, coming through the gloom, down the track which led from the main road towards the field. Then it was another pair of headlights, and another, and another. One more, and one after that. Another. And another. The first pair of headlights had arrived at the pavilion and others were still coming over the hill. They came on and on and on, a procession moving slowly. Each pair of headlights was attached to a car, of course, and I saw that each car was the same, an Austin Mini, each was white, a shade which my father called *Bradford blush,* and each was driven by a woman.

"What *is* this?" said Charlie Laughton. "What the bloody hell's going on?"

"I've taken delivery of these Minis, just a couple," said my father.

"How many?" said Charlie Laughton.

Fifty-seven: I had counted them.

"Without telling me?"

"Glorious sight, don't you think?"

Charlie Laughton's expression suggested that he didn't think so. He was not gracious. "Used hot air for money, I suppose."

"Not even that. They gave me twenty-one days to come up with the cash."

"And how much do we lose if you don't?"

"Don't worry old man, we'll shift them in no time, in no time at all. Porkers on clover, that's what we'll be."

The Minis were parked all over the cricket field. At a signal from my father the drivers turned off their engines and got out of the cars. A regiment of mini-skirted women came towards the pavilion; in fact they were fashion models, hired from agencies in Leeds, Manchester, and Liverpool. The bill was never paid.

"Dolly birds," said Twiggy Fawcett. *"Dolly birds!"*

"Swinging London comes to Bradford," said Diana Laughton.

Still in the priest's outfit, my father posed for a photograph, two women on each arm.

"Father Jack Hamer, with his favourite parishioners," said Twiggy Fawcett.

"He's a card is Jack," said Amos Bass. "I always did say so."

"Amos, Twiggy: I'd like another word," said Charlie Laughton, and to my father: "I'll be coming to see you, Jack, and I'll expect honest answers about just what the bloody hell's going on."

"That's fine," said my father, with a shrug as if to imply he himself didn't have the foggiest. "Whenever."

"Ten minutes. We're leaving," Laughton said to his wife.

She presented her cheek for him to kiss.

"Why don't you see if you can talk some sense into him?"

"I'll do my best," she said, and watched Laughton go off with Twiggy and Amos.

My father kissed each of the four women in turn and suggested that they go inside for a glass of pop. They did, leaving him alone with Diana Laughton. Two conspirators and me, listening in.

"You shouldn't provoke him like that."

"Charlie's alright. He'll be alright."

"I'm getting impatient, Jack."

"Look, let's not discuss you, or me, or your husband."

"That leaves us nothing to talk about."

"The test career of Ted Dexter?"

"What's it going to be, Jack?"

"Not in front of the boy."

"He'll not let on a dickie-bird, he's my chaperone, and besides, we've got a deal, don't we soldier?"

I nodded.

"And I'm not letting you off the hook, Jack. What do you think, you can treat me like one of your tarts?"

"For Christ's sake."

Her face was rigid. "That's it, you *want* me to be a whore, so you can turn round and say you can't possibly do anything but rinky-dink with a woman like *that*. Old man."

"Alright, alright."

"How much do I get? A fiver? Six quid, seven? What's your best offer, Jack?"

As the night went on I remember an atmosphere of hysteria. Cars were circling the field, horns beeping. People were raucous and drunk, clamouring to buy. "Swinging," said my father giving a thumbs-up as he saw a Mini driven by a brunette, then tipping over his hand to signify disapproval as another went by, this time with what he judged a substandard blonde at the wheel, *"Dodgy."*

"Jack, you're off your trolley," Diana Laughton said.

"Insanity," said my father, with his hands in his pockets, leaning back, looking smug, "is a glorious fabric, and sanity is the seamy side. Insanity is the stuff of which dreams are made."

"That's what I reckon myself," said another voice, Schenk's, and my father was surprised, a little alarmed, his back straight now as if he had been fed a poker. How long had Schenk been there, beaming all over his face? "And if you were me Jack you might even say it were my philosophy. Is it yours, Jack?"

My father assumed his old manner. "Don't possess one. Can't afford to, since I know you'll always trump me in that department. You, after all, have the wit and wisdom of a Talmudic sage. And now, if you'll excuse me, I must visit the gun-room."

The gun-room? My father's expression for the toilet.

Diana Laughton's hand was on his sleeve for a moment, perhaps she didn't want to be left alone with Schenk, but my father went anyway, ignoring the gesture, or failing to notice it. Schenk didn't. The gesture was absorbed, filed away.

"Not an easy bloke to get to the bottom of," he said. "And he was such a big shot after the war. All the girls wanted to squeeze his tea leaves."

"I really couldn't say," she said, smiling.

"Must have been quite a let-down coming back here," said Schenk. And then he said, emphasising the point, "Braaaaad-fud," stretching the first syllable as if it were a journey he did not wish to make, and dropping the second suddenly, a man on a noose clattering through the trap door.

"Are you still fucking him?"

"I'll warn you just the one time," said Diana Laughton.

"What do you think, Headingley?"

"My husband is very fond of Jack Hamer."

"Is your dad being wicked with his rasher?"

Diana Laughton raised her arm to strike him and held herself back, quickly lowering it again, but not before Schenk saw that he had scored a hit, and smiled.

A Mexican poet said that memory is a present which never stops going past. Yip-ee-ki-aye! I have my doubts concerning those Mexican poets, because what my memory sees next, after all those heads, yakking, is from a silent movie: Schenk, looking from Diana Laughton, to me, and back again. At first his face does change. Not the smiling expression, but the shape, which seems to become bigger, rounder, transforming itself into something grotesque and inflated, a confident Schenk of a shape which then stays quite still and doesn't move for the longest time. You see, he knew the truth of his suspicion: my father and Diana Laughton were sleeping together again. Now he had only to provide proof and, together with the evidence of my father's swindle, this would be enough to persuade Laughton to let him do what he wanted.

My father was in a bad way when he took Helen and me home late that night. Drunker than I'd ever seen him, and therefore very drunk, he had trouble walking, trouble talking, trouble keeping his eyes open. After ten minutes fumbling with various sets of keys, during which Helen told him repeatedly that he was in no fit state and he replied each time "*Bougrez-off,* my dear, I *am* the greatest pilot," it was into an Austin Mini Cooper S, a tiny white rocket of a car, my mistake, a tiny *Bradford blush* of a rocket, for a nightmare drive. We left some of the Mini's paintwork on the stone boundary wall of the cricket field. We knocked a cloth-capped night worker from his bike in Forster Square. We bashed the bridge at the end of Canal Road and came to a roundabout, which we didn't go round, but straight over. I was quite calm. I knew I was about to die. The Mini hit the roundabout with a series of bangs, seemed to take off, and came down with a thumping crash on the other side.

I don't remember what happened then. Perhaps I was unconscious for a few seconds, or dazed. The next thing I remember is we were out of the car and Helen was on her knees on the road being sick. Splinters of glass were around her feet. The Mini's windscreen was smashed. Flowers and clods of earth were hanging from the bashed-in radiator grille, and the engine was still on, steaming and panting in the dark. My father reeled about. His face was bloody. Wiping a sleeve down his cheek, he looked back to the roundabout. "Bingo! Sex appeal bombing. We just destroyed the flower display. Was in shape of clock."

Helen had him by the arms and was screaming into his face: "Fucking hell, Dad. This isn't funny."

"Is."

"You could have killed us all."

I said, "Come on, Dad."

"Dad, for God's sake," Helen said.

"*Bougrez-off*. Don't love me. Going London. *Bougrez-off* both of you."

He got back into the Mini and drove off.

"I don't believe this," said Helen.

My knees ached from the shock.

"BASTARD," she yelled. She picked up a clod of earth and hurled it after the Mini, which was speeding towards Shipley. "FUCKING BASTARD."

Helen put her arm around my shoulders and hugged me close. "Come on our kid," she said. "Let's go home."

A report on the moving of the pavilion was in the *Telegraph & Argus* the next afternoon, written by Budge Carter, whose misgivings concerning the future of the Hamer family were discounted, or at least mislaid in the rush for colour. Details were given of my father's career, some familiar, others not. For instance: "Jack Hamer," he said, was a "war hero," a "prominent pillar in the commercial life of the city," a "well-known figure on Yorkshire race courses" and "a star of the Trans-Europe car rally of 1958 when, driving a Saab, he had performed outstandingly over the leg which took place on Germany's infamously dangerous Nürburgring circuit." The moving of the pavilion was "a startling feat," "a testament to Yorkshire hard work and grit," "an imaginative publicity stunt which provoked massive interest in the Mini motor cars Jack Hamer was offering for sale," and the party which followed, where a "beat group played pop songs by The Beatles and The Rolling Stones, as well as a tango written by Hamer himself titled "I'm Getting Drunk Tonight" had shown no sign of that much publicised phenomenon, "the generation gap." Young had mingled merrily with old and leading civic dignitaries and even the *Telegraph's* own correspondent had been seen shaking a shoe. There was dancing until dawn!"

A young fellow in a dark blue overcoat came to the door. He had a big round face and Brylcreemed black hair. His smile was so wide I thought his lips must meet at the back of his head, like the cat in the story.

He showed me an identity card. He was a policeman, a detective in the Criminal Investigation Division, name of Weekes. He took out a packet of Embassy and asked if I would mind if he lit up. He had a friendly voice and plenty of questions. Was my father in, did I know when he would be back, wasn't it true that he had a white Mini Cooper S? The previous night some smart alec had driven a Mini just like that through the municipal flower display at the junction of North Avenue and Midland Road. The display had been put together especially for the mayor's inauguration this Saturday; the mayor was very upset about it.

I said I knew nothing.

He took another drag on his cigarette. He stank of tobacco. I pictured him cheerfully chain-smoking in the cupboard where he hung his clothes.

His grin grew wider still, so wide I thought he could swallow me if he wanted. "Little boys what won't co-operate," he said, "gets locked up and the treat for me is I get to forget about the key."

I imagined what it would be like down there in a belly always filled with smoke, swimming in juices, pelted from time to time with chips and fried fish.

"Owt to say to me?"

I knew he would regard silence as the greatest provocation. I told him that my father did indeed have a Mini Cooper S, but it was blue. "Honest," I said, "blue as the ocean, blue as the moon in the song."

"Little boys who lie . . ." Weekes began, and I suppose I would have been worried, had I not been watching the arrival of the cavalry. That's to say, Charlie Laughton, who was walking up the drive. Short unhurried stride, shiny Oxfords, puzzled look in the direction of the police car.

Laughton smiled at me, benevolently, as always, and turned to the policeman. "What's going on here, Weekes?"

"I was looking for Jack Hamer."

"Why?"

Weekes stood up straight, as if he were back in uniform. "Someone ran over the mayor's flower display. It was completely devastated."

"How fascinating. Well, you can piss off now," said Laughton. "I'm hoping that Headingley here is going to invite me in."

"It was wanton destruction of city property. The culprit were driving a white Mini."

"Wanton destruction, and in a white Mini. Oh dear, oh dear. Haven't you looked at today's *Telegraph*? There's a glut of white Minis. They're spreading round Bradford like a disease."

Weekes smiled, and lit another cigarette. "I know you think it's a laugh, Mr. Laughton."

"On the contrary . . ."

"But I'm only doing my job."

"Quite so."

"There's a crime." Weekes smiled still wider, as if to say that, once he got home, he would have a little chuckle over the matter also, but he couldn't afford to now, not right at this moment. "I have an investigation."

"Weekes, for God's sake, he's *not* here. Headingley, is he here?"

"No, sir."

"Satisfied?"

"All right, Mr. Laughton. I'll be on my way. But I have to tell you, I'll not give up on this."

Laughton said, "Quite right." And, when Weekes had driven away, and we were in the house, in the living room, where I'd been trying without success to light the fire, he knelt down and went to work with wood and twists of newspaper. "My God, that Weekes, what a monster. I'll have a word with the Chief Super when I dine with him next week. You're not thinking of becoming a policeman?"

"No, sir."

"Good." He lit the fire and held the front page of the *Telegraph* over the grate while it caught. "Your dad really isn't here?"

"No, sir."

"And everyone's looking for him, as usual."

"He's gone to London."

"The mayor's flowers and a banged up Mini?"

I nodded.

"You've to tell him he must see me. It's important. There are a number of ways this story can end. Survival has to be paid for, but a suitable price can certainly be negotiated."

The fire was blazing now.

He said, "Schenk's a fool to try to ruin your father. Your father's been a fool with the business and he's a fool to run around after my wife. My wife's a fool to listen to a word he says. I'm a bloody fool to have anything to do with any of them and I'm the only one who can't lose in this situation. Tell him my intentions are good."

After that it was two or three identical days: weather fine, nothing much happening. I held the fort. I ate fried bread with marmalade and spoonfuls of drinking chocolate from the tin. I lay on my bed, reading Beatle-magazines (only a week to the concert!) and James Bond novels, wanking a lot. I listened to records and watched TV as late as I wanted because no one was there to tell me to go to bed. Helen was spending a lot of time with a new boyfriend; poor old Victor had been given the elbow. Keith had hired a room in Shipley where his group practised. I saw them only in the morning. I didn't see my father at all. Once, in the middle of the night, I thought I heard a car on the gravel in the driveway and the outside cellar doors banging as they were opened but in the morning there was no car and no sign that he'd been in the house. I supposed it had been a dream.

Then he came back. He took me outside and showed me the car he had been driving, a bright blue Mini Cooper. I asked if it were new. "Not new old man, just altered slightly," he said in a serious voice. "Changed, taken out of itself, given new life, *meta . . morph . . . .* osed. Has anyone been looking for me?"

I told him about Weekes. "I said the Mini you had was a blue one."

"Headingley, you're a mind-reader. Who's Weekes?"

"A copper. He was here a few days ago."

"Placed him. Lanky fellow with a fag in his mouth, met him at the Roses match. Seemed to think that working for Johnny Law was a religious affair. Like being with Albert Schweitzer in the jungle. A strange attitude, Headingley, very strange. What did Charlie want?"

"He said you were to talk to him. And you were to keep out of Schenk's way."

"You know me, son. I'm shockproof, non-magnetic, equipped with an unbreakable self-winding superflex mainspring imported from Switzerland for the job," he said, and started to sing, softly at first, and then with enthusiasm. "Who wants to be a millionaire? . . . Have flashy flunkeys everywhere? . . . Who wants to wallow in champagne? . . . Or own a supersonic plane?" answering each question with the same squeaky response, *"I don't."*

I said, "Dad . . ."

He ignored me, carrying on with Cole Porter for a while, and then changing the melody, it was Gershwin now, "Loving one who loves you, and then taking that vow . . . nice work if you can get it, and if you get it—won't you tell me how?"

I understood why people found him exasperating.

"Did you get me those tickets for The Beatles?"

"Do you know who I am?"

I didn't understand.

"I'm a pianist. The light, it's all soft and gold, a thousand faces look up as I step out to play. I sit down and the orchestra starts up. 'Rhapsody in Blue.' "

Why the euphoria? Because he'd sold all the Minis and everything would be alright with Laughton? Because a woman, Diana most likely, had told him she loved him? Or perhaps he thought . . . The truth is, I don't know. That's what I'm trying to work out, and how it was that it ended, as it did end. Was Schenk's motive greed or revenge or malice? Or were there other causes, of which my father knew nothing? Schenk must have had a reason. That's the terrible thing about villains, they usually do.

He said, "There's something a certain woman has, you'll find that, you'll learn to look for it, not just looks, or sex, but a sort of bloom, and if she has it, she doesn't need to have anything else and if she doesn't have it, it doesn't much matter whatever else she does have."

Then he showed me the pearl, small and not round but shaped like a little pear with a dimple in the side, a real one, he said, which a fisherman called Bill Bass had found in an oyster he netted off Whitby. Bill Bass had given it to my father to give to my mother and my father had somehow, inexplicably, forgotten. Now he asked if he could trust me.

I said, "FULL FATHOM FIVE MY FATHER LIES."

No, I didn't. I said, "Yes, Dad."

He said, "There's a quid in it for you."

"A quid?"

"I want you to go up to Charlie Laughton's house. Tell him that I want to see him but I can't for a day or two. And give Diana the pearl, but make sure Charlie doesn't see. Can you do that?"

I pretended to think. "And you'll get those tickets?"

"Headingley," he said, losing patience. "Just do what I say. Will you? Please."

I walked across the market square in Baildon, hand in pocket, thumb and forefinger rubbing against the slightly rough surface of the object hidden there, the pearl. It was getting dark and I was thinking that the pearl was valuable, that it could be sold anywhere, to finance, for instance, a trip following The Beatles, to London or Paris or Hamburg, even America. New York or Chicago. Bedford Falls. I pictured James Stewart and ZouZou's petals. The pearl was a dream and I was no longer Headingley Hamer but an ace swordsman about to rescue a princess from a tower, an explorer shooting swirling rapids towards the source of the Nile. An adventurer.

Then I met the Irishman. "I do believe the roof's about to cave in," he said, looking up to the sky, his arm pushed inside the window of a letter box. He was small and tubby and wore an overcoat of angry tweed. Was he talking to me, or was he just an Irishman who volunteered opinions in general? "A typhoon, that's what I predict."

A gusting wind rolled clouds towards Bradford and was spreading them densely over the sky. Some were grey, while others were almost black, and one of these, low and to the west, wore a bracelet of bright yellow where the sun was setting behind it, a defiant gesture rubbed out even as I looked, leaving that cloud blacker than the rest. There was drizzle now and, in the distance . . . booms of thunder. The weather was turning in again.

The Irishman staggered as he pulled his arm from the letter box. Trying to regain his balance, he held out his arms like wings. Didn't succeed. Fell down, looked up, belched boozily. The Irishman was drunk.

Still on his knees, he explained, "A duomo is a cathedral in Italy. They are apt to tumble, I'm told, raining bricks and causing general consternation . . ."

A car was at the far end of the square, coming out of the drizzle and gloom, not coming fast, but coming straight towards us with its headlights on full, closer and closer, rumbling over the cobblestones. I saw a mascot, leaping from the bonnet as if about to attack, and I realised that it was a Jaguar, and not just any Jaguar, for there he was, face blurry behind the rain-spotted windscreen, but in typical pose, leaning back with one hand on the wheel and cigar aglow in the other. Schenk. Not so typically, he wore a bow-tie. And there was a woman beside him, another surprise, because the woman was Helen, not looking like Helen at all, with a fur coat and her hair pushed up high in a beehive.

Closer still. I was unable to move, trapped between the wobbling, silvery beams, a rabbit with a fat raindrop splashing on my face. I heard a distant clock striking. A tinny noise. Four, five, six. And then Schenk had his head out of the driver's window, and rain was already darkening the light brown shoulders of his overcoat. He said, "I'd not let a kiddie of mine go walking on his tod on a night like this," and smiled.

I said to Helen, "What are *you* doing?"

She said nothing, so there was a silence, except this was more than a silence, it was a powerful void, a black hole sucking me in. At the time I felt dazed and a little hurt. I realised that Helen had built an invisible wall and placed it between us, but I did not realise why. She had discovered I did not exist, so when I asked again, "What are you doing, why are you with him?" again there was no reply.

Schenk said, "Your dad's a regular villain to send you on an errand on a night like tonight."

How did he know I was on an errand?

I was praying, please don't let him offer me a lift I'll be at Sunday school every week and I won't piss down Hector Boardman's neck and I'll tell no more lies for ever and ever honest amen. But the door was already swinging open, and the feared for invitation was being made. Schenk said he wouldn't even consider the possibility of refusal.

The Irishman meanwhile was staring, at Schenk, and at Schenk's car, and at Schenk's coat, and at Schenk's woman, my sister. Expensive, he seemed to be thinking, this is quite obviously a well-heeled fellow, and inside the Jaguar is the place to be, warm and dry, with the smells of wood, soft leather, and a woman's perfume. And cigars. So he decided to try his luck.

Mistake.

The Irishman pushed me through the door and followed quickly, and while I looked from side to side, panicked, wondering if I could make a bolt for it out the other side, he settled himself, smoothing his spiky orange coat and grasping my arm to prevent any such escape. "Excuse me, sir," he said to Schenk, "I am drunk and temporarily without funds and about as secure on my feet as a tinpot dictator on a greasy pole somewhere in South America and I would be grateful for all eternity if you'd take me to the Midland Hotel and stand me a whisky, a double. It's essential that I get to Tadcaster."

The Irishman smiled, and Schenk smiled back.

Deceptive.

"It's the races, I've a sure thing for tomorrow, Sodom and Gomorrah in the three-fifteen."

I didn't know how it happened. I had, and have, no memory of taking it from my pocket, and yet there it was, the pearl.

"Will you look at that? Will you look at what the boy has? Young he is, and a millionaire."

The pearl was in the palm of my hand.

"A jewel, a gem. I could sell it for you, my boy. Hard as nails at a bargain I am."

Schenk turned once more. "What are you blathering about?"

"The lad has a pearl."

"A what?"

"Never cared for oysters myself. Delhi belly, not quite the ticket after a convivial evening."

"What's that you're saying?"

"My father, on the other hand, liked his seafood very much indeed."

"Well doesn't it take the sodding biscuit. The mick's tellin' the truth," said Schenk.

Helen said, "Where did you get it?"

"You're wearing too much make-up," I said, which was true. Her lips were a garish red, her eyelashes thick and black like the legs of spiders.

"Don't change the subject. Where did you get that pearl?"

"I found it."

"The boy is blessed," said the Irishman.

"He's a little liar," said my sister.

"It reminds me of a woman I knew once who'd seen the Virgin. From Killoran, she was. It was far from being the only remarkable thing about her. She could wrap herself round you like a crafty python, you wouldn't even notice, and get whatever she wanted. I never discovered whether she learned this talent from the Holy Mother herself. Just squeezed, she did, and you didn't feel a thing, like an orange you were, surrendering your pips."

Schenk was looking from the pearl to me, and back to the pearl once more, a stage villain expressing surprise and greed, then, sly as the python in the Irishman's story, his hand snaked out.

"Hey," I shouted, "give it back."

"You should, you know," said the Irishman.

"Tell me, Headingley," said Schenk. "What are you up to?"

"Nothing."

"Did you dad give you this?"

"It's like I said."

"I want the truth."

"I told you."

"You should, you know. Give it back. It's the boy's pearl."

"You," said Schenk, aiming his forefinger like a gun at the Irishman, "out of the car."

"I'll not."

"We can do this hard or we can do this easy."

"It's cold outside. I know, I've been there."

The shoulders of Schenk's tuxedo rose and fell, and when the Irishman answered this shrug with a serene smile I knew that he was being foolish, making another mistake, that while Schenk's shoulders had declared disinterest in continuing this particular conversation, they had some other debate in mind. One of them pushed open the driver's door, both were briefly illuminated by the headlights as they passed in front of the car, and then both reappeared—dewed with rain—after the back door had been opened on the Irishman's side.

Schenk's shoulders issued instructions and Schenk's hands were soon doing their job, pulling the Irishman out of the car and throwing him down.

I'll tell you about Schenk's hands. They were long and pale, with polished nails which curved exaggeratedly, making a shape like a crescent moon at the end of each of his fingers. Tubercular hands, bad hands which might wait for you on a black night in Bradford. They were lifting the Irishman and banging him against the cobbles.

"Call off the dogs," said the Irishman, "you'll break every sodding bone in my body."

Helen had her hand on my arm. She gripped it urgently. "Listen," she said.

"I'll not," I said.

"Where were you going? You'll have to say. He'll not give up."

Schenk's hands were still working on the Irishman, who was silent now, his body limp, bouncing up and down floppily. Schenk's hands let go, and when the body had fallen, a ventriloquist's dummy with the ventriloquist retired hurt, perhaps even dead, Schenk stood over it, exultant, eyes closed and face upturned, greeting the rain:

"AHM THE GREATEST LIVING MAN IN BRADFORD."

"Where were you taking the pearl?"

"AND AHM NOT DISPLEASED."

I wasn't afraid. Imagine you are sitting in an ordinary room. Suddenly you are told that someone you love is behind the door. In that instant everything in the room is altered; everything in it has taken on another look, a more fragrant smell, a richer light. Out there, Schenk is still shouting at the moon and the Irishman's blood

is still mingling with the rain on the shiny cobbles. It is no longer
the Irishman. It's my father. "Headingley," he says, "Headingley
old fellow, I trust you to do the right thing."

I felt very calm.

I ran across the cobbles and jumped on Schenk's back. I had one
arm around his neck, and with the other I clubbed at his head.

Schenk laughed, and I clubbed even harder, beating my fists into
his skull, until he stopped laughing and his shoulders heaved, sending me to the ground. Then it was not the Irishman that Schenk
was standing over, but me. He went up and up and up, like the
beanstalk in the story, the top of his head lost in the sky.

"You hate my dad," I said, "and I hate you."

He leaned towards me and as his grinning head came down from
the stormy clouds I collected all my force into my left hand and hit
him once more . . .

I wish I could assure you that this Bradford variation of David
and Goliath is the way the game ended. It isn't so. In fact I told
Helen I had been taking the pearl to Diana Laughton, got out of
the Jag and ran as fast as I could, stopping only when I was out of
breath and had reached the distant corner where the bell tower was.
Hiding in its shadow, looking back across the market square, I saw
that the Irishman was up on his knees and Helen was pulling at
Schenk's upraised arm—his fist held a cobblestone now. I pictured
dirt beneath those carefully manicured nails, trying to stop the fatal
blow.

In my bedroom there was a big mahogany wardrobe I had an idea
about. Coffins, it seemed to me, had no need of their own shadows.
So they sold them, or gave them away, and the shadows of all the
coffins which had been in our basement were in that wardrobe,
waiting, standing on end, shrugging their shoulders. The door had
a mirror on it which even at night found something to reflect and
it seemed to me that if I opened the door then the coffiny shadows
would march out. This was not a nightmare, but a fear which kept
me awake. On the night I saw Helen and Schenk in the Baildon
market square, there was a twist, for a voice whispered that if I
dared open the door I would find the pearl inside.

I told myself stories to stop myself thinking of the wardrobe. I was a wild and dangerous knight, with my enemies grovelling and my wounds tended by the fairest maids and ladies of the world. I was involved in mishaps and adventures all over Bradford, but always coming out on top like Walter Mitty. I was a Greek god, hurling mountains about. But all the time the room was shrinking. The wardrobe came closer and closer. I was hypnotised by it. In memory, I still am. I see my face, thrown back in dim and fearful reflection as my hand reaches across the end of the bed to turn the key.

The door opened and Helen came in. The room was filled immediately with the smells of perfume, cold air, and boozy breath, all in one whiff. "You should see it outside," she said. "Snowing now. Have you ever noticed how snow makes everything look silver? What a night." And then: "What are you doing, our kid? You'll catch your death."

I got back under the covers.

"Don't say I never give you anything," she said. Giggling, she took off her coat and laid it across the bottom of the bed. "And don't ask me what I had to do to get this back."

She held out her hand and gave me the pearl. As soon as I touched it, still warm from her hand, I remembered, not the promise to my father, but how important I had felt when I walked through Bradford with it in my pocket.

"Love, love me do, you know I love you, I'll always be true."

Helen's voice had a special ease which I'd never heard before, not singing the words so much as caressing them.

I said, "You won the pools or something?"

"We took your Irishman to the Midland," she said. "Kept talking all the time about that bloody horse. God, he was pissed."

When she said it, I felt glad that the Irishman was alright, though to tell the truth I'd forgotten about him.

"I want to go to London," she said. "Don't you?" Closing her eyes, she took herself away from Bradford and told me of the shop windows she was looking into, they were the most splendid sights she'd ever seen, of the fashionable treasures she was touching gently with her fingers, mini-skirts and paisley blouses in cotton, of the models and pop stars and beatnik-booted photographers she saw from the top of a red bus like a skyscraper, of the streets she was strolling along. Haymarket! Piccadilly! The Kings Road! The names were like bells from beyond the stars, she said.

"Jim's to take me there."

"Who?"

"Jim Schenk. Next week, in the Jag."

I said nothing.

"You're a priest, Headingley, that's that you are, a little *monk,* all silent and disapproving, in a cowl."

"No I'm not."

"I used to think of him the way you do. A real bastard, I used to think. But he's not that way at all. He can be sweet and kind and he'd love to be your pal. He was talking tonight about taking you to the football. In Bradford, or Manchester maybe, to see United, you'd like that."

More mute disapproval from me, but then her hands were between the sheets and inside my pyjama top, probing my ribs, tickling, running over my waist, and I couldn't help myself. I laughed.

"Take a pill and pull your leg," she said.

"Give over."

"Won't give up until you beg."

"Stop it."

"Won't give up until you beg."

"Stop it, PLEASE."

Then she did stop. She brushed hair from my forehead with her fingers. "Things can't stay the same," she said. "They have to change. Or else they just wear out."

"Like old tyres?"

"Something like that. I still love you, Headingley."

"The Irishman, was he really alright?"

"Sure. Was that the truth? That Dad asked you to take it to Diana Laughton?"

I assumed a serious expression. What did she want to hear? I asked if she remembered a friend of our father's, Bill Bass, a fisherman. Bill Bass had given it to me, I said, to give to our mother, something for her to remember him by, a *token,* that's what he'd said. I sounded so persuasive I swear I almost believed it myself.

Why did I lie? I don't know, but the important thing was that Helen believed, nodded, smiled, was pleased. CARAMBA!

"Then the joke's on Jim. 'Cos I told him what you told me."

"What did he say?"

"He seemed pleased."

Helen was carried away now with our rediscovered intimacy. She wanted to prove that we were friends.

"Let's go down to the basement."

Not my idea of a journey conducive to friendship. "It's locked," I said.

"I know where Dad puts the key."

"I'm not sure."

"Be great, like old times."

"It's all shut now. It'll be filled with dried-up spiders."

"You're not still scared?"

"Rats the size of ferrets."

"Are you?"

"No!"

It didn't much matter whether she believed me or not. Helen had made the decision in that way she had and soon we were at the cellar door again. She had a torch in one hand, the key in the other, and a face announcing that she was very pleased with this idea. She was on a jaunt, determined that I should have fun as well.

"Remember how there used to be dead bodies stretched out stiff?" she said. "It was great."

We were going down the wooden steps, and my nostrils were filled with the damp smells of mildew and flaking whitewash, but no fruity smell this time, rotting or otherwise, since it had been our mother who had used the cellar to store jams and pickles.

"Do you remember the time . . ."

I said I did.

"Look at that," Helen said. The beam of her torch had picked out three coffins, black, mounted on trestles, in the middle of the cellar. She said, "Weird. No one's been down here for ages."

"Someone has."

"Are there bodies inside?"

"Who's scared now?"

"Let's look."

"Let's go back upstairs," I said, trying not to think of what might be inside the coffins, but finding I couldn't help myself, the pictures just floated up, childish images of death: a woman falling off a horse, a man shot, another standing on top of a building like the Empire State in New York—there were lights running up the side, but what had happened to King Kong?—and taking a step towards the edge then, *paff*, the end.

"Doctors are inventing ways to be rejuvenated," she said. "Did you know that? By the time we get old we won't have to die. You'll be able to live for ever. You'll be able to listen to The Beatles, always."

"Don't," I said, but she had already pushed the lid aside and was asking me to look. I said, "No thanks."

"It's not what you expect," she said.

"I'm not falling for any of your tricks."

"Headingley, I'm not sure I'm not seeing things, I need you to look. I promise."

And so I did.

This is what I saw. I saw . . . No, I won't tease you this time, I'll tell you the truth, and you tell me if you're not as surprised as I was.

The coffin was filled with money. Not coins, but notes: fives, tens, twenties, all in a heap, an incalculable sum. I remembered a film where the villains had bargained to buy a woman, offering cash, jewels, *cities,* fortunes so large they had no meaning, millions which would get together and breed like rabbits. Helen had the lid off the second coffin, which contained another rustling money-mountain, and was rushing to the third. The same: more money. She turned the torch on a fiver she had in her hand. She whistled appreciatively. "Looks real enough."

I asked what we were going to do.

She said, "Spend it."

"All of it?"

"Just some."

Her arms went up once, and again, and then again. The torch showed money as it flew to the ceiling and came tumbling down slowly. Money made a satisfying crackle as I scooped up handfuls myself. Money was soon beneath my feet, in my hair, against my lips, its sound whispering as we tossed it all about. "You were right after all, our kid," said Helen. "We have won the pools."

. . .

We went shopping. For Helen it was skirts, lipsticks, the new Stones single, and a pair of black leather boots from Chelsea Fashions on Kirkgate. For me it was an inflatable Fab Four pillow, a football (I supported Manchester United, for whom George Best—nursing the ball on his instep, evading defenders with a cheeky squirm—had recently played his first game), and a peaked corduroy cap. For Keith it was just the one thing, a guitar, a beauty, a red and white Rickenbacker. The celebrations began as soon as we got home. My Beatle-suit was removed from the wardrobe. My Beatle-wig was combed. While I put on my Beatle-uniform Keith picked the lock on the cabinet in the corner of the living room and Helen whisked rum, brandy, and advocaat into a brown froth which I named *Le Cocktail Ringo*. The froth was consumed at terrific speed. And then I lay on the floor—cap on head, feet up on the coffee-table, head resting on John Lennon's share of the inflatable pillow—and stared out of the window, watching sparks and balls of flame-rimmed smoke burst into the sky from the mill chimneys below, listening to Keith strum the Rickenbacker and sing, waiting for "I Wanna Hold Your Hand," and there it was, my favourite moment in any Beatles song, *"And when I touch you I feel happy inside."* I felt very calm.

Looking back, searching for a pattern in everything that happened, it seems there must have been more, that I must have felt like the character in the song, deliriously, insanely happy, determined to enjoy myself to the full, because that was, I suppose, the last night of my childhood. In fact, I felt none of those things. I remember gloating over the intimacy I had established with my brother and sister. It was me who led the way down into the cellar when Keith asked where we'd got the money; it was me who led the laughter when we saw that it was gone, that the coffins were empty now. *Khazam!* Headingley could do magic.

My father took me to Taylor's Mill, where one of Charlie Laughton's demolition gangs was exploding the cooling tower we had climbed up years before. "Wish it luck," he said. The charges went off with a series of thumps and the tower folded in on itself, pushing up a cloud of dust and smashed concrete. His mood was a little sentimental. He talked about Bradford and how it was changing. He remembered a shop that used to have a big steak-and-kidney pie in the window, not a real one of course, but a fake, about seven feet wide, with steam puffing out through a funnel in the centre. The pie had later become a legend when the shop's window was blown out by a German bomb in the war. The owner had nailed up boards, but left a crack between them, so the people could see the pie was still there, its every breath a reminder that Mr. Hitler would have to do a lot better if he wanted to bring Bradford to its knees.

"Load of cobblers," said my father. "But that's the thing, you see. People need stability in their lives. They want to know that some things don't change. Reassuring, they seem to find it, but they're wrong, of course, things have to change, otherwise they just wear out."

I thought of Helen. I said, "Like tyres?"

"Quite right old fellow, you've picked it up like a true Hamer, and this is my advice to you. Check your tyres and change them often."

Now he was looking at me with an expression so serious it sent my heart into my shoes. I assumed he was going to ask about the money in the cellar, and why I had taken some, but he didn't, it was something else which was on his mind. "The pearl . . ."

The pearl. I forgot to mention what happened. That's not true, it's not exactly that I forgot. I know the pearl seemed like something important after the business with the Irishman and Schenk and my sister selling whatever she had to sell, except she wasn't forced to, she was, I suspect, a bride happily bartered, it's just that I thought, yes, that's it, I thought I'd bring it up a little later.

My father said, "You gave it to Diana?"

"Oh yes, Dad, sure, I gave it to her alright."

"And what did she say?"

This one required thought. I said, "She said it was very lovely. And she thought it was bloody typical of Jack Hamer."

"That's what she said."

I nodded.

"Bloody typical?"

"That's what she said." In fact, that wasn't what Diana Laughton had said. In fact, she hadn't said anything, hadn't had the chance to, because I hadn't given her the pearl. I had lost it playing marbles with Eleanor Burrows from down the street. Eleanor Burrows was a girl with red hair I hoped would kiss me.

"You'd say she was pleased?"

"Oh yes, Dad, that's what I'd say."

"Among the pleasures that I enjoy, Venus is not the least," he said, laughing. "And she gave you something to give to me?"

This needed more thought. I said, "No, Dad."

"Nothing at all, you're sure?"

"I'm sure."

"No message?"

"Just 'Bloody typical.' "

My father was sad then. "Thanks, old fellow," he said, and gave me a pound note.

"That's great, Dad," I said, disappointed with the sum. "I'll be able to get the new LP. It's the concert in a few days."

He didn't take the hint. Instead he told me he hadn't been to a concert for a while. He remembered, when he'd been in the RAF, he and a friend would bribe the duty officer and drive to London, there'd be jazz bands and dancing like he couldn't believe, and women, so many women—if one left, there was always another on the next bus. He said, "Except for Diana. That Diana, she was always different." Presumably she had not used the bus. I wondered where my mother had fitted into the travel arrangements.

I said, "Dad, about those tickets you're getting me."

"Sold out."

"What?"

"Sorry, son, I did try. They'd gone, every last one. I was too late."

Sold out!

"Cheer up," he said.

I was silent.

"There'll be other times," he said, and grinned. He suggested that we go to the covered market. He wanted to pick up a couple of pounds of liver.

Again I said nothing.

But now memory takes me inside the busy market. Hears my feet scratching on the sawdust on the floor. Notes the light which spills from the gas lamps, there's something pearly about it, and also notes the smell of raw meat, and the sweet, sickly taste catching in my throat. Look, over there, a woman is swinging a chicken by the neck. And listen to those two men arguing, shouting at each other like two coal lorries colliding. Look again, there goes the chicken's head, *smack,* against a black marble slab. There is the silence of held breath, for some seconds, before my father speaks.

Once, he told me, on a dark and freezing afternoon, in the middle of what seemed an endless winter, he had been here with *his* father. He had been very young, only eight or nine. "There I was, in baggy short trousers, thinking I was tougher than I was, and my father said he wanted me to see something, it was the goose we were having for Christmas, and off we went, the stall is still there, Bicknell Brothers, and I thought, well, so what, but then old man Bicknell had the bird, alive and I tell you still kicking in one hand, a bloody big knife in the other and I realised what I was going to see was the goose and its cork being pulled. My father made me look. He told me that so long as I looked at things head on, there was nothing to be afraid of. Just not true, old man. There are always things to be afraid of."

He smiled, but as if he had difficulty hiding a fear he did feel. "I miss her, you know."

"Who's that, Dad?"

"Your mother."

He looked down at me with a face like . . . Shall I tell you about his face? I am devoured by comparisons. He wore the face of a mawkish saint. He wore the face of a martyr with a tendency for self-pity. He wore the face parents wear when they are about to embarrass their children. He said he knew Helen and Keith could look after themselves, but I was different, a poor little bugger with no wings to fly. He said, "Your grandma thinks you'll turn out like me. Best hope not, eh?"

"I'll be alright, Dad," I said, puzzled.

"I love you, Headingley, remember that."

He pressed the flats of his hands to his eyes. I didn't understand his mood. It was something I'd never seen before. I was waiting for the moment when he would remove his hands and pull a face to let me know that he was kidding. Instead, something extraordinary happened: he fell to his knees and wept.

I was unprepared. I didn't know what to say. My father's body heaved, and people began to stare. The woman from the chicken stall said, "Isn't that Jack Hamer, pissed as a fucking brewery rat?"

I looked away. I saw a dead pig on a meat-hook; hanging by its milky white feet, turned inside out, the pig displayed its deep red entrails. People were laughing and the chicken woman was saying, "Not unusual, I remember his dad, he were the same."

Shame crawled up my back. I would like to say that I gave her some amusing ideas about what she could do with her chicken. I would like to say that I was a hare unexpectedly caught by a tortoise, that for once emotion got the better of my tongue, and that while I could find nothing to say, I looked at my father with my heart going out. The truth is, I only remembered my anger at his failure to get me tickets for The Beatles. Shame was put to the sword.

My father was still crying, and still on his knees, but rocking to and fro, as if in a trance, with dirt and blood darkening his trouser-knees.

I said, "Dad, who do you like best, John or Paul?"

I'm back in the lecture hall. Hamlet is the tragedy of a man who let down his father, true or false? After all, where was he when he was most needed, when Claudius was pouring poison down his father's ear? Swanning about in Wittenberg. I ask my students what they think Hamlet's father's ghost thought of this filial dereliction. I ask them whether they know what was on *my* father's mind, if he expected help from Helen, Keith, and I. This question raises another: what am I doing, writing about him? I make a suggestion myself: I'm in my room at the Wonderland hotel, I'm up on the fourth floor where everything is dusted white by the plaster which crumbles from the walls whenever a lorry thunders by on the Holloway Road, which is about every ninety seconds, and I'm seeking that which will heal, digging in the past, trying to make it come alive, warm as memory.

Warm as memory!! Prickle me, tickle me: I'm a poet. My girls laugh, bang on cue, and I allow them the comfort of their amusement before suggesting that . . . swaggie, waggie, and shoggieshou, I'm no poet, but a playwright in the revenge tradition. Enter

Headingley (carrying a skull). But revenge on who? On myself, or on Schenk? My father? Am I really like him in the way people say? Ideas of him stretch backward and forward in time. Easing his bladder in the steam and stink of the urinal behind the main stand at Headingley. As absent tyrant, ineffectual ruler of a chaotic household. Grinning boozily. Boozily tearful. It is noon and he is the Scarlet Pimpernel, but darkness falls at five when . . .

I'm in full flow, and a voice interrupts: "You're not in a hotel room at all." It's the flame-haired temptress, in another of those pleasingly brief skirts, but she says, "You're walking through a graveyard with your father's cock in your pocket and you don't know whether to pray to it, or bury it and spit on the grave, or," and here she pauses, smiling with that sweet six-shooter of a mouth, before taking aim and firing below the belt, "put it on a pedestal and *eat it*."

SILENCE!

This is what the next days were like. I have a sense of a pause, and of a hidden God, rigging the climax off-stage. Keith's friends from The Five Shades of Blue would come to the house to listen to music, or practise, or take pills, amphetamines known as "purple hearts." The bass player, he was bearded and warty and the others called him Gimmy because he was always saying "Gimme a fiver," squirted washing-up liquid into the sputnik fish tank and giggled, singing "Da Doo Ron Ron" as corpses assembled on the surface. For a while it seemed that a coi-carp, which my father called Julius, would survive, but then it too floated up, mouth opening and closing, and died in the glistening bubbles.

The police would come to the door and want to know if my father had come back yet. I would say I didn't know he'd gone anywhere. One of them swayed over me and asked—I'm not kidding—"When did you last see your father?" I would say it had been only a couple of days ago. I would warm Heinz tomato soup in a pan.

Twiggy Fawcett and Amos Bass would come to the house with cheques that needed to be counter-signed, for petrol, for car repairs, for the carpenter in Goole who was phoning three times a day and needed his account settled pronto because his daughter was getting married the next week to a professional footballer with Sheffield Wednesday.

"We need them coffins," said Twiggy Fawcett.

"Whooping cough," said Amos Bass.

"Young uns dyin evurryw-air," said Twiggy Fawcett.

"Oh! The calamity of missed opportunity," said Amos Bass.

Schenk would come to the house and take Helen out. She said he only wanted to talk about one thing: our father. Schenk had heard that he was in Glasgow, and London, and Paris, that he had stolen a light aircraft from Yeadon Airport and flown it to Lisbon. Schenk believed none of those stories. Schenk would insist that he was in Bradford. Surely she must know something. Helen would insist that she couldn't care less and Schenk would smile, saying she was right, it didn't really matter, he'd catch up with him sooner or later. He would ask again. He took her to the Midland Hotel where he had booked a room and when they had made love, hit her in the face. Surely she must know something. He hit her again. Helen said she would kill him.

I remember thinking it strange that there should be this fuss. After all, it was not unusual for my father to disappear for a few days; on the contrary, he made a habit of it. Then it struck me that because a fuss was being made, because everyone else—Twiggy and Amos, Schenk, the police—was slightly hysterical, perhaps it was different this time. That thought made a hollow in my belly.

Diana came to the house, just the one time. "Is Helen here," she asked, "or Keith?" They were both out. "Actually," she said, "it's you I came to see."

Me?

She said, "Do you know where he's gone?"

I shook my head; this was easy.

"He said you'd be coming to see me. When I last spoke to him, when he was playing the clown in front of half of Bradford with his bloody cricket pavilion. He said you'd bring the message."

The message? Then I realised: the pearl.

"Did he say anything?"

Did it enter my mind that I should tell the truth? I knew that when my father came back and asked if she'd liked his gift, she'd express surprise, "What pearl?" then he'd come to me and I'd have to admit everything, or at least spin him a good one. I knew also that it could be weeks before he did come back, and by then the pearl might no longer be of importance, might be forgotten. So I grasped at a tactic which I would later use often and without shame. When in doubt, deny it all.

I said, "No, he didn't."

"Nothing at all?"

"Not a word."

"It's important, Headingley."

"He didn't say anything, not to me, anyway."

She was silent. She sank into an armchair and lit a cigarette, even though she had one going already. There it was, smoking in the brass ashtray which my father had found somewhere, Brussels I think, and which was in the shape of a little boy pissing into a pond. She puffed at the second cigarette, and looked round anxiously for the ashtray, so I gave it to her, and then she gave me a little smile as she saw the first. She stubbed them both out.

My father had gone too far this time, she said, and Schenk and her husband were after him. Schenk had been around at their house, drinking, boasting that he would soon be wearing white gloves again and that this time the bullet would have the name John Bertram Hamer written on it. Schenk might be a lousy ham, she said, who wouldn't know a decent line to steal even if it were broadcast by tannoy at the Valley Parade football ground, but she had no doubt that he would hurt my father if her husband told him to. She had a bad feeling.

"Bloody Jack Hamer. He thinks the rest of us are in a cave and it's pitch black and he's somewhere else, out there, waltzing in the moonlight. Well, Jackie, I'm afraid I don't care any more. The cave men can have you."

I imagine a scene in Charlie Laughton's Rolls, at night, with rain teeming outside. LAUGHTON: *Are you saying that my wife is unfaithful?* SCHENK: *Absolutely not.* LAUGHTON: *Then you go to a great deal of trouble to explain an inconsequential occurrence.* SCHENK: *I've been talking to the kiddies.* Schenk says nothing more, he doesn't have to. He turns his head in a certain way and draws on his cigar. Laughton understands at once: Jack Hamer is sleeping with his wife again. LAUGHTON: *Very well, then. Bring me an animal bearing gifts.*

Diana Laughton said, "Do you want to hear about the first time I met your father?"

I said nothing.

"In London, when the war seemed not long over and it still seemed that everyone had been given a break. I was just out of drama school, Jack was going to write a book . . ."

My father write a book? Even at the time this struck me as unlikely; he had been bending it, more than a little.

"I was in a pub, with a friend, Gin and It on the bar, and this bloke comes up bold as a barrel-load of monkeys, that's your dad, he had that same moustache, like he thought he was Errol Flynn, elbowing my friend to one side, and he said . . ."

But I never did get to hear what my father had said in Diana Laughton's version of their first meeting. Instead, her demeanour became businesslike and it was, "I owe you something, Headingley."

"What's that?"

"A kiss. We had a deal, remember."

Her red mouth came towards mine and this time she did kiss me, once, and then again. She said, "That's two, and now you owe me." But when I pushed my lips towards hers she wouldn't let me. She said, "I'll show you where."

I didn't understand. I didn't know what she meant. But, unzipping her skirt and stepping out of it, with one hand on the back of my head, and the first two fingers of the other acting as guides through the stiff black hairs which made a triangle above her stocking-tops, opening intricate folds and furls of flesh, she did show me.

The next day—it was a Monday, the day before The Beatles came to Bradford—I did go to school. Igor Cryer came up in the school playground. I still don't know how the Cryer brothers came by their names. As well as Igor, there was Boris, and little Ivan, whose tonsils had been sliced accidentally by Keith with the fishing rod. Russian names, but I know for a fact that their father came from Morley, not Moscow. Perhaps he was a Communist, or had fought alongside the Russians in the war, or perhaps he merely liked the way the names sounded when they dropped from his mouth. *Bor-is*. Parents can't always control themselves when it comes to names. I know.

Anyway, Igor had a Beatle-badge on his blazer lapel and trousers
that were several inches too short; they flapped around his ankles.
His head was also in miniature. It sat on his shoulders like a pea on
a pie crust, and was on this occasion split by a wide grin. Igor was
excited, not in the mood to bother with formalities: "My dad says
your dad's a regular wrong 'un. A real crook, your dad is, a thievin'
bastard," he said. "Your dad's going t' nick. They'll throw away
t'key. That's what *my* dad reckons."

I said, "Your dad's a fortune-teller, is he? Like glamorous
Madam Sorastro on the pier at Skegness?"

"Your dad's a sack o' shit," said Igor Cryer, moving closer,
noticing the amusement on the faces of other kids who were
gathering to watch the argument. "That's what my dad reckons."

Perhaps I could think of no other reply. Perhaps I knew a fight
to be inevitable, because it was so obviously what Igor wanted. Or
did I feel, at last, anger on my father's behalf? No, I don't think it
was that; had I been Peter in the Garden of Gethsemane I would
have gone on denying Christ after the dawn, all through the day,
and the next night as well. I suppose all through that winter I felt
betrayed by my father and was betraying him in return. The truth
is that I don't know why I did what I did. I hit him.

And what a hit! My clenched fist came up from my knees and
caught him on the point of the chin, making his teeth clatter. Igor
looked surprised for a moment and then went down like an ice-
berged cruise liner.

It was a fluke. I've never been much of a fighter, and most of my
playground scraps had been a few minutes rolling and fumbling
into which neither myself, nor my opponent, put much heart.
Unfortunately, the fluke was seen by Miss Antrobus, now the
headmistress. She was fat, with numerous double chins buttered
over her chest. But she was quiet on her feet, and had a way of
rolling up unexpectedly. She marched me into her study.

"Now then Hamer. What's this all about?"

"All what, Miss Antrobus?"

"You know full well."

I avoided her eye and looked instead at a picture on the wall, an
oil painting of the founder of the school, who wore a beard like
God the Father. There was something intimidating about those
bushy Victorian whiskers. "We are the whiskers of authority," they

said, "whiskers of convention who must be obeyed. Wise whiskers which know better."

"We were playing."

"Really?" said Miss Antrobus. "Look at me when you talk, if you please."

I saw the Antrobus stare, accompanied on this occasion by the Antrobus smile, which was meant to be reassuring. I don't like using the violent stare, the smile was supposed to say, and if only you'd tell me everything then I'd be happy, you'd be happy, and we'd both be on our way.

I said, "I hit him Miss Antrobus. I hit him because I'm confused. Leaving the womb, facing the world, all that growing up stuff. I hit him because he's big and a bastard and he was saying bad things about my father which I wouldn't have minded except that he was trying to insult my brother and sister and me by pissing on the old man. He was pissing by implication. So I had to stand up for the three of us."

You see; I was talkative for my age.

Except I didn't say that. I said nothing, as per. Not a word. I answered the Antrobus stare with one of my own, and threw in a smile.

"Perhaps I will call your father. And suggest we discuss your career at this school over a drink."

I pictured my father and Miss Antrobus, in a pub, up against the bar with pint glasses in hand, discussing religion or health matters or my future. The thought made me smile again.

"You'll stay in that corner until such time as your manners improve. And you stop wearing that stupid grin."

I had been standing there for what was probably only a few minutes, and seemed like fifty, thinking that perhaps I should tell Miss Antrobus what Igor Cryer had said, why should I worry what his father thought about mine? when there was a knock on the door. I was aware of someone coming into the room, and whispering—"Scarborough . . . ," "not sure . . . ," "better come . . ."; I could make out only a few words—and a chair shrieking across the floor as Miss Antrobus stood up.

"Wait here Hamer. You may stand down from the corner."

I turned round. I looked at the bearded gentleman in the portrait, I laughed, I stuck out my tongue, I defied him to talk. "Fuck it fungus-face," I said, "this is 1964, do your worst."

I looked at the door. I see it as it was, open, with Miss Antrobus beyond, talking to my mother. In a panic I imagine the subject of their conversations: me. Another bad report this term, frequently absent, content to rest on non-existent laurels, a special school might be best, for *delinquents*.

But Miss Antrobus is a puzzle now. She smiles, as if she has just been nice to me for hours on end. "I'll leave you then," she says, moving her hands towards my face as if to touch me with her plump fingers, and then thinking better of it. "Goodbye, Heading-ley."

Why is she using my first name?

My mother has dropped her cigarette to the floor and is stubbing it out with the toe of her shoe. She says, "It's about your father . . . ," and my reaction is relief, because it, whatever "it" may be, is not about me.

She has stopped now, as if unsure how to give the comfort she thinks I need, and she pulls me close. Her hands are on my back, pressing my cheek into the silky fur of her coat. From a distance came the sound of a desk-lid banging and a voice calling a class to attention. My mother said there had been an accident, in Scarborough, on the boat, an explosion.

My father was dead.

I saw light shining on the polished wood parquet floor, and a black mark on one of the tiles, a little trench, where something, a football stud perhaps, or a stiletto heel, had been dug in. I was burrowing nose-first into that hole, and then falling, through the floor and the stone foundations, into mud, falling past worms, human bone, and the roots of trees, towards the centre of the world.

The next thing was back at the house, with Helen and Keith, drinking tea and having nothing to say. A copy of the *Telegraph & Argus* was on the kitchen table. My father would have appreciated that the incident had been celebrated by Budge Carter, with some verve.

"LOCAL MAN KILLED ON BOAT," said the headline. "Flames lit the Scarborough sky last Saturday night when *Hello Dixie Minx,* a luxury motor-cruiser," I remembered my father's rather more splendid formulation *motor-boozer,* "exploded and sank within seconds off Flamborough Head." Clothes belonging to my father had been found among the wreckage, though—Budge warmed to the job—"no evidence of the burned remains."

There was talk of "the deceased's eminence on the local scene" and his "distinguishable war record." There was even a photograph, showing my father with a grin and his arm around the shoulders of the Yorkshire cricketer Brian Close. "Happier days for Jack Hamer," said the caption.

There was also a twist. "Top Bradford cops were heading a crack team to investigate suspected fraud"; they were anxious to talk to James Schenk, "former business partner of the dead man," who was also, it seemed, missing from home, "mysteriously." I wondered what was so mysterious about the fact that he had come to see Helen the night before.

"The possibility of foul play has not been ruled out," the article continued, "in this tragic incident."

I thought of the money in the coffins in the cellar. The sum so large it had no meaning was now given a figure by Budge Carter: £68,000. At least, such was the amount suspected to have gone missing from the businesses of those "eminent Bradford entrepreneurs Jack Hamer and James Schenk who, moreover, owed the British Motor Corporation for fifty-seven Mini cars which had been sold and not paid for."

I thought of an idea I'd had, that something would happen to my father when I was twelve years old. I'd assumed that it would be something irrevocable, irreversible, definite. I'd assumed he would die. And now it seemed that he had died, but in circumstances far from definite, circumstances that might even be reversible. I had learned a few things about death from our family's association with the funeral trade. For instance: death generally involved a corpse, and money, not being taken away, but bequeathed, to relatives who sometimes had a hard time keeping pretending they were sorry.

Helen, Keith, and I sat in the kitchen, waiting for our mother to come back. I wanted to ask, "Is he really dead? Did Schenk kill him? What about us?" Instead, I warmed my hands around my mug of tea. It seemed the silence would go on and on. Embarrassment, or an inability to measure our feelings, ensured it did; either way, we never spoke about what happened and, somehow, that fact was to stop us speaking about anything else.

I looked again at the paper. Budge Carter had written another story, about The Beatles; this was the night they were coming to Bradford. "They're young. They're high-spirited and cheerful," he wrote. "They don't rely on off-colour jokes for their fun. It's plain to see why these four, energetic, cheeky lads from Liverpool go down so big." I turned to Helen and Keith but they seemed not to be there, they were already ghosts, faces which had come out of the dark and were now going back to it, vanishing as certainly as my father had.

Part Three

RUBBER SOUL

And then? It was 1981. I was twenty-nine and I lived the suitcase life, losing count of the times I drove across Bradford each week, from wife to mistress and mistress to wife, between Shipley and Four Lane Ends, crossing always through Forster Square, I suppose it was there, with a petrified Victorian wool baron looking on—I would ask myself what gave him the right to be so blankly disapproving, perhaps that stone chain led to a stone half-hunter SHOVED UP HIS ARSE—and the suitcase in question, a blue canvas hold-all, which contained shirt, socks, razor, and several out-of-date copies of the *Telegraph & Argus,* beside me on the passenger seat, that I flicked the switch: Julie off, Barbara on; Barbara off, Julie on again. Friday night was the difficult night, the night I had promised I would always spend at home, and that particular Friday night did indeed find me just outside Shipley, off the Bingley Road, at 24 Hall Royd, with Julie, eating dinner. Lamb chops and me, a light-bulb flickering.

I said, matter-of-factly, "I have to go out."

Julie said nothing.

I made my voice reasonable. I told her she knew the way things were, at work, what with Mr. Hyde and the city in a panic. I was a journalist, I had a lead. I said, "The city never sleeps baby."

"Ha-bloody-ha," said Julie.

"Don't you believe me?"

"It's bullshit this father bullshit."

Pause. "What's my father got to do with it?"

"You've chosen to be haunted."

"It's very simple. I have to go out tonight to work on a story."

Coldly: "Fuck you."

Julie made Lady Macbeth seem weak and infirm of purpose. Once, in the early years of our marriage, conversation had been a struggle, we knew each other so well. Now we heaved words about with the ferocity of prophets in the Old Testament, neither surprised nor concerned if things were broken. I asked what she wanted me to do. It was a fellow who had called me at the office, a little edgy he had sounded, as if he really did know something and was scared. It might be nothing, it would almost certainly prove to be nothing, but what if it didn't, what if it cracked the whole caboodle? I became angry. She might not be believing my lie, but by now I was. I was filled with self-righteousness. I wanted her to see my side. It wasn't a question of choice, I had to do it.

"Don't be pissed off," I said.

"Don't tell me not to be pissed off. Of course I'm pissed off."

"Tell me what you want. I'll do anything."

"Keep your promises."

"I can't do that. Just this one time, I've explained."

"I don't believe you."

"That's unfortunate," I said. "I'm going anyway."

I was more than a prophet now. I spoke in the tone which God found handy when he spoke out of the whirlwind, asking Job if he knew from whose womb came the ice, or if he could lift up his voice to the clouds and cause tropical downpours, or if he could send down lightnings. I spoke as if my tongue were made of bronze.

She said, "You're Prince Myshkin, not Prince Hamlet."

That was another thing about my wife: she was not persuaded by the bronze-tongued approach.

I kissed the top of her head. I told her I didn't know when I'd be back. She should be sure to lock the door behind me, I said, and

I left, not letting her see my expression, which was not that of the Prince of Denmark, nor that of a prophet, nor even that of Jehovah himself. I was grinning like Paul Muni escaped from the chain gang.

My father's father—Bert Hamer, the grandfather I never met—had worked once for a firm of Bradford wool merchants called Rothenstein & Kafka. No joke is intended, literary or otherwise: many Germans came to Bradford at the end of the last century, after the city had sold cloth for uniforms to both sides in the Franco-Prussian war and made itself rich. Rothenstein and Kafka were among them, they built a warehouse and office in Little Germany, three streets north of where the funeral business was to be, and it was there that my grandfather worked in the summer of 1920. He stood at a high desk in a room that seemed all black and white, with hard shadows like an engraving from a book where dragons wait in the dark and angels march towards them from the light, lugging big swords. In this case boredom was the dragon. My grandfather would study reports on the qualities of various wools, and note details in a ledger. He did this day-in, day-out, in air so hot and filled with lanolin and floating tufts of wool that to draw it in was an effort. Each breath had to be squeezed down the throat.

It wasn't as if he would have to stay there for ever. He was being prepared, *groomed,* that was the word my father had used, to take over a sheep farm in the Calder Valley near Harrogate, where the land was lush and green, different from Bradford. This was the more prestigious of the two businesses owned by my grandfather's uncle, Alfred Hamer, whose idea it was that he should get the measure of the wool trade before starting to farm. The idea didn't work out because, one August afternoon, itching inside the heavy suit old Rothenstein insisted he wear, with just one month of his apprenticeship still to run, worn down by the dragon, he left, quickly and without fuss, but taking with him a petty cash box whose polished top shone back a semblance of life. It had in it fifty-four pounds nine shillings and three pence, a lot of money in 1920.

Next stop: London, inevitably, where, inevitably, he was soon relieved of the cash. But he stayed, gambling, sending money each week to Rothenstein (Uncle Alfred had persuaded him not to prosecute), selling furniture to the big department stores which were opening all over London, selling furniture not very well but in the process meeting an Irish Catholic shopgirl, Annie. Marrying my grandfather was, I suspect, the one reckless act of her life. They went back to Bradford a year later, when Uncle Alfred died. He left a will which, though from its obscurity the subject of numerous lawsuits, was clear on at least one point: my grandfather was to inherit, not the farm, but the other family business, the funeral business; revenge, perhaps, for the Rothenstein & Kafka scandal, or perhaps just a joke. Uncle Alfred liked a joke. The trouble was that his sense of humour was intelligible to no one, except Uncle Alfred. Once he had walked down Market Street in a top hat, firing a revolver and shouting Anarchist slogans. When arrested, he had said, "I'm the biggest bastard Capitalist in the entire West Riding." The will might have been an act in similarly confused spirit but, joke or not, our side of the family was to live with its consequences for over forty years.

Bert Hamer died in 1933, leaving my father heir to the business and already very taken with the idea of not belonging. I had grown up asking myself whether I would be like him, as he had been like my grandfather, fearing the possibility, but feeling somehow that it was bound to be, that families—as my father had said—were doomed to walk towards their destiny by proceeding in the direction of their origins. In 1981 home was where I went when I ran out of places.

Here I am, ten minutes after leaving Julie, in the flat off Manning-ham Lane which I left unfurnished apart from a few scruffy chairs and was renting only because it was somewhere else to go if I wanted, which I usually did. I stared at the walls, which were painted white. From time to time I would be stirred by a reflection of a feeling, which would bob in my mind like a drowning man's desperate wave and then go under for ever.

I thought of the policeman Weekes, who had come to see me that day, alone, and as usual, unexpected. Weekes was in the CID now. He made these inspectorly calls, and contrived to time each one so it was a surprise. Over the years he had grown bald and put on weight. He would stand in his blue pinstripe, sucking the peppermints to which he had become addicted since he quit smoking, looking nice and friendly and stupid, showing yellow teeth through a smile which rarely left his face. He was still boring, and a dangerous fellow, asking, as usual, about my father. I asked, as usual, if there had been any progress with Mr. Hyde. He spoke, as usual, about my father, saying he wasn't one to make a mountain out of the proverbial but the fact remained that sixty-eight-thousand pounds had gone missing, in today's terms . . . So Weekes told me what it was, in today's terms. He would do this each time. He would take out a calculator and give me the inflation-adjusted figures. At first the increases had been modest, five or six thousand pounds a year, but in the 1970s, when the Arabs hiked up oil prices, they became spectacular. In 1974 the figure was £140,000; two years later it was £185,000, and a year after that, £220,000. Weekes would report with a frown instead of the usual smile, as if the crime had itself been responsible for Britain's banana-republic economics. I, as usual, explained my theory to Weekes: that Mr. Hyde was someone I had once known, that Mr. Hyde was Schenk. I suppose you want to know how I had developed the theory, it was to do with 1964, at Charlie Laughton's party, when he picked up the head of a drunk woman and let it drop against the paving stones on the terrace. I'd heard that Mr. Hyde did this to his victims, as if he were afraid of their teeth and wished to smash them. And there was something else, which had also happened in 1964. I said that Schenk was a pretty evil fellow and, well, the fact was . . . no!

The fact was Schenk had killed my sister.

Weekes, as usual, reminded me that Schenk had not actually murdered Helen, and that there was no evidence connecting him with Mr. Hyde. Indeed, Schenk had not been seen in Bradford since 1964.

"But don't you worry about Mr. Hyde. We'll nail the bastard. Meantime . . ."

I had told him, as usual, that my father was dead, and Weekes had smiled, as usual.

I thought of Julie. Was she right? Was I really haunted by him?

.   .   .

It's true that I was drifting, weightless. But I was also a juggler, with all the skittles in the air. Watch me later that night, at a party given by Budge Carter, now my boss. The first candidate gave a wary look, and didn't want to talk, but finally admitted she was from London, she had come to Bradford with a friend to see about some work. No, no, I didn't want her to tell me, I would guess. She was a model. No. *Really?* A Ph.D. student trying out for a junior lectureship. WITTGENSTEIN. She was kidding, he was my favourite, absolutely my favourite thinker. The world is all that is the case, *Tractatus-Logico-Philosophicus*. OK, she was right, I could have learned the first line. If I were a con man I would have. It hurt me to hear her say that—how long had she had the jacket by the way; like her I preferred Wrangler to Levi, at least for jackets—more or less accusing me of being a pick-up artist who had learned the first line but she was right there were men with so little respect for women they would do that. Learn the first line. It grieved me that she thought I was one of them. Wounded me, reminded me as it happened, curious this, of something else Wittgenstein had said. Perhaps she remembered the passage . . . what did I do . . . oh nothing much, a doctor at the Infirmary, a surgeon as it happened, now where was I, yes, back with the *Tractatus* and the bit where he proposes that atomic facts are independent of one another, that from the existence of one atomic fact you cannot infer the existence of another. That was the thing about atomic facts. They were out there on their own. At least, such was Wittgenstein's belief and a bleak belief it was, didn't she think, crabby and solipsistic, suggestive of an icy blue heart, but then Wittgenstein had seen the world in a way that could only be described as simultaneously under-emotional and over-wrought, for heaven's sake he would threaten suicide if passing labourers did not smile at him when he took his morning walk, even Goethe had more laughs, and the effect of his work had been after all to shunt British philosophy up a remote siding where semantics and linguistic analysis gathered with other dusty thought-wagons, though I loved that stuff myself, lapped it up, got all of a doo-dah about it, utterly fascinating, and excuse me but what had she said her phone number was? Nonono, I hadn't meant that, I'd got a little carried away, she was so lovely and, *Christ,* she knew I meant no harm, what a dumb thing, Homer himself would have been able to see her beauty. Sorry, sorry. I'd been thinking of something else of Wittgenstein's. Really, I had. Where he says that to know an object it is necessary to know not its external qualities but all its internal qualities. Didn't it suggest to her the possibility that our atomic facts, yes the independent ones who were on their own, should get together and give each other's internal qualities the once over? Wouldn't it be a triumphant empirical application of philosophical theory? No, I wasn't being flippant, I was very interested in Wittgenstein and . . .

Her friend appeared. He was tall, with a long face, white as wax. "Been on a swan downstairs, nothing but a couple of lagers," he said, holding up the bottles and wiggling them.

He said, "Who's this? Another Yorkshireman on the lunatic fringe?" He pushed his face close to mine. I was an atomic fact he didn't like.

I see myself rocking back a little, trying to assume a friendly expression. I said, "Just a fellow with a happy face, and a taste for philosophy."

"Have you been bothering my friend?" His voice was Cockney, angry with the world.

"Absolutely not," I said. "Are you familiar with the work of Wittgenstein?"

"Are you after a thumping?"

"He was only talking," said the woman. "He didn't mean any harm."

"I don't know about that," I said, with a smile, knowing it would irritate the Cockney even more. I could see he wanted to fight; I didn't much care whether we did or not.

"Let it go," said the woman. "He's not worth it."

"Do you really think so? I'm crushed. I was about to suggest that we moved on to religion. Christ on the Cross. Was Our Saviour considering the nobility of man as he died?"

She said, "It's this city. There's a maniac on the loose and it's still full of men who have a few drinks and think they rule the world."

I knew the type. Barbara called them Tetley bittermen. Not that I was one, of course, I was something else again.

A cool customer.

Next in line was a big-hipped social worker. Her face was hard, but she was a simple case. I glanced at my shoe and stutteringly informed her that I was the young C-c-onservative with car and the house on a new estate in Thornton whose apostolic d-d-d-evotion to Th-thatcherism had turned to bile when the ambulance s-s-s-peeding his wife for an emergency appendectomy had run through a red light and into fatal and explosive collision with a tanker . . . b-b-b-b-b-rake failure, due to inadequate maintenance, due to health s-s-ervice cuts. I was overcome. I could not continue. I looked up and . . .

Mr. Holmes, they were the footsteps of a gigantic hound!

Her expression said she didn't know whether to believe me or not, but said also that she was softening, and I knew that if I asked, casually, she would cough up her phone number. So I did, and she did.

Then it was more failure. The fact that I administered a small private charity cut no ice with the woman who ran the coffee bar at the Alhambra Theatre, while my story of working on a commune outside Skipton, talking to vegetables and exhorting them to grow, left unmoved the earth-mother type whose occupation was neither asked for nor volunteered; I think she tagged me from the start.

But now it was the skinny one with big eyes and a classy outfit who said she was a TV journalist in Leeds and whose preference, I guessed from her proprietorial stare, was for blamed men who could be annexed quickly into her life and then blitzkrieged with equal dispatch. So I gave her doom. Yes, I supposed, she was right, I had been something of a prodigy, only sixteen at the time and, to be frank, I'd made a mistake, a big one, I'd told them to stuff it. I'd told them it was my theory that the Stones were finished after Brian's death and my career would suffer if I joined the band. Could she believe it? After that it had been petty crime, ending on a champagne spree all over Blackpool and Morecambe, with money I'd pinched from my landlord when I'd gone to the social for him to pick up two months' worth of his army pension. The magistrate had said I was a determined albeit inefficient criminal. Sentenced me to six months.

Cue for rueful, self-deprecating laughter from me, and from her—the offer. I asked if she was sure, if she really wanted me to call. She did. She was already pulling on her boots and preparing to march into the Sudetenland. No, I assured her, she needn't worry about writing it down. Did she think I could forget? Her phone number was the best news I'd had this week, this month, this *decade*. My brain was a tablet of stone and those seven digits were engraved upon it.

"I'll call," I said, not knowing whether I would or not. Sometimes I did, but more often not, and when I looked at the cheque book, or the scrap of paper pushed inside my jacket pocket, or even on the back of my wrist, I was unable to remember the face, but there they were: JOYCE 355286, TINA (061) 457711, ELIZABETH 249660 (Leeds number, after 7). It wasn't a game I played, but something more, a search, a getting away from myself.

"Working hard, as usual," said Budge Carter.

He knew me, I said.

"Is it fun?"

I told him he missed the point, which was that I pursued women in *opposition* to convenience and even pleasure. That was dedication!

"You know the meaning of the word?"

Budge Carter had been editor of the *Telegraph & Argus* for ten years and had been cynical about my abilities for most of that time, though he had given me my first job, as a junior reporter, and had later promoted me to feature-writer. I was rude to Budge, I went in late to the office and let Budge notice, from time to time I even fucked Budge's wife Katherine, I did everything I could to get Budge to fire me. He liked having me around.

"I don't know why I keep you around," he said. Budge still had the looks of Albert Finney but fleshier now, gone to seed, debauched, not by sex, or drink, but by too much bad news. "I only asked you to come tonight because Kath insisted. Always liked your dad, Kath did. But since you are here, I'm going to say something."

"You love me?"

"Get your finger out."

"Sure thing Budge."

"Or you're gone. Do you understand?"

"Absolutely Budge."

"Bring me a crate. One about Mr. Hyde would be nice."

"I will Budge, I'm just off now, I have a lead."

"You do?"

"Truly Budge."

When in doubt: lie, and then lie again.

What was it about Mr. Hyde? He was mad. What else could he be? He maimed, he mutilated, he raped and then murdered. Women. By 1981, he'd done this at least nine times. I'd come up with the nickname during a slow afternoon at the paper. I'd written: "Bradford is a parliamentary and municipal borough of England, situated in the northern division of the West Riding of Yorkshire, on an affluent of the River Aire, 34 miles south-west of York, 9 miles west of Leeds, 192 miles from London by rail, 202 miles by road. The railway runs straighter, not that it makes much difference, because these days few come here either by rail or road. The great worstedopolis of yesterday is known now as Murder City, its streets stalked by a man who, most of the time, lives a life ordinary as any other, with a job, a family, and a home to go to. But only most of the time. Suddenly, briefly, he transforms himself into the monster who slaughters women and makes monkeys of our police force—MR. HYDE."

I'd been rewarded for that laborious nonsense; Budge Carter stood me a weekend in Scarborough, on expenses.

Mr. Hyde killed only at night, as if after dark Bradford had a nightmare of its industrial past, of a century ago when three hundred mills rattled and roared and belched black smoke, when women were creatures of unacknowledged fear to men, and in this nightmare centre-stage had been taken by a Victorian villain, a modern day Jack the Ripper. But Mr. Hyde wasn't only Bradford's imagining of the beast in man; he wasn't a nightmare, but real, had been made by us, was within us all. Others could not imagine such cruelty. I asked how far is Mr. Hyde from me, and didn't worry too much about the answer.

I'd arranged to meet Barbara after Budge Carter's party. We didn't get as far as her flat. The lift in the tower block juddered and smelled of urine, and had been redecorated with graffiti, but it was there, emergency stopped between floors fifteen and sixteen, after

I said why don't we, and Barbara made a crucifix of my hands at the wrist, tied them with her scarf, hoisted them above my head and attached them to the grille which protected the fizzing light and which seemed to have been placed there for just such a purpose (the power supply winked its appreciation) that we fucked.

I'd first seen Barbara a few months before. She was in a pub with a friend of mine, another journalist, and we spoke. I asked her out. She came grudgingly and was in a bad mood all night. I got drunk and gave her a rose. She wasn't enchanted by the gesture. I asked her out a few more times, and each time she was more grudging. Then all of a sudden she got tired of that and the next night, after we'd seen a film, a comedy about American teenagers in a small town, she sat me down and told me a chunk of her life. Her father was a farmer up Skipton way; he would get drunk and hit her mother. Barbara had done well at school. Got ten O-levels, left at sixteen, bored. Worked as a pub-stripper, making herself find it funny by giving names to the front-row regulars. She had been claiming unemployment benefit at the same time and when she had been caught, prosecuted, and let off with just a warning because of her age, her father had started to hit *her*. She had come to Bradford. At night she had worked behind the bar at The Hand of Glory; in the day she had studied for A-levels. Then she had gone to college in the South somewhere. Got bored with that, took a job selling encyclopedias door-to-door, and ended up back in Bradford. Now she was twenty-two, working at the city library, not an environment I'd have predicted, hating Bradford and dreaming of escape. Like me, and Billy Liar in the film I mentioned.

Relationships are confused agreements. No one is sure of all of his or her own needs, let alone those of the other. But terms, even if not discussed, are soon decided; a necessarily incomplete contract is drawn up. With Barbara and I it had been early on. Part of the deal was based on Barbara's fear of Mr. Hyde, a fear shared by every woman in the city. It had been while she was working at The Hand of Glory that Barbara had known Muriel Kalevsky, a prostitute with a prostitute for a daughter, who had been one of his first victims. Muriel Kalevsky was walking home across wasteground when a man came at her with a hammer. She survived, but a part of her brain was crushed. Now she walked Bradford, urinating, screaming, with a picture of Mr. Hyde locked inside her head.

Once Muriel Kalevsky had invited Barbara to run her fingers along the scars. Barbara admitted a terror of Mr. Hyde, but was reluctant to let it determine her actions. Hence my insistence that she should, if she wished, tie me up, or use handcuffs. Confused, perhaps disgusted, perhaps even a little excited, Barbara became an accomplice. It was more than OK by me.

Barbara had found a sanctuary in art. Stuff littered the floors of her flat. I picked up a canvas. It was mostly red with a toothless mouth howling in the bottom corner. A light piece. I listened with no great concentration as she told me a story which involved meeting her friend Brigid, who I apparently thought was pretty, a curry in a basement somewhere, and an encounter with, and subsequent trouncing of, a Tetley bitterman. I didn't fancy being a Tetley bitterman going up against Barbara. She opened a bottle of red wine. She drank a glass, gave me one, and, ignoring my protest, refilled her own. Sometimes, when she was drunk, a chaos would swell up inside her and threaten to take me over.

"You look beautiful," I said.

"I look like seven kinds of hell."

"No you don't."

"Suit yourself." She downed another glass.

I said, "Let's fuck again."

She said, "How are you? What's been happening?"

"Fine."

"Is that it?"

I shrugged.

"You're a ghost. Do you know that?"

I smirked.

"We meet, we fuck, and it's as if you're not there. What do you dream about? What do you fear? Tell me about your boy. How is he?"

Did I mention I had a son? Tom, aged five. "Fine."

"Look, here he comes. A suit of clothes with nothing inside. You're invisible."

"Sleep with me and I'll be one visible fellow."

"You're a moral bankrupt."

I saw a wide stone staircase leading up through cloud towards bronze doors and a plaque saying THE BANK OF MORALITY.

"I'm going to leave her."

"I don't want you to make any promises. You know that."

It was another part of the contract with Barbara that she didn't want to play the game: will he, won't he, will he, won't he, won't he leave his wife?

"The marriage is over."

"That's up to the two of you, not me. It's not my problem."

"I want to make it your problem."

"Why are you telling me this?"

I said, "It *is* your problem."

Barbara gave a deep and mechanical sigh. She said, "Let's fuck."

Badababing.

Then it was the handcuffs, and as I felt my cock, guided by her hand, push inside, I whispered, "Imagine I'm him. Think of it. Me doing the things Mr. Hyde would do."

I was a bad journalist. I was lazy and enjoyed it. Since I made up what I wrote I reasoned that the paper gained integrity every time I didn't do a story, which was usually. I was bored with my job. Budge Carter wasn't bored with *his,* he was bored with the news. Stories were like crates, he said; they might differ in size, but each presented the same problem. He had to decide where it should be stacked and with what prominence. When Mr. Hyde committed a murder, for instance, Budge was presented with a very unwieldy crate. The matter was of no other concern to him.

I sat at my desk with a bad stomach. At the far end of the harshly lit, open-plan office two men were making too much noise laying in electric spaghetti for the new computers. An iron hat tightened around my head. I thought I would vomit and failed to notice Budge Carter's approach. "Ah Headingley, my good friend. Rough night?" he said, looking around, checking that he had the attention of Gines and Gawthorne. He did. They were the other feature-writers. I think of them as twins, their faces pale, white, and round. I think of them as clocks. They had no wish, other than to beat time with Budge Carter.

Budge Carter said, "Good to see, isn't it lads? Comforting. We say snap and here he is, beavering on our behalf. We'll never be short a crate, not so long as Scoop Hamer is on the premises."

Gines and Hawthorne chimed in unison.

He continued, "Oh yes, we can learn plenty from Hamer. You must have noticed that one thing's for sure in Bradford at the moment. No dice with the chicky-dees. Bloody Mr. Hyde! He's not done any of us any favours. Women no longer dress like teenage temptresses. Men can't even talk dirty. None of which affects Scoop. With women he's like a kid running down the streets after a fire engine. Tells them he's ashamed to be a man. Tells them that some men are different. That Mr. Hyde, he's done Scoop a favour. He fucks and doesn't phone wherever possible. Do you know how he does it?"

The clocks did not.

"Is it money?"

The clocks were dithering.

"Not on the wages I give him. Is it religion? Does he pray each night to a higher power?"

Again: blank ignorance from the clocks.

"Does he buggery. For some it's a still point of certainty in a shifting world. Look at our friends the Pakistanis. They believe alright. I saw a skinhead the other night, thought he could Bradfordise one of the brethren with a Stanley knife and a piece of paving stone. A few blows to the Islamic bounce. Won't make a blind bit of difference, because they're not persuadable. They're on a crusade. There is no God but God and it's theirs and he doesn't buy his fish and chips at Harry Ramsdens. But Scoop here wouldn't believe in a higher power, not if it came up and whacked him over the head with a crucifix the size of the one on that mountain in, where the hell is it in . . . ?"

"Rio . . ." offered one of the clocks.

"Rio de Janeiro," said Budge Carter. He continued, "No, I think we have to face that religion has nothing to do with it. Desire, now there's the thing. With me it faded a while ago. I'm in calm waters. Haven't felt desire for years now. But desire alone is not enough. It's in a bottle like a genie waiting for the top to be taken off. There has to be opportunity as well. And do you know why Scoop gets so much opportunity?"

Budge Carter, motor running and well warmed up, didn't wait to hear what the clocks thought about it. "Because he never does any work. Scoop would miss the crate if he found Mr. Hyde at home having tea with his wife. Well, today's going to be different.

Today he's going to see the Queen and bring us back a crate. You know about the Queen?"

Gines and Gawthorne: indecision crawled over their normally blank faces. The Queen? Of course they knew, but was Budge talking about *the* Queen? They didn't know, and Budge was, as usual, enjoying their uncertainty. The clocks were ambitious. In time they wanted to go and be clocks in London, on Fleet Street, where the big clocks ticked, and for that they needed Budge Carter.

"It's her birthday. Fifty-five, she's going to be. Hamer is going to approach the throne. His father's been there already, of course, many years ago. Pushed his sceptre right up her red carpet. I'm talking about the actress Diana Farrell."

Gines and Gawthorne understood now. It was a joke. They chimed again; I laughed too. "Budge, do you enjoy cunnilingus?" I said, smiling.

"Just go to the crate shop and bring me back a crate of one thousand words. You could do with some credit round here," he said, not bothering to smile himself, but instead turning to Gines, or was it Gawthorne, and shaking his head and tut-tutting about an article written by whichever one of them it was. If they thought stuff like this would wash in London, they were sadly mistaken. "You'll be crate slaves in Bradford for the rest of your born days, just like Scoop here."

Diana Farrell lived outside Whitby, in a big Jacobean house on a cliff, not far from where my father had found the cricket pavilion. She had divorced Charlie Laughton and had been married again soon after, to a rich aristocrat. It was in 1967, I suppose, or perhaps early 1968, that she had gone back to her own name and to her career. Success came quickly. When she opened in New York in *Hedda Gabler* streets had to be closed off so she could walk in safety to the waiting limousine. At the time her lover was a glamorous American senator (later assassinated). The servile Duke had been understanding. After that, she never lost her fame. Quite the reverse: there were appearances in prestigious British films, based on even more prestigious British novels; there was the work for charity; there were photos with minor members of the Royal Family, in which she took care not to look too much more stylish than they. No wonder the press loved her.

First, she said, "Hello Headingley, I've seen your name in the paper. I always assumed you'd turn up one day."

She said she wanted to see me from behind.

"Excuse me?"

"Go on, turn around," she said, and so I did, apprehensive of the effect I made and why she wanted me to make it. "You have your father's legs," she said.

"Really?" I said.

"They're short."

Next, she took me into the living room which was huge. Logs spitting in a marble fireplace. Gold brocade curtains. Paintings in dull oils of family members and landscapes so vast human figures were lost inside them. Silver tea service on a table. Diana Farrell poured.

"Do you ever hear from him?"

"Who?"

"Jack."

"What makes you think I would have?"

"Not in all this time?"

"No."

"You think he's dead?"

I told her I was sure of it.

"He had a lot more up top than that fellow Schenk realised. Even Charlie underestimated him, and Charlie was a cunning sod himself."

"Poor old Charlie."

"Yes, poor old Charlie. Worn out by his climb to the top."

We talked some more, about me, a subject which didn't seem to interest her much. She said, "So that's what you've done with your life?" She was older, much richer, obviously, and a little colder than I remembered. Her clothes were expensive, and she wore too much make-up. She wasn't quite real.

I decided to upset her. I told her something had been troubling me all these years: the pearl and my loss of it. "I was supposed to give it to you," I said. "A love-token, or something."

She shrugged. Her face showed no surprise. She lit a cigarette.

She explained that the pearl was to have been, not a token, but a sign. When it came she was to have gone to Yeadon Airport, where my father and a small aeroplane would have been waiting. A flight across Europe and then a boat from Lisbon. My father had wanted the adventure to start there, the traditional jumping-off point to the new world. He had spoken of Humphrey Bogart and Ingrid Bergman in *Casablanca;* she had reminded him that Bergman had gone to Lisbon without Bogart. "Buggered up the ending, didn't they, those Hollywood chappies," my father had said. "Me, I believe you can rewrite history."

That sounded like him.

She said, "I'll tell you something, about that pearl." Another dainty puff on the cigarette. "I wouldn't have gone."

"No?"

"The first time I saw your father he had his arms held behind his back with two men holding him. Great gorillas, they were, he owed them money and they wanted it fast. He told them a story, he was coming into some cash later in the day, and he did. He won three hundred playing roulette at the Embassy Club, but he blew the lot on me. Champagne, a Chanel, dinner. The gorillas never found us, Jack said they were up a tree eating nuts, and we checked into the Savoy, where he seemed to be well known, but by another name, Sir Spencer Somethingorother. I thought, I want you, you *are* life. I was wrong. He gave those wonderful performances, so much energy, but he gave them for an audience of one. Himself. He was the most self-regarding man I ever met, and I was very much in love with him for a time. I suppose some people blamed me for marrying Charlie, your father did, he said I was only in it for the money. But Charlie and I rubbed along. Marriages are two islands, sometimes too close, sometimes too far away, but usually within conversational distance. Your father was at the other end of the world, like Krakatoa East of Java, a disaster waiting to happen. If you happened to be around, he'd take you down with him."

I'm not sure when I knew I would have to seduce Diana Farrell. Was it when she told me that her husband was in London for the week, attending a debate in the House of Lords? Or when she asked me, "And you never left Bradford and now you work for the *Telegraph & Argus*?" Or when I saw her ask herself how it was I seemed so much less of an adventurer than my father? Or when I saw the late afternoon sun catch her black hair and realised she was still handsome, perhaps even beautiful?

This is how it was. We went to a restaurant, in Scarborough, high above the promenade, looking over the turgid grey sea. A storm was on the way. Wine and food were ordered. Waiters hovered around her celebrity, like gulls over a rubbish tip. I was a man, much younger than her, with an expression showing eagerness, perhaps even tenderness. Flattery was routine issue.

"You're so beautiful," I said. She smiled without moving her head, and accused me of being insincere. Then she said sincerity was never to be trusted. I smiled back: thank you.

"That film, the last one, set in India, you were stunning," I said. Another smile from her: of course. "Film itself was lousy."

"I know," she said. "I couldn't understand that."

I observed that such mysteries did happen and there were hundreds of things in the world that could not be understood by even the greatest intellects.

Her look: is Headingley for real?

I listened. Appeared to listen. It was a trick I had, I could gaze into a woman's eyes and my silent gaze would talk, saying you're lovely, or intelligent, or lovely and intelligent and so sensitive, or vulnerable, or angry and with such good reason men really are pigs I'm different. My gaze would add that I was intent on learning the secrets of their soul, that if only they would give it me I would mend their heart, but if they were just interested in a quick poke that would be fine too. Consider what a devil of a figure I was, leaning forward, chin cupped in hand, eyes dewy, not listening to even one word. Why do women fall for it? Are they stupid? They are! At the end of dinner Diana Farrell asked if I would like to come back to the house for a brandy.

We were a little drunk. I reminded her of the last time we met, in 1964, when she had come to our house. If a life is capable of being changed, she had changed mine that day. She asked what I meant. I said she knew very well, she said not, I said really, she said no, but then kept up the pretence no longer and delivered an unrestrained burst of laughter.

I said, "Was I any good, back then?"

She said, "You were so scared I thought you'd piss your pants."

We went to bed, and I found again the pearl I had lost, it was round and hard, a little button of flesh; that's to say, I sucked her clitoris. This was the part of sex I enjoyed, not because the woman felt pleasure but because I gave it. A woman once told me a man had attacked her with his tongue as if trying to stub out a cigarette. Not my style. I was a cunt-connoisseur. Bushy cunts, shaved cunts. Cunts like orchids. Cunts with flaps of extra skin hanging loose. Cunts that stank. Cunts that were clean. Cunts that were perfumed, but not so strongly that I couldn't taste beneath a tang of blood and urine and sweat. I was a gentle God, down there among the cunty whiffs. I kissed the thigh. I ran my nose through the stiff and glistening hair. I let my tongue enter the cunt, a little. My lips found the clitoris and covered it, gently, my tongue came and rested on it, gently. My ears were radar, alert to sounds of excitement, telling me when to stop and when to begin again, and all the time my prick grew harder, keeping time with the upward beat of their excitement. Sometimes, as they came towards orgasm, I would begin to masturbate. That's how it was with Diana Farrell. As soon as she began to gasp, I looked down and an image of my prick was in my mind. It was big, its head huge and swollen, and swaying monstrously, too big big big to be contained by this mere woman. I was an angry God now, and as soon as she had come, when her head was to one side and she was breathing deeply into the pillow, I rose up and, planting a knee on either side of her chest, beat myself off. Sperm flew all over, down her cheek, on to her lips, into her hair, her eye. A gob landed on the tip of her nose. I slapped her face.

Kapow!

She said nothing. She cleaned herself with tissues from the box on the table by the bed. Then she said, "You know, I'd almost decided I liked you. You awful little shit. You awful little *bastard*."

I smiled. "Does this mean the interview is over?"

She said, "But of *course*, I forgot. You are!"

"What?"

"An awful little bastard."

"So."

"I mean, you're a bastard, literally, isn't that right?"

I let alarm run up my face like a flag of surrender.

She looked at me for a while, then laughed. "They never told you? That you were born after your mother and father were divorced. That you were the result of a second-rate coupling in the back of a car. That they stayed together, hating each other, for seven years, just for your benefit."

"Legitimacy is an unimportant concept," I said. "Christ was God's bastard after all." I grinned.

"You knew?"

My brother Keith had told me some years before.

I said, "The details of family life. The Hamers have never been very good at them. Historically speaking."

"You smug little shit."

"Not me."

"I'll tell you something you don't know."

"And what's that?"

"I heard from him the other day."

"Who?"

"Your father."

"I don't believe you."

"Believe me. He's back."

She was smiling, savage now. I didn't hit her this time; I spat in her face.

This is what happened after my father vanished in 1964. To be brief: after Helen died, Keith went off with his rock band to Brighton, and it was decided I should live for a while with my grandmother. I lay on the bed in the small back room where I slept, listening to The Beatles. When winter turned to spring, I played cricket with other kids from the estate, setting up stumps on wasteland, fighting for the ground with gypsy children who lived in boxy tin caravans. It was nine months before I went back to the grammar school, and soon after that my mother came to Bradford to organise the sale of the house we had lived in. She said she would soon be taking me with her, to live with her, but it didn't happen. Her husband took a job he had been offered in Hong Kong and so I stayed at my grandmother's until I was seventeen.

She died three years later. I stood by the window in her bedroom, watching drops of condensation as they chased each other down the glass and made pools on the ledge. She was in bed, with a book beside her on the turned-back sheet, *Stories from the Bible,* she had given it me years before, and I had been reading aloud to her: the story of the prodigal son. Believe it or not. She talked about my father. She loved him still. Even as a boy, she said, when he was four or five years old, he would sneak off, bold as you like, and would walk beneath the counter at the Luxor Cinema in Saltaire to watch Rudi Valentino again and again, dreaming dreams he didn't understand, but which must have touched something deep inside. My father always had a romantic heart, she said, and restless feet. She said, "You'd like to see him again, wouldn't you? You think he's alive, don't you?"

I was twenty-one, with an oily tongue, already working at the paper, already seeing Julie and chasing other women all over Bradford. I knew what was required: a little lubrication. I should take her hand and say, "Yes, Gran, of course." Instead, an honesty attack: I said, "No, Gran, I'm sorry, I wouldn't like to see him," and I added, "I hope he is dead."

In fact, I had often thought that my father was alive. In the years immediately following his disappearance I had seen him, not often, but quite clearly, once in the street, once in a pub, and three times on a summer afternoon at a cricket match. Each time I had rushed up with the words spilling from my mouth, only to realise it wasn't him. So I wasn't surprised when Diana said that she had heard from him. Nor did I believe her: I presumed she had spoken out of spite.

Besides, as Bradford had changed, so it had become impossible to picture my father within it, and Bradford *had* changed. Paris was built for art and learning, London for government and trade, but Bradford was built for one thing only: to make wool. The great mill buildings were not just places for the creation of wool and wealth, however, they were monuments, like cathedrals, and the owners expected them to last as long. In 1875 it seemed they might be correct. There was a greater proportion of millionaires in Bradford than anywhere in Europe, and in the decades that followed cheap labour was brought in, first from Poland, from Germany and Italy, and, finally, in the late 1950s, from Pakistan. But spoilsport science created synthetic fabrics, and history dictated that these be made very cheaply in Taiwan and South Korea and Hong Kong, parts of the world that were not Bradford. Thus the city retained the cosmopolitan flavour which immigrants had always given it, while losing its means of making money. A decline began, which could not be reversed.

Cities, like people, have myths, they have states of mind, and the spring of 1981 was the time of Bradford's nervous breakdown: unemployment twenty per cent; a crisis in housing; wool industry in a mess; white skinheads attacking Asian mini-cab drivers; Asian youths, fearing such attacks, making petrol bombs in basements off Lumb Lane; prostitutes working in pairs, one holding a knife while the other fucked a man. The weather was correspondingly dismal. Storms had flooded basements all over the city, flushing out sweat-shops that had operated underground for years, using immigrant Asian labourers, who now emerged blinking, dazzled by the dull grey Bradford light, as if they were seeing it for the first time. Each street had a bad story attached to it. You heard them all the time, told dead-pan. A man's face was slashed here. This is where the windscreen of a truck was stove in by someone with an iron bar. The driver? His head was taken clean off. Look, just over there, see that wall with the white-painted slogan, a bloke was knifed there Tuesday. And, always, the details of his crimes repeated over and over, the three-syllabled name tap-tapping the beat of Bradford's funeral march, you heard: *Mister Hyde . . . Mister Hyde . . . Mister Hyde*.

It wasn't my father's city any more. It was mine and I was numb to it. I no longer had feelings. I no longer had feelings about feelings. You'll have noticed, as I proceed, that sometimes I don't tell you the room was *alpha*, the weather *beta*, and that bird's face quite definitely *omega* (it wasn't that I didn't respect women; I didn't think about them at all, and they occupied most of my thoughts). This isn't because I won't be bothered with such de-scription—although, believe me, that to-ing and fro-ing, that way people will have of coming into rooms and going out again and, oh no, here she comes again, it's very hard work—but because my concern is more usually with emotions, and their lack.

Once I asked Barbara if she thought me immoral.

Barbara said, "You live always on the surface of things. You have no sense of your own actions and how they affect others. Nor do you understand your emotions. You're one of those characters in Homer who spills blood and brains and smashes the other fellow's teeth with a bronze spear and then wakes the next morning with a clean slate just as if it were the first day of his life and goes out and does it again."

She wanted to help. She sat cross-legged on the red bean-bag in her flat in the tower block, holding my hand, telling me I was making the same choice all the time, namely to believe that I was like my father and doomed to re-enact his mistakes; I could as easily make another choice, to be different, she said, but I wasn't listening. I stared at the purple birthmark on her left shoulder. I thought about morality. Morality didn't have to be a bank account running into the red, it could be something else, like the weather, say, which had to be dealt with, but which could be forecast: conscience close to the average, ethical dilemmas moving in from the West Country, heavy humanism and unexpected honesty in some districts; you get the idea. And because morality was predictable, it could be dealt with and avoided. The trick was . . . *carry an umbrella!* That way anything was permissible. Fuck this, suck that. Nothing was serious. Obsessed with keeping my head dry, I failed to notice where my feet were—on the edge.

And then my father did come back.

Budge Carter found out I had botched a crate. That's to say, I had invented a story, about a pub off Manningham Lane, The Perseverance, where one of Mr. Hyde's victims had been, I had said, a regular, and had slept with a score or so of the other customers. Porkies, I'm afraid. There had been letters, phone-calls, *complaints,* and an angry landlord was threatening to sue the paper. Was I worried? I had my feet up.

"Why?" said Budge Carter.

Gines and Gawthorne were two happy clocks.

"Perhaps I was tired of not doing the things that should not be done. History in the making, today as yesterday. Nobody's interested in the truth. Nobody who reads the papers."

"I'll discuss that particular remark at a different time."

"Whenever you like."

My phone was ringing. It was my wife, talking calmly at first, appreciating what an imposition it must seem to ask this question, but she was interested to know, and so was our son, *when the fuck would I be going home?*

Budge Carter had turned to Gines and Gawthorne. He said, "Tell me he doesn't do it to make me look bad." But the clocks shook their heads and told him no such thing; in their view I did it to make him look bad.

My hand covered the receiver. I said, "Go fuck your wife, Gines. Everyone else in Bradford has rashered it, even Gawthorne, though she said he was every bit as incompetent as you."

"What's that?" said Julie.

"Nothing much."

"So?"

"What?"

A lot of things were mixing and moving. The clocks had their heads together, whispering. Budge Carter was moving towards me with warning finger raised. Julie was saying, "When will we see you? Not that I'm convinced I want to. You know what you are?"

"I'm sure you'll tell me."

"The sort who arrives home, says "Where's my dinner, suck my cock, is that the time already, I'd better be going.' "

"Listen, I'm bloody busy."

"You're a bloody disgrace," she said, and hung up.

Budge Carter said, "This could cost us, if he goes to court . . ."

"Don't worry, I'll go see the bloke, get it sorted."

". . . and even if he doesn't it could still cost us."

My phone was ringing again. Julie, I presumed, getting ready to shoot another earful.

"How much?"

I picked up the receiver. "Hello."

"Hello, Headingley old fellow," said a voice, which I recognised at once; odd, but I did. "It's your dad."

What did I feel then? Surprise? No. Curiosity? No. That a door was opening, as if in a fiction, and the past was marching through to put its boots all over my future? Not precisely. I felt calm. I felt nothing.

"Hello," I said. "How are you?"

Staring at me, Budge finally said, "You really are a careless bastard, aren't you?"

"Certainly."

"Who's that?" said my father.

"My boss. Budge Carter."

"Budge. The one Helen used to fancy?"

"So she said."

"Wrote some unkind words about jolly Jack Hamer?"

"Now he's tearing me off a strip."

"In a spot of bother, are you? Don't tell me you've taken after the old man."

I held out the phone to Budge Carter. I said, "It's my father. Perhaps you'd care for a word."

For a moment Budge's face was a blank. Then he roared, and turned to the clocks. "He's a joker isn't he? That's why I keep Hamer in the crate factory. It's a variety show free, gratis, and for nothing."

The clocks smiled thinly; they were not pleased.

"It's no good," I said to my father. "He won't talk to you."

"Bloody hell, Headingley. What are you playing at?"

"What are *you* playing at?"

"I'm back."

"So I gather."

There was a pause.

I said, "Well."

He said, "Fancy a jar?"

The Hand of Glory was old Bradford, a huge palace of a pub, all dark wood, dull brass beer pumps, and cut-glass mirrors which reflected wall after wall, reinforcing its Victorian spaciousness and solidity. It was at a crossroads in Little Germany which, some two hundred years before, had been Bradford's place of execution. A form of guillotine had stood there, on a stone scaffold which still remains. In those days it was deemed so necessary to protect the infant wool trade that magistrates were empowered to judge without trial, and sentence to death, any offender caught stealing cloth. Inevitably, false accusations were made, and innocent men killed, so another law was passed, a bizarre law, to the effect that if, after the signal to release the blade had been given, the criminal was so nimble as to pull his head away, then he should be allowed to jump from the scaffold and go free. My father said this had happened to Great-great-great-great-uncle Jeremy Hamer, though he had not been quite quick enough. "He left something of himself behind.

The top of his head was flat as a billiard table," my father said, "oh, yes, he was a very odd fellow indeed was Uncle Jeremy."

We met at nine o'clock. Outside it was raining and the streets were empty. Inside it was hot, crowded. And noisy. Voices shouted in English, in Polish, even in Urdu. Non-Islamic drinking was in progress. I found my father with a large scotch, looking at home, near the back door. Pubs were his burrows, and he seemed to have an exact knowledge of their topography. He preferred those which offered escape front and back and, if possible, to the side. He always sat near an exit. "Hello son," he said. "Large one, with a chaser?"

My first impressions? He hadn't changed very much. Had lost some hair, was a little fleshier in the face, walked to the bar with shoulders rather more hunched, came back showing a rounder belly than I remembered. But, recognisable at once: John Bertram Hamer; my father, dressed in blue blazer and grey slacks, with the thin moustache shaved off and the flair for melodrama seemingly intact. We drank in silence, as if we were lovers so familiar we no longer had anything to say. I bought the next round, he the one after that, and then another from me. The jukebox played a bouncy pop tune.

"You're alright?"

"I'm fine," he said. "Bloody hell, yes. God yes, I'm right as rain." He said, "Tell me how you've been."

"I've been fine. You?"

"Fine, fine, apart from my liver. And a bit of a toothache. What about your mother?"

"She's fine. I spoke to her the other day. She sounded fine."

"And Keith?"

"I'm not sure. He's in Paris, I think. We haven't been in touch."

"I expect he's fine."

"He could always look after himself."

"That's right. I'm sure he's fine."

"I'm sure he is," I said.

"I heard about Helen."

I said nothing.

"I know how you must feel about it."

Like hell he did. I didn't want to talk about it. Vaguely angry, I felt my face flush. I looked at my watch and told him I had to go. He didn't seem disappointed. "Bird?" he said.

. . .

"Your father?" Barbara said.

"That's right."

"Not your stepfather. Your *father*. Your father-father who no-body's seen for half a century and might be dead?"

"Sixteen years. And five months."

"You're winding me up. This is just another story."

"He drinks Johnnie Walker Black Label. As well as Famous Grouse. I thought he was strictly a Famous Grouse man."

"You're telling the truth?"

"Yes."

"My God."

"Am I?"

"That's not even funny." She wanted to know what we'd talked about. Had I asked him where he'd been? What had made him leave? And come back? Who had he been with all this time, did I have another family somewhere? Had I told him that the police were looking for him? Had I told him about her? About my wife, my son?

I said we had omitted to discuss any of these things.

"How do you *feel*?"

I shrugged. I said . . . you know what I said. Just fine.

"You're extraordinary," said Barbara.

She took me to bed. There were to be no handcuffs tonight, she said, kissing me gently, they weren't required, I could fuck her for as long, and as slow, and as hard, as I liked. I could do anything I wanted.

I couldn't get an erection.

She said I was upset; I said not. "You should be," she said.

"He mentioned he'd been in Johannesburg."

"All this time."

I shrugged.

"I'd like to meet him."

"He'll probably try to seduce you," I said.

It was The Hand of Glory again. I introduced Barbara to my father, who made a fuss of buying her a drink, settling her in a chair, and lifting the palm of her hand to his lips and kissing it. "Headingley," he said, "when are you going to make an honest woman of her?"

"Headingley already has an honest woman," said Barbara. "I'm his less than honest one."

"You're married?" That was my father, to me, in a tone of surprise.

"With a son," said Barbara.

"You didn't say."

"So what do you think of my dad?" I said to Barbara.

"Very handsome, very charming," she said. "I suppose your brother must have collected those attributes." She said she'd heard he'd been away for some time; very direct, Barbara.

"I have been in the heathen lands of the Amorite, the Hittite, and the Girgashite."

"Girgashite? So that's what Headingley is full of."

"I like her. Some women preach at you. This one looks a lecture," said my father. He added, beaming, "Byron. Good fellow. My inheritance."

I said, "More drinks?"

They were talking about South Africa when I came back from the bar. He told the story as if it were a serenade. He had been a representative for Dunhill. His job had been simple, to drive around in an open-top Bentley, painted red and gold, the company colours, with a boot full of cigarettes which he handed out at polo matches, embassy shindigs, and any society party to which he could get himself invited; a somewhat archaic system of public relations, Barbara said. My father agreed. But parts of South Africa were like that, he protested, kissing her hand again, like England after the war, rather amateurish, decent fellows doing Mickey Mouse jobs.

"The place disgusts me," said Barbara.

"Good fun," said my father.

I asked what had happened to the money, the sixty-eight thousand pounds, over three hundred thousand in today's terms.

"Oh *that*," said my father.

"He's still after you by the way," I said.

"Who?"

"Weekes."

"I blew all that within a couple of years."

He had taken the money. I suppose that was something else I'd known all along.

"Bloody expensive business, buying false passports, giving yourself a new life. And then it's an easy way to spend money, South America."

"South *America*," said Barbara.

Before he could elaborate, something happened, seemingly undramatic, but of great importance. A woman made her entrance. And what a woman! This one will be trouble. Myth would linger on the moment. Consider Tristan after he has drunk the love potion, overwhelmed, pausing because he somehow knows what he does next will be of terrible significance, then looking up, his nervous glance meeting Isolde's, to find their eyes threaded together, pearls on a string. In a film there would be a surprising cut, or the camera would be held for slightly longer on the face, or would move in smoothly for a close-up, and you would know, faster than you can say D. W. Griffith, men will die for this.

She was tall and blonde, too skinny. Mid-twenties. Face an oval mask, pale and without expression. Not beautiful, but she made you think she was. Her first line? "Hello Jack, sorry I'm late." Not exactly a belter.

"Vickie's just come up from London," my father said. "Vick, I'd like you to meet Barbara, and Headingley, my son."

"Hello," she said.

"Hello," said Barbara.

"Hello," I said; not "hi there" or "hel-*lo*," just "hello." Meet Mr. Cool!

"Another round?" said my father, and went to the bar. He looked back, smiling, and gave the thumbs up.

I began. Where had she met Dad?

"In London, about six months ago."

Was that long after he'd come back?

"I didn't know he'd been away."

She liked him at once?

"I was curious."

Why?

"I have a curious nature."

About everything?

"No."

Was she sleeping with him? No, don't answer, I followed up quickly, my apologies, that was impertinent. I smiled.

"Yes, I am," she said. "Your father is a wonderful fuck."

This wasn't what I needed to hear. I remembered an old Warner Brothers cartoon. Wile E. Coyote, busy trying to dynamite the Road Runner, fails to see an oncoming train. Then he does notice; big close-up, as he is about to be smashed, of his pupils shrinking to pin-pricks—WAAAAAAAAAGH! Vickie would make me feel I had much in common with Wile E. Coyote. No Iago, Headingley; he too was a less than competent villain.

"And he sucks my cunt all night if I ask him to."

Funny, I told her, that was one of my preferences; did she think it was in the genes?

She answered my smile with one of her own: "Is the interrogation over now?"

My father came back from the bar, with a tray this time, and on it two rounds of drinks. His grin went from ear to ear. He beamed, and sang "Getting to Know You." He set down the tray. "This is the business, isn't it? There's nothing better for a fellow than being among friends and family, and the next round already in. What do you say, Barbara?"

Barbara didn't say anything for a while, because Barbara was busy looking at me with a less than friendly expression. I maintained a smile. She looked away and said, "How do you find Bradford? Changed a bit, I should imagine?" which prompted my father to tell the tale of Bradford's misfortunes, as he saw them. First, there was Mr. Hyde, buggering about. Second, the place was unrecognisable: Charlie Laughton and his boys had knocked down most of the old city and built stuff that was like sticking pins in a fellow's eyes; he'd been to see where the funeral business had been and found it replaced by a restaurant called something like Mr. Pumperninck—a real bugger's muddle. And money, it seemed money had taken a look at Bradford and decided somewhere else was the place to be; so many men, so few jobs, almost as bad as his grandfather's time when the mill gates would be shut in the face of anyone who came after the morning hooter. Last, worst—the cricket. When he had been here Close, Trueman, and Jimmy Binks had been top of the heap. He spoke their names as though they were heroes from Homer. Now, disaster! The question wasn't would Yorkshire take the championship this year, but would we win a single game?

"God has opened his bowels," he said. "We're in the shit."

"They're talking about letting in players born outside Yorkshire," I said.

"The whole country's going down the drain."

"Isn't it just?" said Vickie. "I need a pee."

My father watched appreciatively as she took her long legs to the ladies. "What do you think?" he said.

"Attractive," I said.

"*Attractive?* This one's been causing car smashes since she was thirteen years old. She's a cracker. I took one look at her and realised she was a situation, quite definitely a situation. It was in a bar in Rio de Janeiro."

"That's funny," said Barbara.

"Copa," my father sang, "Copacabana."

"She said you met in London."

He took it in his stride. "Did she? I suppose she did. Barbara, are you someone I can trust with a secret? I think you are. I know you are, so I'm going to tell you something about Vick, the Honourable Victoria, who I love and adore and live for. She makes things up. It's true. Bradford pork pies it all over the shop, I'm afraid to say, and generally takes a dramatic view of herself. Like an actress in a film. The director chappie's said to her 'First half, good girl; second half, bad girl,' and she's not sure which half she's in. I've spent my life getting into situations with women like that."

"*Femmes fatales?*" said Barbara.

"They're the ones."

"It's something you choose to believe, that a woman is that way. All men do. It's an idea they have, it's what they want."

"Not me. I've spent all my life looking for the other. Someone I could depend on as they depend on me, no it's true, someone whose dream would be my own, someone with whom every hour would be a soft hour of love, someone like . . . Barbara," he said, and then he laughed, to let her know that *he* knew he was being absurd, to let her know also that, in some mysterious way, which probably even he didn't understand, he meant it. I had to admire the old sod.

"Headingley," he added, "I hope you appreciate what a lucky fellow you are. Does he appreciate it, Barbara?"

"I don't know," she said. "Do you?"

"I do," I said, watching Vickie as she came back towards the table; again, her legs. "I do appreciate it."

"Here she is," said my father, looking up, "she walks in beauty like the night." He looked at each of us in turn, an actor judging the response of his audience, and laughed again. Barbara laughed too; even the ice-maiden allowed a smile to melt her face a little. How did he get away with this stuff?

"Vick, you go and sit next to Headingley," he said, with an air of protection. "Headingley, you and Vick are two of my favourite fellows on this going-to-the-barkers planet and you would be doing your old man a great service if you became good friends."

I was willing. I told her about me, about the *Telegraph & Argus,* filling her in with stories of Budge Carter and the two clocks, and a few confidential details concerning Mr. Hyde; I asked about her, pressing for details with some firmness and, I thought, no little charm. She was polite, but unforthcoming. She would keep glancing towards my father. He was silent, with his head inclined just a little towards Barbara's, listening. She asked was it true he had gone away and why had he come back?

My father winked. He raised a finger and went tap-tap-tap against his reddened nose. "Boodle," he said, which prompted questions with the eyebrows from Barbara. *"Cash,"* he said, and then there was more eyebrow music, further nose-fingering. "Great boatloads of it."

Vickie decided we would be friends after all. She told me about her life in London. She could have had a career, she and a friend had come up with an idea for a television show which one of the independent channels had wanted to buy. But she wasn't sure she wanted a career. She had no particular desire to go through those battles. Her life was split, she said; she wasn't quite sure what she wanted, except to be dependent on no one. There had been a time when she had taken drugs, heroin, and had since decided life was best lived without crutches.

"So why are you here with my father?"

"He lives to the sound of a trumpet."

"You enjoy that?"

"He's fun to be with and I don't have to take him too seriously. So many men are death. They try to take you over like the plague. It's look at my car, look at my job, look at my dick, look at ME! Your father's courteous. He listens to what I say."

"I need to be educated about women."

"You don't say."

"I'm afraid I do say. I'm looking around for someone who might be prepared to take me on. I warn you, it will be a big job."

Before I went further with the issue of my needs, I looked from Vickie to Barbara, who wasn't thrilled, and back again. From now on, I decided, everything was going to be good. Better than good. Perfect. I looked at my father and smiled. "The elephant, we're going to see the elephant."

"Meaning?" said Vickie.

"A little code between father and son," said my father, unperturbed, grinning. And then: "Headingley. Book me the royal suite on your ocean liner. And set sail for the shores of Africa."

At the time I really wasn't bothered by my father's reappearance. On the contrary, I saw it as a challenge, a chance for a game, and I thought that so long as I kept moving, nothing would hit the bullseye of my being. I told myself this behaviour came from an impulse towards freedom; thus my wife was surplus baggage, and it was as if my son Tom didn't exist at all; I rarely thought about him. It didn't occur to me that, in removing myself from my responsibilities and my own opinion of myself, I was setting myself up to be hit. I was so easy to read, such a simple target for feeling. Feeling would smack me in the end.

I stopped going to the office. I spent time alone in the empty flat off Manningham Lane. I spent even more time with my father, and Vickie. When landed with Tom for a day, which was inconvenient, and unusual (who *was* this intense little boy?), I took him with Vickie to see the cricket pavilion. Once there I told the story of my father taking it to pieces plank by plank, and moving it from Scarborough.

"Who did that?" Tom asked.

"Your grandfather."

"Why?"

"Because he's your grandfather," I said, and suggested that he get out of the car and play.

"Dad . . ."

"Go on."

". . . it's raining."

"Tom!" I said, firmly.

"Nice little boy," Vickie said, when he had gone.

"He is," I said. Tom kicked at a stone. He made wings of his arms and was running towards the middle of the field. I imagined the aeroplane noises he would be making.

I tried to take her hand in mine, but she wasn't falling for it. She said, "What are you up to?"

I replied, "I'm not sure," which wasn't true, I'm afraid.

It's the Headingley Hamer Memorial Lecture on . . . seduction. I start with the history. The seventeenth-century seducer, I remind my students (did I mention that only women attend, only women are allowed?), was on horseback, leaving verse on the balcony and manure beneath the window. The eighteenth-century seducer, on the other hand, was a man of the Enlightenment, an atheist, an anarchist who held convention in contempt and was a threat to society. Look at Don Giovanni: the rebellious libertine who chased his own destruction. Moving ahead to the nineteenth, we meet Count Dracula, seducer as vampire, who was a threat to the sexual, rather than social order. The problem for those Victorian fellows with whiskery chops and unread volumes of utilitarian philosophy was that Dracula was Semtex between the sheets; the legend was that he drank women's blood and gave them pleasure, the implication was that he was a guy who liked to go down, and didn't care about the time of the month. The women are silent. They stare at me with angry faces. But what about our own time? There can be no question of the seducer as a threat to any order, whether social, sexual, or religious. A lie is a tiny seduction, I tell them, though a seduction is not a collection of tiny lies, rather one lie pumped up big, the effortless assumption of another identity. The modern seducer pursues, not pleasure, not really, but loss of self; women's eyes are mirrors in which he sees someone else reflected. Not me, never me. The trick is to find that other self.

Vickie said, "I see right through you."

Where are you, other self?

"You want revenge."

Other self, other self!

"You want to fuck me to get back at your father."

"That's not so. Vengeance doesn't come into it. I want to fuck you, period."

"Why?"

"Why? Because there's a hole between your legs you dumb cunt!"

No, no, no: of course I didn't say that. Before I tell you what I did say, I should mention what I told my women about the human brain. I told them it is divided into parts. There is a part which sets us above the ape. We also have the part which differentiates between ape and horse. Lucky us! And somewhere, at the very back, in a dungeon of the brain, is the part which hasn't changed since we came from the ooze. I picture a reptile, a tail-less amphibian of the genus *bufo,* a toad which squats at the top of my spine. When sex is a possibility, a jingle of keys, the dungeon door creaks open and . . . hoppety.

I said, "Because I find you intriguing and I want to know you better."

Croak!

"Because you're the most beautiful thing I've ever seen and I'm nuts about you."

Croak!

"Because I'm drowning in my life, and I believe I could change with you."

Croak, croak! Then another approach: "My father used to tell me when I was a kid, the thing he was most afraid of, that he'd end up selling rubber ducks on the Golden Mile in Blackpool, he'd be an old man, and he'd die in the street with strangers crowding around. And it probably will end like that. He's never had an attachment that mattered more than the next pint, the next fuck, the next trip to see the elephant. And I've always told myself these stories of escape, I make myself characters in them, act them out, make them live, but because they're stories, I behave as though they're not happening to me. I'm very much afraid."

"Of what?"

"That I'm like my father."

"You don't seem like him at all."

"Maybe you're right," I said, and smiled at her. "I expect you are."

I looked out through the car window into the rain and saw Tom, in the middle of the field, still an aeroplane, zooming.

I spent a night with Barbara. The next morning I couldn't find my underwear. She held out a pair of red cotton panties, saying, "Wear mine."

From me, the usual: "Why are you so pissed off?"

"I'm not."

"You think I've been spending too much time with Vickie?"

"Not at all. She's your father's girlfriend. You're playing the dutiful son."

"Then why are you angry?"

"I'm not."

"I'm always losing stuff in this bloody flat."

"Wear mine," Barbara repeated. "Scared your cock will vanish?"

I put on the panties.

"No size problems there," she said, inspecting me.

"Get your skates on. I told my father we'd meet them at eleven."

"I'm not coming."

"Don't be ridiculous."

"I'm being ridiculous?" she said, and let me have it. The way I was behaving? Was all the more depressing because so predictable. She refused to involve herself in whatever game it was I was trying to play with my father.

"We'll talk when you cool off," I said.

"Don't bother."

"No, no, I want to, we will," I said, and made for the door, once again disguising the joy of a chain-gang escapee.

My father, Vickie, and I went to meet Charlie Laughton, at a pub a few miles outside Harrogate. The car park was stocked with fancy cars—Jaguars, BMWs and Mercedes, an old Rolls with white ribbons tied to the mascot. "A county transaction," my father decided. "Money marrying money." He sniffed the air. "A reassuring smell, I always think."

My father was at home in pubs, not at home. Pick a pub. Some would be foul, with carpets tugging at your shoes, and reeking of beer and stale cigarettes; others would seem trapped in an older time—in Yorkshire there were pubs which hadn't changed since the beginning of the century; others still would be like this one near Harrogate, with real ale on tap, horse brasses on the walls, and men in green waxed jackets talking about milk surpluses and the European monetary system. My father's procedure was always the same, however. He would swing in through the entrance and pause, looking around, checking the exits. He would amble to the bar where he would stand, legs apart, hand on the counter, smiling his pleasure at the barman or, better still, barmaid. He would inspect the parade of bottles upside down in their optics as if they were soldiers who had served with honour in many campaigns. He would survey his fellow drinkers, smile, and crank up a conversation about cricket or racing or politics. He would be Jack Hamer.

"Johnnie Walker," he said. "Three, large ones, and another for yourself my dear." The barmaid, a blonde, about forty, in a green dress, smiled; barmaids were created for my father to endear himself to. He turned to Vickie. "Wouldn't you say I'm quite a card?"

She said that he was quite ridiculous.

"Below the belt," said my father, not bothered. "Definitely below the belt."

Vickie went to an empty table and sat down. She had spoken only three sentences to me all morning. These had been: "No," "Yes," and "Beats me." You don't want to play? Alright, alright, I'm a game show host, so they were: a) "Sleep well?"; b) "Eat breakfast?"; and c) "Where's Dad?" Now I bet you wish you hadn't asked.

Back to Vickie and my father. I wasn't displeased. I presumed she and my father had been arguing, which was fine with me. I picked up the three glasses and, while my father paid, followed her to the table.

I told her she was in fine form.

"I'm bored."

"Something which happens to you easily?"

"It depends on who I'm with."

"Well now. Isn't everything tickety-boo?"

That was my father, back from the bar. He had a finger in his mouth and was frowning, rubbing at his gum as if his tooth was causing him trouble.

"Vickie's bored," I said.

"We'll have to seduce her out of that."

"What do you propose?"

"I propose," he said, "that we go back to the tribal caves and consider what it is that a woman really wants from a fellow. I propose . . ."

But then it was the entrance of Charlie Laughton, a bustling entrance, impossible to ignore because Charlie Laughton has expanded like a balloon. He has become the sort of fat person fat people stand next to so they look slim by comparison. And he is not well: he pants for breath; the flesh on his face sags from the bone. In addition, there is something fearful in his appearance, as if he worries constantly about what's going on behind.

Charlie Laughton: his life since 1964 had been a wild parade. He had been wrong in supposing that he could not be harmed by the quarrel between Schenk and my father. He had been held responsible for defrauding the British Motor Corporation of cash accrued from the sale of fifty-seven white Minis; no court, since he had been able to lay most of the blame elsewhere, but there had been a scandal and, a year later, there *was* a trial, this time concerning his property business, when it was revealed that over several years he had bribed several civic officials to win several million-pound building contracts. Charlie Laughton went down for eight years and when he came out he found that he had lost the lot—business, reputation, wife. Giants tumble. For a while he drove mini-cabs, and still did, but now owned his own firm, which is why we were at this pub: he had a block-booking from the wedding party.

"Jack," he said. "Sorry it had to be Harrogate. I know you can't stand the place. But business is, and I have to watch the pennies."

"Very canny. I'd forgotten you're half-jock."

"An ancestor was mentioned by Robbie Burns. One of the lesser poems, I'm afraid."

My father smiled. "Good to see you, Charlie. You look dandy."

"It's been boom and bust and it'll be boom again. Just watch.

Two lots of them are at it. Big boys, from London and Europe, buying the place up for a song. In ten years Bradford will be different again, spanking new and ready to go to the dogs. Right now, it's a unique opportunity for someone to get in the middle."

"You'll be making your move?" said my father.

"You know me, Jack. I always did like Italian history."

"Speaking of which . . ."

"He's here."

"Schenk?"

"The bugger's in Bradford right now. I treated him like a son and the bugger stabbed me in the back."

"So did I."

"It was just a tactic with you, Jackie. You were in a mess and you saw a door marked "EXIT." Trouble was you had to step on me to get there. It was different with Schenk. He vanished when I needed him and it turned out he'd been ripping me off for years. A thou' here, a couple of thou' there. He planned it all along. It was *strategy*."

"Water under the bridge. Let it go, Charlie. You had Diana, you had the big house, you had the Mayfair flat and a brace of Rollers, your requirements were Veuve Cliquot and China tea and a certain *eau de cologne* from Jermyn Street. You lived Charlie, no two ways about it."

"And will again. We both will."

"How is Diana?"

"If there were a nuclear war, she'd end up in the winner's enclosure. When she divorced me, not long after I was nicked, I thought I'd do the decent thing, told my people to let her have a hundred grand, didn't want to leave the girl with no roof over her head."

"Quite."

"Within a year she'd rogered half the American senate and married a toff, a duke no less, had several *miles* of roof over her head. Big house out Scarborough way."

"I have to go to Scarborough."

"Business?"

"I've some money stashed. You're getting half."

"Why?"

"For the trouble."

"Like you said, water under the bridge."

"All the same."

"That's very civil. You know why you've come back?"

"Why's that?"

"You *know* why. Schenk. Your return . . ."

"It isn't a sign, Charlie."

". . . is a fucking sign. I'm going to kill the bugger."

Vickie had been sipping her drink, and looking from one to the other. She didn't seem to believe what they were saying. I presumed she saw two frail old men, a little sad, each supporting the other's sense of self-importance, and I was offended on their behalf. What a thing it was, I told her, to have seen Charlie Laughton and my father in their prime! The whole of Bradford had made way for them. She was unimpressed. They were like film stars, I said. She lit up a Marlboro. What would it take to disturb her clarity and calm?

The wedding party came from a room upstairs. The bride had brown eyes and a delicate face. She was dressed in white; I doubted whether it was a cynical gesture. The groom had a proprietorial arm around her waist and she picked confetti from the shoulder of his jacket. They kissed, while a young squire with a boil on his neck swayed like a tree in a stiff breeze, muttering: "Champagne, champagne." Overcome, with emotion, or wine, other guests gave similar performances. "Further *premier cru,*" they brayed. "CHAMPAGNE."

My father stood up. He spread his arms, like a conductor motioning to the orchestra, as if he were about to start making music. And that's what he did. "My friends," he began in a loud voice. "My very good friends, you take me back more than thirty years."

Puzzled murmurs from the wedding party.

"To 1946, and the time of my own marriage, to the beautiful and brilliant mother of my son here. As you can see just from looking, he took after me. Poor bugger."

Laughter and applause from same.

"It's been said that marriage is only a trick to make a housecleaner think she's a householder. But the man who said that was Irish, and a homosexual."

More laughter, louder applause.

"And my dear," he continued with a nod in the direction of the bride, "you look like a real bobby-dazzler. Doesn't she?" Heavy-headed nodding from all directions; their heads seemed made from lead. "She *is* a bobby-dazzling little angel and she'll remember that all unhappy marriages come from the husband trying to use his brains. I know she won't let that happen."

Yet more, louder still. The barmaid came out from behind the bar with a tray; on it were several bottles of champagne. Corks went bang, tall glasses were handed about. "Ladies and gentlemen," continued my father, raising his. "I will detain you no further. Just let me add that my own marriage gave me my best years. A toast, then! To marriage, to the future of this handsome couple. I know it will be a happy one. And the champagne's on me."

Wild cheering, and my father sat down. I said to Laughton and Vickie, "Bullshit, my dad wrote the book."

They laughed, but my father shook his head, he had not been joking. Suddenly he was mournful. He asked me to remember the story of my grandfather. The Harrogate farmlands should have been ours. "There was a fortune in it," he said, "That's the thing about this country. If you own land, you're never short of money." He spoke of the enlivening effects of money. "That's where my life went off the rails, you see. No land and therefore no money, really. I'd have been happy as a farmer. I'd have been singing happy songs all day if I'd been a farmer." He drew a romantic picture of himself. He had not been to blame. Others, history itself, had been to blame. He nodded at the party-goers. "This should have been you and me."

I looked around. They were celebrating a wedding. I'd always imagined, despite his irresponsibility, perhaps because of it, that my father celebrated something else: life itself. Perhaps I was wrong, perhaps this was the world he had aimed for, dreamed about, regretted all these years—a world of tweed. He said, "Things could have been different."

Sing me a sad song!

I said, "Dad, those people are bad jokes. Stooges. They're in the pockets of the government."

He said, "What's wrong with the government?"

Thus: my father, the outlaw.

I said I was surprised.

"Why?" said Vickie.

"Because *he* is different. These people would send you down, Dad. It's people like you these people want to see in jail."

My father was silent. A voice came from the other side of the bar, sank, and kept popping up again like a cork. "Rolex watches . . . are going for a song in Pudsey . . . I have a weakness for Rolex watches."

"Why would they send him to jail?" said Vickie.

"Because he's a crook."

"True," said my father. "Teerr-*oooo*."

"Is it?"

"Oh yes," he said. "Me and Charlie stole the Crown Jewels. Made off with them from the Tower. Cool as several cucumbers in an open top Bentley S type. Our getaway was down the Strand at a ton plus."

"Charlie?"

"Mr. Laughton here. A gangster I used to know."

"Jack," she said, but looking me in the eye, "I dislike men who boast."

The groom came up. He thanked my father for the champagne; my father waved aside his gratitude—it was the least he could do. "Let's get in another round," he said.

"Excuse me for asking, sir. But were you in the services?"

My father admitted, with an expression of becoming modesty, that he had been in the RAF for six years. I liked the "six years"; in other words, he had been in from 1939 to 1945, when the frying pan was spitting.

"Fighters?"

"Bombers. Blenheims and then Lancs."

"Bloody good show, sir."

"Nothing much, you know. Most of the time it was boredom at 250 knots."

"I'm going into the army myself, Paras."

"Got yourself a commission?"

"That's right, sir."

"Your dad must be a proud fellow."

"He's just over there. Come on, sir, I'll introduce you."

"I'd like that."

It was a conjuror's trick. The opportunity was there, and, *pfuft!* he was gone. Even Vickie was left blinking. "Does he do this often?"

"One of his specialities. You'll come to admire it."

"I doubt that." She said she would go and sit in the car. She would leave if we weren't out in ten minutes.

My father stood, legs apart, rubbing his nose, listening to a story the groom was telling. I thought about his attitude to me. Probably too complicated to talk about; but what if it wasn't, what if it was very simple? After all, I was not: rich, famous, expansive in character, a professional success. I had a beached marriage and a son I scarcely knew. What had he expected? A mansion with a Ferrari on the gravel driveway and a rolling green estate to which I would point, boasting that I had made this with my two hands. Dad, one day it will all be yours!

"Not lost his touch, the old bastard," said Charlie Laughton, admiring Vickie's exit.

"Fuck him," I said.

In the car Vickie had her nose in the local paper. She crossed her long legs and one shoe fell off. There was a carelessness in the way she displayed her body, and a nervousness. She wanted men to notice, she hated men to look. I asked what was in the news. She read a story about a woman who had been attacked by a man with a hammer as she walked home from the bus stop. Had it been Mr. Hyde?

She said, "Your father. Is he really . . ."

"A crook?"

"Is he really?"

"You don't know the story?"

"No."

So I told her about Schenk, Laughton, and how my father had embezzled the sixty-eight thousand pounds etc. etc. in today's terms, how he had faked his own death and vanished, how somehow I had always known he would come back, how the policeman Weekes was still looking for him. Note: Vickie now has the information necessary to send my father to jail. The bitch!

"Do you think there is some more money?"

"Precision on the point, as on most points where my father is the sole authority, is impossible."

"But you I can trust?"

"Absolutely."

She told me about her own father, who had also been a pilot, but in peacetime. His jet had gone down in the North Sea when she was seven and he had been killed. Throughout her childhood her mother had said to her, "Don't cry, Daddy wouldn't have liked it." She remembered him as a man who didn't smoke, didn't drink, and didn't laugh very much. "Cold, I suppose," she said. "A bit of a bastard." His grave was in Scarborough.

"We could go and look," I said. This time she let me take her hand, and smiled, a little warily.

I proposed we leave, and let my father make his own way back to Bradford. She seemed to be thinking about it, but then there he was, coming across the car park, sidling between a Mercedes and a BMW, wheeling about, doing the tango with no partner. He had something on the sleeve of his jacket. It looked like an armband. Only when he got in did I see that it was a white garter, the bride's presumably.

"Here we are," he said. "All bright and breezy and brisk as bottled ale."

Julie was furious. "Why do you do these things?"

"What's that?"

"Have Tom and I offended you in some way?"

"No."

"Do you actually want to humiliate us? Is that the idea?"

"I can't explain. It's something in my head."

"Bloody right. You should be committed."

Running, nothing if not true to form, I made for the door. I said, "Look, I can't go into this now, Budge is on my back about a story. I'm going to be out of town for a couple of days. I'll see you later."

Julie said, "Don't count on it."

I saw myself up in the sky, in the hushed marble halls of the Bank of Morality, where I presented my cheque to a clerk. He examined it, and keyed numbers into a computer, at which an alarm bell rang, not a clanging sound, not a *noise,* because such would not be permitted in the Morality, but a faint buzzing in the distance. Yet: consternation! My clerk went to his superior who in turn shook his head and walked quickly to *his* and then it was an unseemly scramble across the chequered floor to a bearded figure of stern aspect— yes, the great banker himself—who turned the cheque between his fingers and announced: "This account is . . . *overdrawn*."

They say it can happen two ways. It might be a question of the once-and-for-all spree, a murder or a betrayal or a rape; on the other hand, it might be a slow, almost unconscious using up of resources, a lie here, a failed responsibility there, a broken promise, an adultery, but they all add up, and the result is the same. You are finished, broke, no-good. I imagined the advert: Headingley, derelict, stumbling beneath a railway arch with a plastic carrier and a can of supercharged lager; he *used* to be with the Morality.

Did I worry? No, no, no, no. No.

I went to my father. I suggested that since the three of us, that's him, me, and Vickie of course, wanted to go to Scarborough we should get in a car and *just do it,* tomorrow, or the next day, or the day after that, and I started in about what fun it would be, we could stay at a hotel, hire a boat, go fishing, whatever, what did he think?

My father said what he thought: *"Avanti!"*

In Scarborough we stayed at The Balmoral. My father had been there before and, for reasons only too easily imaginable, called it The Immoral. It occurs to me that when I think of my father, myself, and sex, I picture a battlefield. I remembered myself aged nine, at a cricket match, late afternoon of a blazing day, with two friends from school, waiting for my father and seeing, when he did arrive at last, that he was staggering drunk. I had been filled with nine-year-old rage. That was the night he brought the prostitute to our room and argued with her about how much he should pay. I had wanted to kill him.

We ate dinner at the hotel. The restaurant was empty and our voices carried. Vickie looked good and didn't say much. My father was in a gloom. He talked about going to the bar for something he portentously called *the big drink;* in other words he was convinced he was going to die. He said, "Like 'The Dead End Kids' of cinema fame, I have no rosy future." He wanted to go to bed early. We had adjoining rooms on the first floor, facing the stairwell. In the corridor, my father apologised for his mood. He had been thinking about Charlie Laughton. "Poor sad old bastard," he said, "like yours truly."

"Come on," said Vickie. "You're not so bad. For an old man."

He threw his arms around us both. He became sentimental. He said, "I've missed you, son. I'm looking forward to spending some time together."

"Good-night," I said, disentangling myself, smiling at Vickie.

I woke in the middle of the night. The digital alarm clock said 3:08. I thought I heard knocking at the door and someone *was* there, Vickie, with a bottle of whisky cradled in her arm. She wanted to see her father's grave.

"Now?"

"Now," she said.

I made the face of a man resigned to having a restless night. But inside I was grinning like you-know-who.

This is how it was: moon out, strong wind up, cemetery gates locked. But we found a way, by the side of the football ground, down an alley over which the old grandstand loomed, creaking in the wind as if about to collapse, and through a gap in the black iron railings. We were in. Vickie strode ahead and I followed, moisture from the long grass soon soaking my shoes.

Many of the graves were in disrepair. Stones were smashed and scarred, roofs and doors caved in. From inside a mausoleum came sounds, not ghostly, but the shuffling of feet, and gasping laughter. Homosexuals, cruising. Look: a couple holding hands, another kissing, and there, a third, lying naked in the grass. Elsewhere a man was draped over a cross in the attitude of Christ crucified. His jeans were at his feet, where a second man knelt and took an erect cock in his mouth.

Vickie marched on, past the mausoleums, through a colonnaded semi-circle, to an area where the graves were more recent and stopped in front of one which was fighting a losing battle with the grass. She pushed the stems aside to reveal white lettering on a black headstone: JOHN ALEXANDER BRENAN, 1930–1962. She unscrewed the cap of the whisky bottle, drank, and, without turning, held out the bottle. The whisky went down, warming my stomach, and I gave back the bottle.

She said, "And for you?"

I said I was alright thanks, then realised she was talking to the grave.

"Go on, have a drink, have a drink with me. I insist," she said, and upended the bottle. Its contents glugged out and splashed on the grass, filling the air with the smell of whisky. She tossed the bottle away and I waited for the sound of breaking glass, but it didn't come. My mind had a brief picture of the bottle, unbroken, on its back in the long dewy grass.

She said, "Let's fuck."

I said, "Excuse me?"

"I want to fuck now."

"Just like that?"

"Why not?"

Barababoom!

I suggested we go back to The Balmoral; she wanted to do it here.

Again: "Excuse me?"

"I want to do it here. My father's down there."

I was hesitant, but her expression was determined. She wasn't smiling. She appeared to expect no pleasure from the activity. She said, "I thought you were the eager one."

I wasn't sure what I felt. Yes, I was: I was aroused, of course, watching Vickie take off her leather jacket and hang it on the headstone, unbutton her shirt and then take my hand and place it round her naked waist. She unzipped my fly.

We began to fuck. I thought. Men do this while fucking. They think while they are fucking, not of fucking, but of football, or the books of the Old Testament in order; I knew a fellow who learned passages of Wordsworth for the purpose. Others think toady thoughts of violence and rape. Me, I'm always in a bar, a big place, cool and well lit, and I am talking to four different women, but not at the same time. I talk to them discretely, and discreetly; none knows of any of the others, and none ever will, because my plan has compass-point simplicity. North is pretty, a young executive, brought up in Mile End. Her voice still has that Cockney twang. I suspect she has on fancy underwear, not Bond Street fancy, not that fancy, but Marks & Spencer fancy; I suspect also that she's on the prowl for a husband, someone aggressive and pushy. So I'm in computers. I paint a picture of company life. The picture is a Shakespeare tragedy and it's me, gory knife in hand, Macbeth-ing it to the board room. East just wants a love affair, an adulterous one, since she's married already. A nurse, she has recently discovered that her husband sleeps around. She considered slitting his throat with a scalpel, but that was too easy. She wants sex and anarchy, a release of rage, which is fine by me, I tell her, I'm a bomb-chucker myself. South is Jane and the sane, supportive, and affectionate embodiment of all the name implies, so I become a Jane of a man, a social worker in need of kindness and nurture, which is fine by her. And lastly, West, who wants to discuss the political situation in Latin America. Which is no problem.

I was fucking Vickie slowly and then withdrew, dropping on my knees to the dripping-wet grass. I kissed her thighs and nosed towards cunt. I was sucking her clitoris when she lost control of her bowels for a moment and farted in my face, an exhalation which smelled, this is true, of champagne. Well, not precisely; but I loved it, because I am in command, an air-traffic controller with a hundred jets on the screen, monitoring flight-paths, issuing orders in a robotic tone.

The politico West is keen to play a game. Where and when in history would I most like to have been? I tell her that spot was surely right now in Nicaragua, riding under fire with the rebels. *Sandinista hoy!* East is informed of the occasion I tried to shoot my boss with a crossbow. That was when I still believed in the hoax of nine-to-five, and he still had the scar. South, on the other hand, hears of my afternoons spent cleaning floors at the local asylum. And what of North? Have I forgotten about North? What a question! Striding over, diving in front of the brilliantined wide-boy whose tie is a bomb gone off in a paint factory, I tell her of a new club, some friends and I are off there in a couple of minutes, and would she? Of course she would!

I stood up. I rubbed my cock in her wet pubic hair and saw pleasure on her face, an expression of happiness, almost innocence. That's not true; I made that up. At that moment Vickie had the blankest face I've ever seen. Its lack of expression was startling. I pushed my cock in once more.

The wine-bar Oscar Wilde is still at work. I tell East I'm thinking of packing in my job altogether, in about two months time, to travel and, she knows, take stock of my life. After all, who needs work? It's the curse of the drinking classes. I smile, noting with some concern that North is moving from her allotted compass position. It's a smooth apology for East and I head off North just before she strays into forbidden territory. But I'm rattled. What was she thinking of? "*Hello* again," I say. "I've just been chatting with a bloke over there who was exiled from Chile. I asked him if he ever felt homesick. He said, 'Show me a man who longs for jail and I'll show you a warden on his day off.' I laugh, but North lifts her foot and rubs the toe against a black-nyloned calf. She puts her head on one side. She says, "Yew are funn-ay."

Vickie said, "Don't stop."

I said, "Who are you? Why are you doing this? I haven't seen my father for fifteen years, I didn't know whether he was alive or dead, he comes back with you. I feel . . . I don't know what."

She said, "Get on with it."

West won't. West can't. West isn't. West *is*. Ignoring all the rules. Determined to destroy the compass. Distracting the juggler. Behaving with blatant disregard of air-traffic procedure. West is *talking to South*. There is no precedent. The warning systems bleep and wink. West and South are together, staring at me. Inoperative lodestone, magnetic chaos: the needle spins and spins.

I'm fucking Vickie hard. Her legs are criss-crossed round my back. My hands hold her arse to prevent it bumping too hard against the gravestones. My breath comes in rattling wheezes. My mouth tastes of cunt and phlegm.

East has joined West and South. Disaster is imminent. They advance towards me with awful purpose. Screw connector gone. Mid-air collision . . . jet-fuel *whoomphing* . . . binnacle blasted . . . skittles tumbling. Ladies, please!

I came. I came with my buttocks thumped by her heels and I broke out laughing. "You're beautiful," I said, "and I love you." I meant it. I longed to fall in love. I put on the act of falling in love, I found myself doing it more and more often, I fell in love with almost every woman I met, and despised them even if they didn't love me back.

I said, "Did you enjoy that?" and wished that I hadn't. I waited for her reply. It could be crushing. It *would* be crushing. I was afraid.

Instead it was routine, and delivered with a smile: "Thank you, that was very nice."

"Don't tell me," I said, "tell your friends."

She laughed then, and looked at me warmly. I said, again, that I loved her.

"You are impressionable, aren't you?"

"Am I?"

"I'm trying to work out whether you're like your father in that respect."

"Do you know us both that well?"

"I'm not sure there's that much to know. The two of you are only mysterious to yourselves."

We didn't go straight back to the hotel. Instead we walked along the promenade. In the distance the surf made a noise like applause in a football stadium. I held Vickie's hand, saying I wasn't sure who had been the seducer here. She asked if it mattered. I said, "If you let yourself be fucked . . ."

"You will be," she said.

"Exactly."

I mentioned the habits of the black widow spider; she mates and then she kills, with the male spider not even attempting to survive. I spoke also of other species of spider, where evolution had allowed the male to fight back. Some would begin their seduction with an offering of prey, still alive, with which the female would stuff herself. While the female belched, the male would fuck in safety. In other species the male performs a dance of courtship, around and around, enmeshing the female gradually in a web. Fucking would take place when she was completely tied up, then the male would be on his bike. Way to go! That was a style I admired. Still other males would kidnap pre-adolescent girl spiders, tie them up, not feed them very well, keep them weak but protect them from other predatory post-adolescent man spiders until they were sexually mature and then . . . *biffbangbonk!* the consummation devoutly to be wished.

"Oh really," said Vickie. "That's very interesting. So what type of insect are you?"

· · ·

The next morning my father said he had his business to take care of.

"Your money?" Vickie said.

"And someone to see." He said he'd meet us in the coffee bar across the street. I was pleased, but, when he'd gone, and I said to Vickie, "Fancy a fuck?" she wouldn't let me kiss her, saying she also had something to do.

"Fine," I said, as if it didn't matter. "We'll do it later."

"Maybe," she said, and I thought of eternal innocence that allows no evil. Alright, a stinker; I thought of fucking her again, of why it was some women got their hooks into you. I decided I did love her. I went to the coffee bar and waited. The place was run by two men, Italian, Salvatore and Enzo. Salvatore wore a tie and a Harris tweed sports jacket, he seemed to be the boss, while Enzo had on a blue waiter's jacket of shiny nylon. They could barely stand the sight of each other. Their present dispute was over a tub of tomato slices. Enzo would pull it to his side when he had to make a sandwich; Salvatore, who prided himself on his precision, would snatch it back and, staring at the counter to make sure he had got his geometry just so, return the tub to its proper place. He would glare at Enzo, not straight in the face, but courtesy of a mirror opposite the counter. The ritual was enacted each time someone ordered a sandwich.

Enzo was frying bacon when my father came back. "A bacon buttie," he said. His nostrils expanded, drinking in the smell. He smiled, and said, "There were times when a fellow would have killed for a bacon buttie."

I didn't ask him what times those might have been.

"Strange the things you remember. The time I left, in 1964, I tell you, Headingley, it was like fifty cats fucking a Ping-Pong ball. All hell was on. Johnnie Law was after my arse, that bastard Schenk was doing his best to put me six feet under, and Charlie Laughton had washed his hands of the whole caboodle. As far as he was concerned Schenk could go ahead and I could go for a shit with a blanket. It was all I could do to retrieve the situation. I gave money wings to fly with. Fifteen hundred quid for a new passport, another fifteen on a plane for one night, foreign currency at three times the odds, two ton plus for a birth certificate. Expensive business, popping your clogs. You'd think that stuff would stick and it did. But what

I really remember is something about you, a silly thing, really. You'd asked me for a model aeroplane, a Focke-Wulf 190D, couldn't find the bugger anywhere, had to get the 190A, realised it was all wrong of course, what you wanted was the night fighter. I gave you the thing, you didn't say a word. Just binned it. I'd had a few and at that moment I was lit-up like Regent Street on Christmas Eve. I thought I'd belt you to the other side of kingdom come. If that wasn't enough I turned round and saw the fish in that bloody stupid tank, all dead, with bits of their skin flaked off, little coins on top of the water. I felt as if the walls were coming down. I was crying my eyes out. It was a rotten moment. Then you came back in and you put your arms round my waist and said, "Don't worry, Dad, it'll be right." Do you remember that?"

I didn't.

"I've thought about it a lot. I didn't want to do it, you know, just pick up the cricket bat and bugger off like that. I had to screw them first. It was out of my control."

Vickie came up. We spoke for a while, about nothing in particular, and then she said to me, "Will you still be here in twenty minutes?" I said we didn't have anything better to do, so I imagined we would, and she was on her way again. "See you later," she said. And, a cheerful afterthought, from the door: "Bye Jack!"

My father lifted his coffee-cup and sipped. I saw the black hairs which sprouted from his nostrils. I saw also what he was asking himself: why Vickie had spoken only to me. "Is she brassed off do you think?"

"Beats me," I said.

Salvatore watched Enzo in the mirror. Enzo picked up a cocktail stick, thrusting it into a triangle of bacon sandwich with the passion of a betrayed lover knifing the villain in opera.

"Funny that," said my father.

"She's a funny girl altogether."

He was a dog with a bone, worrying at it. Then it came. "Bloody hell," he said.

"What?"

"You corked her. That's it, isn't it?"

I said nothing.

"Come on. That's something you can't have forgotten. Did you cork her or not?"

"Since you insist: yes, I corked her last night, or she corked me to be more accurate."

"Where?"

"Does it matter?"

"Yes it bloody does."

"On her father's grave, in point of fact."

"You're lying."

"Alright, I'm lying."

"You're not lying."

"Any way you want."

"You're making this up. You didn't cork her at all."

"Suit yourself."

"On her father's grave? I don't believe it."

"She's an imaginative girl."

"What the bloody hell were you up to?"

It was a moment to relish. I assumed an expression of surprise. Hadn't he guessed? "Seeing the elephant."

I walked along the promenade down to the harbour. The weather was hot and sticky, tropical; thick air pressed on my skull. A trawler had come in and was emptying its nets. Gulls shrieked for fish. I walked back towards the beach. Vickie was there, building sandcastles with some kids, not far from the water's edge, which was fine, but Barbara was also there. A complication.

I said, "What are you doing here?"

"Vick called and suggested I come."

"I needed an ally," said Vickie.

"How nice," I said.

"How do you like your sandcastles?" said Barbara.

"Round or square or with a hole in the middle?" said Vickie, not bothering to suppress a smug smile.

I'm painting a picture and it shows my fear that Vickie was a predator, you know the type, she would bite the head from a man's cock and spit it out to see whether it lent a certain something to the pattern on the carpet. As you will remember, Barbara said this was something men like to believe about women, just another fantasy, and prevalent in these times when women have been getting more clout and men have been getting more and more antsy. Barbara was right, of course, but that doesn't mean I wasn't; because this male fear is unreasonably, unjustly, even luridly held, it doesn't mean it isn't so. Enjoy those double negatives? Just remember: we've got Mr. Hyde on *our* side. Feel nervous at night? *Sayonara*, ladies.

I asked Vickie what her game was.

"What's your game?" I said.

She looked over my shoulder. "Look, here comes your dad. Isn't he fab? Do you think he knows somewhere we can go for dinner? My treat."

That night he flirted with them both, looking at each in turn as if she were the most beautiful, the *only* woman he had ever met, listening as if he had never heard anything so moving or intelligent or wonderful, and, when asked, talking about himself in a quiet, modest tone. His stories? They were:

1. Of flying: of being in his Lancaster at twenty-five thousand feet over Cologne and thinking that everything else had ceased to exist, even the white bursts of anti-aircraft fire were part of a dream in which he was alone and invulnerable; of being in a hot-air balloon above the veldt, with one of his South African girlfriends, two thousand feet up and the gas hissing loudly, but still able to hear conversations from the ground below, a weird and beautiful thing, he said, the voices were quite clear, as if coming up a funnel created by the wind.

2. Of being on the run: of befriending a police officer wherever he lived, winning his trust, and putting himself in his hands. In Durban, for instance, when a telegram arrived from the Bradford CID, saying Inspector Weekes had heard Jack Hamer was in South Africa buying and selling Rolls-Royces for King Hussein of Jordan, his friend the Durban detective had filed a reply to the effect that King Hussein had neither met, nor heard of, nor wished to hear of, the criminal Englishman Jack Hamer.

3. Of childhood and of gambling: of cycling to Blackpool and back in 1931 with the Saltaire Athletic Club, coming home late and with the skin scraped off his knees from a fall, and not taking a bath but instead hiding in the stables where the funeral horses were kept, watching his father play brag with the employees, using an up-

turned coffin for a card table; of winning five grand on the ponies in São Paulo, backing an outsider because its name was Coffee Bar and he ran one, in Rio.

4. Of families: of a woman he knew in Brazil, Maisie, who owned a hotel as well as the coffee bar, of the child to which she had given birth, a son.

"So you see," he said, "Headingley has a half-brother on the other side of the world."

"Is that true?" I said.

"Would I tell a lie?"

"Tell us about Maisie," said Barbara.

"Why did you come back?" said Vickie.

"Maisie was fabulous. She was American, you see, born in a puritan town in New England, but not tight with her cash. Dressed like something out of the fashion pages. Gucci on her feet, Chanel on top, and things underneath that were just indescribably nice."

"Why did you come back?" said Vickie.

"Keen on the gee-gees too. In fact that was how she came to be in Brazil. Her first husband . . ."

"Why?" said Vickie, stuck in the groove.

My father at last acknowledged the question. "I'd nearly done it a couple of times. Once I was even on the boat, a white hull it had, with the name in black, *Ludwig Beethoven*. Just after dawn, with a mist still on the bay, and a porter bringing my suitcases on board. What was his name? Gone now. Anyhow I looked at his face and at his ears, he had boxer's lugs, red and swollen with blue veins standing out like rivers on a map, and it came to me that I wasn't going to go through with it. I saw myself, with Maisie, at the hotel, on the terrace, with milky coffee and bread for dunking. Heaven! I'd have been off that boat no quicker if its cargo was nitro-glycerine."

I had watched him, asking myself if these stories were lies, knowing it was unimportant to him because, in the drama of their telling, he felt them so truly. It was a feeling I knew; words could rope facts at will.

Barbara asked what had been different this time, why he had come back.

"Boredom," he said, and made a noise from the back of his throat, a glottal shrug. "I was bored."

"And your money?" said Vickie.

"What money?" said my father. And then: "Oh, *that* money. Well, of course, since it was here, I thought I might as well come and get it. No harm in it."

Barbara didn't know what they were talking about, so Vickie explained, it was money my father hadn't been able to take with him because he was in such a chase to get out of the country, he'd left it in a sack, like a burglar caught in the act. My father laughed, throwing back his head, and they joined in.

Oh what a charmer!

I was silent.

He said, "I went to see an old friend today. Diana Farrell, the actress, you know, star of stage and screen. Fabulous lady, an absolute cracker. Headingley knows her, don't you son?"

I wondered what she had told him, about the pearl, about me. I didn't feel panicky about it. My response was the usual no response.

He said, "She asked after you, old fellow. Quite surprised me. Didn't know she'd remember after all this time. Famous lady like that, busy, must have all sorts on her mind."

"I interviewed her," I said, "for the paper. Not long since."

"That must be it," he said. "I always did like Diana. Clever lady. Look how she took old Charlie to the cleaners. And she's not lost her looks. In candlelight . . ."

"Candlelight? You were there in the middle of the day," I said.

"Went down to the cellar, old man. In soft yellow candlelight she could be thirty years old. The elephant was viewed," he said, looking at me all the time, smiling, as if to say I had made the choice, not only by fucking Vickie, but by rejecting the intimacy he had offered, and it was fine by him. His cool smile said *it's war old man*.

I was woken again in the night. As before I thought someone was knocking. Then I realised the noise was different. There was a banging, a woman's voice—Vickie's?—saying something I couldn't make out, some giggling, more banging and, quickly after, a gasping sound and a long exhalation. *Aaaaah*. Then, silence. I got out of bed.

The corridor was empty, but I heard two women talking; flat vowels, Yorkshire accents, getting louder as they came up the stairs.

"I've not seen hair like it. 'Cept mebbe on a race horse. It were beautiful," said one.

"He was Italian. He definitely had look of an Italian," said the other.

I thought I would go back into the room but, looking down, I saw a fat white slug which had left a glistening trail behind it. The voices came closer.

"Did you see your Jimmy's face? Really hacked off, he were."

"He were not well suited."

"Still, I could go some of that Italian."

"Oh aye. Bin there, done that, got me T-shirt."

Looking again, I realised that the object on the carpet was no slug. It was a used condom.

Two blue-rinsed heads came into view, then two pairs of tinted spectacles and two lipsticked mouths, laughing raucously. I bent down and picked up the condom. I went back inside the bedroom and shut the door softly. There was the hiss of nylon as the women went past, and their voices, growing faint.

"You'll be goin' straight to bed then?"

"Like 'ell, I will. I'll wait while my Jimmy comes and put 'im to work. 'Ave 'im tell me a funny story."

"Yer lucky. That's the trouble with my Ted. He's never funny by vocation, just laughable in 'imself."

I tried to work out what must have happened. Perhaps it had been my father, fucking Vickie up against the door, to get back at me. What an outrage! The condom was still warm from the sperm inside. I thought about evolution. Nature favours that which exists already. But any change may result from reproduction. Variation occurs at random. So: I might have been doomed to be a mere copy of my father; or, I might have been the rebel egg which would overthrow all he stood for. I tell you, that theory of evolution, it cuts no mustard. Where's the use of it? I sniffed, I dipped a finger and I dabbed it on my tongue. Sticky, with a tang of salt. More dipping, dabbing. I'd show the bastard.

The light went on. Barbara asked what the fuck was happening. "Go back to sleep," I said.

"What's that in your hand?"

"Nothing."

"Looks like a condom."

"It is not a condom."

"You disgust me."

"Do I?" Naked, I stood by the door, with my toes scratching against the harsh texture of the carpet, and held out the condom, saying, "Is this the stuff from which I was made?"

I announced that I had hired a motor-boozer. The four of us would go for a cruise. Leading the way along the harbour wall, I promised adventure. There was a fridge on the boat, in which I'd made sure plenty of alcohol had been stored, and we would get geesed, royally stinking. As we cruised out beyond to sea I made martinis the way they should be made, the way Diana Farrell had taught: Gordons, Noilly; chilled glasses, and olives from a jar I had brought with me. My father was at the wheel, at my suggestion, and Vickie and Barbara were below, with me. We did get stinking. And then I took off my clothes. I said, "I am very sensitive and I need a lot of love."

Vickie and Barbara laughed, as I had thought they would, and so I smiled as well and sloshed martini about, saying come on, they should get their clothes off, it would be a hoot, and when they exchanged a look, each questioning the other, shrugged and laughed again . . . *bingo!* We took mattresses down from the bunks and lay them on the floor of the cabin. They undressed. I felt buoyant, light-headed.

I had my lips on Vickie's thigh when footsteps came tapping down the companion-way. My father. But who then was steering? An automatic pilot? I had a sudden picture of the boat sailing blindly on to rocks or smacking an oil tanker in the belly.

He said, "Well, shoot me down, everything is going very well in the best of all possible worlds." Within seconds he too was naked.

Barbara inspected us both. "Vaudeville lives," she said.

"Absolutely," said my father. "I've said it before and I'll say it again. We're a grand team, Headingley and I. None better. Isn't that right, son?"

"Right," I said without enthusiasm.

He launched himself and came down with a thump on the mattress. "Burn my clothes, I'm in heaven," he said.

The situation was not yet a farce, but nor could it be described as a success. Only my father kept up the pretence of passion. Maybe it was no pretence. He moved easily between Vickie and Barbara, now kissing, now murmuring endearments, now giggling and rolling on his back like a puppy. I was beginning to understand that he was capable of unself-conscious action in a way I was not.

I looked at his penis, which was nut-brown in colour and fully erect. Uncircumcised, like my own, and with more wrinkles. Odd, I thought, that a penis should be like a face, or a heart, that it should age. I had once been inside it, an adventurer with yet-to-be-revealed personality problems. I imagined myself there now waiting for the orgasm which would rocket me into Vickie or Barbara.

He had his head between Barbara's thighs. Slurping sounds suggested he was working hard with mouth and the tongue. Her expression seemed to suggest that, all in all, she would prefer a cup of tea. Was that how women thought? Were they always this bored? She winked at Vickie, who winked back; lovers who would steal a man's shadow.

I slapped Barbara hard on the face. Vickie gave me one in return.

"Bastard," she said. "Don't dare do that again."

"Oh bloody hell," said my father, raising his head. "What now?"

"It's your son, being a dick," said Vickie.

"As per usual," said my father.

"You said it."

"Can't you do *anything* right?"

And then, wham-bam, it was a different tennis match.

I said, "Some things."

"Name one," said my father.

"I fucked Diana Farrell."

His expression: *what?*

"She didn't mention it? I'm not surprised. Fucked her both front and rear. Buttfucked her until she bled."

My father looked at me with great intensity.

"Vickie too."

"If we're on that particular subject, and a fine one it is, I corked Barbara."

"Barbara?"

"She was magnificent. And so was I. Her precise words my dear fellow. 'You were magnificent.' "

"Vick begged for more."

"Had to slap her down."

"Corked . . ."

"Her . . ."

"Andherandherandher"

"More than you."

"Better."

"Fucked . . ."

". . . fucked."

". . . fucked . . ."

". . . . . fuckingwellfucked."

"Did that one in the lav."

"Down an alley."

"Up the Amazon."

"In the lift at Brown–Muffs."

"Underneath the podium at Nuremburg."

". . . all night . . ."

". . . . . . . all week . . ."

"Corked for a month straight."

"Boffed longer."

"More."

"BETTER."

Joyous songs upon the billows!

Barbara stared at my father and me, seemingly unsure whether to hit me or to laugh out loud or to tell us to stop behaving like children. Vickie was unconcerned. She ignored us and began to put her clothes back on. Barbara did begin to laugh.

My father continued, "Your mother, in a lay-by outside Otley, the back of a Rover, never known anything like it, she was like a wild thing, almost bit off the end of my nose. You were a child of passion, old man, no doubt about it."

"Bastard!"

"Got that wrong, Headingley. *You're* the bastard. And a great disappointment to me."

"Oh that's rich. You're so entranced with yourself. The lovable old dog, the old rogue, the pirate who's spent his life on the edge.

What crap! You're a joke. Don't you hear us laughing at you. Ha-ha-ha! As a human being you're a piece of shit. You know what you've amounted to? Nothing, just one fat zero. You've pissed your life up the wall. The morning comes and it's dried out and there's nothing left, not even a stain, just a bad smell. And I'll tell you something else. You've been a bloody awful father, to me and Keith, and to Helen."

"Don't bring my daughter into this."

"Murderer!"

"You bastard! You miserable little bastard! I demand your respect!"

And then? I couldn't help myself. I was twelve years old, filled with shame and anger and fear, saying, "It would have been better if you had died," and then recapturing an even cruder emotion, it was tea-time and I was having a tantrum, waving a custardy spoon above my head, that's it, I was in nappies, *"I wish you were dead."*

There are little lies, so tiny it doesn't much matter whether you do or you don't, such as me telling Julie I was going for a drink with the clocks from the office when in fact I would be alone in the empty apartment, drinking coffee and staring at the walls. And there are the in-betweeny ones, involving, say, adultery, told off-the-cuff but prepared with care. Ideally, lies of this nature should be as close to the truth as possible; dying relatives are handy. Then there are the big lies, elaborate lies, great whoppers with the precision of a Bonaparte battle plan and a nasty sense of humour.

Consider this.

It was in the icy Bradford March of 1921 that the executions went wrong. Three men were hanged; not only were their necks broken, their heads were pulled right off. The mess was followed by a fuss. Word got about, and the condemned of Bradford did not go quietly to the scaffold but died kicking and screaming. Down in London, the bureaucrats went to work, keen that there should be no repetition of the errors. First of all they decided that Bradford should no longer be allowed to run their own show. Hangings would be staged in the South, in the capital, in London. Then they hired new executioners, an entire family, grim men from *Lancashire,* who knew about physics, weights, and gravity's insistent demand, and took care in the precision of their work. But that wasn't enough. They needed a system. So they sat down with all the available statistics and psychological reports and came up with one.

Imagine: you have been tried, found guilty, sentenced; you are in the death cell, fourteen feet by fourteen feet, with little furniture, just a bed, a bookshelf, a wash-basin, a lavatory, and a wardrobe at the back. This is it, your final home. For three weeks you will be here. You sit, sleep, and read. Perhaps you masturbate. In the morning you splash water on your face and you eat the breakfast which comes on a wooden tray. You sit. You stand. You sit. You examine the cell door, which is made of steel plate and painted grey, it looks heavy and unbudgeable, with a peephole at the top. From beyond it you hear the trudging footsteps of the men who guard you. Occasionally you hear their laughter, and when they come in you can see they are bored. Sometimes, when you are on your own, you have the sense of being watched. Through the door. The door comes to fascinate you. It represents the possibility of escape: they, the people of the outside world, your loved ones, are out there, beyond it. But as escape-fantasies recede you think of something else. The door is danger, the end of your life, for it is through the door that you will be taken and killed. So more than anything you come to dread the door. You fear it. You develop the attitude of your ancestor in the cave, looking out with terror towards the unknown you know lies beyond.

It is morning, *the* morning, nearly eight o'clock, the morning of your final day in your final home. You wait for the prison bell to sound, you will it not to, perhaps some miracle has occurred and time has stopped, but there it is . . . *dong* . . . *dong* . . . *dong* . . . and black-suited men of calm and kindly appearance come through the door. These men are not, however, your friends. You think about resistance. Perhaps you can spread your arms, hold yourself inside the cell, but there is nothing to grasp on to.

You do not notice until too late that three of the men in black have business at the bottom of the wardrobe. You notice only when the wardrobe is wheeled away—they've lifted it and put on smoothly-oiled castors—that, behind you, in the part of the cell you thought safe, the back of your cave, there is *another door,* a second door which swings open on to the courtyard where you are to be executed. The scaffold is there, only yards away, a short walk across wooden planking. You're in a daze. ANOTHER DOOR! You do not kick or scream, you are only just beginning to consider the enormity of the deception when you are taken outside by the executioner, whose dark Lancastrian pride it is that he will have your hands tied, head hooded, and neck snapped in the noose before the prison clock completes its eighth chime. Your final thoughts are not of fear, or of your family and loved ones, but of the dreamer who worked at a desk in an office in a building in London and imagined a wardrobe of wheels. Crucially, as he had known you would not, you do not make a fuss.

It was after the incident on the boat that my father, together with Vickie and Barbara, sent me on an adventure. What I found at the end of it was a dodgy wardrobe, a wall that moved. Barbara came to me. She explained that Vickie had a problem. As I probably knew, Vickie was from a well-heeled family in London, her father had been, like mine, in the RAF, but later, in the 1950s, he hadn't flown in combat, he'd always been disappointed by that, and afterwards he had made a bundle on the stock exchange. Her mother was a painter.

I nodded, yes, yes, though I had knowledge of only some of it.

Barbara went on. When she had been eighteen Vickie had run away to America. She had worked as a cocktail waitress in Houston, fallen in love with a fellow, a Texan, a drug addict who had died. When she had come back to England she had married a rag-trade millionaire, a Greek with a Ferrari and a front tooth missing. He had wanted to conquer new territory; he would inherit many acres of old territory, but that was back in the Mediterranean. So he had decided he would open a club, somewhere in Chelsea. He would put black marble on the walls and mirrors on the floor, and his money and Vickie's smart connections would be the guarantee of success. Or so he had thought, and at first he had been proved right. The club was a runaway. Then Vickie had become involved with one of the regulars, someone she had known for years, he ran a PR company in the West End, and it was so on and so forth, and then the Greek had become suspicious and *dedumdedumdedum,* rows, and he had started beating her up. She had sued for divorce, and he had taken her to lunch at an excellent restaurant and had warned her that if she went ahead with the action he would fuck her up very good indeed. It might not be tomorrow, or the next day, but I will destroy you, he had said. She had gone ahead anyway, and had lost the case when his lawyers produced fake evidence concerning her drug habit.

I said I didn't understand; surely her application for divorce couldn't have been turned down on those grounds? Oh no, said Barbara, *that* wasn't the problem, the problem was that there was a child, a little boy, and Vickie had lost custody.

I saw a chance too good to miss. I went to Vickie and reviewed things with her. I was sad and cheerful in the proper places. To lose a child was like someone removing your guts with an ice-cream scoop. I had tears in my eyes and I meant them. I said of course it made me ashamed to be a man. But to get back her child was not impossible. I would develop a plan. But first it was bed. Afterwards, when we had fucked, I believe I said, "You're beautiful, an enigma, maybe you can't be solved, maybe you don't want to be solved. I'm in love with you Vickie. I do, I feel . . . ashamed. I've said that to a lot of women. But with you I mean it."

She told me then about the man who had been her husband's partner in the rag-trade. The Greek had a system for dealing with the Inland Revenue; it was complicated, it was based in fact on the labyrinth at Knossos. The partner knew enough about this to have the Greek jailed for tax evasion, and when he and the Greek quarrelled, it seemed the secret of the labyrinth would be revealed. But the partner had been killed. Of course the Greek had been suspect number one, but so long as his nerve held the only man who could damage him was an accountant, who knew all there was to know about the firm. His name was David Lightowler, a thin man with bad skin. He had disappeared. Bought off, or threatened, or both.

"He lives in Bridlington. I know you'll laugh but I don't even know where that is."

I said it wasn't far from Scarborough. I said I would go if she thought it would help.

My father said, "We've been a regular pair of real buggers. But now there's a chance to do something right for once, something with nothing in it for us. We can save her life."

So he and I drove to Bridlington. The address Vickie gave me was in an estate where each street was named after an American astronaut, row after row of houses, small and identical, built in garish orange brick; they looked like toys put there by a careful child. Many of the houses had lace curtains in the front window, behind which figures were glimpsed. The curtains were not to stop you looking in, but to prevent you seeing them looking out. This was the new England which my father found so strange, like science fiction. He did not know what these people thought or felt. He could not guess at their dreams. At the end of Neil Armstrong Way two teenagers were swinging on a young tree; the tree was a bow, bending, bending, and for a moment threatening to spring back and launch them into orbit. Then it snapped, a sharp sound that echoed like a gunshot.

We found the house. We walked up the path, I knocked on the door, and when it opened I saw a wardrobe, moving smoothly away, leaving me in front of the drop. My heart went down to my bowels.

It was my wife.

"Hello, Headingley," she said, matter-of-factly. "You look grim."

"Just surprised."

She said to my father, "You're Headingley's dad, aren't you? There's something in the eyes, and the way you both stand with your feet at ten-to-two."

She and my father exchanged a few remarks, I was still too surprised, too dazed, to take them in, but I was aware of a lot of smiling and nodding of heads. And then: "I'd like to meet that grandson of mine."

"He's at school, I'm afraid."

"A pity."

My father took me by the arm and said he had to get back. He was going to leave me to it. Naturally, I wanted to ask him what the hell was going on; naturally I didn't, couldn't, wouldn't have even if Julie hadn't been there. My tongue was sandpaper. "This isn't about saving Vickie's life, old man, it's about saving *yours*," he said in a whisper.

"Do you really have to go?" Julie said.

My father was a portrait of regretful candour. "I'm afraid so. Don't worry, I'll be back now I know where you are."

Like a film moving very slowly he backed down the path, facing us, with one hand in his RAF blazer pocket and the other held high in a wave. "Good luck, Headingley, see you at The Balmoral at six, we'll have a couple of quick ones," he said, opening the car door and getting in. "Goodbye, my dear. Don't be too hard on him."

"Why not?" she said, and they both smiled.

We watched as the car moved towards the end of the street, swerved to avoid the two teenagers who were prising loose a manhole cover, and turned into Scott Carpenter Close.

"I was expecting a man with two heads, or The Creature from the Black Lagoon. He seems very charming."

"Don't you believe it."

"A bit of a twinkle in his eye, but alright."

I could only shrug.

"I'll make some tea."

She turned and walked rapidly inside the house. What was going on?

I notice that my women are not paying attention. I smile, I bring my papers together with a confident snap, and they ignore the gesture. They actually begin to talk among themselves. I raise my voice, it's a favourite subject: having one's sexual cake and eating it, but it seems to make no difference. I command silence and insist that they show proper respect. This gets their attention, at last. They stand up, but I soon notice that this is not an action of feminine obedience. They surround the podium in a loose semi-circle, and *what's my father doing here,* popping up at the back of the hall. I try to shout, "I'm the only man allowed in here," but one of the women already has a gag in my mouth and the flame-haired temptress reaches into her bag and pulls out a thin-bladed . . . MUTINY!

I have never denied that I am less than perfect. But did I deserve this? Consider the facts. Julie was having an affair with another man. Julie knew, and had known for some time, about Barbara.

They had *spoken on the phone*. They were quite friendly! Oh, but it gets better. Julie had decided to leave me, and she had arranged with Barbara, who had in turn fixed up the tawdry little lie with Vickie and my father, that I should be brought here to Bridlington so she could tell me. It was an outrage. Ladies and gentlemen of the jury, if you please!

In the living room, on a coffee table, was a framed photograph of Tom and a statue made from milky glass, showing the god Apollo about to catch the lissom Daphne, only to find, before he could embrace her, that her protector Zeus was turning her into a laurel bush; Apollo did not look pleased. Julie had bought me the statue, years ago, an ironic gift to mark my birthday, or our anniversary, or an indiscretion she'd found out about; I can't remember. I wondered why she'd brought it with her.

I realise I haven't told you much about my wife. I'll give it to you briefly: a small figure, dark hair, dark curry-colored eyes. A teacher, and determined. We had met when I was twenty-one, and she twenty, and she had rolled down the slope of a lawn towards me in Lister Park, arriving at my feet like Cleopatra in front of Caesar. Something about her had reminded me of my sister, and we had married eighteen months later. She had assumed that marriage meant fidelity. As I had assumed she had assumed. I had been arrogant and blind, as she took no particular delight in telling me that day in Bridlington, when she had told the rest, the worst.

I was shattered.

"How's Tom?" I said.

"Fine," she said. And, coldly: "Now that I've said my bit, you'd better go. Ted will be home soon."

"Ted? Who the fuck is Ted?"

"I'm not going to get into this."

I apologised. "Look," I said, "I'm a little confused." I was still trying to register the enormity of the tremor. "You're leaving me?" I said in an every day sort of way. Was I dreaming?

"I've left you already."

I see I said. I'd known Julie for ten years. I knew everything there was to know about her. Even her bad temper was predictable. Yet here she was, not being Julie at all.

"You're leaving me?"

She said nothing.

"Let me get this straight," I said. "For Ted? *Ted?* Does he smoke a pipe?"

She crossed her arms as if the gesture were an obscenity.

I asked myself the predictable question: how could this have happened without my seeing? It had, I had to deal with it.

"Look," I said, "I'm sorry. I didn't come to argue."

"That's good."

I felt ridiculous. "I feel ridiculous," I said.

"I'm not surprised."

"No," I said. "You don't understand."

"Oh diddums. Poor complicated baby."

Very well, I thought, have it your way. I began to get myself under control. I told her I knew my behaviour had not been good, alright, an understatement, my behaviour had been very bad indeed. I had been selfish, thoughtless, and cruel, and I could expect nothing better than her anger. But, in the last few days, with my father having been back, I had felt I was changing, I was at last implicated in my life and able to take responsibility for it. I had been adrift, perhaps still was, but I knew I could put down anchor, if she would help.

"I don't believe you."

"Believe me," I said.

"It's too late, Headingley. There's a limit beyond which someone's nerves can't be torn and still alive. I feel numb to you now."

"So that's it?"

"I'm afraid so."

"A divorce, and you trot down the yellow brick road with the pipe-smoker?"

"I do, yes, I do think we'd better think about divorce."

It occurred to me then I had meant what I had said. It's true, at that moment, I did feel I was changing, and I did need her belief.

So I said, "What can I say? You're right. Let's shake hands and call it a day."

I held out my hand.

"Just like that?"

I said, well, wasn't just like that just how she wanted it.

"No, not that way."

"You've made your decision."

"Talk to me a little. Tell me about you."

Imagine yourself in a small, suburban living room with a carpet whose colour is, say, a friendly red. You are with someone you know well, a lover or perhaps even a spouse, with whom you have argued, who has told you everything is finished, but who has shown you a little hope. You are: a chess grandmaster, or a fencer trying to recover a disadvantageous position, or a general at a moment of crisis. You are not sure you want to win, but rules are tyrants: you must try.

I told her about my father. I was honest, that's to say I didn't mention anything about Vickie and Barbara, but was straightforward about the other facts: namely, that I didn't know how his mind worked, that his energy made me feel like an old man, that he filled me with love and hatred and anger, that I couldn't talk with him about this, that his presence was a problem likely to tip over the wobbling and slowly moving cart of my mind.

"All this is a big change for you."

"Not much. Only like Pompeii."

She laughed then, and I thought I had a chance. Her body moved towards me, a little, an unconscious movement.

Imagine such a moment, a hushed moment when the lover, or spouse (perhaps you've been unfaithful; have you been unfaithful, to a lover or, you know, the other, or to a belief?) is once again showing an emotion. True, it's only pity, but don't knock pity. Pity often wins the day, and right now, with all in the balance, you must use every available weapon. Your next move?

Mine was to lean forward, gently, and try for a kiss. Her hand was on my chest, not an unaffectionate gesture, but still holding me in check.

She said, "Same old Headingley."

Game over, battle lost.

"Another cup of tea?"

"No thanks."

Imagine, finally, the aftermath, the wondering whether to lose your temper and say there'd be another day, another battle, a bloody fight for custody, but deciding that now wasn't the moment, the peck on the cheek, the goodbyes as if to a stranger, the closing of the door, the rose bushes (Ted, the ruthless pruner), the trying for some reason to avoid the cracks as you walk down the garden path you have just been led up.

I stood in the street, taking deep breaths. The air was filled with the smell of paraffin. The heavy, sickly fumes made me a little faint. Someone was giving a barbecue, I thought, or else the teenagers had moved up to arson, but no, there they were, leaning against a lamp-post, whistling at a pretty girl who waltzed by on thin legs. I realised I had left with the glass statue. Had I picked it up without realising? Had Julie given it to me as I left, another ironic gesture?

I asked the kids where the bus station was.

"Not far," said one.

Something cracked inside me. I was a child holding on to something too big. My self-absorption began to slide away.

"He's crying," said the other. "Look at him, he is, he's crying."

"It's alright, mister," said the first, "really it is, it's alright."

I was on my knees, sobbing, staring at the ground. Pieces of Apollo and Daphne, broken now, were in my hands. I remembered my father in Rawson Market, at the time of his darkness and fatigue, preparing to leave behind everything but himself, also on his knees, also in tears. From far away came the mournful ghost of a ship's horn hooting.

The lobby of The Balmoral was filled with old-age pensioners. A spotty man in a red blazer was trying to shepherd them into an orderly flock but instead they shuffled all over, some still in their slippers, zombies released, not from a horror film, but from a nearby Butlin's camp.

The desk clerk gave me the notes with a smile, as if pleased he knew something I didn't. I opened Vickie's first: "Something came up," it said, "catch ya later." Barbara's was less ambiguous, more blunt: "This is probably the only time in my life when I've behaved like Headingley Hamer. Don't try to keep in touch."

Turning away from the desk, I was faced by an elderly couple. The man had a face like he was eating a lemon, the mouth wrinkled and sucked in. The woman held him by the arm. She was spruce in a red dress with a floral pattern, and though she looked younger, she probably wasn't, it was just that she carried the years more easily.

"Oooh, George will yer look at him," she said, evidently talking about me. "Lovely green eyes, don't you think?"

George looked at me, saying nothing.

"Oh aye," she said. "Lovely."

She bet that with eyes like that I broke all the girls' hearts. "Don't you think so, George?"

George neither agreed nor contradicted. I gagged on his stench of urine and clothes left too long in a cupboard. I saw with a certain horror he might have been the same age as my father and I realised something that may have seemed obvious. I was afraid of my father because he was old; in him I saw not only the present, my personality, but also the future, my death. I went back to reception and asked the clerk to check that there was no message from my father. There was nothing.

I got the train to Bradford. An idea came on in my head like a light bulb: this is it, I've had enough, I'm leaving for good. I walked out of the station and down the hill towards the city centre. I would catch a bus home and collect a few things. Then it would be the Intercity to London. On the other side of the street, at the edge of a pedestrian precinct, a policeman, in a uniform, was blowing his whistle and pointing. At me? There were a few moments for me to feel panic and then I thought, no, not at me, but at this fellow who is coming at me like a sprinter, faded-denim knees high and fists pumping above his head. He cannoned into my chest, and spun away, shouting, "EXCUSE ME." Now he was sprinting again and the policeman, joined by two colleagues, was after him.

I went towards Ivegate. A crowd had gathered in front of the black stone splendour of the town hall. A woman was on the steps making a speech. I didn't try to listen to what she was saying. I didn't care. There were angry faces. A woman pushed her face close to mine and tried to say something but I refused to listen. A policeman on a grey horse pushed through the crowd, aiming blows downwards with a long truncheon. I tried to hurry on but the crowd was moving now, in the opposite direction. At first I was carried backward in a slow, steady crush, then there was a wild surge and I was swept off my feet. I realised it would be impossible for me to get where I wanted to go. The crowd was a brute with ideas of its own.

If I could get to the edge of the crowd I would wait until this was all over. It was a struggle, but I made it. I would get a couple of drinks. I sat in a pub and did just that. Someone had left a copy of the *Telegraph & Argus*. "MR. HYDE OR RACIST COPYCAT?" said the headline. The story was written in typically plodding style by Gines and Gawthorne. An Asian shop keeper had been slashed with a razor and an Asian girl, seventeen, had been found on wasteground near Lumb Lane, disembowelled and murdered. A local politician had appeared on the TV speculating that the attacks had been racially motivated and had not been made by Mr. Hyde. There had been a demonstration the previous night and the owner of a Lumb Lane curry restaurant had died during a police search. Further demonstrations were expected today. At least the clocks had got that right. I had a couple more drinks and thought how the story would have been crisper if I had written it.

Looked again at the paper. A story on page five said that Charlie Laughton, Bradford businessman, one-time husband of the famous actress Diana Farrell, had been found dead in the back of a mini-cab. Foul play was not suspected. It was believed he had suffered a heart-attack.

Poor Charlie! Dead Charlie now. Drank a few more, had a little cry, not for Charlie. Thought about Julie. How could she do that? Two-backed beastliness with a pipe-smoker. Ungrateful bitch! Thought about my father and Vickie and Barbara and the trick they had pulled. Buttonholed a man at the bar. Told him to look about him, at the glasses, tables, mirrors, beer pumps. Everything was dead. Even him. Especially me. I was the nasty product of a faithless age, an age with no myth. Look at the Muslims. And the feminists. They had theirs. They believed. Heaven help us if they got to-gether. When we arise in the morning, behold, we are all dead corpses. Look out old man, I told him, and look here, I'm seeking a religious experience. Drank some more, cried some more, railed at women and the state of the world. Fuck them all, fuck all wardrobes!

At last the landlord got sick of my self-pity. I was ejected, and outside I found . . . showtime!

Thick coppery smoke rolled down towards me. A crowd moved in the opposite direction, up the steeply sloping cobbles to Cross-ley's Mill, and I went with it. The mill was on fire. The lanolin-soaked boards kindled easily and windows began to blow out, one and then another, now another, showering glass and revealing as they popped the derelict machinery in the weaving shed. A rafter fell noiselessly. The shell of an old generator glowed red and then exploded; perhaps an acid battery had been left inside. Everyone in the crowd cheered. The heat of the flames was on their faces. A bale of wool, burnt to a cinder, came from a glassless window and didn't fall but was carried upwards on a gust of wind. It seemed to float, from this distance like the banknote of Schenk's which my father had turned to a butterfly so many years before. In the distance I heard sirens, coming from all directions, all over the city. I cheered as well. Bradford was burning.

I didn't see my brother Keith often, sometimes only once a year, and though in recent years, the last four or five say, we had been comfortable with each other, I felt, not scared of him in the way I had once been, but in his shadow. Therefore I absolutely refuse to describe what Keith had been doing since 1964. Here's a character you'll have to create for yourself. Perhaps he is famous, an actor or a rock star. Or has he turned about and walked towards the middle-of-the-road? In which case he might be a lawyer, an accountant, a moderately successful businessman, number three at a firm which manufactures Oralsure, the Rolls-Royce of toothbrushes. Or perhaps he is a megalomaniac who believes himself the Harley-Davidson of contemporary poets. A barman, a bus driver, a Grade III university lecturer. An insurance man. A psychiatric nurse, an escaped mental patient with a history of violence.

Consider now: his clothes, his politics, his sexual proclivities, and possible connections between the three.

Perhaps he has had: a breakdown, a skin-graft, a debilitating nine-month attack of hepatitis.

A sex change?

No?

You don't feel inclined to play God?

Alright.

Here is the truth. Keith's story, and the story of The Five Shades of Blue, the group he had been playing in when my father left Bradford, had been a story of the 1960s. One of the group had become a builder's labourer, one had died from a heroin overdose, and the other, Gimmy, who had squirted washing-up liquid into the Sputnik tank and killed my father's fish, had grown his hair even longer, had added a few more warts to his already warty face, and was now the millionaire leader of a heavy-metal group. After Helen's death, Keith had left the group, and school, and had gone to live in London, earning a living as a musician. For a while he had been successful. He could have joined The Rolling Stones. Alright, it's a bit much asking you to believe that, but it's true, he was asked, in the summer of 1969, eight days before Brian Jones was found face down and drugged and dead in his swimming pool. Jagger and Richards had already decided he was on his way out of the band, which was why they went to Keith, whose reply was superb. He said, "My father thinks it would be an unwise career decision." Then disaster smacked into his life with the inevitable impact of a bus with no brakes. That year he lived in London with a woman, doing the things people of that time were supposed to do: fucking, dancing, smoking dope. They discussed the revolution. They speculated on whether it would be a month or a fortnight before it arrived to sweep away the banal values of English society. In preparation they read the Marxist works of Herbert Marcuse and the necromantic ones of Aleister Crowley. Remember, this was 1969. Frisbee-ownership was the mark of intellectual achievement.

And Keith was on the way up: guitarist, lover of a woman with full lips and hair the colour of Pacific sand. Everyone was agreed: The Rolling Stones needed him, not he them. He was going to make it big on his own, and it was while he basked in the radiance of this certainty that he went back to the flat one afternoon and found the living room empty, the kitchen empty, and the bed-room, empty. Not so the bathroom, and there he saw: sodden towel snaked across the floor, mirror misty with steam, drops leaving a dull brass tap, one and then another, bouncing into the bath where his girlfriend Jane lay with a movie smile on those Monroe lips. Her head rested on her left shoulder, as if there were fur or something else soft there—she liked soft things—and she wanted to rub her cheek against it. He saw the colour of the water and his first thought was that she must have been trying a new bath oil. The thought was wrong. Cuts ran up the inside of her arms, straight and deep, and not red now but almost black: like looking inside an ants' nest. She had opened her veins. He remembered asking what had happened to the razor. A picture went through his mind of it down there below the surface, its edge against the enamel of the tub, or against her wet and still-warm flesh. He said he still couldn't touch a razor-blade without a tremor.

Keith had fallen apart. Played truant from his life. Like my father, he had vanished; unlike him, he had not run off with sacks of other people's money, and he had kept in touch. Once in a while, a postcard would arrive from California, New Mexico, Hawaii, Australia, India, Tibet, and even, on one occasion, Finland.

When he came back he had lost sixty pounds and much of his hair. He had taken to wearing a beret. He kept a bedsit in London and still moved around a lot, but usually within Europe; Paris one year, Milan the next, or Lisbon, or Brussels. He was, I suppose, a bohemian. How did he make money? He was reticent on the subject. He still played guitar and admitted that sometimes he dealt in antiques, as well as books and rare prints. He was an expert on the topography of East Anglia and from time to time he would walk into a dusty, damp-smelling shop in an obscure Midlands town and emerge with a book on *Wool Manufacturing Techniques in Norfolk, 1610–1750* or *Doomy Folk: Life in the Fens* which he would sell to a dealer in Pennsylvania for thousands of dollars. He was known in the trade as Doctor Death, because of his cadaverous appearance. He knew people wherever he went and had been married five times. No one ever accused him of being afraid of commitment.

Not like me.

Keith wrapped bony arms around me and pulled me to his chest. He had been in Paris when he got my message and had come as soon as he could. "So where the hell is he?"

"I'm not sure."

"You lost him already?"

"We were in Scarborough."

"You *misplaced* the old man."

"I think he's with someone."

"A woman?"

I nodded.

"Not one of your girlfriends?" said Keith. "Maybe Aristotle got it wrong after all. Some things never change. He's the way he was and you look like you've had six kinds of shit kicked out of you."

I smiled: true enough.

"So what are you going to do about it?"

The answer was, is, that I had no idea. What happened next between my father, my brother, and myself was in no way planned; but it was a strange sort of accident.

This is how we got the gun.

The Hand of Glory was empty but, even so, the air was stuffy, so stale with beer and cigarettes it seemed no wind had blown through for years. Keith and I sat beneath one of the carved mirrors, pints of beer barely touched on the table in front of us.

"Your problem . . ."

"Yes."

". . . is you never did leave Bradford."

"I know."

"This city, I tell you, it still affects me. Last time I was in here they had Jim Reeves on the jukebox. Has he asked about Helen?"

"We didn't get round to that."

"But he knows?"

"I suppose."

"He probably doesn't feel anything at all."

"Probably not."

"The old sod."

"Yes."

"Jesus, Headingley. Is that all you can say? I think about her, often. I *dream* about her. Remember what she used to say about the corpses in the basement, how she used to say they sang to her."

"That was crap."

"I hear them."

"I never heard them. I *never* heard them."

"In my dreams she comes with them all, with Amos Bass and Twiggy and Billy Crow, and they stand in a field and sing. Bradford is burning."

"Bradford *is* burning."

"I know, I know. I don't know."

"Dead people in a field? Singing?" I said. I took Keith's face in my hands and kissed him on the lips. "You're so full of it."

The pub doors swing open and the air is disturbed, a little, you can almost see it, a jelly wobbling. A man is there: small, black, dressed in grey shoes and a creamy jacket, flattened nose like a boxer. He stands quite still, sweat on his forehead reflecting light from the mirrors, as if suddenly overwhelmed by something he has to free himself from. Freeing himself from it, smiling, he goes to the bar.

"Flash Leonard Maclaren," said Keith. "Last I heard of him he was running a club in Manchester. Was shut down when some poor bastard found his shirt stuck to his back with a switchblade. We could score some dope. Maclaren always knows the man."

Maclaren had got his drink. He looked over at our table. Glasses were raised. Eyebrows were hemmed and hawed, and we followed him to the toilet. The barman looked at us in disbelief. How could three people be so obvious about dealing drugs?

Where the bar was cavernous and hot, the toilet was cavernous and cool, with grey marble on the floor and thin light issuing through windows of frosted glass.

Silent.

Another man was in there, thinner and much taller than Maclaren, a giant in a shiny blue suit. Where had he come from? I hadn't seen him come in. Perhaps, like my father, he judged places according to whether they had exits both front and rear. Maclaren smiled; the man who had come from nowhere did not.

"Who are the pinkies?"

"These guys are friends."

"Not friends of *mine*. I got the friends I need."

"Hey man, it's cool," I said.

Observe the naturalness of the fellow, this Headingley!

"*Hey man,* just listen to this, he says it's cool," said the man in the suit, smiling. He had his hair slicked back and wore many gold chains. A black jaundice seemed to have deepened the black of his skin. He might as well have had a sign stamped on his forehead: EVIL DUDE DRUG DEALER. One of the chains jingled as he moved a wrist upwards, slowly.

A gun was suddenly at the end of that languid wrist, and pointing at me. Nor was this any ordinary gun; it was huge. He said, "Now then, Mr. Pinkie, my good friend, my *man,* there's a riot out there and the pigs are hitting citizens with sticks and shields and a brother I knew, a guy who had served me food, who had eaten with me, who had shared my table, was killed last night and you think *it's cool*?"

The sound of water rushing came from the urinals.

"You wanna new hole in your face?"

I coughed on disinfected air.

"You know what this is? A .357 Magnum, just like the one Clint Eastwood uses. *Blow your head clean off,*" he said, but with no smile and with the gun still aimed at my head. "*Make my day*. You think that would be 'cool'?"

I said nothing. There were yellow splotches on the floor and a vague mist was rising; outside it was sunny. I was looking down the barrel. It was like . . . Of course I did not think the gun was like a penis, or like anything else for that matter, what I really thought was that it could be the end of my life, now, and I had a picture of myself, nose down on the cold marble, watching blood—hey, this is mine!—as it spread thickly in a pool, taking my last breath, of Dettol and piss. That was how extinction could be.

"No," I said.

There was a silence. Maclaren had that look again, as if he was fighting to free himself from something.

"A warrant card!" he said. "You ever seen one?"

"*What?*" said the man with the gun.

"The real thing. Taken from a fucking DCI, a fucking Detective Chief Inspector in the fucking drugs squad, only last night."

"No use to me."

"No use at all, man, but *amusing*. This guy came into The Persy last night, with a yellow and green hat, oh man he looked like he was in fancy dress, and he was talking like he was in *The Black and White Minstrel Show*, Bob Marley this, ganga that, so we took him outside, took off his pants, and tied him to the bumper of his car. Not a hair on his head was touched."

"It does make me laugh."

"Yours, man. It's yours, I mean it. It's a gift."

"Thanks," said the man with the gun, and, not a laugh, but at least a smile. "It *is* funny." He balanced the gun on a ledge in the tile. He turned the warrant card in his fingers. "Now: what am I going to do with the pinkies."

He turned to me. "You want to buy the gun, pinkie?"

"No thanks."

"No thanks. Very polite. But you didn't understand what I said. You *want to* buy the gun. We're talking about a statement here, not an interrogative."

"You want to sell me the gun?"

"Give pinkie the Nobel Prize!"

Appreciative laughter from Maclaren, who was smiling more happily now. "Come on, make my friend happy, buy the gun. I'll throw in the ash for nothing."

"How much?" said Keith.

"How much do you have?"

We had eighty-five pounds.

"The very sum I had in mind."

Keith handed him the money, he handed me the gun. "Wasn't loaded," he said, reaching into his left waistcoat pocket. "Just the three bullets left, unfortun-a-te-ly." He stretched the last syllables while we thought, as he knew we would, of what had happened to the other three. I stood there stupidly, gun in hand. He gave me the bullets.

He said, "It has been a unique pleasure doing business with you," and walked to the door. He paused for a final thrust: "So long, *brothers.*"

Then it was Maclaren, as we came out of the toilet: "Don't worry about it, he hates white people, it's one of his manias, he's got quite a few, he thinks he's the angel of death, he comes, he goes, you never know when, he could fuck up a Stradivarius just by looking at it."

"For a moment I thought . . ." said Keith. "You know. I was scared."

"Wrong. *Terribly* wrong. He quite liked you guys. If he hadn't . . ." said Maclaren, leaving the sentence hanging, and leaving me with a ton of metal in my raincoat pocket. Once again I felt stupid, as if I were a character in a play. I didn't know what to do with the gun. Throw it away? It wasn't something you could just leave on a table in The Hand of Glory. Now I know that props have a way of imposing their own logic.

We found my father, eventually, in The Oddfellows. He was drunk and with a woman, which was true to form, though the woman was not Vickie, or Barbara, as I had expected, but a skinny thing called Nancy, a dental nurse on her day off. My father had met her the day before, when he went to have his tooth fixed.

"His head was buzzing like a hive of bees," she said. Her accent was Northern Irish, very soft. She turned to Keith: "What would your name be?"

"Keith," said Keith, staring at my father.

Then it was my turn.

"Headingley," I said, also looking at him.

"What do you do?"

"What?"

Nancy's elbow jabbed me. "What's the matter, not interested in girls? I asked you what you did. I'm expecting a reply. Or do you plan to send a telegram?"

"A journalist."

"A *writer*?"

"Of sorts."

"I was a writer. Well, like you, a writer of sorts. I was a typist." She continued: she had also been a barmaid, a bank clerk, a waitress, she had sold insurance not very well at all and had travelled with an English repertory company in a farce called *The Tart and the Vicar's Wife*. She had played both roles.

"I'm twenty," she said. "And I cleaned house once for this fellow in London, really ugly he was, he'd been a welfare officer in Glasgow, turned out he was nothing but a pimp. Used to boast that one of his girls earned five thousand pounds a week. More than I get in a year dental nursing."

"Did you consider the job opportunity?" I said.

"You," she said. "You're nothing but a saucy devil. Do you believe in alternative medicine? That's what I've been practising on your dad. Quite an abscess he's got there, just waiting to explode, could go off like a balloon. But an operation won't be necessary, once I've got on top of him. I'll make it go away by effort of will, well not exactly by effort of will. Sex is surgery for the soul."

My father looked at me. I suppose my face must have been showing something, amazement probably, because he threw back his head and gave the Hamer laugh. He was enjoying himself. I imagined him in Brazil, in South Africa, all over the world in situations like this; admirable circumstances for a fellow to see the elephant.

"So," said Keith. "How's tricks, Dad?"

"You're Jack's son," said Nancy.

"That's right."

"Me too," I said.

My father wasn't listening. He grinned boozily, and downed another whisky. I wondered about Vickie and Barbara; if they weren't with him, then where were they?

"Dad," I said. "Where are they?"

"Who?" The voice was Nancy's, not his.

"Barbara."

"Who's Barbara?" said Nancy.

"And Vickie?"

"Who's Vickie?"

"I say, Headingley. Would you mind doing the honours? Here's a tenner. Mine's a Johnnie Walker, you know, large one. And get a half-bottle of the same, just to be on the safe side."

He was in a fog.

"Come on old man, a fellow could die for a drink."

"We're all dying, and that's it."

"Will you just listen to this?" said Nancy, giving me another in the midriff. "He's a philosopher."

I went to the bar and got the drinks.

Then I was Mr. Jovial and Hearty. I asked whether he wouldn't rather be somewhere quieter, where we could have a drink and a good old chin-wag, after all there was so much catching up to do. He merely stared into the glass I had just given him. It was Nancy who replied.

"A private party," she said, "that would be excellent."

"Nancy," I said. "Keith and I would like to speak with our dad alone."

"Are we off now then?" she said.

I said, "Do you mind, we'll meet you later?"

"Is this place far? I tell you what, you and Keith go ahead, I'll bring your dad on behind. We'll follow."

"No, no," said my father. "Want to talk to Headingley. Played nasty trick on Headingley."

"What was that?" I said.

"Vickie, Barbara, and me, we conned him. Sent him to see his wife. But they conned me."

"You don't say?"

"Do too. It was the double-whammy. We fucked you, they

fucked me. This was their life, these were their purposes. Went off with my money when we were in Bird. And good luck to them. Damned attractive woman."

"I don't believe you."

"Absolutely old man."

I didn't want to believe him. On the other hand: where *were* Vickie and Barbara? "This life business," he said. "I don't mind telling you, Headingley, I'm a worried man. Look, I'll knock on my head. Sounds like a coconut doesn't it? That's because I'm perplexed."

We got him out of the pub and into the car park. He gulped in air and windmilled his arms, trying to sober up. "Fuck and fuck off," he said. "Maybe that's what it's all about. The world must move on. Man must move on." He sat down with a bump on the concrete and contemplated his shoes, which were yellow under the sodium street-lights. "Always tell a gent by the state of his foot-wear. Look at the gleam on those brogues. Like gold. What do you say, boys?"

Keith and I struggled with this truculent freight. He didn't want to get up on his feet.

"Sod the both of you. I say they're the toe-clobber of a gent and no question."

Nancy came up and asked if we were managing. If we wanted her opinion, it seemed pretty much like we couldn't keep the old boy in hand. We needed help.

"The target for tonight," said my father. "Is somewhere in northern France. Sex appeal bombing."

"We'd better get him up on his feet," said Nancy.

I told her Keith and I would manage.

"I'll help."

"It's alright."

"I insist."

I put my face close to hers. "Piss off," I said.

"Don't fool around," she said.

"I mean it. Put it this way, if you don't piss off I'll thump you one."

Was I serious? She wasn't sure. I raised my fist and she stepped back, a little afraid now. My heart did a jig around her fear. For some reason I reached inside my pocket and showed her the gun. "Fuck off," I said. "Cunt."

She stared at me, certainly not as she had in the pub, as if she were about to launch into discussion of ley lines or the lost crystals on which were encoded the secrets of Atlantis, and not as she had only a few moments before, but with a new awareness, as if she had at last recognised I wasn't her, I was different, a terrible confirmation of everything she feared about my sex. I was Mr. Hyde!

We got him into Keith's car, which was rented, and new, with the seat covers still on. Smells of plastic and a sickly pine air-freshener. My father was in the back, happy with the half-bottle, not noticing that Nancy had run into the pub. He wouldn't stop talking. "Take time," he said. "Damned if I understand it at all. There's this idea that time just goes tick-tock, and the Devil himself, probably he looks a bit like a pirate, a bit like that Aussie quickie, what's his name, Dennis Lillee, anyway Old Nick is there with a cricket ball, tossing it from hand to hand, saying 'life,' " he slapped his hands together, " 'death,' " another slap, " 'life,' " and so on, regular as, well, clockwork, counting and counting, each cricket ball slap sending us closer to the grave.

"But you see it's not really like that, not all the time. I remember, I was flying, this was in the war of course, things looked pretty hairy, and that old chestnut—your life flashing before your eyes— well, I assure you old man, it started to happen, and it was in the smallest detail as if everything had been written in a handy handbook and someone was up there in my head, not hollow like a coconut in those moments, reading it out, except I could see it all of course, my head was so clear, like I'd had a whiff of very strong mustard.

"There I was at the *conversazione* in Saltaire, with Lillian, it must have been one of the very first times we went out, just kids, only sixteen or so, and she was in a red dress, matched the fire in her hair, and Charlie Payne, running around her he was, sniffing like a ferret, asking for the next waltz. Now the thing about Charlie Payne was that he was five feet nothing but he had this giant chopper. All Bradford knew about it. That chopper of Charlie Payne's, it was a legend. So Lillian has the dance, she comes back and I ask what was it like and she says, 'Fine. Except he had this filthy great pipe in his pocket.'

"There I was, in the Odeon, with Jimmy Randall, we'd be no more than seven, should have been at school I suppose, but Jimmy's dad, who was a little funny in the head, had given us ten bob, a fortune then, and told us not to bother with school. So, it's Jimmy and me, in the front row, right beneath the Wurlitzer, loud laughs and snotty noses, watching Dougie Fairbanks, not reading the cards but making our own lines come out from his lips, making our own swashbuckler. 'Still enough strength to run you through, you cad!'

"There I was aged three on the step outside the kitchen door. I've just filled my pants with shit and my mother is there, she doesn't have to say anything, the reddening of my face is punishment enough.

"There I was in my first job, before the war, before I came into the business, that's where I met Lillian, a curvy little thing in grey overalls, it was at Butterfields and I was in the office that made up the wages and one week the driver and the guard were both off sick so it was me they picked, 'Git thissen off to that bank, Jack,' which I did and collected the money in big sacks, forty grand it was. And I thought: I could have it away with this lot, easy as pie, but my conscience said 'No.'

"And there I was, getting on for thirty years later, I've done the dirty on Schenk and Charlie Laughton, and I've got the money from the Minis, a tidy bundle, and there's my conscience again, 'NO!' it says, this time with an exclamation mark. So what do I do? I leave anyway. So I reckon your conscience has to be a big empty room where one door closes and another swings open.

"And there I was, there I was, there I was . . . The point is, of course, what if somewhere I'm still in the Lanc with the starboard inner gone already and the starboard outer not too clever either, reliving every moment of my life, that's to say, I'm there for ever, in that somewhere, and perhaps—who knows?—there are other somewheres and in each of them I can never catch up, because each moment that passes is another that I'll have to relive in glorious Technicolor. So what do you think about that?"

Then he passed out. "Thank God for that," said Keith.

We dragged him up the two flights to the front door of the flat off Manningham Lane. The scrape of his heels on the linoleum was like cats fighting. We got him into the flat and sat him on a wobbly dining-room chair, oak, one of a set of three, they were the only furniture in the place, I'd bought them from the white-haired fellow who'd once been a doctor and now had a junk shop on Manningham Lane. How much had I paid? Five, I think, or had it been a tenner? Keith fetched a bucket of water from the kitchen and emptied it over my father's head.

That woke him up. He made loud snorts and shook his head, spraying water over the floor and walls. Little beads ran ran ran down the white paint. He stared at Keith and seemed puzzled, as if seeing him for the first time. I wondered whether he would ask what had happened to Nancy, but no, it was something else: "Now who are you? Not you Headingley, I know you, but the other fellow, with the funny hat. He was in the pub. He's here right now."

"Dad, it's Keith," said Keith.

"Keith?"

I thought he would say something along the lines of "Sorry, son. I left you in it," or "Good to see you old man," or maybe just "Hello," something which would break the ice, since there was ice to be broken, without question, after all it had been Keith who had been taken to the police station in 1964, it had been Keith who Charlie Laughton had come to see to ask if he knew anything about the money which had gone or about the cars which my father had sold without paying the manufacturers, who were now after *him,* it was Keith who had been left in the shit. But no apology was made. Instead he swigged from the half-bottle of Johnnie Walker.

"I've never seen that fellow before in my life," he said.

"Dad, it's Keith," I said.

"That's not Keith. Keith's my son."

"He doesn't recognise me. Hasn't the foggiest."

"I'm hungry," said my father, as if this too were a statement concerning his own nature or the nature of time. He smacked his lips loudly. "Right now I could get outside a rainbow trout. And a dish of Jersey spuds, sweet and buttery."

Keith said, "I don't believe it. The fucker doesn't know who I am."

"With nutmeg. Yes, nutmeg! But not too much."

Keith said, "Dad. Pay attention."

"What's that?"

Keith shouted, "LISTEN!"

"I'm all ears. Even my tootsies are lugs. Look!" He waggled a toe. "Are you paying attention down there? Listen to the man with the head furniture."

Keith said, "Right now. Is there anything you want to say?"

"What's that? *Want to stay?* So you're giving me the deeds to the ranch?" His gaze slid over the dodgy chairs and the rotting bare boards. "Well, very generous of you and all that, but this is one ranch I'm not sure I want, pardner."

He hummed the theme from the TV show *Bonanza*.

Keith said, "Give me the gun, Headingley. You're going to die. Do you understand?"

"Little Joe! Little Joe!"

I took out the gun, but didn't give it to Keith.

"I say, Headingley, I haven't thought of that for years, that's what I'd call you and you'd get angry because you liked the fat one with the tall hat."

"Hoss," I said.

"Hoss. That's right. And once, when you were watching, you were making one of your plastic aeroplanes, a twin-engined thing . . ."

"A Bristol Beaufighter."

"And you swallowed the tail-plane. We drove to St. Luke's Hospital at twice the speed limit, do you . . . what's that you've got? Looks like a gun."

Stage-property logic was taking over: what is shown in the second act must be used in the third.

Keith said, "You're going to die."

"What?"

"I always hated you, you bastard."

"What?" said my father.

"Headingley and I are going to kill you."

"You miserable fuck," I said.

"You can't do that."

"Why the fuck not?" said Keith.

I said, "We're going to blow your head off."

. . .

Let's get Freud into the act. Alright, so in some areas he is a questionable authority. He believed, for instance, that "jokes could not be dealt with otherwise than in connection with the comic." Listen to that applause: *way to go Sigmund!* When it comes to myths of the father, however, Freud is our man. He knew all about the loving father, the cruel father, the father the son must avenge, the father the son must carry on his shoulders, and the lost father, the absent father, the prodigal. My father had always come into this last category and he himself knew it. Rather, he gloried in it. He would evoke *David Copperfield* and Mr. Micawber. "Talent, Mr. Micawber had, Capital, Mr. Micawber had not," he would say, adding his own twist. "Talent, Jack Hamer has. Capital, he has also, but with a regrettable tendency to use as income faster than it can accumulate." Thus: the prodigal. But in the last weeks, since he had come back to Bradford, my father had moved up a step or two, more than that, in fact right to the top of the pyramid of the father myth, located somewhere in Thebes with an ugly dead bird at the bottom. He had become the father the son must kill. Traditionally, stories of this sort work out in a certain way: the father gets dead, the son gets dead also, and if he doesn't he becomes The Man Nobody Wants to Invite to Dinner Again. Think of *Hamlet,* where the ghost of Hamlet's father demands that his murderer be killed in turn. But the murderer is Hamlet's uncle, now married to Hamlet's mother, so Hamlet must avenge his ex-father by killing his new one. Two father-myths are thus combined and nobody is surprised when Hamlet doesn't make it through the fifth act. Best thing all round, reflects Headingley, seersucker-wearing drama critic in the front stalls. Think how tricky Elsinore small-talk would be, were he left standing.

What I'm saying is this, that stories where sons decide to kill their fathers tend not to work out well, it's the nature of the genre, and since I'm the teller here and you're the reader, we have a relationship from the jungle ("Me Tarzan, you come to tree-house, listen to improbable tales of adventure"), I thought I should warn you: despite the knockabout stuff this one will also end badly.

Where was I?

With a gun in my hand and a situation out of control.

Keith was hysterical, red in the face, screaming that I should give him the gun.

"That's a gun," said my father.

"I'm going to shoot you."

"No you're not."

"Oh and why's that?"

"You're my son."

The gun went boom, which was surprising, and quite nice.

My arm jerked up and, as if attached by a wire, a chair cushion, not from the chair my father was sitting in, but another, was lifted into the air and hurled against the wall.

I moved closer, holding the gun at arm's length with my right hand locked over my left wrist, as if I were on TV. It was at that moment, I think, that my father realised we were really trying to kill him. Imagine you are watching a film: the lens zooms in close on my father's face while, simultaneously, moving quickly away, producing an effect of vertigo, as if the hero is on a crowded beach and realises the man-eating shark is there, only yards offshore, preparing to attack. You see: fear, and that's what I want you to picture when you imagine my father at this moment. He had seen a threat to life and it was me, about to fire again.

"Headingley, you're drunk."

"No, you're drunk."

"You're right. I am drunk. But you're the bloody nuisance."

Turning to Keith, ignoring me, he tried to bluff it out.

"Headingley is an uncivil sort of fellow," he said. "Don't you think this is remarkably uncordial behaviour? Nancy wouldn't like it. Remarkable popsy, that. She knows all about guns. Worked in a circus with some fellow she knew from Londonderry. He'd knocked about with the IRA. Ended up doing eight to twelve for armed robbery. He needed the cash, you see. Politics and poverty just don't get along very well."

Keith said, "Get closer. *Shoot the fucker.*"

I was telling myself, line up the front-sight, don't pull the trigger, squeeze it.

"Oh no old man you can't shoot me."

"Says who?"

"You're forgetting about time. You see, I'm not really here. It's the night of June 12, 1944, a hundred-ship show over Frankfurt, flak popping all over the place, five minutes while we drop the load, just a few minutes. T for Terence has taken a hit, right up the rear. Nasty. I've seen it happen before. They'll be washing tail-end charlie out with a hose. That was Burgess. Fancied himself the Romeo, a regular canteen cowboy. Not any more.''

Boom!

And strike two: this time it was the turn of a tile behind the gas fire; fragments leaped up, spun in the light, slowly, tiny shapes of brown and red, it seemed that I saw each and watched them all as they came tinkling down.

Now I had one shot. My father was in a panic. He ran to the door. Blocked, by Keith. Shouted wildly and ran to the window. Stuck, too much Dulux gloss, courtesy of my decorator, the grue-somely named E. T. Deadman. Now the victim-to-be was beaten and in retreat, sliding along the wall from the window to the corner of the room, where he bumped down and hugged his knees to his chest.

Keith said, "Give me the gun."

I told him I would handle it.

"Don't fuck up."

"I'll *handle* it."

"Make the fuck sure you do."

"Watch his head. It's about to go pop like a toad run over."

Enter the brothers Hamer, B-movie hoods!

I know, you're thinking that Headingley has lost contact with reality, and his feelings. I had. And you want to know what I felt? I know what I felt. Exhilaration, power. I was about to destroy him and I felt *great*. I was tap-dancing on the grave of my history. So much for the taboo against patricide. I wouldn't be just killing my father, I'd be killing something of myself, something I would be better without. I'd swallowed a hundred suns.

In the corner, he was getting ready for a last throw. He made a face like a rat: nose screwed up, squinty eyes. Then he gave me his warmest smile. "Step outside," he said. "We'll settle this like men. Or are you chicken?"

This was supposed to be cunning? He thought I'd fall for this? I felt the urge to spit in his face.

"Don't be absurd. I'm going to kill you now, with this," I said, waggling the gun. "Boxing gloves will not be required."

"This is bloody diabolical."

"I know."

"This really isn't fair at all."

"Who taught me that life is supposed to be? Not you, that's for sure. The only thing you ever taught me was how to tie a half-windsor knot, a difficult skill, a skill I value, getting that triangle just-so and tucked into the collar, but it's not the same as 'Son, here is all I have learned, the ABC of how to be a man, here are the keys to life itself.' " I gave him one with my shoe, and then another. Boot, boot! "You old git."

"Quit pissing about," said Keith. "Shoot."

I paused, relishing the moment of essential desire and gratification. To kill your father! It's suicide, without the obvious disadvantage. And I pulled the trigger, knowing this time I could not miss.

I missed.

"You missed!" said Keith. "I don't believe it."

I had missed.

My father was inspecting the hole, large as a grapefruit, which had been punched in the plaster behind him. "That's not a gun," he said, with his hands in his hair, perhaps contemplating what had nearly happened to his head. "It's a sodding cannon."

Keith and I exchanged a look. He shrugged, I shrugged. What now? We were confused.

But from my father, resignation at last! He didn't know I had only three bullets. Naturally he presumed I had three more. His face said he knew it was all over. His expression was doleful.

He said, "I used to see myself as a bird, flying from one thing to another. I thought I'd never come back to the nest, but I did, I'm not sure why. It wasn't the money. I didn't give a damn about the money. I only went to get the money because it was in Scarborough and it was so close and Vickie and Barbara seemed pretty damned keen on the idea, no wonder since they were planning to pinch the lot. Good luck to them. I hope they enjoy spending it. I don't give a damn. I've been taking things as they come. I wanted to see Headingley and Keith and Helen, I was looking forward to seeing her, she was the best of all of you, always the best, she had such grace, and life, and she was a jewel in the palm of my hand and it hurts here . . ."

Tearful, he fingered the conventional point on his chest, unaware he sounded like Henry Irving, in the Palace Theatre at the end of Manningham Lane, dying theatrically. Keith had his hand over his mouth, like a bad boy in the back row. I caught his eye. I too began to giggle.

My father, meanwhile, was failing to appreciate the hysterical humour of the situation.

"It hurts here that I'm not going to see her again. And I'll tell you something else. I'd been away all that time, I'd been all over the world, and I was alone and I was bored. So bored I was ready to rush into Bradford, black filthy Bradford, and kiss the ruddy town-hall steps."

Which was of course a cue for his sons: laughter.

"Go ahead," said my father, suddenly angry. "I don't give a toss."

"Go ahead, he doesn't give a toss," said Keith, trying to be grave, but unable to keep it up.

"So why don't you? I wish you'd never been born. You were the result of second-rate couplings, it's a miracle you were conceived at all, and no surprise you turned out to be a pair of miserable milk-soppy buggers," he said. His voice was honeyed malice. But then he yelled: *"Shoot me!"*

I was out of control now, with my head down between my knees, laughing so hard I was scarcely able to breathe. The words came between gasps, "No . . . more . . . bullets."

He didn't understand.

I dropped the gun. It fell with a clatter.

"It's empty."

"No more bang-bang," said Keith. "I'm going to pee my pants."

My father still hadn't got it. He moved across the room. His progress was furtive, as if he thought we would use violence to stop him, then he picked the gun up quickly, raised it, and pulled the trigger, *click!* And again, *click!*

"Well, I'll be buggered," he said.

An image popped up—from childhood, a light shining all of a

sudden through a hole in a curtain—of my mother and the brown-eyed handsome man. I said, "If such is your preferred *modus operandi*."

Then there was a strange noise, an animal noise which grew louder and louder, until it filled the room. My father was howling.

"I'm going to kill *you*," he said, charging at me with his arms outstretched, but he made no better job of it than I had, because his hands were shaking so much, from rage, or from shock, that he couldn't get a grip on my throat, and because Keith picked up the chair whose cushion had been shot away and brought it down over his head, which caused, not pain, but rather surprise since my father's head popped through the hole where the cushion had been and his arms were no longer outstretched but trapped by his sides, held prisoner by the wood frame.

He blundered about: "I'll have your balls, you little fuckers!"

It would be wrong to say that the clumsy attempts at murder, the business with the chair, and the hysteria of three men who did not know what they felt about each other provided a catharsis and that fifteen minutes later they were sitting, comfortably, chumming it up, warmly, debating Hamer family history, reasonably. There was no such scene. Things did calm down, however. Keith freed my father from the chair, I brought three glasses from the kitchen and splashed whisky about, and we stood at a distance from each other. The intensity of what each of us had felt was reflected in the silence of the other two. The silence was awkward and went on for a long time. After a while Keith asked how Tom was, and Julie. I explained, she'd left me, taking Tom with her, and he said sorry, sorry, he remembered that I'd told him before. My father talked to Keith, apologising for not having recognised him, and asked how he was, what he did, if he'd been married, and if he had any children. Keith explained that he'd been married five times. None of the marriages had lasted very long. No kids.

"Let's be honest lads," said my father, sadly. He was sober now; fear seemed to have done that to him. "We've not been top of the averages in this department. Not a wild success with women, any of us. Not exactly. My fault. The old man didn't offer much of an example. Did I? I fucked up good."

Keith didn't say anything; neither did I.

My father wept, silently and steadily. I looked at him, looked down at the floorboards, turned to Keith and asked: "What now?"

"I don't know," said Keith.

We spoke as if my father were not in the room.

"Maybe I'll go to London tomorrow. There's a girl in Paris, I promised I'd pick her up a pair of ear-rings."

"Maybe I'll come with you."

"Why not? Get away from this place."

"Don't go lads," said my father. "Stay a while. Let's get to know each other. Like a real family." He staggered, and spilled whisky from his glass. He looked pathetic, guilty, desperate. His unhappiness made me embarrassed. I wasn't sure what to say. I didn't know whether I wanted to hurt him or not. There was another silence.

And another twist: look, the door is opening and here are three policemen in uniform, they're plodding in, followed by Weekes, wearing his blue suit and smelling of peppermints, with Nancy close behind. It was she who had gone to the police, and Weekes who was now directing the scenario. At a nod from him one copper went through to the kitchen, another came and stood by me, while the third went over to Keith. He himself picked up the gun, as if he had known he would find it, just there, on the floor. He smiled and then quickly straightened his face, as if that particular gesture was not in the script; he didn't wish to gloat.

"That was a very wrong thing you tried to do, and I hope you're ashamed of yourself," Nancy said to me. "The police are here and they'll be taking you to jail for sure." Then she whispered in my ear: "Who's the cunt now?"

"This is the one," said Weekes, placing a hand on the shoulder of my father, whose response to the touch was calm and smiling.

"Hello Weekesy old man," he said.

"Long time, Jack," said Weekes, and his hand tightened its deliberate, almost friendly grip. "Now then, lads. Do what you have to."

The uniformed police surrounded my father, and one of them read him his rights, reading from a card to be sure he got it spot on.

". . . right to remain silent."

Nancy watched the handcuffs put on. "Not him. Him and *him,*" she said, pointing at Keith, at me.

". . . anything you do say may be taken down and used as evidence in a court of law."

"Those two." She stood in front of Weekes and pointed at us. "Say something, Jack, tell them."

"It's all hunky-dory Nan, don't worry. These fellows are doing their job, that's all," said my father. "Isn't that right, Weekesy?"

"That's right," said Weekes. "How've you been, Jack?"

"Grand."

"You're looking fit."

"I'm *grand*. And yourself."

"Oh, middling, middling-to-fair. You know how it is."

"I do, you're quite right old man, I do."

There was a silence, and some uneasy shuffling about, and then at last Weekes said: "Come on, Jack. Let's be having you."

"They were trying to kill him," Nancy said, but it was as if she wasn't there, for Weekes had the face of a man who has seen a vision, long hoped for and at last witnessed.

"Suck my pig," he said. "I've only gone and caught Jack Hamer."

At first my father was on remand outside Leeds, in Armley, a bad jail, overcrowded and violent, where he was bunked with a Liverpudlian who had held up a betting shop using a toy gun. It could have been worse. In the next cell one man stabbed another in the leg with a sharpened spoon after an argument over whose turn it was for the *Playboy* centrefold. The Liverpudlian's name was Leonard Swales Mosby. He was generous and funny, with a red face and cheeks scarred by acne. He called my father "The famous Elizabethan adventurer Sir Jack De Fucking Hamer, on account of the dead posh way he talks."

I reported the trial. That was Budge Carter's doing, of course, his little joke. The clocks appreciated it; they ticked their amusement and paraded it on their otherwise blank faces each time I came back from court.

"Been to Sunday school lessons?" Gines would say.

"Learn anything from the master criminal?" Gawthorne would say.

Then the two of them would start up with the theme from

Batman, and it would be Budge's turn: "Watch out Robin. Here comes . . . *The Joker!*"

I smiled, I laughed, I played it any way they wanted. Even when Schenk made a brief and mysterious appearance at the trial, sitting in the visitors' gallery, dressed in an expensive suit, smiling as if he had somehow been responsible for my father's capture, and disappeared again, leaving me puzzled and anxious, even then I wasn't going to let them know what I felt. Since I didn't know exactly what I did feel, this might not be saying much, but I wasn't going to let them see *anything.* "Gines, you know you really are very good," I would say. "You too Gawthorne. I don't think Budge knows how good. Budge, do you know how good these two boys are?"

"Fuck off," Budge would say. Or something.

I wrote the stories: "WAR HERO ADMITS TO FRAUD!"; "BRADFORD MAN STAGED HIS OWN DEATH SAYS KILL ME AGAIN!"; "HOW TO SPEND A FORTUNE IN FIFTEEN MONTHS!"; "HAMER GETS SIX YEARS! *Shouts 'See you in Hollywood' as led from dock!*" Even Budge said they were the best work I'd done and, I suppose I shouldn't have been surprised, there was a call from Fleet Street. I was offered a job in London.

"Well done Scoop," said Budge Carter, as if he really was an editor from one of those films Helen had liked so much. "Always knew you had it in you. Those were good crates."

Gines and Gawthorne were without expression. Their worst fear had come suddenly true. The clocks ticked slow. I would go to London, they would stay, here, in Bradford, and what if it were for ever?

Julie called. She wanted to know about my father. I told her the truth: that they hadn't even given bail because they were afraid he'd jump the country, that he'd added at least two years to his sentence by calling counsel for the prosecution "old man" throughout the trial, that he didn't care for slopping out, or carbolic soap, or the smell of a thousand men in a building together, but was more taken with prison food than he'd thought he would be.

"You've seen him, in Armley?"

"A few times."

"So?"

"So what?"

"What do you feel?"

I was silent.

She said, "You don't know what you feel. As usual. You don't feel as though you're really there."

I told her she'd got that wrong, I didn't find myself observing myself and him, I was a participant alright, but it was with an avant-garde theatre group performing somewhere remote and right-on, Hull perhaps or Lancaster, and I was required to masturbate in public while wearing boxing gloves. During my visits to Armley he had been embarrassed, had laughed too much, and had called me "son" very often. I had replied without thinking and had often glanced towards the younger warder with the Zapata moustache who had always responded with a smirk which seemed to suggest he knew about my habits and character—I was a liar, a wanker, a nose-picker, a reveller in sexual perversion—and that because of these qualities of mine he would make my father's life a misery for sure and perhaps even introduce him to a couple of characters who worked in the prison hospital and had revolutionary ideas about trepanning.

Julie said, "Are you OK?"

"I miss you."

"I miss *you*."

"There was something strange, at the trial, someone turned up, an old enemy of my father's. A very nasty fellow."

"What did he want?"

"I'm not sure, and then he vanished, like a ghost."

We chatted some more about the trial, and my father, and this and that. I said, "We could go back. As we were the first day in Lister Park."

"It isn't the first day Headingley."

"It could be."

She said she knew what would happen: I would go back to spending one night with her, the next with Barbara, telling lies with face-straining solemnity, as if the biblical tone made them credible.

"Not me," I said.

That brought a laugh. We were enacting a familiar scene now. "How can you read me so wrong?" I said.

"Do you think I do?"

"I love you. I have always loved you. I will always love you."
She hung up.

One day, a few days later, a few days before I was due to go to
London, a Thursday, an unusually warm day, Gines and Gawthorne were absurd in baggy shorts I remember, she came to see
me. I leaned back—feet on the desk, arms behind my head, oh I
was casual—and watched her nervous progress across the office,
knowing I had won, because she could be here for only one reason:
she wanted to try again. I considered my position. I could be
neutral, I could be forgiving, I could be angry. Or superbly dismissive: *go get buttfucked by a magician!*

But she wasn't here to talk about that, nor did she want to know
if I was seeing Barbara, or Vickie, or someone else, she wasn't
interested in any of it. Something had happened. She fiddled with
her brown leather bag, it wouldn't sit just so on her shoulder, and
for some reason I remembered her nervousness in banks, she hated
banks, and a time, years before, when we had been making love and
she had whispered, *"Inconnu,* stranger."

"Julie, what is it?"

Her head cracked and for a moment I was inside, pulling up her
dreams like fish: here's one, she was surfing, on a glide down a
wave like a tube which she knew would fold in on itself before she
came out, another, on the run with a middle-aged Conservative
politician who was disguised, for some reason, as a Rastafarian, and
a third, with a storm roaring and howling outside and Julie in the
loved familiar world of her grandmother's bedroom with soft sheets
pulled to the chin and the overwhelming smell of camphor.

She told me that Tom was dead.

I know, you're thinking that I've told you before about death,
that my mother died, and my father. This time, as with Helen, it's
true. Reality had come in with a surprise. Julie wasn't crying. Her
face was blank. Our son had been killed, knocked down by a car
outside the house on Neil Armstrong Way. Tom was dead.

Part Four

GOING TO SEE THE ELEPHANT

I didn't go to Fleet Street. I went to High Royds, the mental hospital I told you about, with the towers like rockets on a launch pad, and I'd been there, I don't know how long, a week, a month, a *while,* I'd lost touch with time, when I met the Devil. It was in the garden, where I walked each afternoon. The garden was silent, enclosed, with crisp hedges and lawns cut with such unnerving precision that they might have been diagrams.

He was an unthreatening presence. True, he made me feel like a child and he did have on the uniform, that's to say, he was dressed in black from head to toe: black shirt buttoned at the collar, black suit, black boots. What struck me was his gentleness. "I have just been to the bank," he said, in a husky voice, so soft it seemed to be on the point of drifting away. "Do you like banks?" I said I had no strong feelings about banks one way or the other. He whispered that he hated banks. He always had such trouble in banks. "Ask me anything," he said. "Anything at all." So I asked about where he lived. What was the landscape like? Aside from the obvious— murderers, rapists, blasphemers—who, and what, else had been sent to hell? Were there: politicians, Ford Sierras, suits by Cecil Gee, muggers, mini-cab drivers, movies with Shirley Maclaine, cricketers who had played for Surrey, estate agents, debt collectors, grey shoes (I imagined rooms, entire stately homes, stuffed with grey shoes), condoms, cocktail bars, and prizes for poets?

We discussed metaphysics to the accompaniment of the *adagietto* from Mahler's Fifth. I looked around the garden. I saw no orchestra. I asked the big things, the obvious things: life after death; heaven and hell; the world outside the self and its existence; the survival of the planet. Given that he, the Devil, existed, and presumably God as well (he smiled, a little ruefully), and God was omniscient, seeing both future and past simultaneously, he knew what I was getting at, the old free will thing . . . in what sense can a human being be said to make any of his or her choices freely—or is it that God is merely a story invented by man to explain his own sense of helplessness?

He smiled again. "Yes," he said. "God is merely man's invention. Through every abyss I still carry my beneficent Yes."

The next day he was more assertive. I noticed that I had been mistaken about his appearance, or else he wasn't the same, that's it, he was changing as I stood on the gravel pathway, it was in his eyes, even as I looked they were in retreat, moving back and back, until they were set so deep in his skull that they seemed at the end of a long, black tunnel. He invited me to consider one year, the year 1979. On the night of the general election, in May when Mrs. Thatcher had been elected Prime Minister, I had been busy elsewhere, being unfaithful to my wife, and not for the first time, having told her I would be covering the poll count at Bradford North. An earthquake in China, the Wakefield pit disaster, these had been treated by me with the disdain of a Parisian. Israeli tanks in the Lebanon? Had passed me by. The early exploits of Mr. Hyde had not, however. I had recognized their potential from the start to effect the seduction of women who allowed me to take them home and then, sometimes, inexplicably, foolishly, offered to make me coffee. In one case, he said, it had been little short of rape. I had held her cunt firmly with one hand while caressing her breast with the other. "Really," said the Devil, "you're not much of a citizen. Don't you believe in anything?"

I told him that I was not, had never been, and had no intention of becoming, a religious man.

"Funny things can happen," he said. "Sudden things, violent things, like that, or like being hit by a runaway bus."

I did not believe, I said, and therefore he did not exist.

"De-lovely, de-lightful!" he said, laughing. "Have it your way. I don't exist."

I went up the steps and into the main hospital building. He was in the corridor which was too hot as usual. He leaned against a pale yellow wall dripping with condensation. He fanned himself with a magazine. *The New Yorker*. My attitude? Was cool, I ignored him, my feet squeaking across the spongy linoleum towards the end of the corridor, where he was when I arrived. Hail friend! "Heading-ley," he said. "The end of the world is coming. Or so they're saying in Composure, Iowa. See, you were right. It *is* a town in the American heartland! And they've got the new Messiah. I know, I know, we've heard it before and everybody gets a little frisky with the millennium coming up. Nutcases, or another of the bank manager's tiresome little games to keep my hands full. I have to leave you."

I said that was a terrible pity.

"Yes, but I'll be back," he said. "Later. Tonight. You see, for me there is no time. I move hither and thither. It's very convenient."

I said, "I am no longer afraid of you. I am no longer afraid of the universe."

"Oh, really, that's good," said the Devil.

"I have seen my father. He is old now and has told me to be ready. And I am."

"I see," said the Devil.

"I will dive deep to the bottom of the sea and find there the watercress of immortality."

"Of course you will," said the Devil. "But tonight I'm going to scare the life out of you."

I did not see him at first, but I sensed his presence, and I knew that this time, if I were unfortunate enough to see him, he would be very different. I ran. I hid in a dark place. I had been clever, I had tricked him, but there was a scuffling sound, like the scratching of a hoof, and I realised I had not run quickly enough, so I stood quite still, not daring to move. He was there, and I set off again, and again, and again, only to find that each time he reached my place in the dark before I did. I was forced to change my tactics. With infinite caution I moved away from the door, tiptoed across the linoleum and opened another. As my eyes became slowly accustomed to the blackness I saw that I was in the hospital gymnasium. Looking around for somewhere to hide, I tried not to think of how afraid I was. I was very afraid. A phrase popped into my head: every man has a right to the pursuit of happiness. Jefferson. Or did he say property, the pursuit of *property*? And would that lead to a variation on Lenin's formula? *Happiness* is theft? No, I remember now it was Proudhon, not Lenin, who said property is theft. Lenin set out to prove him right and ended up proving just the opposite in a way. DON'T YOU THINK?

The gymnasium door fell in with a roll of thunder. There was lightning and the Devil stood there like the Devil should, tall, with scaly thighs and huge red bat's wings, spread out against Bradford black clouds. Horns grew from his head and in one hand he held golden arrows of disease. His eyes were on fire, though his face was not the Devil's face, but Schenk's.

He said, "Give me back my dignity."

I didn't understand.

His voice was booming now, "GIVE ME BACK MY DIG-NITY. CONFESS TO YOUR SINS. YOU ARE TO BLAME FOR MY FALL."

I was to blame for *his fall*? Alright, I shouldn't have expected the Prince of Darkness to be a reasonable fellow but, even so, this was steep. Now the Devil moved back and I saw someone else, a chirpy looking fellow in brogues and three-piece pinstripe, with a ledger under his arm. The Morality Bank manager himself!

"Please tell him," said the Devil, very respectfully.

God looked at me over half-moon spectacles. "Yes," He said, "I have consulted The Big Book and I'm afraid there can be no doubt, you *are* to blame."

I had a session with Dr. Austin. He was a Scot, from Edinburgh, educated at one of the snooty academies and then the university. A thin man with glasses and a forehead going back like a not-too-tricky ski slope. Waspish. Believed the soul to be located in the liver, and nursed his regularly with Glenmorangie single malt. He was dazed and smiling, the better, I suppose, for his own session, at lunchtime, in The Lord and Duck, three pints of Tetley and a couple of stiff ones. He asked me to tell him about my wife and son. I told him I had no wife and son. I had never had a wife and son.

"And your father?"

"I had, I do, doesn't everyone? He's a tax collector, lives in Godalming and collects butterflies with a net."

"He numbers lepidoptery among his hobbies?"

"He's a driving instructor, you should hear some of his stories, madmen ramming into walls, letter boxes, even supermarkets, gear boxes dropping out of the car when punters change straight from fourth to first. I'm surprised he makes it through the average week."

Dr. Austin made a steeple of his hands.

"He's in the wool industry. He practises the martial arts and his girlfriend's a dancer from Barcelona."

"What about you?"

"I am Mr. Hyde."

"You know that can't be true. Mr. Hyde was caught some time ago. He is a man called Kipling, a driver for a big firm of demolition engineers. He has confessed. The police are satisfied they have their man."

"The Devil organised that."

"I see."

"He's behind it all. I met him up at Undercliffe, near the mausoleum, the one with the sphinxes. There he was. His voice. He told me what to do. Details as if they were on a shopping list. Name. Date of appointment. Nature of punishment. They had to be corrected."

"You've been having bad dreams?"

I said, "I've been thinking about my wife and my father and the son I lost. About the mess I've made of it all. I spoke softly and it was the truth. Very occasionally I would feel a calm at the centre of myself and I would think of these things. I would remember the day Tom had been born when I had walked the hospital wards, posing as a surgeon.

"I see, I see," he said. A phone was ringing in the adjoining office, his secretary's. "Will you excuse me?"

When he'd gone I looked at the notes he'd made: "EGOMA-

NIAC"; "DELUSIONS OF GRANDEUR"; "THIS ONE'S A WHOLE SUIT SHORT OF THE FULL DECK." Were these really about me? I heard his voice from next door. For some reason he spoke in a wildly exaggerated version of his own Scottish accent.

"Aw no no, I'm afraid Dr. Austin cannae come to the phone. He's been taken poorly. In fact, they're wheeling him away on a trolley at this precise moment. Aye, it's true. Think I'm bloody daft, make up a thing like that? Aye, I'll make sure he gets the message, aye, aye, no, thank *you*," he said, and hung up.

"Not Helsinki," he said when he came back. "Helsinki's late. That was Johannesburg. Bloody South Africans." And then he looked at me, perhaps thinking his behaviour might be considered odd. Even I, in the state I was in, considered it odd. He sat down, straightened the blotter on his desk, gathered himself. "Maureen's not in today. A most unreliable customer."

I was silent.

"Please go on. You were telling me of your chats with the Prince of Darkness."

"I made them up. Wholly fabricated. Stories I tell myself to tell to you," I said. He glanced at his watch, and looked anxiously towards his secretary's office. The phone was ringing. Perhaps it was Helsinki. I wondered about Helsinki.

"Good session," he said, "you're *admitting* to your lies now. Good progress."

In fact, my meetings with the Devil were neither dream nor invention. They were as real to me as the manicured lawns and Dr. Austin's office, as real as Dr. Austin himself. They seemed so then and they do now. What happened at High Royds is therefore uncertain in my mind. My brother Keith told me recently that the undertaker Twiggy Fawcett was a patient there at that time. Twiggy had lost his mind when he buried Amos Bass at Undercliffe. It had been a summer day, so hot that the pavements of Bradford seemed to glow here and there with real fire. He had climbed to the hollow steel globe which stood at the top of the Provident Insurance building on Hustlergate. He had stood inside and had shouted his anger at a changing world. With him he had Amos Bass's collection of old records and he had sent the heavy black discs spinning down, one after the other. From that height the performances of Noel Coward and Laurence Olivier at 78 rpm were dangerous projectiles. Twiggy had been arrested and then committed. I know now that he died while I was there and I'm trying to remember whether I spoke to him or not. I like to think I did. Memory shows his skeletal frame stalking me round the edge of the hospital cricket field as we reminisce about my father. Memory may be lying, as memory will, creating a film, vivid and brightly coloured, but glimpsed only through narrow chinks.

I was late. I didn't have a chance to go to the bathroom. A silver-grey car, a getaway Jag like the one Schenk had driven, was at the bottom of the steps which went down to the gravelled hospital driveway. Behind the wheel? A visitor, a middle aged woman in a fur coat, reading the *Financial Times*. Very plummy. So I was discreet. I pissed against the front tyre on the *passenger* side.

I got on the bus. There was a silence. James Cleugh, Big Tom, Edgar Potter, The Straight Man, and even Bob from Thirsk with his grinning face, the face of a natural underdog, always eager to please, they all sat and stared, without a word.

"They're frightened of you," said Jolowicz, the driver.

I said nothing.

"Because you're fucking crazy. Because you stare at them when you're awake. Because you scream your head off when you're asleep and give the rest of the fruitcases bad dreams. Last night you were running up and down the ward. You tried to open the bars on the window. You were howling, and there wasn't even a moon."

"You're so . . . *there*," said James Cleugh, whose use of language was so imprecise that it had acquired its own poetry. "So . . . *big*. Like *nnnghgh*."

The bus jerked forward. Each week there was an outing like this, to a cricket match, to the cinema in Guiseley, for a walk on Ilkley Moor, to nowhere that was very far from High Royds. We went first that day to the parsonage at Haworth, where Jolowicz gave an alternate version of Bradford's favourite page in literary history: The Brontës. "First act: three screwy virgins live with big-pricked sibling Branwell! Back story between first and second acts: Branwell boffs the lot, just *hoses them down,* WHOO! Second act: Branwell gets his, serves him right! Third act: three demented sisters write works of towering genius about men with big equipment! Any questions? Back in the bus, then. We're going to Bolton Abbey."

Jolowicz was an actor, with a small company in Leeds, but unlikely to find himself playing the romantic lead. Prematurely bald, with a gawky figure and an elongated face like a horse, he was no oil painting. He drove the bus to earn extra cash. He was funny, in a wildly aggressive way, and spoke in an accent that was located somewhere in mid-Atlantic.

"Let's do a poll," he said, when he had got us back into the bus. "Hands up the screamers! Hands up those who shit in their pants!"

The Straight Man gathered the rest around him, a hen protecting her brood. If he could have moved them any further away, he would have, but they were already at the back. "You're the crazy one," said The Straight Man. "You're the one they should lock up."

Jolowicz was loving it. "Hands up anyone who thinks he killed his mother! Or fucked her!" said Jolowicz. "Edgar, don't be shy now, your secret will be safe. This head of mine, like Fort Knox."

None of this touched me. It was a long way off. I had my knees jack-knifed to my chin and I picked at the seat cover. The feel of it, stiff and prickly, a hedgehog given a short back and sides, made me shiver. I was in a fog. It's not just that I was going to pieces, breaking up, it was happening as well to the world out there, outside the bus. Watch: we're passing a Shell station, and the pump attendant, a young kid wearing patched jeans, is talking to a man in a BMW, Mr. Paisley Tie & Braces, he doesn't have time for this, he has a business to run, give me back my credit card, and a hurt expression is on the boy's face when suddenly the garage is gone, not just out of sight, but no longer there, *exploded;* for a moment I see the attendant, quite still in the flames, smiling, then he is gone.

No one had noticed a thing. Jolowicz's lips were going up and down, so I assumed he must be talking, and The Straight Man was shaking his fist. I closed my eyes, opened them again, and tried not to resist what I had seen. I would go to the back of the bus and take another peek, perhaps by staggering, well, lurching was more like it, *reeling,* just look at me, I would regain my balance, and the vision would disappear.

It didn't.

Fire chased the bus towards Bolton Abbey.

Helen, Keith, and I had gone there once with our mother for a picnic and because Helen wanted to see the monastery, which had been in ruins since 1536, when Henry VIII had decided he wanted the Church's land, and the lush meadows which rolled down to the River Wharfe. My mother had said it was a beauty spot, very nice if you liked that sort of thing, which she didn't especially, but at least it was somewhere we were unlikely to bump into our father with one of his floozies.

Helen had been before, on a school trip. She wanted to show me something else, she said, when we had looked at the broken walls of the monastery. I remember a feeling of alarm; I didn't want to go with her and did not, of course, have the courage to say so. Not uncommon for me in those days. This was during her Edgar Allan Poe period.

We walked through a meadow and along the river bank. Dewy grass turned my light brown shoes to chocolate. Helen talked of dead people, and the way they sang. Something happened to the voice, it grew deeper, richer, more honeyed, though not in all cases, there were the freaks, she even knew one man whose dead voice had assumed the mumbling tones of Popeye the Sailor. "Of course no one sings with *him,*" she said. "That would be quite out of the question. It would do terrible things to the harmonies."

The path took us up. We were no longer walking on grass, but on the flat top of a bank of shiny black rock. Here the river had been forced into a funnel no more than nine feet across. Water rushed through and plunged down in the direction from which we'd just come.

"Can't you hear them?" said Helen.

I heard only the water.

"There's a chorus down there. They're rehearsing *Oklahoma.* You want to know how?"

I didn't, she told me anyway.

"There's a cave."

"There is?"

"This is how it works. See that rock there, it's very hard, that's why the river is so narrow here. I don't know why, it's geography or something, but below the top it's different, the rock is soft, it's been worn away like Coca-Cola eating your tooth, and there's a big cave filled with water, and dead people, because if you go in there . . ."

She pointed to the heaving, boiling, hissing water.

". . . you go down into the cave and you never come out again."

"That's not true."

"People step in, or try to jump across and don't get there. Or they get to the other side and can't find their feet. Just think of that. You're all right and then . . . *splash*. Shooting down and your lungs bursting like balloons."

I peeked down, and then across: an easy jump, that's how it looked, it could even be less than nine feet.

"Our dad did it once, that's what Mum says, she tried to stop him. It was when they were courting. I bet you can't do it."

I remember thinking: "I'm good at games."

Helen said, "Go on, our kid. Jump."

Jump.

"Don't jump!" shouted The Straight Man. He was on the opposite bank, waving his arms and leaping about. His arms looked outrageously long. "Wait, don't do anything. JOLOWICZ!"

I looked into the swirling waters. Was I going to do anything? No. I wasn't.

Suicide, I remark (yes, it's another Headingley Hamer Memorial Lecture), is rarely a philosophical decision; to kill yourself only because there is no point to life, no meaning, seems pretty dodgy to me, life being its own point, life being the day to day living of it etc. until the last syllable of recorded and so on and so forth, life being a struggle we have to struggle through and death being a definite sign of slacking. My students, my women, are silent, because they are there no longer. The hall is empty. I realise that to have done it, to have gone down into Helen's cave, to have jumped, would have merely been a gesture, an act of self-pity, not despair, or madness. It didn't come to that. As I've said, I'm no hero. I lacked the nerve. Easier to go on.

Jolowicz came running up. Pale, sweating, shirt spattered with mud from a tumble he'd taken during his breathless dash across the meadow. He said I'd scared the shit out of him. We trooped back to the bus. A fine rain was falling. There was smoke from leaves burning in the cemetery and a Mr. Whipped ice-cream van was parked by the Abbey gates. I bought a strawberry double cone. That night it was different again. The Devil did not come and I sat on my bed, crying like a child. My hands were clenched tight into fists. I repeated my name again and again and again.

What is a life? Mine, then, in those years, was made up of little things. I came out of High Royds, I didn't move to London; nor did I go back on the *Telegraph & Argus,* though Budge said my job was waiting. Instead I worked as: barman, cab driver, hospital porter and dark-room assistant to an Irish photographer whose neurosis it was that he didn't like any picture he took. Sometimes I fell back. If I saw the word "Devil" in a newspaper or magazine or book I would cut it out and then cut the word into five letters and then throw each letter into a different bin, as if by scattering the sign I destroyed what it signified. I tried not to read too much.

For six months I was a salesman with builders who had a development on the edge of Bradford. I think, I'm not sure, that the company had been responsible for the estate in Bridlington where Julie had lived when she left me. This time it was seventy houses, seven streets, each named after a British admiral. I shared an office with Brian, who had a pair of sunglasses he rarely took off and whose telephone patter I tried to imitate. "Marilyn," he would say, or Alan or Meg or whoever. His voice was a whine from somewhere near London, one of the Home Counties, Essex probably. He sounded pedantic, as though he were always explaining things to slow children. "Brian Graham here . . . *Brian* . . . I'm bereft . . . *beside* myself . . . you don't remember . . . your offer . . . not wishing to push you . . . that's GREAT! . . . oh, Marilyn . . . did you get to see that film the other night, you were going with your new . . . right! . . . brilliant, isn't he Spielberg? . . . the Dickens of our age . . . yeah, did him in school . . . remember that XR3i I had, I'd hired it, took you in it up to Ramilles Street? . . . had it up to 105 on a run down to Brighton at the weekend, I never go more than 80, I didn't even notice it . . . *cocooned* . . . that's what I was . . . I'm a sedate driver . . . a sedate kind of a bloke all in all."

Brian told me he had been in the army. He had terrifying stories which were told offhand, with the sunglasses still on, and I didn't know whether to believe them or not. I envied Brian his certainty. He was my age and had presumably endured misfortune, the occasional kick in the groin, or the heart, yet he still believed life was something you reached out to conquer. I shook my head at the stories, *amazing,* and knew I was expected to offer some of my own. That's the way it is with men who don't know each other. First of all jokes erupt like a bad attack of pimples. Then reminiscences are exchanged, but only those shaped by frequent retelling, sculpted and polished into anecdote, thus removing any danger of revelation. This is where I made my mistake. I told the story of Jolowicz and the visit to Haworth, from which Brian deduced I had been a mental patient. I might as well have spat in his beer. For a while the sunglasses stared at me, insect-eyes asking themselves whether they shared office and executive toilet with a feared species . . . *loser.* But Brian was a decent fellow, he wanted to give me the benefit of the doubt, and we continued to get along well enough until the morning, a month later, when I saw the "D" word on an inside page of his *Daily Mail.* That did it. I snatched away the paper, cut out the word with an artist's blade I kept in my desk, scalpelled the word into, you know, was able to dispose of "D," "E," and "V" in bins we had in the office and ran into the street to find two more, shouting over my shoulder, "Take my calls, would you? Just taking out the rubbish. Back in a jiffy." Brian said nothing; I was fired the next week.

It didn't matter. I got another job and, after a while, even the "D" word didn't bother me. Not that I was fully recovered. I had a trembling hold on the real. I would imagine myself playing cricket, walking to the centre, nodding at the keeper, perhaps offering a little smile, looking around, thumping the bat against my boot as I prepared to face the first delivery. These games were always at Windhill, where my grandfather had played with Learie Constantine, where my father had made love to Diana Farrell, and where I would walk towards the square from the pavilion he had built, with my cuffs buttoned at the wrist. I would shrink the field in my mind so boundaries wouldn't be too difficult to hit.

I worked as a waiter in a big hotel near the railway station, discovering that my rubbery attitude to the truth was useful. A waiter has to be amiable, confused, flirtatious, invisible, or superbly arrogant and dismissive, depending on the need of the customer. Many roles were required each night and I was good at them all.

Women? Ceased to be a problem, since I no longer chased each one I met.

I had slept with Barbara when she was in Bradford, shortly after I came out of High Royds. She had wanted to explain what had happened between her, Vickie, and my father. No, no, I had said, don't bother, but she had insisted. The two of them had run off with the money which my father had gone to Scarborough to collect, but all they had got for their trouble was a bag filled with notes which were damp and green with mould and, in any case, of a type removed from circulation years before. She supposed it had been my father's joke; certainly it had given her and Vickie a surprise when they tipped the bag's contents on to the bed of the suite they had booked at the Ritz. Barbara was living in London now. And Vickie? Had disappeared. Even Barbara didn't know where she was, or so Barbara said.

I had slept with Julie, four times. The experience was strange, at once familiar and comfortable, yet haunted by the awareness of what we no longer had in common. Afterwards, each time, when we were curled up together, she had cried. Our divorce had come through and she had married the pipe-smoker.

I had lived for a year with a woman I had met when she had knocked me over with her rusting Ford Cortina. I was her lamed duck, and then, one day, she had lost interest in healing me.

I had slept with others, from time to time, not many.

What else?

I noticed that women were different, not in general, of course, but in their attitude to me.

Let me explain, there are certain things which don't change, that haven't been affected by economics, or education, or fashion, or feminism. I'm thinking of the first look most men give most women. This look asks two questions. Would I want to fuck it? How do I make her? Notice, only with the second question need the existence of another individual be considered, and then only because tactics are necessarily a consideration. Morality does not come into it, or even manners. I don't imagine it's fun for women, being on the receiving end of this each day, but they've learned to ignore it, or deal with it, or turn it to their own advantage. In any event a law has evolved, and it's a constant. No Einstein is going to come along with a new suit of clothes for this one. It's Hamer's Law of the First Glance and the Glance that Is Given Back: the glance says *this is what I want,* and the glance that is given back replying *I know and you are a beast.* Women do make exceptions: with the blind, for instance. This is a mistake: the eyes of Mr. Hyde do not need to see; they would prefer to, but it is not a necessity. But what I'm saying does not concern the beastliness of blind men, what I'm saying is that women looked at me with the same absence of suspicion, even the same compassion, they normally reserve for men crippled in some way, men assumed, correctly or not, to have no penis. At that time I was no Don Juan, and certainly no Napoleon; I even had trouble seeing myself as Hamlet. As the English poet said, I had spent my life, both interest and principal. I hate those English poets.

It was Bradford, in the summer of 1989. Mr. Hyde had been caught, but the city was still rich in opportunity for vice and violence. What remained of the industrial architecture had been blasted clean and was regarded as a new kind of beautiful. Some of the warehouses and weaving sheds were functioning once more, as restaurants, art galleries, and centres to which people could go and enjoy "leisure." Bradford had become a tourist attraction. Twiggy Fawcett and Amos Bass would have run up a routine on the subject. There was talk of a boom, of Bradford being restored to something like its Victorian vitality, but no one believed it, not really, because Bradford had been so sick for so long.

It was only the Pakistanis, the Moslems, who dreamed with passion; their dream was the one the English had dreamed in their time of power and conquest, that they were chosen, that it was their duty to make the world a mirror in which they would see the reflection of *their way* staring back. Some months before, they had set fire to the book of a writer who had offended them. A mosque was being built near Forster Square.

The *Telegraph & Argus* had a report about the property developer responsible. His company was based a few miles away, in Leeds, and his name was Melrose Gadney. He made the usual statements. He was ahead of schedule. He was performing a service for the community and for the future of Bradford. He was using Irish labour flown in. When asked if he was a relation of a famous Bradford artist with the same name, he said, "A distant cousin, I do believe." Beside the article was a photograph of a sleek man in a suit with a glass of champagne in his hand and, in his mouth, inevitably, a cigar. He was older, but I recognised him: Melrose Gadney was Schenk.

I went to see Budge Carter. He was stouter, more impressive. He had grown into a commanding sort of man. Heat swam up from the street and past the window of his office. Bradford was shimmering. I asked what he knew about Melrose Gadney. He knew for a start that his name was not Melrose Gadney.

"That's his joke," he said.

I said that Schenk had a bent sense of humour.

Budge Carter registered the information that I knew him. "Of course. He was a friend of your dad's. Way back."

"Not the word I'd have chosen."

"Weren't they partners?"

"Schenk was bad luck for him. My sister too."

Budge asked if I remembered his wife. I didn't ask where she came into it; nor did I say I remembered her only too well, from the days of cunty whiffs. I kept my face blank and said I did. He told me that soon after his marriage in 1964 Schenk had threatened to slash her face because of a story Budge was about to write concerning a suspected murder. A solicitor's clerk who had been found in the back of a car on the promenade in Scarborough, dead. So Budge had felt cheapened, and had been fearful of discovery, but he had fudged the crate. The story had gone in the bin.

Schenk had turned up again a few months before, calling himself Melrose Gadney. Nothing illegal about that: he had changed his name by deed poll; but at the reception where Schenk announced that, as well as building the mosque, he was negotiating to buy the whole of Saltaire for redevelopment, Budge had recognised him at once, as I had, and had decided to have someone do some poking about.

One of the new clocks excelled at legwork and tracked down a man who had worked for Schenk, a Pakistani, very frightened. "This bloke said that Schenk had other businesses around the city, sweat-shops making clothes, paying slave wages because he knew they were illegals, immigrants, and threatening to turn them over if they tried to leave. Also that he himself had come in illegally and Schenk had set him up with a phony identity, got a name from a grave up at Undercliffe, applied for a new birth certificate, passport, the whole number. Now he was having to pay Gadney's people to keep the secret. He reckoned there are a couple of hundred who are in the same boat. Schenk calls them his dead souls."

"Could you confirm the story?"

"Could we buggery. And then the bloke disappears. Scared, I suppose. Or dead."

There was another rumour, he said, about Schenk (sorry, but *Melrose Gadney,* I can't bring myself). He had approached the chiefs of a property company, noting they were about to have a problem with an office building they owned in Hull. They had been puzzled. They had known of no such problem. It was when Schenk, using the same tactic he had with Charlie Laughton, had blown up the building that they decided to make their enemy their friend, offering him a seat on the board.

"One day he called, I'm talking about Schenk, and you should hear him talk these days. Like a cabinet minister. He told me he'd heard we were doing a story. He said, 'You have disadvantages.' I said, 'What disadvantages?' He said, 'You have scruples. You have a wife and children and I know where they live.' "

"What did you say?"

"I said I didn't respond well to threats."

"What did *he* say?"

"He said he wasn't making a threat. And he was a legitimate businessman now, with a company that had been praised by the government for its imaginative use of labour. And that the story we were working on was a dead end, if I understood his drift."

"Always the subtle fellow."

"So we did the other story. How a bunch of micks is building the Temple of Allah! How Melrose Gadney is a businessman for our age."

Budge Carter smiled. People told him he was a boring fellow, he said. That was fine. Being comical got you nowhere in the crate business. You had to play on the front foot with a straight bat, usually, but this time he was quite prepared to be devious. Before, when he had known Schenk, he had felt a helpless and directionless rage. Now he knew better. Schenk thought of himself as a Bradford style emperor. Schenk was going to come down with a crash and Budge Carter would be responsible for his fall.

I drove to Leeds. I walked around the city square, stopping each time at the building where I knew Schenk had his offices. I felt somehow that a part of me was there, inside, up in the penthouse with Schenk. I took an aimless stroll up to the town hall where big stone lions stood guard and strolled back again. I went into a phone box, called his office, and hung up when a woman's voice answered. I stood once more on the white marble steps of the building. I didn't go in.

My father came back. The last time I'd seen him he'd been in jail. After his trial, in Bradford, in 1981, he had been moved to a prison for white-collar criminals outside Manchester. Compared to Armley, where he had been on remand, this was a holiday. "Like an Ealing comedy," had been his verdict. He had pointed out the various characters. "See the chap over there, the bald one, sweating like a porker on heat? Used to work for the big fellow. He was a bishop. Down south somewhere, Home Counties job. It's not as if I have a good opinion of the man and the way he behaves, or even of the Church, many's the time I found Fatty Lawrence out of his tree in the pub and had to borrow his collar and do the whole bit myself, dust to dust, I can still remember that routine, but I don't mind telling you . . . A bishop. I was surprised. I mean, how can life be that hard in those houses they get? Very select properties God lines up for his top executives. Him? Bank manager. Mind like a trap. But some pair of legs took him for a ride, it was fur coats and Aspreys this and Costa del that. Good for her. He got caught with his rasher in the till. That one, him by the window, computers. Big fraud, makes me look very small beer. Oh yes, a good quality of customer. I keep expecting Alec Guiness to walk in."

I had sat opposite him in the visitors' room—it was low and the walls were painted glossy grey, it stank of a hundred men sweating—with my fingers drumming on the Formica table top, not really knowing what I was doing there, not knowing what I felt. My father had greeted me with tears in his eyes and a wet kiss on my cheek; he had seemed to expect something in return, a recipro- cal gesture, but I hadn't been able to respond. Somehow nothing had been settled. There had been a storm, but no clear air after- wards. Who was this man? I had nothing to say to him.

I asked if everything was alright. Was there anything he needed?

"I'm chipper," he said. "A hundred and ten per cent. This place is a doddle. Piece of cake."

"That's good."

"How have you been?"

"Fine. You know, fine."

"High Royds?"

"Wasn't too bad." I nodded. I was conscious of my head going down and up, down and up. I thought it might drop off. "Yes, not too bad at all."

"Fancy one of us ending up on the funny farm, eh?" he said, laughing the raucous Hamer laugh. "Hard to believe."

I tried to smile; I felt myself drifting. He realised he'd struck a bad note.

"I'm sorry about Tom. I know it's hard to talk about, but I wanted to say how sorry I was."

"Thanks."

"Makes me think about Helen. Makes me count my blessings. That I've still got you and Keith. I've still got my sons."

The display of sentiment made me angry. I wondered what right he had to be emotional about me and my life. I felt savage. I said, "The last time I saw Keith he told me he'd sooner stick needles in his eyes than see you again."

My father took this without blinking. He told me he was having trouble with his eyes watering. Bloody contact lenses! He still hadn't got used to them. He told a story about an Englishman, an Irishman, and a Scotsman called McBagpipe.

"Come again, son," he had said.

I had said nothing, and I hadn't.

After that? For three years he had been in London, living in a club for ex-servicemen which he would leave each morning for no purpose other than just that, to leave, and to which he would return each night to sleep in a narrow bed in a tiny room on the fifth floor. His window overlooked the Thames. He watched the brown waters, moving slowly. Just like his life, he thought. He wrote letters, telling me what he did. During the day it was the churches and the streets, he reckoned he had been in more pubs in London than anyone alive, he could stand in Mayfair or Bow or Ealing and locate them blindfold, by smell. He made occasional trips to the country to buy cars, Porsches and Ferraris, which he sold at elephant profit to young men in double-breasted suits. He sat in cinemas and cried without knowing why. The letters would always end the same way: "Thanks for caring for me, son. I love you—Dad."

Then he had met a woman, it had been in the bar at the Ritz, somewhere he wouldn't have minded dying, he said. Her name was Jessie, she was a widow, in her forties, still beautiful, and she owned a hotel in a cold Scottish town made from granite. She was on a weekend trip, stayed for a month or more while her sons Sinclair and Alexander ran the hotel, and when she did at last go back it was with a piece of freight they hadn't bargained for—my father. He and Jessie travelled a lot, and between times he managed the hotel, played golf, ate plenty, and put on weight. He bought an old Jag. He wore his RAF blazer and refused to cultivate the Scottish taste for adding Coca-Cola to whisky. I think those years were a happy time for him. But Jessie died from stomach cancer and there was a bitter argument over the will: she had meant to change it and had forgotten, or she *had* changed it and the amended version had gone missing; I never found out. Sinclair and Alexander got the hotel. They told my father to clear out the day after their mother's funeral. Puzzled, a little surprised, he said he would leave the next morning but when he came to look for the Jag found that it was gone, they had already sold it. He caught the train to London, resuming as before, in the serviceman's club, in the same room, as if his life with Jessie had been a dream.

We drove to Leeds, to Headingley, in a red sports car he had bought, an Alfa Romeo. He wanted to see David Gower, whose elegant off-drives he admired. We sat in the sun, watching Gower knock up sixty in no time at all, then slash outside the off stump and get himself out, caught in the gully. He walked to the pavilion, bat under arm, ruffling his hair, wearing an absent-minded grin. My father thought that was the way to go: carelessly, but with style.

We didn't talk much. We drank. It was two pints (Tetley bitter) before one, chilled white burgundy with lunch at a local fish and chip restaurant, more beers in the afternoon, a half-bottle of champagne in the shade of the sponsor's tent in the tea interval, and large whiskies in a cavernous pub not far from the ground at close of play.

"It was the first time I've been at Headingley since I came back," he said. "Felt nervous about it before. Didn't know if any of the fellows would recognise me, didn't know how they'd react if they did. Everything was dandy. Hamilton, at the gate, he even touched his cap. 'Long time Mr. 'amer,' he said. They were pleased."

"Why wouldn't they be?"

"Bloody marvellous day," he said. "Think I'll come tomorrow."

By then we were so drunk that we gave up the idea of driving to Bradford. Instead we took a taxi to Leeds station and got the train. My father insisted on travelling first class and we found a compartment. It was then that the blood drained from his face. "To tell the truth I feel a little queer," he said, and tried to laugh. "Get bad marks for that answer." He had aged ten years in a minute. Eyes fixed on a spot between his feet, he took deep breaths and a terrible rattling came from the back of his throat. I thought he was going to die. But he recovered, a little, and smiled. "Oh bloody hell," he said.

"We'd better get off the train," I said.

He tripped and fell on the platform. People came to help, but my father stayed on his hands and knees, struggling to breathe, first of all, and then, having recovered himself a little, and realising he had lost a contact lens, moving his palms over the oily concrete, as if trying to brush it clean.

He went into hospital three days later. When I saw him he was sitting up, propped against three pillows, wearing light blue pyjamas. "I see they've got the usual number of assorted little darlings," he said, his eyes tracking a nurse as she squeaked down the ward on black shoes with thick rubber soles. "There's a Welsh girl who's an absolute cracker. Food's not so bad. I'll put on a bit more weight, be out of here in no time at all." They did tests. His heart was weak, one kidney had failed and the other was about to. His liver was also in bad shape. "They cut off a slice and sent it to lab boffins," he said. "Who reckoned it was one hundred per cent Johnnie Walker."

I spoke to the doctor. He was small and simian, from Sheffield, with glasses. He took me to the consultant. He was tall and dressed like a dandy, from Pakistan. They wanted to operate. One kidney would have to be taken out and the other lowered by an inch so a length of clogged artery could also be removed. If my father did not agree, he would die within days. But I should prepare myself. He was so weak there was a chance he would not survive the surgery. He said he had explained this to the patient.

I went back. "Dad," I said. "Why didn't you tell me?"

My father was sullen. He said, "At ten, an animal. At twenty, a lunatic. At thirty, a failure, and at forty, a fraud. At fifty, a bloody criminal. At sixty I just wanted to see my family again. Doesn't look like I'll see seventy."

"You'll have to let them operate."

"I've just remembered something I thought I'd forgotten a long time ago. I could only have been six or seven years old and my dad took me into Rothenstein and Kafka. You know the story about the cash box?"

Yes, I said, I knew.

"He wanted to see old man Rothenstein about something, I can't remember what, *that's* gone, anyway the point is that at this place they got samples from all over the world. And not only wool. Camel hair from Egypt. Buffalo skins. And they'd just got in a bale from Shanghai. Pig-tails. It's true, they'd all been chopped off after some state decree and someone had the bright idea of sending them to Bradford. Don't know what they thought we would do with them. My dad took one of these tails, it was slick with grease, and stuck it to the back of my head. Doesn't that beat the band?"

He smiled at the memory. "You know what my dad called that place? 'A vault with bloody mummies in it.' Anyway, I kept the pig-tail there for days, it began to stink, but my dad called me 'The Chinaman.' I liked that, it made me feel close to him, as if I was part of his world, as if he and I were in a club."

I said, "Dad . . ."

He said he had been thinking about my mother. He remembered their wedding again. He had had an idea of what his wedding would be like. Everyone would cry! Everyone would kiss everyone else! Every man would look with envy at the groom waltzing with his bride! Everyone would get drunk! Everyone would be relieved when it was over!

"And you know something Headingley," he said, his eyes following the progress of another nurse, a redhead who came towards us pushing a trolley with a big urn on it. "That's just how our wedding was. What a day."

"Tea for you, Mr. Hamer?" said the nurse.

"Very kind of you, my dear," he said. "Very kind indeed." And with those words he turned to me, saying softly, but not so softly the nurse couldn't hear: "Isn't she a picture? I think she may be the most lovely thing I've ever seen."

Smiling, she gave him a cup.

"I love you," said my father. "I have always loved you. I will *always* love you."

She was sharp with him now. "None of that nonsense, Mr. Hamer."

He was not deterred. "This is my son," he said. "He's also unattached."

"No wonder," said the nurse, pushing the tea-trolley as if it were an engine of war.

My father sipped the tea, remarking that it was a little cold. He put the cup back in its saucer, and set down the rattling pair on the table in front of him. He tried to grasp my hand but his grip was so weak that his fingers fell away. He said he was very scared.

The days wore away. At last he agreed to the operation. I went to see him the night before. He read me a story from the paper. The male heir to a gin fortune had been found in a gent's lav', wearing stockings and a garter belt. The image delighted him. "Makes me glad I'm a whisky drinker," he said, roaring with laughter, and then remembering something. "You like gin martinis, don't you?"

"That's right."

"Never quite trusted this martini-swilling side to your character."

"Diana Farrell taught me to make them. At one of those parties, when I was a kid, everyone fucking like the world would end at midnight."

He cleared his throat. His expression told me we would be setting the record straight, man-to-man. These conversations often seemed not to work. There was sentimental statement of emotion and, at the same time, a forced jocularity. Our previous relationship had been poor preparation for this.

"Must have been rotten for you. All of that. Sorry."

"Not really."

"Really?"

"Really."

"Really?"

"Really."

Oh how English!

"Now Diana, there was a character. Poor old Charlie Laughton. He couldn't handle her. Inevitable that he'd end up the way he did, six feet under, pushing up the tax bills. Now Diana, *she'll* end up in the House of Lords. Buried in Westminster Abbey. A bequest to the nation."

"Probably."

"In the RAF they said I was a fearless man but she scared me, I'll tell you that for an empty bottle of Carlsberg."

"And my mum?"

"She believed in the subtleties. Might take years to pay you back for something. Like running away with Dewsbury. Whereas Diana, she favoured the more direct approach. Physical violence. She clobbered me on the head with a golf club once. A number seven iron."

He lifted his hair away from his forehead to show the thin white scar, a three-quarter-inch diagonal.

"There's something else you ought to see, not important, not *really*," he said, "but you should know about it."

He leaned over and opened the door of his bedside cabinet. Water trembled in the jug on top, threatening to slop over. Muttering, he searched for a while, or at least made the pretence of searching, and pulled out an envelope. "If the worst happens, and I do pop my clogs, don't say anything, I'm only saying *if,* then you should know about these."

He opened the envelope and spread six pieces of paper in front of him on the turned-back sheet.

"I'm very much afraid that I've been a bad boy," he said. "And if they find this little lot they'll probably have me in the clink again. And if the worst—I know, I know—then they might come to you."

I asked what he was talking about.

"These," he said, moving three of them to one side, "are in my name and *these*," the three remaining, the other side, "are not. Now what have we got here?"

I realised: they were birth certificates. The certificates were yellowing and stiff, as if soaked in water long ago. We had: Spencer Lewis, date-of-birth 17.3.1920; Albert Rich, 1.1.1923; and Daniel Defoe Shalloon, 9.5.1919.

"Daniel Defoe Shalloon?"

"He's Irish, you see. Look, it says, born in County Antrim. Likes a bit of a bash, does Daniel, and knows when it's night because it's dark outside," he said. "I've been using these to claim pensions in three different London boroughs. Lambeth, I think that was Albert Rich, and Westminster and Hackney but with those two I can't quite figure out who I was where."

"And the other three."

"They're all in my name, but you'll notice that the dates of birth are different."

He had been drawing state pensions on these as well, and other benefits, allowing the government to keep him in the style to which he had become accustomed. I imagined him pulling up in the Alfa outside various dole offices around the country, perhaps with some dolly in the passenger seat. Won't be a moment sweet thing!

"Make them pay for the entire caboodle. The buggers owe me after all. Of course, these are a bit of a problem really, because even the Social Security might notice that three lots of the lot have been claimed by John Bertram Hamer. Sooner or later. Later, hopefully. But it goes to show, no short measures, much better to be *completely* dishonest."

I shouldn't have been shocked. I had seen no reason to suppose he had become a conventional citizen. I was surprised, however, by the impressive scale of the enterprise. In 1964, when he had done the bunk to South America, he had bought many documents, reasoning that a fellow could not have too many identities, that extra one, the one you thought an indulgent one too many, could prove the most useful one of all.

He moved the certificates around, first this way, now that, and back again, his fingers working with deft conjuror's swiftness. "Spot the real one, old man. Find the lady!"

I threw my head back and laughed raucously. The Hamer laugh: I thought he would appreciate the gesture. I said, "You crooked old bugger. If moral choices were marked out of ten, we'd neither of us be *magna cum laude*."

Perhaps it sounded awkward; perhaps he refused, at that moment, to be teased. Suddenly he was petulant.

"I was a war hero, you know," he said.

My voice was soft. "I know."

My mind retreated into noises, the man in the next bed, who was always asleep, turning over and sighing, the clunking doors of the hospital lift, the hum of traffic outside.

"Sorry, didn't mean to snap."

Another silence, less awkward.

"I'm a bit shaken up. Sorry old fellow."

"It's all right," I said. "I understand."

He asked about Helen. He said he'd never heard the whole story and I thought of the oddness of his life, that it made him stranger to so much that should have been familiar. Why had I never told him before? He hadn't asked. I saw him in Rio, staring at a wall, announcing "My name is Albert Rich."

"Tonight?"

"I want to know."

It had been in the months after he had left, when Helen, Keith, and I were living in the big house, on our own, though our mother came to visit at weekends. Keith was with his rock group much of the time, they were playing at dance halls most nights, were beginning to be known. Helen was still seeing Schenk, and it was Helen who looked after me. She washed my clothes. She made me go to school. She fried up huge meals—sausages, eggs, mushrooms, bacon, bread dipped in the hot fat, and baked beans swimming through grease towards the edge of the plate—and bet me two shillings I couldn't eat them.

Then, one afternoon, she came home, turned on the gas, and put her head inside the oven. But she had forgotten that gas was no longer taken from coal but piped in from the North Sea and was therefore not poisonous. The stuff was making her sick, not killing her. She turned off the gas, thought for a while and, no, did *not* light a cigarette thus exploding the house and herself. She considered the possibility, but rejected it because it would have appeared an accident, as if she had not chosen to die. Instead she opened door and windows, and sat down to write another note, explaining the details. She ran water into the bath, climbed in and slit her wrists with a razor-blade, taking care to slice, not across, but upwards, along the length of the arteries. Always decided, my sister, always thorough.

I came back from school. I found the kitchen empty, the living room—empty, but not so the bathroom. It wasn't Keith's girlfriend who killed herself, but Helen, and me, not Keith, who found the body. The cuts ran up her arm, straight and deep, and not red, because they were already beginning to congeal. The blood did still move, but very slowly. It was like watching, from a distance, a mass of tiny creatures, dark and seething.

The autopsy revealed she was five months pregnant; her letter named Schenk as the father. He hadn't come to the funeral, up at Undercliffe. By then he had vanished, and the police were looking for him, as they were for my father.

He listened in silence, without expression, until I had finished, and then went at it. "That *bastard,*" he said, so loud that the man in the next bed woke up, looking surprised. "That fucking bastard." The red-haired nurse speeded from the other end of the ward, a finger pressed to her lips, making *shushing* noises. I would have to leave, she said, if there was another disturbance. I promised we would be quiet.

He did not recover his calm for a long time. He was panting for breath. His face was ashen. He said, "As soon as I get out of here, I'll see to the bastard. Mark my words."

"Right."

"Frankly I'm surprised neither you nor Keith ever did anything about it."

I said, "What would have been the point?" I did not say that I was not impressed by his dramatics, that both Keith and I blamed him almost as much as Schenk. Those had been bad days for Helen, after they had both disappeared. At first I was surprised he didn't see it, then I realised it was predictable, he was such a self-obsessed old bugger.

"Do you know where he is?"

"I don't," I said. I know, but that was a lie to him, not to you.

"We'll have to find out."

The man in the next bed had gone back to sleep, and the nurse was back at the desk with the anglepoise lamp. My father had also regained his composure. He settled himself among the pillows. He asked what I thought Helen's life would have been. I replied that even had it been hard, she wouldn't have let that stop her. Rip-off artists, lame-duck men, bad-news bosses—she'd have dealt with them all. She would have raised children, two or maybe three, on her own, holding down both a day and a night job if she had to. She would have been a hero.

"Do you think so?"

"You've only got to think of her to know that."

"She was a wonderful girl, wasn't she?"

"She was."

"A wonderful daughter."

It struck me that there was so much more to say about Helen. It struck me also how badly equipped we both were to say it. Emotions were icebergs we smacked into by accident, discovering they left holes.

It was time for me to go. He was glum now, so I made up a story, about a girl I had to see in an hour or so, a blonde, on the skinny side, she smoked Marlboro cigarettes and was causing me trouble. She kept me at arm's length. Wouldn't let me get close. Seemed to think love was better when not possessed. Or perhaps enjoyed the spectacle, me making an ass of myself, night after night.

"Blondes," he said, with sympathy. "Never met one yet that couldn't wreck a city. What's the plan? Dinner?"

"That curry place in Shipley. It's very good."

"Don't try to kiss her."

"Really?"

"Absolutely not. But don't be cool either. Be intimate, let her know that she's a still point and your life is spinning around her. But don't say anything."

"No?"

"Make her *feel* it."

"I'll try."

"Don't try, son. *Do it*. See the elephant."

I stood up. "Good luck for tomorrow," I said.

"You'll come on Monday then, eh? I expect I'll be ga-ga for a day or so after the op. Maybe the anaesthetic will induce a dream of sexual glory. I'd like that." He laughed, and motioned for me to kiss him on the cheek. "What do you reckon to the chances?"

I gave him the kiss. "It's a racing certainty," I said. I stood up. I was surprised to feel a pain in my chest. The pain was a bird and an almost imperceptible fluttering of wings kept it poised too close to my heart. I thought I would cry. I walked away, eyes fixed on the light which came from the anglepoise lamp and seemed to bend and wobble before it landed in a yellow oval in front of the nurse. I was convinced I would never see him again. I didn't look back.

What is a life? An adventure, a daring ride to an unknown destination? A formless journey? Or one which is planned, where the pilot carefully monitors the glowing dials—food, sex, family, home, money—on the control panel in front of him? My father's hadn't been that. His had been a life of uncertainty, of unfulfilled potential. At the end of the war, when he left the RAF, he really was like a film star, larger than life. Perhaps the mistake he made was in coming back to Bradford. London might have been a better place for him. Then again, perhaps not: his character was a cracked box from which stability would always leak. Just when everything seemed set, and success assured, things would run riot all of a sudden, turning against him, and he would be the one doing the running. He would always make sure of that. I suppose the difference was that my father did make the journeys most men only dream about, the detours and little trips on the side, away from his responsibilities and his opinion of himself. He was energetic, raffish, anarchic. Desire meant nothing to him. Only pleasure was important, and then only in the moments of gratification. For such a moment he would rupture any circumstance. At the same time he was sentimental, secretive, and constipated about money. His had been a life of rolling mercury.

. . .

I went to the hospital. It was a leaden summer afternoon. He was still unconscious, they said, and I should come in again, see him the next day. So I did. He was sitting up, but looking weak. He waved his hand at the grapes I brought and decided he didn't want any after all. The simian doctor with the spectacles took me into his office. He told me they were optimistic. The operation had gone better than even they had hoped. My father would be alright. They expected to be able to let him out in a week or so. A part of me was disappointed, I'm ashamed to say. I had built myself up to enjoy the drama of his death. He had upstaged me yet again.

My father came to live with me in the flat off Manningham Lane. It was furnished now, and had been repainted, grey and grey, the colours in which philosophers see the world, but I wondered if he remembered when Keith and I had tried to kill him there; if he did, he said nothing. The operation had turned him in on himself. His appetite was poor and he didn't talk much. He watched TV with the sound turned up loud. Even this didn't engage him. Soap operas, films, news programmes, cartoons—all were viewed with a blank expression. He was in a stupor, from which he woke occasionally to deliver fizzing monologues about his bowels. His turds—their colour, their length, their consistency and, most particularly, their regularity—were an obsession. After a while they ceased to appear at all. He sat on the toilet, grunting with pain.

"Been regular all my life. Nine o'clock every morning, set my watch by it. Three days now," he said.

Then it was four, and five, and six, until at last, the local GP, who had been calling each day, gave him an enema. An hour later his bowels opened in a rush, a deluge so sudden it prevented him getting to the bathroom in time. "Oh Christ," he said, staring at the mess, "who'd have thought the old man had so much shit in him?" He wept at the humiliation.

I sat him in the kitchen and gave him a glass of orange juice. We both had a laugh and I went back into the living room. Toiling with a sponge and a bucket filled with disinfectant, I thought: *What compassion! What a splendid fellow this Headingley is! Are you watching God?! How much morality do I get in the bank for this?! Bet I'll be getting my credit cards back soon!*

I scrubbed all the harder.

After that it was more constipation, more groaning, and more TV watching at ever more deafening volume. Added to which: complaints about numbness in his legs. I told myself to be compassionate. He was sick, he was old, he was my father. I sat at the table by the window with my back to the room. I filled my tumbler with whisky, I tried to read, I tried to keep calm. At last I snapped. I pulled out the plug and tossed it aside with an operatic gesture. *Mori!* We went at it like Callas and Gobbi in the second act of *Tosca.*

"What the bloody hell's the matter with you?"

"Nothing."

"Are you bored?"

"No."

"Do you care about me?"

"Of course."

"You're bored, aren't you. Look, I know, it's a terrible imposition my being here."

"Not at all."

"You're disturbed."

"No."

"That's it. You're disturbed about something."

"I'm not."

"You're my son and I love you and you're disturbed."

"I am *not* fucking disturbed."

I plugged in the TV again, turning the volume up full.

"Missed the beginning of *Miami Vice,*" he said, looking at that night's *Telegraph & Argus.* "Says Crockett and Tubbs investigate the disturbing case of a psychopathic child murderer. Like that. Disturbing. Should think it bloody well is ... *disturbing*. What a world. Missed the beginning."

I told him he would catch up on the story.

"Not the point. Like the beginning. Like to look at the Ferraris."

And so it went on, through grey, oppressive, and sticky-hot days. I was relieved, every third day, when the district nurse called to give him a check up, stayed for a little longer than the GP did, and I would walk in Lister Park, or go to the art museum where I inspected garish Victorian paintings of naked women lugging big spears. But he tried to put his hand up the nurse's skirt, she refused to visit any more, and it was a week before I managed to persuade the doctor to send another. Then he collapsed again.

He was back in hospital, the same bed as before, with the same patient next to him, except the fellow was awake now and complaining. "I've been ill for thirty years," he said, to no one in particular. "It's been shitty, in and out of places like this. Shitty shitty life for thirty shitty years. Shitty food, shitty doctors. End it quickly, Lord, end it quickly."

"Oh hell," said my father, staring at him, flushed for a moment from the burrow of his own illness. "It's Bob Hope."

This time it was the consultant who took me into his office and this time the news was bad: the operation hadn't gone so well as they thought. My father had another problem. The veins in his legs had narrowed so badly that no blood was getting through. There would have to be another operation.

"To open up the veins?" I said.

"We tried that already," he said.

I won't report the rest of the conversation in all its meanderings until I at last got the point: that they would have to amputate, otherwise my father's legs would turn gangrenous, and he would die. The consultant thought it might be easier if I were the one to tell him.

My father took it without a blink. "Out of the question," he said. "Not happening. Won't happen. Can't happen. Remember a chap in the war, a sparks, took a piece of shrapnel in his thigh, nasty wound, they were all for chopping his leg off, he wouldn't let them, told the buggers to bugger off, *bougrez-off,* he said, fancied himself as a man of the world, *bougrez-off,* he'd sooner have it done with than be a hopalong, so they didn't and three weeks later he was playing football. So much for medical science."

I said, "Dad . . ."

"No bloody way."

"Dad . . ."

"Bougrez-off."

I brought him in a portable TV. His pain was worse. The fellow in the next bed was always awake now and always complaining, but my father didn't care, or rather he didn't notice, he was always in the company of something else, his illness. Sometimes he would observe it. He said, "Did you know you can take a piss without knowing it. When you're awake I mean, not when you're asleep, anyone knows *that*. I'm here with the telly on, watching the cricket, and I'll take a piss without knowing about it, without feeling a thing. I find it quite remarkable." But more often he *was* his illness, it had taken him over, and it wasn't a laugh to talk to, since its dialogue concerned pain, drugs, bowel movements, and not wanting to eat, or not being able to.

Sometimes, rarely, the illness took a vacation and Jack Hamer was there, for a while, and usually frightened. He had misplaced his watch. He would not open his locker to search for it, because he knew the locker was filled with lizards, their scaly bodies piled on high on top of each other. He had woken in the middle of the night and seen that the fellow next to him was dead. No one had noticed. He had asked the night staff what they were doing, letting him lie there and they had told him the fellow was perfectly alright. When my father had looked again he had seen that the man was indeed dead and was not the usual fellow, but himself. He dreamed of the lizards, their black and gold eyes without expression and yet shining terribly, so bright he could see them through wood.

He refused to talk about the second operation. I didn't blame him, and nor did the consultant, who said it was a decision only my father could make, but said also that my father would have to be discharged, he had been in for two weeks and the bed was needed. "The GP will let us know when he absolutely has to come back," said the consultant, not meaning it to sound ominous.

At home he was constipated again, and the GP gave him another enema, but this time it wasn't shit that came from his bowels. His blood was gleaming at me from the white linoleum of the bathroom floor. He said it was the lying down that did it, and the standing up and the walking and the stretching and being. This business of living, it was killing him, he said, and smiled.

There were times when we did hate each other. He hated me for carrying him to the bathroom, for cooking his meals, for clearing up his mess, for my tolerant smiling. I hated him for being ill, for being about to die with so much unresolved *stuff,* for not dying quickly. I would be in the bathroom, with the taps on and the extractor fan belting, and I would shout into the bowl of the flushing toilet: "DIE YOU FUCKER." I felt guilty, of course, but think about someone you care for, haven't you ever wished them dead, haven't you ever thought life would be easier if they were?

He began to hallucinate.

"Helen's been in," he said. "While you were at the shops. She brought her kids in. Grand lads. One of them's going to be a copper. A Hamer in the ranks of blue. Who'd have guessed it?" He laughed and grabbed at my neck with bony fingers, mocking the voice of a plodding policeman. "Headingley, you're *nicked*."

He told me he was a captain on a ship who'd had a disaster that morning. He'd leaned over the side to shout an order and his teeth had fallen out, both upper and lower plates. "I know where they are," he said, darkly. He didn't wear false teeth.

There were other times when he was quite clear and he would want to talk about the country and its management, or cricket, or women. He admired Mrs. Thatcher. He watched her on the TV and referred to her as Boadicea. "Quite frankly, I'd like to suck her box." Speaking of which, he said, he wanted to know what I was up to in my life. He asked about the skinny blonde.

"Still giving me the runaround."

"You've corked her?"

"Oh yes," I said.

"Bloody good show."

It was during a lucid spell that he saw an interview with Melrose Gadney on the local TV news.

"Sod me, it's Schenk," he said.

"Can't be," I said.

Schenk was pictured on scaffolding, at the top of the nearly-completed mosque, grinning.

"Just take a look," my father exclaimed, pointing at the screen.

"Dad," I said. "You're seeing things." Schenk was in Saltaire now, walking towards the gorgeous façade of the abandoned mill building. "It's in your head, the whole show's up there. It's your knowledge-box, on the blink again."

"My knowledge-box is just fine," he said, and there followed some minutes of Hamer Ping-Pong, him on one side of the net, and me on the other, at first denying there could be any connection

between Schenk and this other fellow—what was his name?—
Melrose *Gadney,* but then pressed into confession by the sullen
ferocity of his play: yes it was him, and no there wasn't any point
in talking to Budge Carter because I had done so already. Schenk
was a swift and evil villain, that was Budge's opinion, and we were
better off keeping away from him.

My father lamented his illness and the chance that had given him
such a son. He became tearful. He asked God what he had done to
deserve such ingratitude. He wasn't asking me to kill Schenk. He
was only asking me to meet the fellow, to get the lie of the land.
Well, if I wasn't going to, it was no skin off his nose, I could fuck
off.

I clapped my hands, once, and again. *"Bravo!"*

"Piss off."

"Bravo! You were magnificent."

"I'll do it myself."

"I'll go," I said.

"I'll phone right now."

"I said, I'll go."

He apologised. He reckoned I understood, he knew he shouldn't
lose his temper, but seeing Schenk like that, talk about bowling a
fellow a googly; after all, Schenk had as good as killed Helen, and
had told Weekes to be on the lookout when he came back to
Bradford.

"We don't know that," I said.

"The bastard was at my trial," he said, "grinning like he'd sent
me to the taxidermist."

"That's true."

"He'd been after me for years. I know *that.* Tell him I want to
meet him."

"Why should he talk to you? Or me?"

My father was confident. Schenk was vain and boastful, he said.
"Bastard'll want to rub our noses in what a success he is," he said.

I met him at Saltaire. He had an office on the top floor of one of
the mill buildings. He was wearing a dark grey worsted suit of
expensive cut. He stood by the window with his back to me,
watching his reflection in the glass, and he didn't acknowledge my

presence until I was half-way across the room when he turned, playing a scene: the corrupt mogul is assailed by his past, and is unperturbed. There was a jar on his desk. Dark, bulbous forms were inside, squashed together in liquid. "Pickled bird," he said. "A favoured delicacy. An old lady does them for me. Quail. Shoot them, up in Scotland, the Borders. Try one."

I said not.

"Life is life and time is short," he said, spreading his arms. "Why not have fun with friends? Did Budge Carter send you?"

"No."

"Because Budge believes he's in a fight and he'll lose, he'll look for me but I don't go to battlefields any more. He'll be alone with his rasher in his hand. Which brings me to the question: why *are* you here?"

Schenk still had a full head of curly hair. He seemed not to have aged, as if he had somehow been the recipient of an energy my father had lost, and looked, if anything, trimmer, stronger than he had before. Staring, he took a cigar from a box on the desk and rolled it between his plump fingers. Alight now, it stared at me also, saying I am Schenk, I am powerful now, I dare you to respond. He said, "I know why you're here. Because Jack is dying, and the past. You might even be here because you have a gun and mean to shoot me. Do you have a gun, Headingley?"

"Maybe."

"I heard you tried to kill Jack with one, you and your brother. Happy family, the Hamers."

"It was a long time ago."

"Like the House of Atreus."

"Anyway, where did you hear that?"

"It was *all* a long time ago. We played out a fierce little game, your father and Charlie Laughton and me. Shall I tell you something?"

I shrugged.

"I did run off knowing your sister might do something stupid," he said. Then: "I was behind Weekes catching up with your old man." And then: "I did kill Charlie Laughton and used Mr. Hyde for cover. And I raped his wife."

I don't know what my expression was, but he laughed at it. "No no no," he protested. "NO! Just joking."

"About all of it?"

He shrugged.

"Tell me."

He was bored with the game. "I was sorry about your sister. She was really rather a lovely girl."

"My father would like to see you."

"Why?"

"I imagine he wants to talk about all of this."

"Nothing in it for me," Schenk said simply. The tip of his cigar was an orange glow in the darkening room. From below came the sound of the Skipton train. "If I did see him I might tell him things. I might tell him he's going to die leaving you and your brother and nothing else. Not a trace. The door will close and it will be as if he never came into the room. And I wouldn't want to do that. That would be telling him I hate him, which I do, but hate doesn't solve problems. Business solves problems. Money solves problems. When it all blew up in 1964, when I lost a lot, thanks to your dad, I went away and made more."

"How?"

"Does it matter?"

"Probably not."

"Dealing," he said. "In wool, in aeroplanes, in arms."

"Really?"

"You don't believe me?"

Now it was my turn to shrug.

"Shall I tell you your dad's problem?" he said, and didn't wait for a reply. "Your dad's problem," he said, "was that he wanted to make the rest of us chase his tail in a today which he should be seen to waltz through with no trouble at all. He never thought about the future. After the war he left it to everyone else to build him a nest, a new life, a castle in the air. And everyone else said, 'Screw you, Jack.' Me, I adapted. I *am* the time. Shall I tell you about the future?"

"Please do."

"*Green* money, that's the thing now, money which wants to save a forest in Brazil, money which cares about people, about the world, money which persuades itself it cares, or pretends to care, because that's what it needs to do to protect itself, because otherwise it will be swallowed up again by nature . . . *chaos*. Conservation! That's what I've got my eyes on, that's where I'm making my next millions. Money which wants to keep the shell of old Bradford and let a new Bradford grow inside it. Those eco-minded dollars, they're swimming the Atlantic towards me. Keep me in Havanas for a long time."

The room was almost dark now. His voice was coming from the shadows. "So, Jack Hamer's boy has come to see me. How is he?"

"Not so bad. And yourself?"

"Me?" he said, surprised I needed to ask the question. "I'm happy as a bear at the fair. I never imagined I would become this respectable. I'm *improbably* successful. You just have to decide."

"What?"

"Do you want it?"

"What's that?"

"Bradford."

I didn't understand. I sensed him studying me, from the gloom behind the desk, as if his eyes could see in the dark.

"I'm offering you a job," he said. "I can make you like me."

None of this was what I had expected. His matter-of-fact tone suggested he was serious, and I wasn't sure whether I cared or not. I thought of Schenk's driven career, comparing it to my father's, and my own, both of which had such a ramshackle quality, an air of drift. Looking out of the window, I saw floodlights go on, and suddenly there were the streets of Saltaire, the main weaving shed with its palatial appearance, and the mill chimney, over two hundred and fifty feet tall, built to resemble a Florentine campanile. There was Bradford, a glow in the distance, a promise.

I said I didn't want it.

I said I'd think about it.

I said, "I do."

My father—thin and grey, wearing only pyjamas, no slippers—was out of bed, sitting in a chair, staring at his feet, which were no longer like feet, but huge things, black and bloated. The muscles in his legs had wasted away. Ulcerous sores had made holes in the skin. Yet all the time I had been with Schenk he had fought with himself, keeping his mind above the gluey mess of the illness, so he could ask, as soon as I returned: "How did it go?"

I said, "You're half-naked. You'll catch your death."

He said, "Sod that."

"He didn't want to see you."

"Fuck that for a game of soldiers."

"I think he's scared of you."

"So he should be. But you fixed it alright?"

He tried to stand, but flopped back into the chair with a bony thump, fighting for breath. The skin seemed to be melting from his face. His flesh was slushy grey. Surely he couldn't live more than a few days. I said, "A week Saturday."

"That long?"

"As I said. He's scared."

"Gives me time to get ready, I suppose," he said, and I could see that he was pleased, that for a moment he was able to see Jack Hamer as he had been, in the days of his pomp. "We're going to kill the bastard."

Was he joking? He wasn't.

"I know lads in London. They'll come up on the train with a couple of sawn-offs."

He looked at me as if he expected a protest. I said nothing.

"They'll do the job for two hundred pounds. Go back the same night." He was concentrating hard, perhaps making a picture of the event in his mind, a pair of heavies swilling lager in the buffet car on the way back to London, pleased with a job well done; it seemed to amuse him. He said, "Assassins on an away-day."

Again: he was serious. Now I did try to reason with him, but he wouldn't listen; it was as if, in his illness, he was capable only of obsession. "Give me the number. I'll set it up," I said, which was absurd, because I wasn't going to make the call, but I felt tired, and the situation was getting out of hand, so I thought I'd better do whatever was necessary to shut him up. I presumed he'd forget about it.

"Get some rest," I said.

He relaxed and closed his eyes. He said, "I'm glad you're with me now."

I believed him about the fellows in London. The subject of his underworld connections had come up before. I'm thinking of the forged documents, and the time he'd mentioned that if I ever had personal bother he knew someone in Heaton who did a respectable job with a baseball bat for the price of a couple of bottles of scotch. Nor was I especially troubled by the arrangement I seemed to have made with Schenk, which I could break. Nor by the perspective the proposed murder offered on my father's moral universe; that, I'd known for a long time, was astronomical disaster. The problem was elsewhere. I remembered an occasion, it must have been in 1963, that very cold winter, driving with him from Manchester: warm car, the smells of leather and whisky, and "Please Please Me" by The Beatles on the radio. We had passed the *Daily Express* building, which was lit up like an Atlantic liner, with the presses running. Thirty minutes later we had been crossing the Pennine mountains, in fog, and he had fallen asleep at the wheel. The car had started to snake along the icy road so I had leaned over and had popped his left eye open with my thumb and forefinger. He had been startled, but once he had realised what had happened, he had said "Damned cool, Headingley." Remembering this, I felt a glow in the belly. The problem was that he refused to allow the ease of such memories.

I have been describing these things to make some sense of what happened between me and my father; at the same time, I am turning events into a story with the story's tricks, its jokes, its woes and happinesses, its—at last—honesty. A story is a seduction. Are you listening? Are you pretty? I am in dread of not moving you.

I understand now, my father's bad temper, and his sudden obsession with Schenk and settling the score, these weren't ends in themselves, but useful—if unconsciously evoked—irritants, specks around which a pearl of concentration might grow, signs that he wasn't giving up, that he was fighting, not just raging against the dying of the light, but spitting at it. They were also more than irritants, or signs, they were parts of his own need to explain. Schenk was the villain of his story, as he is of mine. For me, Schenk had been a shadowy presence, changing and terrible, but almost an abstraction; now he was a confusing temptation, a bad book with a surprising page; whereas for my father, Schenk had been terrible and real, a twisted version of himself. He had yearned to leave Schenk behind, and sometimes seemed to have succeeded, only to find that Schenk was there, always, like his own shadow.

. . .

He collapsed again and went into hospital for the third, and final, time. They put him at the other end of the ward this time, near the night sister's desk, and the way out, as if to hurry his departure. The consultant said my father's legs were too far gone to operate, and anyway he was so weak now the shock of surgery would kill him. It would be a fortnight at most; drugs would ensure his comfort. So he was going to die. I still didn't quite take it in. A fortnight? I wondered how it left me with regard to Schenk.

My father had other, unexpected, concerns. He sat up in bed, his hand on a Gideon Bible, grinning broadly. He leaned forward and whispered that Helen had been to see him again. She had confirmed that he was immortal. He said, "We all are, old man. So it's alright. Isn't it the business? A load off my mind, I must say."

Was this the morphine? For most of his life his only reverence had been to a reckless quest for adventure. Now he spoke of his mother's faith, and how he had been raised Catholic. In the next days he spoke, not of Schenk, but of the need to see a priest and make confession. Perhaps, about to die, he was turning to his God. Very understandable. However, the way he lowered his voice for churchy talk, the sanctimonious expression which would fall gently on his face, these things made me wild. I felt like leaning close and whispering poison: *you're talking crap you old fraud and in any case you'd better pray your God doesn't exist otherwise it's the eternal toasting fork for you buster*. Then I was guilty. I told myself to remember: he was an old man, sick and sad.

He said, "All my life I wanted to be someone who counted. And I suppose that hasn't happened."

Oh tragedy!

Stop it.

"Now it doesn't matter. I'll have plenty of time to prove myself, plenty of time to meet women and learn how to deal with them right. I've never been much good without a woman."

"Why's that?"

He didn't reply. He issued the demand: "Stories."

I filled him with anecdotes from my time on the *Telegraph & Argus,* and a few juicy religious ones of my own.

"Not those kind of stories."

"What kind of stories?"

"You know what kind."

I softened. I told him I was seeing the blonde again. His mood brightened, so it was more, about a woman who liked me to come in her face, one who was virtuous and thought me—could he believe it?—*naive but beautiful,* another who wouldn't let me do anything except suck her cunt and instructed that I wear my glasses while doing so, a fourth whose taste was for fucking in public, notably in an alley in Little Germany, not far from that pub, The Hand of Glory.

"That's it, old fellow, cork them all," he said. "Cork the lot while you've still the chance."

I wondered how this squared with his reborn Catholicism.

He wanted to hear these stories not, I think, because he was obsessed with sex but because, historically, sex had bored him less than most things. He could concentrate on it when his mind was fading. Still, during all our conversations there was the likelihood that he would tire suddenly, stop in mid-sentence, if he happened to be talking, and fall asleep. Then I would sit by the bed, reading a page or two of a book, but most of the time letting my mind go blank. Imagine that consciousness is a lantern. I did my best to keep mine dull, like the one Aladdin found. My dread was of rubbing it, making it glow, summoning a genie. Genies have a way of bouncing back at you: like morality, they make promises which turn out to be demands.

I would wait for my father to wake up, or until someone told me it was time to go, and then I would go home. Or not: often I would sleep in the back of my car. The pretty nurse, the redhead, had a name for me: she called me "The Zombie."

One morning I found my father on his feet, which was rare, and on his way back from the bathroom. He walked with determination. He motioned me to follow him to the side of the corridor. We stood in a doorway. He was very pleased to see me, he said in a whisper. He wanted me to understand. At night the hospital was transformed. People were drifting in under cover. Sleeping in the beds. An Irishman named O'Rourke seemed to be controlling it all. O'Rourke was riff-raff and he was collecting more of the same, refugees from asylums, from jails, from the *Department of Health and Social Security,* and he was bringing them in. They were after something for sure. What it was, he didn't know, but Jack Hamer was on their trail. He could spot the conspirators, easily, because they were made of straw. He could see it poking through the legs of their pyjamas and from the back of their imperfectly fitting uniforms. They left trails.

Uncertain how to respond, I neither contradicted what he said nor went along with it, but changed the subject. Blakey had scored a good eighty for Yorkshire that day. I gave an account of the innings which, of course, I had not seen. I said, "First ball: a drive through mid-on, to the boundary like an arrow." I stood up, using a rolled-up newspaper to mime the stroke. "What an opening!"

My father was exasperated. "You don't understand," he said. "They're all selling property. They're playing hit and miss. Do you understand?"

I stood there, quite still, with the newspaper poised at the top of the follow-through. A male nurse watched me from the end of the corridor.

"Hit and miss. Bear and bull. An annual income in excess of two hundred grand."

I was feeling stupid with a rolled-up newspaper grasped in both hands and my father shouting: *"Do you understand? HEADING-LEY?"*

He had everyone's attention now. The corridor was an ant's tunnel of purposeful bodies. I tried to calm him.

"It's all right Dad, I do, I understand."

He was frantic. "I don't know where it will stop," he said, stamping his feet with his head in his hands. A male nurse hurried towards us on squeaky shoes like cornish pasties. My father looked up at him, saying, "It's human guinea pigs."

"Is it now?" the nurse said.

"Deny it if you dare."

"I don't," said the nurse, soothingly.

"It's hit and miss," said my father, as we led him back to the ward.

We got him into bed. The nurse went to work with syringe and bottle. It was necessary to keep increasing the dose, he said, and this was affecting my father's mind; I would have to accept the fact that he might be like this from now on. He might not recognise me.

The thought must have risen up just as he was losing consciousness. For a moment he was lucid, his voice quite firm: "Headingley, old man. Don't forget now will you, about Schenk?"

"No, Dad."

"The lads from London. *Promise.*" Before I could reply his eyes closed and his mouth went slack. Soon he was snoring.

The suicide commands his own death. Most of us don't, we don't run joyfully towards it and fling ourselves into its arms, like lovers at the end of an opera. Most of us do not choose when to die, and we do not choose how. How simple if it were a matter of saying, "I rather think I'd like to go in this way, at this moment." Unfortunately, death is a process which has to be proceeded through, an event in life.

I'm sure my father had contemplated death, in the war, for instance, when he had concrete evidence of its possibility every time he flew—KERRUMP! there goes C for Charlie—or when Diana Farrell had held a knife to his throat during a binge in Mayfair in the 1950s, or when Schenk was on his tail in 1964, or when Keith and I had played out the farce with the very big gun seventeen years later. I'm equally sure he wouldn't have seen it like this. Me neither. I'd had in mind the holding of hands, the exchanging of confidences, an understanding, a true intimacy at last. I was pleased, of course, that he was no longer in pain, though it did occur to me that the non-pain-registering part of his mind might still be aware of the imminence of his death. Might still be terrified, hence the need for the hallucinations. But I felt cheated. I had wanted to ask: *Come on, Dad, what are you thinking, what's it like? You screwed me around, I mopped up your shit now teach me SOMETHING USEFUL.* Instead his death was a morphine-raft, and set sail for the gulf of paranoia.

O'Rourke brought in more of his friends. My father knew what he was after. O'Rourke was in with Schenk. The two of them were taking over the hospital, and already so confident of their power that they no longer bothered to hide during the day. They marched up and down bold as you like. His voice was thin and hollow as he said this, and then he suddenly became angry. "It's Schenk. The scoundrel. How dare he tell me that? I warned him before. I don't care how powerful he thinks he is, I'll not be treated in this shoddy manner!"

The red-headed nurse came, with another, to remove my father's dressings and put on clean ones. His feet were entirely black now, Bradford black, with white ooze seeping. The air filled with a sickening stench.

"Bit on the ripe side, your dad, isn't he?" said the sister.

"Where's my watch?" said my father. I wondered if he too smelled the gangrenous fluid.

"Like cheese left in a spermy sock."

"The bugger's had it away with my Omega."

"Oooh, look at this, it's really horrible."

The red-headed nurse invited me to look inside the stinking bandage she had removed. Something was there. It was small, and stiff and black, almost like charcoal, as if it had been burned. It was one of my father's toes.

She shrugged, and made a little smile. She wasn't being callous. By inviting me to see comedy in the situation, she was offering her comfort, she was telling me that, bad though it may be, and it is, this is what happens, it's part of life. I tried to smile back. I tried to think of a joke in return, look, here's my dad, not just dying, but *rotting,* but I couldn't, I couldn't manage even the insincere smile.

"O'Rourke! Think of the bills. Come in with me. Strasbourg, that's where we'll go, for a regular lost weekend. Soon as I get my watch back," said my father, evidently not believing in his own power to persuade, for his voice was thin and hollow, bleak, like the wind in a graveyard, like the wind at Undercliffe.

I said, "Dad . . ."

"Let's leave Schenk out of it, eh? Got no sense of humour. He'll be dealt with. He'll not touch us. We're outside time."

It was useless. He didn't know I was there. I wanted to run, away from the ward, away from the hospital, away from Bradford as far as possible.

. . .

Schenk's murder was all over the *Telegraph & Argus*. He had been killed by shotgun, in his Rolls-Royce, the previous night, stalled at traffic lights in Forster Square. His chauffeur, who had seen a dark Ford Capri speeding away, had called the police, and they had found Schenk already dead, sprawled in the back with a jar of pickled birds, also caught by the blast. I imagined Schenk's last moments: watching his own blood froth over smashed glass and quail meat; the whiff of vinegar startling his nostrils. Budge Carter's clocks had some fun with the detail of the pickled birds; while Budge himself, the problems of libel and reprisal removed, had even more fun with the remarkable career of Schenk, also known as Melrose Gadney, also known as Redbecker, who was described in terms which would have been unflattering to Heinrich Himmler. "This wicked man, this evil man, whose criminal empire extended throughout the entire north of England, from Blackpool to Scarborough, from Sheffield to Barrow-in-Furness, whose crimes included murder, fraud, and the exploitation of immigrants as slaves, who was implicated in the death of one former partner, Charlie Laughton, and the imprisonment of another, who, in the opinion of a distinguished former colleague . . ."

. . . that was me; *distinguished?* . . .

". . . was responsible for at least one of the vicious attacks on women normally attributed to the mass murderer known as Mr. Hyde . . ."

And so on. Budge's sentences grew longer and more pompous in proportion to his indignation.

My father was delighted. He was sitting up, with the paper beside him. Though still very weak, he had now forgotten O'Rourke. "Bloody good," he said, grinning at me. "Excellent show."

"Very bizarre," I agreed.

"If you need help . . ."

"Why should I?"

"*If* you do, I know another fellow in London, he could come up tonight, very good, look after you for a ton, just while the fuss dies down."

I understood. He believed I had killed Schenk, or he wanted to believe it, which gave me the same problem. I said. "I *see*. You think . . ."

"Old Budgerigar reckons it was a business rival, perhaps even the IRA." His voice was very faint. "But we know better, eh son?"

I had gone up in his estimation enormously.

"I shouldn't think there'll be a problem with the coppers. Be glad to see the back of him, I should say. Weekes'll probably stand you a drink. But even that bastard must have had a friend. One who might come looking for you."

I said it wasn't a problem.

"Don't be so bloody stubborn. Take advice about this one thing," he said. He slid the table close to his chest and wrote with a stubby pencil on the back of an envelope. "Important. Call tonight. Tell him Jack Donne put you in touch."

"Jack Dunn?"

"That's D-O-N-N-E. Like the poet, our joke, so he'd know I was no impostor. And another thing."

"What's that?"

"Stay in a hotel. Don't go home tonight."

"A hotel?"

"Promise," he said. He was quite fierce.

"I promise," I said.

"Good." He lay back on his pillows, and grinned. He believed I had killed Schenk, or had paid the London boys for the job, and done it to please him. Probably he was hoping it had been me, so he could applaud my thrift as well as my filial commitment. But that wasn't what made me angry. What made me angry was that he thought I had taken something he said so seriously, because I didn't, even then.

He was very tired. I saw what an effort it was for him to keep his head upright. "One more thing," he said, his voice almost exhausted. "All that about Helen paying me social calls, and immortality, the religious stuff, I could see what you wanted to say. You were right. It was crap."

I said nothing.

"Just crap. Scared, I suppose, so I made it up. I wanted to believe."

"And O'Rourke?"

"O'Rourke?" he said.

"Was he crap too?"

"You haven't seen him have you?"

"No."

"If you do tell him the deal's off. Tell him his lord and master is dead, done for by Jack Hamer's son."

I tried to remember the last time he had been so pleased with me. I thought it had been when I was eight years old and was given such a good school report that he assumed I must have bribed the teacher, or blackmailed her. "Dad," I said, "I didn't do it."

He wasn't listening. "I don't believe in God, or country, or anything much, that's the thing of it. But you and I, it's been a struggle, but we've found each other, we understand each other now, and that *is* important. I love you," he said, raising himself a little and stretching out his hand towards mine, but I caught hold of air, because he fell back, asleep, before I could take it.

I drove around. The city was quiet. I got out of the car. A walk would clear my head. I bought a coffee from a stall. The town hall clock struck one, a line of street lights went out on Ivegate, a man limped into the pedestrian precinct with a sherry bottle cradled in his arm, and rain began to thicken the Bradford darkness.

My father died in his sleep in the night.

It's easy to take a body from a hospital. After the registrar has signed the death certificate you only have to ask, which is what I did, once they'd given me my father's, in an opaque bag of grey plastic, I drove to the coast stopping at a garden centre outside York where I bought a small urn. I had a picture in mind of my destination, a beach which at low-tide stretched so far out to sea that it seemed to lose itself in the horizon. It was a few miles north of Scarborough, I had been there once, when I was a child, with my grandparents. I guessed it was near Filey.

I found the beach at about seven. I made a phone-call to Coleridge, an indolent fellow with interesting connections, and said I needed material for a big bonfire. Could he help? He had come into possession of a lorry-load of Swan Vesta matches, of which he had two crates left, mine for fifty pounds. I said that would be fine. I waited in the car until near-dark and decided against it. I made another phone-call, cancelling the Swan Vestas, and drove back to Bradford. I set fire to my father's body in the cricket pavilion at Windhill.

Standing on the rise at the far end of the field, an hour after midnight, watching the flames as they climbed higher and higher, up into the cool air, I remembered that other night, one of my father's great nights, the night of the Minis, the climactic night of the scheme he had devised to fox Schenk and Charlie Laughton, twenty-five years before, when fifty-seven pairs of headlights had come over this hill, each pair seeming to hang for a moment before sweeping down towards the field and the newly built pavilion. I remembered also the drive which had happened after, in a Mini Cooper S, when he had almost killed Helen and me. The fire was at its peak now. The roof fell in and the balcony came down with a crash, showering sparks and flaming embers. I heard approaching traffic, but what came this time were fire engines and screaming police cars. I reflected that this, at least, would have pleased him: his final exit was causing maximum inconvenience.

I went down there at ten the next morning, when most of the official vehicles had gone; only an ambulance and one car re-mained. The policeman Weekes was poking around in what was left of the pavilion. A mistake he had made in the Mr. Hyde investigation had stopped him going as high in the police force as had once seemed likely. He didn't seem surprised to see me.

"I suppose it was your dad," he said. "We found the remains of a body." He pointed to an area of the blackened concrete founda-tion; it had been roped off. The rope, I noticed, was yellow.

"He died three nights ago. At St. Luke's."

"I checked," said Weekes. He seemed old and ill. He was tired of it all. He said he'd decided to let this go. It was the right thing, he thought, or at least he hoped so, but if anyone discovered the truth we'd both be in it; so we'd both better watch out.

He watched in silence as I scooped up the ashes.

He heaved a heavy sigh: "Now fuck off out of my sight."

I drove to Leeds, to Headingley, with the ashes in the urn in an Adidas bag I had bought, but there was no game that day and the ground was closed, so I went to the motorway. Headed south, to London.

. . .

The name was on a white sign from which letters had fallen: wo-e—and. The building had once been a monument to Victorian solidity and substance: five storeys, entrance with pillars, servants' quarters at the back. Decline began when the wrought iron railings which once guarded it from the street were ripped up during the war and melted down for tank armour. Decline was accelerated when a widow named Irene Krumpholz became the owner. She had the good idea of turning it into a hotel for itinerant Irish workmen, and the bad one of opening on Festival of Britain Day, June 25, 1951, thus guaranteeing that the intended clientele would never cross the threshold on point of political principle. Decline became irreversible in the 1980s when the Holloway Road became a major route through London. Lorries thundered past all day and all night. This seismic assault rattled glass in the windows and shook plaster from the walls. The linoleum which covered the staircase and corridors was painted with a thin coat of dust. Walking through the Wonderland, I was Man Friday on Robinson Crusoe's island. I left footprints.

I stayed for a week. Or perhaps it was ten days. I talked to no one. There was no one to talk to, except the urn on the mantelpiece. Twice a day I went for a walk, hurrying down the stairs, turning my eyes from an area of dripping damp plaster in the corridor because, each time I did look, I imagined something buried inside, still alive.

I called Keith in Paris. I told him our father had died. He sounded neither shaken nor surprised, and asked when. I said a while ago.

"What does that mean?"

"A week or so. Ten days maybe."

"Ten days." Now he was surprised. "Did you tell Mother?"

"No."

"You tell *anyone*?"

"No."

"The body?"

"Burned him in the pavilion. After that I tried to get into Headingley. That's where he wanted his ashes spread."

"Jesus," said Keith, softly.

"I've got them here, with me now, in an urn, it's not very nice actually, a nasty sort of plastic."

"Are you alright our kid?"

Our kid. That set me off crying.

"Listen. I'm coming back tonight. Don't worry. I'll take care of everything."

I didn't think I was late. Perhaps I made a mistake about the time, perhaps I was confused by the hectic drive north and the surprisingly sultry heat which smacked me in the face when I arrived in Bradford and made me stop for an iced drink at Burger King. I'd certainly intended to be on time, but when I got to Undercliffe they were waiting. That's to say: Keith; my mother, in a black dress, and her husband; my ex-wife, and hers; a woman who I knew was a great aunt, who I hadn't see in twenty years, and whose name I had never been able to remember even back then; a number of old faces I didn't know, and a few younger ones; Mosby, the Liverpudlian who had shared a cell with my father in Armley; gap-toothed and still grinning, Billy Crow, an old man now, standing next to Budge Carter; and Barbara, who was with Vickie. She waved, as though her being there were the most natural thing.

Keith came over. He wore a black suit with flared trousers and lapels like a Vulcan bomber. I told him he looked preposterous. He ignored this and asked where the hell I'd been.

"You said two-thirty."

"Two-*fifteen*."

"Sorry."

"You're a selfish sod, you know that?" He told me the trouble he'd had, squaring it off with my mother about the fact that my father had been dying, had actually died, and I hadn't bothered to inform anybody. Then he softened. "How are you?"

I said I was the better for seeing him.

"Likewise," he said. He smiled. He hummed a few bars of a song I couldn't place. "So where is the old fucker?"

We looked down at the Adidas bag, we looked up at each other. For reasons that were less obvious than they may appear, we started to laugh. We laughed not because my dead father was inside an

Adidas bag and the situation was comic, it was, but because we were both a little hysterical, sweating in the heavy atmosphere. Steamed-up brothers.

He said, "Take him out."

"Here?"

"What the hell do you think? Over there?" He motioned with his head towards the mourners. My mother was looking in our direction. She would come over in a moment or two. "Do it now. Quick, I'll put myself in the way."

"I'd have bet my life I was early. Christ."

Keith giggled. "In the shit again."

"What shall I do with the bag?"

"Bury it with him. Perhaps he'll be going on his holidays."

"I'll leave it."

My mother was on her way. She had that carrot-topped, purposeful, prime-ministerial look about her. "What are you two playing at?"

"Hello Ma," I said.

"We're on our way," said Keith.

"No sweat," I said.

"This . . ." her arm gestured around the cemetery ". . . it's so predictable. I wouldn't count on you two to get yourself drunk in the Tetley brewery. It's a scandal."

Keith tried to calm her. He said not to worry. The priest was a cool customer, an anarchist. I know, you're thinking, an anarchist *priest,* but that's what Keith said, and if such a character did exist, Keith was the man to find him. Keith explained that the priest had taken a hefty bribe to perform the ceremony; he'd be talking to nobody. So you see, Mother, Keith said, nothing would get in the papers.

"Neither of you understand, it's not that, you haven't seen the grave, oh what a mess," she said, and then saw the urn. She paused. She saw the urn. She seemed to shrink, as if someone had let the air out of her.

My mother had remarried, and was happy, "so far as it goes." Her words, not mine. She kept in touch, asked if I was healthy or needed money, and dreaded the truth because she was touched by my griefs as though they were her own. I felt close to her, in a way, but her influence on my life had never been like my father's, though he had been absent for most of it. Chairwoman of the Dewsbury Conservatives, bridge-player, gardener, fruitcake-baker, she inevitably cut a less glamorous figure than he did, which is not to say that she was less remarkable, just that it was hard to see her as a character from myth, which is what I'd tried to do with my father all along. I called her: *The Lillian*. For a long time I presumed this wasn't her story, but that's not so, I realise now that she has also shaped it, and me, though with different tools. She had been forced to save herself. Who knows what strength it had taken to leave him, and Helen, Keith, and I? Sometimes I would see a glimmer of her loss, and this—suddenly she notices the plastic urn containing not many of my father's ashes—was such a moment. Her face filled with grief.

"Oh Jack," she said. "You poor old bugger."

The priest was in a hurry. He gathered us round the grave and began the service. I saw at once what my mother had meant. There was a problem. That was down to Billy Crow. Billy had remembered the funeral of my father's father, Bert Hamer, whose coffin had been lowered into a grave fully twelve feet deep, and had decided that his old boss, his friend, my father, deserved even better. He had come to Undercliffe the night before and had shovelled each spadeful himself. I looked over the edge. I couldn't see the bottom, and imagined the urn, vanishing like a stone in a well, picking up an irresistible momentum as it spun to the centre of the earth. "A fifteen footer," said Billy, proudly.

My father stood up from the bench where he had been sitting and came towards me slowly, slapping one hand against the bag of Tate & Lyle sugar he had in the other. He said he had been buying sugar in bulk and would soon be pouring it into the petrol tank of each non-Hamer hearse. It would be funeral chaos, and victory *at a stroke*. This was my father as I first remembered him, in his late thirties, raffish Jack Hamer, Fred Astaire dancing, about to let go with a gorgeous Gershwin tune. He peeped into the grave. "One thing about Billy," he said. "He could be relied on to dig a spectacular hole."

"If that one had less brains his head would ring like a bell every time he put his cap on. I always told you he was a liability." This was Schenk, but the Schenk I had seen a few weeks before, dressed in grey worsted, and carrying a recent magazine which had an article on the subject of his own murder. He too peeped down. "I tell you, Jack: if there'd been more hours in the night, you'd be heading to Australia."

Schenk advised me to chuck the ashes in. He was curious to see just how far down the urn would go. And he wanted to be on his way. He had business, green dollars to attend to. "Let's get it over with," he said.

My head was a machine not running the way I expected. Those billions of neurons had sent my father and Schenk, and now Helen, in her thirties, very lovely, laughing because she knew something I didn't: the facts of my life, the secret of my future. If only I would go and talk to her, she said, I could make sense of it, I could decipher the moment I was living. I saw her, I saw them all: my grandmother, Twiggy Fawcett and Amos Bass, the drunk Irishman from the town square in Shipley, RAF crew my father had flown with, women he had fucked, barmen he had bothered. And Tom, who had taken Helen's hand.

The priest looked at me expectantly. So did my mother, Keith, and Diana Farrell. Didn't I mention? She had arrived late, in style and in Chanel, wearing too much make-up, as if she had stepped from the set of the American soap opera in which she now appeared from time to time. She had gone first to my mother and embraced her, then Keith, and then me.

The priest had his hands together and was making discreet tossing motions. Keith nodded: *go ahead*. I was surprised that they hadn't noticed my father and the rest who, led by him, were singing now, going at it full tilt, a song of the dead: *"Yes, we have no bananas."* I stepped forward with the urn.

"Dust to dust," said the priest.

". . . we have no bananas . . ."

"Ashes to ashes."

". . . tod-a-aaay . . ."

As the ashes spilled out, falling with a sandy rush into the grave, carrying with them each page of my father's history, I had a picture of myself, in the pavilion, seeing his brains bubble inside the cauldron of his head, telling myself I must save the dreams that had been there. I also remembered the second half of the promise I had made years ago, so I cupped my fingers and took back a handful.

Going to see the elephant: I always meant to ask my father where he had heard the phrase. I didn't tell you before. It was used by soldiers in the American Civil War to describe the fear, the excitement, the strangeness, and even the charm of battle. For my father, it had applied to peace as well as war. Now large things, like an elephant, are graceful, it's a necessity, otherwise they would be in trouble; if they fell down, for instance. Look at my father: despite his irresponsibility, his languid and sometimes ridiculous posturing, his awful death (the idea of the *good* death has credence only in the minds of priests and politicians), I think that he too had an unselfconscious grace. He was often on the point of falling, and it would seem he had, but he would always recover himself, somehow. He had a knack for life, no, that's not quite it, he was selfish, the knack was for *his* life. Perhaps it was enough.

I spoke to my mother at the end of the funeral. It was how is everything really?, the usual promise to be in touch more regularly, this and that, then she said: "You don't have to try to be like him. And you don't have to try not to be. Give him up."

I said I knew, but thanks.

In the distance, on the other side of the valley, lightning flashed and there was thunder. There would be a storm soon.

I said goodbye to Keith and Diana Farrell, shook hands with Mosby and Billy Crow, hugged my mother and Keith, kissed Barbara, Vickie as well, and stayed after they had gone, waiting, watching the sheeting rain come closer, falling on Heaton, falling on the Manningham Mills and on the football ground, and when it came to Undercliffe, spattering the sphinxes of the Illingworth mausoleum, then bouncing like fish-hooks off the creamy gravel pathways, I turned up my face and I felt something I couldn't identify at first, but then I knew, it was the death of Bradford, I knew also that though I had been trying for years now I could leave at last, so I drove to Leeds, reached Headingley just after close of play, ignored the policeman who stood on the roped-off wicket, and tossed up the last handful of my ashes, watching them fall where Hutton had once stood, and Bradman, and then I came back here, to a dusty room in the Wonderland hotel at the dodgy end of the Holloway Road in London, to sit and force myself to think about my father, me and the women we knew, or thought we did, not understanding that I would be obsessed, that I would wake in the night crying, or shouting, or laughing, remembering him as he sprinted down the prom at Scarborough acting out how Trueman put the frighteners on the Indians in 1951, *had them 12 for 8 old man oops! there goes another bouncer,* but hoping that through telling the story I might learn something, how to feel or, at least, how to appreciate that I had time for adventures, time for my own elephant, a fancy hope, to think I might change, might begin to begin my life again, a ridiculous hope, and I don't know if there's a chance, perhaps not, but I have learned one thing—ask me now about my father and I will say that he is dead, and that when I look at the back of my hand I see him there.

About the Author

RICHARD RAYNER was born in Yorkshire and educated in Bradford, in North Wales, and at Cambridge. He is the author of *Los Angeles Without a Map*.